OTHER MATADOR NOVELS BY BILL PAGE

The Moon on the Hills (2009)

The Sower of the Seeds of Dreams (2011)

One Summer in Arcadia (2015)

www.billpageauthor.co.uk

THE
DECEIVERS

BILL
PAGE

Matador
9 Priory Business Park,
Wistow Road, Kibworth Beauchamp,
Leicestershire. LE8 0RX
Tel: 0116 279 2299
Email: books@troubador.co.uk
Web: www.troubador.co.uk/matador
Twitter: @matadorbooks

ISBN 978 1789018 189

British Library Cataloguing in Publication Data.
A catalogue record for this book is available from the British Library.

Printed and bound in the UK by TJ International, Padstow, Cornwall
Typeset in 11pt StempelGaramond Roman by Troubador Publishing Ltd, Leicester, UK

Matador is an imprint of Troubador Publishing Ltd

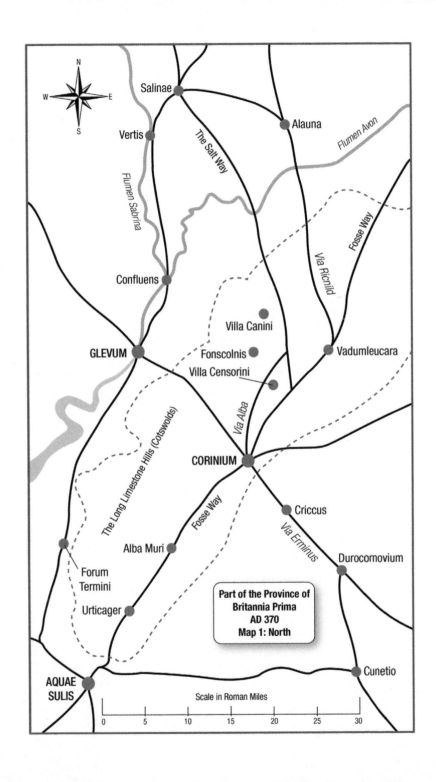

N
W   E
S

Salinae

Vertis

Alauna

Flumen Avon

The Salt Way

Flumen Sabrina

Confluens

Fosse Way

Via Ricnid

Villa Canini

Fonscolnis

Vadumleucara

GLEVUM

Villa Censorini

Via Alba

CORINIUM

The Long Limestone Hills (Cotswolds)

Criccus

Fosse Way

Via Erminus

Alba Muri

Durocornovium

Forum
Termini

Urticager

**Part of the Province of
Britannia Prima
AD 370
Map 1: North**

Cunetio

AQUAE
SULIS

Scale in Roman Miles

0   5   10   15   20   25   30

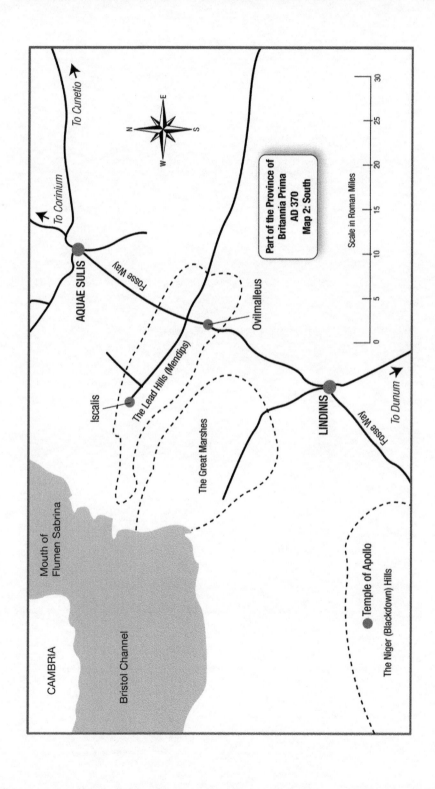

CAMBRIA

Mouth of
Flumen Sabrina

Bristol Channel

To Cunetio

To Corinium

Fosse Way

AQUAE SULIS

Iscalis

The Lead Hills (Mendips)

Ovilmalleus

The Great Marshes

LINDINIS

Fosse Way

To Dunum

● Temple of Apollo

The Niger (Blackdown) Hills

Part of the Province of
Britannia Prima
AD 370
Map 2: South

Scale in Roman Miles

0 5 10 15 20 25 30

CHARACTERS

appearing or mentioned in the novel

Many of the characters appearing or mentioned in *The Deceivers* first appeared in earlier novels, ie:-

The Moon on the Hills (Moon)
The Sower of the Seeds of Dreams (Sower)
One Summer in Arcadia (Arcadia)

Θ indicates that a character is dead by the time *The Deceivers* begins.

Antoninus (Lucius Flavius Antoninus) Θ: Born AD 346. Inherited Villa Censorini (Chedworth, Gloucestershire) on the death of his father, Censorinus. Half-brother of Trifosa. Arrested in early July 370 on a charge (fabricated by Sabinus) of involvement in Valentinus's failed conspiracy in 369. Murdered shortly afterwards by Julius Castor on Sabinus's orders to prevent him proving his innocence. *(Arcadia)*

Bodicca: Odd woman in her mid to late thirties with a strong, expressive face and thick auburn hair, beginning to grey. Lives at the foot of the Hills in a circular stone-walled house beside the stream that rises from the spring inside Vilbia's temple. Always seems to know more than she reveals. Probable associate of Vilbia, although exact relationship unknown. (*Moon*)

Canio: Aged 31. Ex-soldier. A big man with a closely-cropped black beard, which does nothing to soften his somewhat wolfish appearance. Now owner of the Villa Canini (Spoonley Wood, near Winchcombe, Gloucestershire) and styling himself **Aulus Claudius Caninus**. His wealth derives from the acquisition of gold looted in the aftermath of the *Barbarica Conspiratio* of 367. It had been hidden in a lake in the Great Marshes of what is now South Somerset to which, in the summer of 368, he travelled with Vilbia to fulfil his promise to the dying Orgillus that he would throw the Hecate figurine into that lake. (*Moon, Sower, Arcadia*)

Censorinus Θ: Father of Antoninus (by his wife) and Trifosa (by a slave). Died in February 370 and was not mourned. (*Arcadia*)

Civilis: Actual historical character. In 368, after quelling the invasions of the *Barbarica Conspiratio* and offering an amnesty to deserters from the army, *Comes* Theodosius arranged for a man called Civilis to be installed as civil governor of Britannia, presumably occupying the office of *Vicarius* and based in Londinium. All that is known of Civilis is that he was "a man of fiery temper but uncompromising integrity." (Ammianus Marcellinus xxvii. 8)

Eutherius: Apothecary with a little shop in Corinium. Ostensibly a very old man. Mentor to Vilbia, but his influence over her was diminished when she acquired guardianship of the Hecate figurine through her association with Canio. Consequently he is somewhat antipathetic towards Canio. In *Sower* he told Canio of the myths associated with the figurine when they met on a snowy January night in 370. (*Moon, Sower*)

Eutyches Θ: Late *vilicus* (bailiff) of the Villa Censorini estate. Betrayed Antoninus by supplying Sabinus with samples of his letter seals, which Sabinus then applied to forged letters to implicate Antoninus in Valentinus's conspiracy. Subsequently disappeared, almost certainly murdered on Sabinus's orders. *(Arcadia)*

Felix and Senuacus: Bailiffs on Canio's Villa Canini estate. *(Arcadia)*

Julius Castor: Soldier of about Canio's age and size. Primicerius of Sabinus's bodyguard troops. *"Pale grey eyes in a face so set and hard it might have been cast in bronze."* On Sabinus's orders he arrested Antoninus that night in July 370 at Villa Censorini (in Canio's presence), then murdered him and Lunaris on the road back to Corinium. *(Arcadia)*

Lunaris (Quintus Macrinius Lunaris) Θ: *Agens in rebus* (intelligence officer/secret policeman). His hatred of Antoninus's family first led him to blackmail Canio into helping him spy on Antoninus, and was then harnessed by Sabinus to assist him in incriminating Antoninus with forged documents linking him to Valentinus's conspiracy. Having served his purpose and to ensure his silence, on that July night in 370 he was murdered by Castor, who then claimed that Antoninus had attacked Lunaris before being killed by his soldiers in self-defence. *(Arcadia)*

Orgillus Θ: Deserter encountered by Canio and Peltrasius in June 368. He was carrying a figurine of the goddess Hecate, which he claimed to have stolen from a temple sacked by himself and fellow deserters some months before. Stabbed to death by Peltrasius. Before dying he told Canio of a lake on the south side of the Great Marshes and of the looted gold that was hidden there. In the deluded belief that Hecate will bring him back to life if it was done, he begged Canio to throw the figurine into the same lake. *(Sower)*

Pascentia Θ?: Saturninus's lover. Born following the relationship between a married woman and a young pagan priest, she was sold as a slave to an elderly wine merchant, who married her following the death of his first wife. Both she and her husband were believed to have drowned when their ship sank in a storm when returning from Burdigala (Bordeaux) where they had a vineyard. This happened several years before the opening of *Moon* in 367. *(Moon)*

However, at the end of *Sower*, Vilbia tells Canio that she had herself recently been to Burdigala where she met both Pascentia and Saturninus. While believing that Vilbia is not telling a deliberate lie, Canio is still uncertain if this is true. *(Sower)*

Peltrasius: Soldier in his early twenties. "*A young man, but one from whose face all trace of youth and softness had long since fled.*" Believing it to be gold, he took the Hecate figurine from Orgillus, then threw it away into the undergrowth when he realised it was only made of *orichalcum*. Stabbed Orgillus to death when he tried to escape. *(Sower)*

Sabinus (Caristanius Sabinus): *Praeses* (governor) of the province of Britannia Prima, the capital of which was Corinium Dobunnorum (Cirencester). Held the rank of *vir perfectissimus*. A man "*nearer forty than thirty, with a smooth, bland face that could exhibit benevolence or severity whenever it chose, although Canio suspected that only the latter would be unfeigned.*" Determined to acquire Villa Censorini, he trumped up a charge of treason against Antoninus and then had him murdered in the hope of being given the villa as a reward for exposing a "traitor". In the event, he was only granted a lease of the property. *(Arcadia)*

Saturninus Θ?: The principal character in *Moon*. A soldier. Once Canio's immediate superior. Had a prophetic dream that he would be killed by a man called Caelofernus. Disappeared under mysterious circumstances on the night of the full moon in May 367 after apparently meeting Pascentia and then travelling with her to the shore of the Seven Estuary, near which Vilbia subsequently found an old tombstone bearing the name Caelofernus. *(Moon)*

Trifosa: 22 Years old. A Christian. Beautiful and enigmatic half-sister of the late Antoninus, the only man she ever really loved. Father was Censorinus, mother was a slave. Sold to the previous owner of what became Villa Canini and so became Canio's mistress. Fled Villa Canini following Antoninus's burial, suspecting Canio of complicity in his death. *(Arcadia)*

Valentinianus I: Actual historical character. Emperor of the western half of the Roman Empire from 364 to 375. Said to have had a horror of magic and sorcery. Also to have had a hatred of the expensively dressed, the educated, the wealthy and the aristocracy.

Vilbia: 18 Year old priestess of the goddess of a spring whose temple is situated on the scarp edge of the Cotswold Hills some seven miles north of Villa Canini. Slim, with a pale intelligent face and abundant dark red hair swept up into a tightly coiled cylindrical bun on the top of her head. Put Saturninus in mind of a young hawk, fierce and beautiful.

Conducted a séance for Saturninus when he was searching for Caelofernus *(Moon)*. Accompanied Canio on his long journey to the Great Marshes, where she became keeper of the Hecate figurine and, Canio fears, may thereby have been transformed into something more than mortal *(Sower)*.

In *Arcadia* she carried a message to Antoninus from Trifosa warning that his life was in danger, meeting him one dusk on the steps of the old temple near Villa Censorini. A warning which Canio subsequently helped to negate by fabricating "proof" that the danger was past. *(Moon, Sower, Arcadia)*

The Hecate figurine: An ancient *orichalcum* (brass) figurine of the Underworld goddess Hecate, reputed to contain those pomegranate seeds that Persephone did *not* eat during her first stay in the Underworld after Hades had abducted her.

It is about five inches high and almost black, except for one small spot on her *stola* where the metal gleams dull yellow.

Her unsmiling face has an austere beauty and she wears an ankle-length long-sleeved *stola,* gathered at the waist by a belt from which hangs a coiled whip. She holds a short sword in one hand and a flaming torch in the other. Curled protectively around her feet, and forming the base of the figurine is a great hound, its lips drawn back to reveal cruel, pointed teeth.

One of the most enduring of the Greek myths says that, because Persephone ate some of the pomegranate seeds – some versions say four, others six – she is compelled to return to the Underworld every winter, although she is released every spring to bring warmth and new life back to this world.

A less well-known myth claims that Hades believes that if he could find and destroy those surviving seeds, then Persephone would be compelled to remain with him in the Underworld forever, and in this world summer would never come again, replaced by an endless winter.

But Hecate, who escorted Persephone out of the Underworld after her first captivity there, is supposed to have hidden the seeds in an *orichalcum* figurine of herself, and Hades has never been able to find them, although he desperately wants to. It is also said that Hecate dares not carry the figurine on her person, for fear that Cerberus, Hades' guard dog, might detect the seeds as she crosses the Styx on one of her frequent visits to the Underworld. *(Sower)*

CHAPTER ONE

18th October AD 370

The dreams still came. By then it was past mid-October, almost at the end of the grape harvest, and more than three months since Trifosa had vanished on the evening of that long July day when, together, they had buried Antoninus above the vineyard on Coel's Hill.

In the depths of the ever-lengthening nights he would see her approaching silently from out of the darkness. And always Antoninus would be at her side, as though his death had made them inseparable as they had never been in life, or at least not since they had been children together at Villa Censorini.

She never spoke, but he could read the accusation in those forget-me-not-blue, unblinking eyes. In vain he would protest that he had played no part in the murder – that Antoninus had been the victim of Lunaris's malevolence and Sabinus's coveting of Villa Censorini. Yet still she came, unbelieving and unappeased.

But then, three nights ago, he realised that the dream was slowly changing, the image of Antoninus fading until, by last night, it had become so indistinct that he could barely make out the man's face.

It was then he first noticed that Trifosa was no longer wearing her silver chi-rho ring – the ring which Antoninus had given her when they were children, and which he had seen her slip onto the little finger of the dead man's left hand as he lay in his stone coffin. The same ring he had subsequently found on the turf above the grave, then tossed into the air and lost some two weeks later when riding back from Fonscolnis, vaguely angry and more than a little drunk.

So was it possible that, wherever she was, the pain of her own memories of Antoninus was fading too? And if that were so, perhaps there was only one thing preventing her from returning to him – the lingering suspicion that, by conniving with the late and unlamented Macrinius Lunaris, he had played some part in bringing about Antoninus's murder.

But where was she now? In the days that followed her flight he had ridden endless miles around the countryside, asking everyone he met if they had seen her on that night, or on subsequent days. Nobody had, or if they had would not admit it. Yet surely these last dreams were urging him to find her, telling him that she wanted to be found, that she wanted to be convinced that he was innocent of Antoninus's murder. And when convinced, then she would come back to him.

The one person he had never asked while searching was Vilbia, fearing the questions she might ask – questions about why Trifosa had fled away, and where he was when Antoninus was murdered.

Which was why he still hesitated to go to her, although her temple of Leucesca, goddess of the spring, lay only seven miles away to the north of his Villa Canini. Instead, he found himself lingering in the vineyard and the pressing house, finding things to do that would normally have been done by his bailiffs, Felix and Senuacus.

But at last, when nightfall was less than two hours away, the compelling need to know at last overcame the doubts and fears. Saddling Antares, he started up the track on Coel's Hill which led to the high Salt Way.

As he rode past the grassy mound beneath which Antoninus lay buried, he found his eyes unwillingly straying towards it. With an effort he turned his head away and stared straight ahead, hurrying Antares on.

All around him he saw what were essentially still the landscapes of summer: mostly-green trees, blue sky, and the sun, already quite low in the west, warm on his back despite the cool breeze which sighed mournfully through the aging leaves.

And later, as he rode first north along the Salt Way, then north-east along the path that followed the scarp edge of the hills, most of the trees were still in full leaf, although the signs of summer's dying were all around. Several ash trees on the plateau itself had already lost half their yellowing leaves, their skeletal branches stark against the skyline.

Summer's life-spirit was slowly but inexorably shrinking back into the earth to await the coming of spring, which then seemed so far away. It was a depressing thought. He urged Antares into a trot until, at last, they arrived at the path which led down the slope between the beeches to the clearing where Vilbia's circular stone temple stood.

He caught sight of her the moment he entered the clearing, standing in front of the little stone house on the far side. With her simple off-white *stola* and dark-copper hair coiled in a tight bun on top of her head she looked not a day older than the sixteen-year-old girl who had come to his room in Corinium on that June day two years before, asking what he knew of Saturninus's disappearance.

If she was surprised to see him, or anyone else, so late on that autumn day, it did not show on her calm face. In fact, it almost seemed as if she had been expecting him. Slightly uneasy, he rationalised – telling himself that she must have heard Antares clopping down the path. Thankfully, there was no sign of her great black hound, Cerberus, as she called him – as a joke, or so she claimed.

Antares neighed in apparent recognition and she smiled. At the horse more than himself, he suspected – but perhaps it was only his conscience that made him think so.

'Welcome to you both – although it's a strange time to come visiting, isn't it, Canio?'

'It is, yes. I meant to come much earlier,' he replied, dismounting and letting Antares' reins trail on the grass. 'But there were problems with the grape pressing that had to be sorted out.' The lie had slipped out almost without conscious thought, and was immediately regretted. He paused, then admitted, 'Actually, that's not true... You met Trifosa, didn't you?'

'You know I did. And now she's gone.'

So she knows. No point in asking how, I suppose. 'Yes, she's gone – but I don't know where.'

'And now you do want to know.' It didn't sound like a question.

'Yes... did she come this way?'

'When was it that she went away?'

He suspected she already knew, but... 'Early July.'

'Over three months ago.'

He waited for her to ask why he had not come sooner, but it seemed she had another question in mind. 'Tell me, why did Antoninus return so soon from Durobrivae, when Trifosa said she believed his life was in danger from something in these hills?'

'He came back because he thought that Macrinius Lunaris, that *agens in rebus* who wanted to destroy him, was dead. So both he and Trifosa naturally thought that the danger was past.'

Vilbia appeared puzzled, although he doubted that she really was. 'So *that* was why he came back. I heard tell that, while he was away, a fragment of a star fell from the heavens and struck Villa Censorini, right above his empty bedroom. Which seemed to prove that the dream that came to Trifosa really had been a warning from the gods – which he heeded and went away, and so escaped death... It was a fragment of a star that actually hit the villa, wasn't it, Canio?'

So she didn't believe the story about the falling star either. 'That was the other reason he returned.'

'Oh, so there were two reasons why he came back. One genuine, and the other—'

'And the other faked by me and that bastard Eutyches,' he admitted. *So she did know.* He wondered how... *Unless Trifosa had told her?*

She showed no surprise at his confession. 'Did Trifosa know you had?'

'I didn't tell her.'

'But she suspected?'

'Perhaps: she never said. Did she come this way?' he asked again.

And again she ignored the question. 'Perhaps we should look into the waters of Leucesca's spring to discover where she is now – if the goddess is willing to tell us, of course.'

And we will look, and I will see nothing, and then I will go on my way, still not knowing where she is. He was about to politely decline her offer, when the thought came that this might be her indirect way of letting him know where Trifosa had gone, without actually breaking a confidence. So... 'Yes, why not – let's do it now.'

'No, not yet. We must wait until it is fully night, the time when the creatures of darkness walk the woods. I will go into the temple now and make everything ready. Come to me when you can count at least ten stars in the sky.'

'It's quite cloudy,' he pointed out.

She looked up at the darkening evening sky. 'The wind is blowing the clouds away; it will be clear soon. Trust me.'

For Canio, waiting impatiently beside Antares at the edge of the dark trees, time passed maddeningly slowly. With increasing frequency he scanned the irregular oval of sky visible above the clearing, but dusk had long since given way to full night before he managed to count ten stars winking coldly in the ink-dark sky. Away to the south, through the clouds which hid its face, he could detect the faint glow of the moon, still some three days from full.

He walked across the clearing, rapped twice on the heavy door, lifted the latch and entered the ambulatory, where a solitary candle feebly illuminated the remembered brightly coloured frescoes on the plastered outer wall.

'I'm over here, Canio,' came her voice from the cella, the inner heart of the temple.

Easing between two of the smooth stone columns which separated the ambulatory from the tall cella tower, he made out her slim figure standing on the far side of the circular font. Carved out of warm yellow limestone, the font was a long arm's span across and rose some six inches above the mosaic floor. Back in June the *agens in rebus* Macrinius Lunaris, now safely dead, had contemptuously urinated into it. He had never told Vilbia of that incident, and had no intention of telling her now, but here, encircled by the darkness, the memory made him uncomfortable.

She gave him a faint smile, then turned and unwound a fine chain from a cleat on the far wall. As the chain fed through her fingers he saw a triple-spouted bronze lamp descend from the gloom above, until she halted it some three feet above the font. Taking a taper from a fold of her *stola* she brushed past him and lit it from the ambulatory candle. Reaching over the font she held the taper above each spout in turn until the oil vaporised and ignited with a splutter. She blew out the taper and with a gesture of her outstretched hand invited him to crouch down beside the font, before herself kneeling on the opposite side.

He looked down into the dark but air-clear water, seeing the faintly shimmering reflections of their two faces, separated by the images of the three bright flames of the lamp. He glanced up at her, but at first she said nothing, and the only sound was the soft lisp of the water overflowing through the lead-lined opening in the side of the font, just below floor level, on its way out to become the headwaters of the stream which wound down through the wood to the lowlands below.

He found his eyes trying to focus simultaneously both on the reflections and on the muted multicoloured pebbles covering the bed of the spring. Together with the soft murmur of the overflowing water they produced a strangely hypnotic effect, and he began to feel slightly light-headed, his awareness of time and place beginning to grow hazy.

'Leucesca, Leucesca, goddess of this spring,' came Vilbia's voice, little more than a whisper but sufficient to break the spell. 'If it pleases you to do so, show this man, Canio, where he might find the woman, Trifosa.' She repeated this invocation twice more, all the while staring down into the clear water.

In the font Canio saw nothing, except the pebbles and the reflections. He was now almost certain that Trifosa had come here as she fled on that July night. Vilbia had never asked why Trifosa had left, which surely meant that she already knew – and who but Trifosa could have told her? So was Vilbia now going to pretend to see, in the waters of the spring, the place where she thought Trifosa might be found?

Time passed. Raising his eyes a fraction, he covertly studied Vilbia's face as she gazed intently into the water. She seemed confused, but even as he watched the puzzled expression slowly turned to one of alarm. Suddenly she looked up, and for a long moment they stared directly into each other's eyes, before Canio peered down into the font to see what had startled her.

For a heartbeat he saw nothing different, then realised that the upside down face in the water opposite his own was no longer Vilbia's. It was now that of an older woman, coldly beautiful, but stern and unsmiling, her eyes seemingly fixed intently upon him.

Instinctively his head jerked up to see who it was that now knelt on the other side of the font. To his intense relief it was still Vilbia, and down in the water of the spring the reflection was once more her own. But that momentary illusion of the strange woman's face had unsettled him. Uneasy now, he deliberately let the mystification show on his face.

But before he could ask, Vilbia said abruptly, 'It seems that Leucesca has chosen not to show us where Trifosa can be found... unless you saw something?'

He hesitated, wanting to tell her, but equally unwilling to appear foolish. Or, worse, for her to admit that she too had seen the face. 'No, I didn't see anything... are you quite sure you didn't either?' he could not stop himself asking.

She shook her head. 'No, nothing of any consequence... nothing concerning Trifosa. It would seem that your journey here has been wasted.'

'Perhaps... but not entirely wasted though – it's been good to see you again.' But she seemed lost in thought, and when she didn't reply he stood up and stretched. 'I'd better be on my way then.'

She rocked backwards and rose gracefully on her toes. 'If you wish, you can stay the night in my little house. I'm sure the bed won't be as comfortable as the one you shared with Trifosa at Villa Canini, but it'll save you and Antares a ride home through the dark.' And before he could ask, she added, 'I won't be needing it – there's someone that I have to see tonight, so you'll only have Antares for company.'

'That's all right, he doesn't snore – although your bed might be a snug fit for the two of us... What someone?'

'Oh, nobody you'd know,' she replied lightly, gliding past him and moving out towards the gloom of the ambulatory. Then she halted and slowly turned to face him. 'But why now, Canio – why, after more than three long months, have you come to me seeking Trifosa?'

So Canio told her about the dreams in which Trifosa appeared, she still vivid and alive while the image of Antoninus was fading. And that he interpreted those dreams as meaning that she would be willing to come back to him, if only he could find her and convince her that he had played no part in Antoninus's murder (although he was acutely aware that it would have been more accurate to say that he had played no willing part in it).

Vilbia listened in silence, then said gently, 'But Canio, they were *your* dreams – yours, not hers. So perhaps they only told you what you wanted to believe... I have to go now. Please stay here for as long as you like, but be sure to extinguish the lamp and candle before you leave.'

But he had no wish to linger inside the temple: in his mind's eye he could still see that strange woman's face and unsmiling eyes staring at him. Yet by the time he had snuffed out the four tiny flames and made his way out into the dark clearing, Vilbia had disappeared. He called her name several times, but there was no reply.

CHAPTER TWO

19th October

Canio stayed awake long into the night, but Vilbia did not return. Eventually he kicked off his boots and slept in her little bed, finding the blankets faintly damp, as though they had not been used for some time. But if she did not sleep here, then where? As he lay in the darkness, listening to the sighing of the wind in the trees and the occasional scuffles and unearthly squeals of woodland creatures fighting and dying, the disquieting suspicion returned that perhaps these days she did not need to sleep.

Waking at sunrise, he waited until mid-morning, but still she did not come. And as the time passed, so the conviction hardened that she would not return until she was sure he had gone. He could understand why: she must suspect that he had once again demonstrated a capacity for betraying someone who considered him a friend. But it still hurt.

Saddling Antares, he rode the seven miles back south to Villa Canini.

In the vineyard the last of the grapes were being picked. Along the rows of vines Felix was slowly driving the small one-ox cart, into which several of the residents of the villa and outbuildings, including old Diovicus and Regina the cook, were tipping wicker baskets as soon as they were filled (or half-filled, in the case of Diovicus) with bunches of plump black grapes. They were slicing them from the vines with small, sharp knives, which they pushed back into the sheaths on their belts before heaving the baskets over the sides of the cart.

As Canio approached he heard the gleeful shouts of several small children as they ran up and down the rows, the dark red juice of illicitly eaten grapes staining their chins and hands. He gave them his best ferocious roar and shook his fist, then watched in amusement as they scampered away as fast as their little legs could carry them.

He rode on a few yards, then twisted around in the saddle to see them peeping out from between the tall reeds growing on the banks of the little brook – the brook which was formed by the confluence of the two small streams between which, further up the coomb, his villa stood.

He exchanged a few words with Felix, who maintained (in the face of Canio's undisguised scepticism) that the children had only been helping themselves to the few grapes that the pickers had thought too small or over-ripe to be worth picking. Then, after crossing the stout timber bridge that spanned the deep gully in which the south stream ran, he continued up the coomb. At the great aisled barn below the villa he turned Antares over to Austalis, the blacksmith-cum-ostler, then walked back down to the press house.

Inside that large timber building he found Senuacus, bare-legged, treading the grapes inside a waist-high vat constructed of timber staves bound with hoops of wrought iron and raised up above the beaten-earth floor on several large blocks of the local limestone.

Crouching beside a short pipe projecting from the base, Aniceta, Trifosa's maid, was juggling a pair of pewter flagons, substituting the empty one for the full one, before pouring the contents of the latter into one of several dozen enormous clayware jars sunk up to their middles in the floor at the far end of the press house. A large square of sacking tied over the mouth of the jar served to strain out the pips and stalk fragments.

Canio waited until the last drops of this current first pressing had been collected, then helped Senuacus clamber wearily out of the vat.

'Sticky work, Master,' he remarked, as he collected his boots and walked stiffly out of the press house, on his way to wash his legs and feet in the waters of the north stream, which bubbled down the slope only a few yards away.

Adjacent to the vat stood the press. It consisted of a large slab of limestone, set slightly sloping, its interior hollowed into a shallow basin with a smooth, polished surface. From the lowest point in the surrounding kerb a spout projected. Suspended above and across the basin was a long, wide beam, formed from the trunk of a young oak, adzed flat and smooth on its underside.

The low end of the beam was pivoted in a squat timber framework. The other end was suspended by a rope and pulley from a high horizontal cross beam supported by two vertical posts. The free end of the rope was wound tightly around a large iron cleat fixed to one of the vertical posts.

Unbuckling his sword belt, Canio propped the scabbarded *spatha* up against the wall, picked up a broad-bladed wooden shovel, reached over the edge of the vat and began scooping out the pomace of trodden grape skins, pips and stalks, and slopping them down onto the basin, directly under the beam.

'Ready to catch the juice?' he asked Aniceta, as he smoothed the tenth shovelful down, then leaned the shovel against the press house wall.

'Ready, Master,' she nodded, and placed one of the pewter flagons below the spout, then hastily backed away as Canio began unwinding the rope. As the rope came free from the cleat, Canio felt the sudden shock on his arm muscles as he checked the beam's drop, before lowering it onto the pomace. Releasing the rope, he straddled the free end of the beam, adding his own

12

weight to it, and after a few moments heard the juice of this second pressing begin to splatter into the pewter flagon.

'That's a lovely sound, isn't it?' he remarked to Aniceta, pointing towards the rapidly-filling flagon. 'You are keeping this separate from the juice from the treading, aren't you?'

'Of course I am, Master,' she said patiently, 'just like I did last year, and just like Diovicus did in Aurelius Charax's day. The best juice is in the first seven rows of jars, and this from the pressings goes into the rest.'

And before Canio could reassure her that he had only been teasing, she continued, 'And the pomace that's left after pressing all goes into those big bowls over there, for whoever should want it to help themselves from – but only after Regina has taken as much as she needs to make those little sweet cakes of hers.'

'Quite right,' Canio confirmed, studying the way her breasts swayed under her *stola* as she twisted sideways to deftly change flagons. Aniceta was a pretty girl; not as beautiful as Trifosa, but then who was? Several times in these last months he had found himself tempted to coax her into the bed that he and Trifosa had once shared. But so far he never had, and perhaps he never would – for what secrets and suspicions and fears had Trifosa shared with her maid, and what questions might they prompt her to whisper to him in the depths of the ever-lengthening autumn nights? And sleeping with her might banish the dreams of Trifosa, dreams he did not want banished.

He was still watching her, contemplating what he would probably never do, when he heard rapid footsteps outside, and in the moments before Felix appeared assumed that it was Senuacus returning.

'Soldiers! Four of them – coming down Coel's Hill!' the bailiff announced, panting slightly.

Canio swung his left leg over the beam and dropped down onto the press house floor. 'Four – what in Hades' name can they want?' he muttered.

'Trouble – that's what they always want. If they can't find it, they bring their own,' said Felix, adding, 'The one in front had a helmet with a big red crest.'

'*Merda*!' Grabbing his scabbarded *spatha*, Canio pointed to Felix and Aniceta in turn. 'Wait here, both of you. And if they should see you and ask, tell them that I'm around somewhere in or near the villa, but you don't know exactly where.'

'Do you know who—?' Felix began, but Canio was already out of the press house and didn't catch the rest of the question as he hurried up the gentle slope towards the villa courtyard. Once inside the villa he strapped on his sword belt and made his way down the east wing corridor to his bedroom.

Closing the door he selected a key from one of his belt pouches, and with it opened the nearest of a pair of oak chests which stood on the mosaic floor in one corner of the room. Taking out a small, sheathed dagger he tucked it into the top of his *bracae* trousers, so that it was hidden below his knee-length tunic. After re-locking the chest he strolled back along the corridor to await the coming of his unwanted guests.

He did not have long to wait. As he neared the main entrance doors he heard the thunderous clatter of hooves crossing the bridge over the south stream. Stepping back a pace, he watched through a gap in an unlatched shutter as the four soldiers came trotting under the arched gateway in the courtyard wall.

'Julius Castor, you damned turd,' he murmured. 'So it is you.'

He continued watching as Castor rode across the courtyard, dismounted and threw his reins carelessly to one of his men, then stared around him, the expression on his face a mixture of irritation and puzzlement – presumably at the apparent absence of people.

Castor set his right foot on the bottom step, but before he could advance further, Canio had taken two quick paces and flung open both leaves of the door.

Quick as a cat, Castor jumped back, his right hand grabbing for the hilt of his *spatha*. The two men were about equal in height, but, as he intended, from the top of the steps Canio towered some twelve inches above Castor. The two men stared at each other, Canio keeping his face expressionless, and Castor's face too, after an initial flash of anger, giving nothing away.

In the silence which followed it seemed that neither man was willing to be the first to speak. But the advantage was with Canio, and it was Castor who said stiffly, 'Claudius Caninus, the *Vir Perfectissimus* Caristanius Sabinus extends his greetings and requires that you attend upon him at his residence, the Villa Censorini.'

'Still called Villa Censorini, is it?' Canio asked, affecting surprise. 'I thought Sabinus would have changed its name by now.'

'The *Vir Perfectissimus* has no intention of changing the name,' Castor replied coldly. 'It is the one by which our sacred emperor, Flavius Valentinianus, referred to the estate in the deed by which he granted the *Praeses* the tenancy when it became imperial property, following its confiscation. Confiscation which, I would remind you, resulted from the treasonous conspiracies of the previous owner, your friend Flavius Antoninus.'

'If he was a traitor, then he was no friend of mine,' said Canio, deadpan. He knew full well that Sabinus had only been granted tenancy, not ownership as he must have hoped, but he enjoyed making Castor say it out loud, guessing it was a cause of resentment to Sabinus and thus to his dog Castor as well. 'Tell me, is the rumour I've been hearing true?'

'What rumour?'

'That bids are being invited for Villa Censorini's lands. Not the villa itself, just the estate lands. They say that Emperor Valentinianus is always looking for ways to fill the imperial coffers, armies being such expensive things to maintain.'

'I can't say I've heard any such rumour.'

Which was not surprising, since Canio had only that moment made it up. 'So what exactly does Sabinus want the pleasure of my company for?'

'The *Vir Perfectissimus* did not inform me, but you can be assured that the matter is one of some importance.'

'And when does he want me?'

'Now, of course. That's why we're here.'

'To escort me there and make sure nothing nasty happens to me on the way?'

'We would be failing in our duty if we did not.'

'How reassuring. But at the moment I'm busy with the grape harvest, so I must decline the *Praeses* kind invitation.'

'It isn't an invitation, Caninus, it's a summons,' Castor said bluntly. 'The *Vir Perfectissimus* requires your presence now.'

'Oh, I see. Then be so good as to tell Sabinus that I shall attend upon him shortly – after you and your men are safely back in your kennels.'

Canio took a fierce pleasure in seeing the anger flash across Castor's face again. 'I could insist that you accompany us.'

'My name's not Antoninus.' Canio let the fingers of his left hand rest on the hilt of his *spatha*, easing it slightly in its scabbard.

'With four against one it wouldn't matter what your name was.'

'You think so? First it's four, then it's three, then it's two, then it's one, then it's none… I've done it before, against the Alemanni, and they were big lads too.' It was a lie, of course, but it produced a gratifying shadow of uncertainty on Castor's face.

'My orders, Caninus, are to deliver you safely to Villa Censorini. You have nothing to fear from us.'

'Did you say that to Antoninus too?'

'The traitor Antoninus was killed in self-defence when he attacked my men after murdering the *agens in rebus* Macrinius Lunaris.'

16

'I never doubted it for a moment, as I'm sure Sabinus knows. I'll be at Villa Censorini sometime this afternoon. Tell Sabinus that. And now I'm sure you have other important duties to perform, so I won't ask you to wait.' And Canio waved as if in farewell.

Castor hesitated, which Canio found reassuring, because in that hesitation he read Castor's instinct to do violence to him warring with what he assumed were Sabinus's orders to get him to Villa Censorini unharmed.

'Very well, Caninus. If that is the way you wish to proceed I shall advise the *Vir Perfectissimus* to expect you this afternoon... but Caninus, if you don't come, then I can assure you that *Praeses* Sabinus will be most displeased, and will waste no time in making his displeasure felt. Do you understand me?'

'Only too well. Enjoy your ride back – and do try not to murder anyone on the way.' Canio waved farewell again, and watched as Castor hesitated, then, stiff with anger and affronted pride, remounted, kicked his heels into his horse's flanks, making the beast whinny sharply, before trotting briskly out of the courtyard, the other soldiers trailing behind.

Canio watched them go. Hearing a slight rustle of cloth he turned to see Regina standing behind him. 'How did you get here?'

'I came back from the vineyard while you were in the press house, Master, in case you wanted something to eat... Do you think it was wise to make that wicked man angry?'

'No, not wise at all. But sometimes a man can be too wise for his own self-respect – not that that's a problem I usually worry about. Anyway, since you're here, I do want a bite to eat before I set off for Villa Censorini – so what delights have you got hidden in that kitchen of yours?'

'Only bread and cold mutton, Master – I've been in the vineyard picking since the dew dried off the grapes.'

'Cold mutton will do me fine… You haven't asked why Sabinus wants to see me.'

'Would you tell me, Master?'

'Probably not, even if I knew – which I don't.'

'Then it's as well I didn't ask, isn't it, Master?'

CHAPTER THREE

Canio stayed for a while in Regina's kitchen, eating bread and cold mutton, washed down with a rather pleasant South Gaulish wine (brought in two barrels from Glevum docks only a week before, and costing two bright gold *solidi* each). Then, when he reckoned that Julius Castor and his men were at least halfway back to Villa Censorini, he strolled down to the great aisled barn and helped Austalis to saddle-up Antares again.

As he rode past the vineyard he asked Felix which way the soldiers had gone.

'East, up Coel's Hill, towards the Salt Way – same way as they came.'

'Right,' said Canio, and headed south, towards the valley leading up to the minor road which passed through the market settlement of Fonscolnis.

When Felix heard where he was going, the bailiff had asked if he wanted himself and Senuacus to accompany him, seeing as they considered themselves to be his bodyguards. Canio had declined the offer, reasoning that, if Castor were lying in wait somewhere, then his best defence would be Antares' speed. Felix and Senuacus could be useful bully boys on occasion, but he doubted they would be much use against trained soldiers.

The early afternoon October sun was still pleasantly warm as he rode the ten miles south, passing through Fonscolnis and then following the little River Coln until he arrived at Villa Censorini.

Things had changed in the three months since Antoninus's death, and not for the better. As he approached the villa, Canio noticed three heavily armed soldiers stationed in the broad, watchtower-flanked gateway that gave access to the lower courtyard. In the summer there had been the sounds of children's voices coming from the courtyard, but now there were none. Strange, he reflected, that he should have noticed their absence more than their presence.

When he was yards from the gateway, Castor appeared from the entrance of the right-hand watchtower. The man must have been waiting for him, wanting to savour the moment. 'Ah, Caninus, so you've arrived at last. Be so good as to dismount and wait here while I inform the *Vir Perfectissimus* that you have at last found the time to attend upon him.'

Canio watched as Castor strode away across the lower courtyard towards the enclosed cross-gallery which separated the lower and upper courtyards, mounted the flight of steps and disappeared through the gallery gatehouse.

But he did not dismount, which seemed to make the guards uneasy. Perhaps, he thought sardonically, they were wondering if they should repeat Castor's instruction, but did not quite have the nerve. Then one looked as though he were actually about to do so, but Canio fixed the man with an unblinking stare until he looked away. Time passed. Canio was not surprised: he had guessed that Castor intended to make him wait, which was another good reason for not dismounting.

At last Castor reappeared from the cross-gallery. Canio slid down from the saddle and led Antares into the lower courtyard, then waited for a groom to take him: he wasn't about to trust the horse to one of the soldiers.

'Your sword belt, if you please.' Castor held out his right hand, palm uppermost.

Canio had expected as much. He unbuckled the belt and handed it to Castor, complete with scabbarded *spatha*.

Castor tossed it carelessly to one of the soldiers. 'Follow me.' Without looking back he began re-crossing the lower courtyard. Canio did as bidden, noticing as he did so that two of the soldiers, including the one with his sword belt, had swung in behind him.

Castor led them up the steps and into the cross-gallery, turned right and continued down the gallery until it opened out into a large room in the north wing. This room, paved with a geometric mosaic, Canio remembered as the reception hall, which served as an anteroom to the two formal audience chambers, which themselves lay behind the pair of tall double doors in front of him. Both sets of doors were closed.

Signalling Canio to halt, Castor rapped twice on the nearest of the doors, waited until a muffled voice from inside called, 'Enter,' then opened them and went in, closing both leaves behind him so quickly that Canio was unable to see who was inside, although he assumed it was Sabinus.

Moments later the doors opened again and two soldiers came out, followed by Castor. 'This way,' he said briskly, and led Canio into the audience chamber. Neither the two new soldiers, nor the pair that had accompanied him from the lower courtyard, followed Canio into the room before Castor pulled the doors closed again.

Sabinus – Caristanius Sabinus, *Vir Perfectissimus, Praeses* of the province of Britannia Prima – sat on a large throne-like chair on a raised dais which occupied the whole of the polygonal apse in the far wall. It occurred to Canio that the arrangement was deliberately mimicking the apse in the great basilica in Corinium, the place where he had last seen Sabinus, as the man sat hearing the pleas of petitioners on that endless day back in July.

Castor took up position at the foot of the dais, below Sabinus's right hand, but it was neither Sabinus nor Castor that held Canio's attention.

'*Salve*, Peltrasius.'

'*Salve*, Canio,' replied the soldier standing opposite Castor, below Sabinus's left hand. 'You remembered my name then?'

'And your ugly face. How's Galenus?'

'Dead, so I heard.' Peltrasius did not say how, and Canio did not ask. Peltrasius was still a young man, twenty-two or twenty-three perhaps, but whatever softness of youth might once have existed in his features had long since shrivelled away. And as the face, so the soul behind it. The army often did that to men, unless they were already like that when they joined, which, Canio suspected, Peltrasius probably was. He and Castor were a matching pair.

'So you remember each other, Caninus. Excellent. Now be so good as to listen to the story that Peltrasius is about to tell.' And Sabinus indicated with a slight gesture of his open palm that Peltrasius should begin.

'In the autumn of last year, when I was stationed at Lindinis—'

'From the beginning,' Sabinus interrupted.

'But Canio knows that part of the story, sir.'

'Are you questioning my orders?'

'No, sir; of course not.'

'Then let us hear the complete story.'

'Very good, sir... From the capture of the deserter, Orgillus?'

'Of course.'

'It was, as I recall, about the middle of June, two years ago, when myself, Galenus and Canio—'

'Claudius Caninus to you,' muttered Canio.

Sabinus shot him an impatient glance and gestured Peltrasius to continue.

'The three of us were riding a patrol some half-dozen miles south of Corinium, when we captured a deserter, a man going by the name of Orgillus. While searching him I discovered a small *orichalcum* figurine, a representation of what I now know to be the pagan goddess Hecate.'

'Describe it for us, this figurine.' Canio noticed that Sabinus seemed to be gazing at some point in space above Peltrasius's head.

'It was about so high,' said Peltrasius, holding the index fingers of both hands between five and six inches apart. 'A woman in a long *stola*, carrying a sword in one hand and a torch in the other, both held upright. And there was a dog, a sort of hunting hound, curled at her feet. And the *orichalcum* was black with age, with only one small spot on her *stola* polished bright.'

'And when you shook it?' Sabinus prompted.

'I think I may have heard something rattle inside, but I can't be sure. I only held it briefly.'

'Why only briefly?'

'Because I hurled it away, sir, as far as I could into the undergrowth.'

'And why did you do that?'

'Because it was a pagan idol and I thought that was the correct thing to do – what our sacred emperors would have expected me to do, sir.'

Canio gave a grunt of amusement. 'You only threw it away because you realised it wasn't made of gold.'

Sabinus ignored Canio. 'How did this Orgillus say that he had come by the idol?'

'He never said, sir. Before he could be questioned further he was killed attempting to escape.' Peltrasius paused and glanced quickly at Canio, as if expecting him to say something.

But Canio said nothing, although he gave Peltrasius a sardonic leer which was intended to say, *The man was unarmed and defenceless and you stabbed him in the guts, you turd.*

'And that was the only time you ever saw the idol – you never saw it again?'

'No, sir, I never did. Although afterwards, as we were riding back towards Corinium, this man, Canio, halted, saying his horse had gone lame. And I didn't see him again until late that evening, back in the city.'

'So you suspected that he had gone back and retrieved the idol?'

'Not at the time I didn't, sir, but now I'm certain that he must have done.'

'And why is that?'

'Because, in the early autumn of last year, when I was riding through the hilly country some miles to the west of Lindinis —'

'The Niger Hills, I think you called them.'

'Yes, sir; the Niger Hills. I and several of my fellow soldiers took shelter from the rain in the ruins of what had once been a large pagan temple. I believe it had been sacked and burnt during the *Barbarica Conspiratio*, and by then nobody was living there, except for a strange old man. A priest he was, or claimed to be, although we suspected he was mad.'

'Why mad?' Sabinus asked. *Rhetorically, just for my benefit*, Canio thought. Peltrasius's tale had a well-rehearsed smoothness.

'Because, sir, he would stop everyone who happened to pass by, asking them if they knew of the whereabouts of a small *orichalcum* figurine of a goddess. And from the way he described it, I realised that it must be the same figurine I had taken from that deserter, Orgillus, the previous year. So I asked him why he wanted it, and he said that it was the most valuable thing in all the world, to those who knew its secret.'

'And what was its secret?' Sabinus asked.

'He wouldn't tell me that, sir, although when I told him that I might know where it was, he said that if I were to bring it to him, he would take me to someone who would make me a rich man.'

Canio thought he knew who that someone was. He told himself that he didn't believe that Hades even existed, but nevertheless could not stop himself thinking, *Yes, my boy, I wish he had taken you to him – and then left you in a place from where you could never return to this world.*

'So as soon as you got leave, you went back to the place where you last saw that pagan idol and searched for it... even though you knew it was only made of *orichalcum*?'

It occurred to Canio that Sabinus enjoyed seeing Peltrasius squirm. Which was fine by him. He also noticed that Sabinus's face seemed thinner than he remembered it from the summer, almost gaunt, like that of a man who hasn't been sleeping well. Conscience paining him, he hoped.

'I had thought it was *orichalcum*, sir, but because the priest was so anxious to get his hands on it, I suspected that I must have been mistaken and it really was made of gold.'

'But you never found it.'

'No, sir, I did not, although I searched for half a day.'

'And there, Caninus, the matter might have ended... But then it chanced that, a month or so ago, Peltrasius became one of several soldiers from the *Jovii* assigned to my personal bodyguard troops in Corinium. And there he learnt that a one-time fellow soldier, a man who used to go by the name of Canio, had suddenly become very rich about two years earlier – something that must have happened only a few months after Peltrasius had thrown away that supposedly worthless idol that the mad priest appeared to value so highly.

'So that set him wondering whether you, Caninus, had gone back on that June day and retrieved the figurine. And he further speculated that the idol was the source of your wealth. Exactly how such a thing could have been accomplished I neither know nor wish to know. Peltrasius assumed it was done by enacting some obscene pagan ritual, details of which I have no wish to pollute my mind by learning or even conjecturing. In short, Caninus, he believes that you practised sorcery, those forbidden acts so rightly abominated by our beloved emperors, Valentinianus and Valens. And so he very properly reported his suspicions to Julius Castor, and Castor, of course, informed me.'

So why, Canio wondered, if Peltrasius really did suspect that he had obtained his wealth by proscribed means, hadn't the man attempted to blackmail him? It was certainly something he himself might have considered doing, had their positions been reversed.

Then, remembering their mutual antipathy, he realised that Peltrasius would have hesitated to approach him alone, fearing that he might subsequently have vanished from the face of the earth. Which, he reflected, was something that could very well have happened.

Sabinus's voice broke his train of thought. 'Thank you, Peltrasius. You may now resume your duties.'

'Yes, sir; thank you, sir.' Peltrasius sounded relieved. He saluted Sabinus and Castor and hurried out of the audience chamber, giving Canio a sour glance as he went.

Sabinus waited for a few moments, then at his signal Castor opened the doors again and Canio heard him send the four soldiers away.

Canio tried to guess what was coming next. Was Sabinus really going to bring a charge of sorcery against him? 'You don't seriously believe what that cretin Peltrasius said, do you – about me going back for that worthless figurine?'

Sabinus eyed him coldly. 'What you really mean is, do I believe that you practised black magic with the figurine and became rich as a result?' He snorted in what Canio assumed passed for amusement. 'No, of course I don't – do you think I'm a complete fool? I suspect that you acquired your wealth by more mundane means – although probably no less criminal. I do, however, believe that Peltrasius was correct in believing that you went back and retrieved the idol from wherever he had thrown it.'

Canio shook his head. 'No: the one and only time I ever saw that damned thing was when Peltrasius threw it into the undergrowth. And if you don't believe I wanted it for criminal purposes, why else would I want it?'

'Quite possibly because you suspected that Peltrasius was wrong, and it really was made of gold? I don't know, and in truth I don't really care. But whatever your reason, I'm certain that you went back and found it.'

'But since I didn't, it must still be where Peltrasius threw it.'

'No, it's not.'

'Are you sure? Peltrasius could have missed it, even if he looked in the right place, which I doubt.'

'He could indeed. But a week ago I sent him and Castor to search the area again, and again they found nothing.'

'And did they find what was left of Orgillus's body? It should still have been there.' *Or it would have been, if I hadn't taken it away and buried it.*

Sabinus glanced at Castor, who shook his head.

'Well, there's your answer,' Canio continued. 'Orgillus wasn't dead; wasn't even as badly wounded as we all thought. He must have retrieved the figurine and made off with it. It's the obvious answer... Why, if I might ask, are you so interested in a little scrap of old *orichalcum*?'

Sabinus hesitated, as if considering, then said, 'What I am about to tell you is in the strictest confidence, not to be repeated to anyone. Understood?'

'Understood,' said Canio. Not that he could have said anything else.

'It so happened that, some ten days after I first heard about that figurine, I travelled to Londinium for my quarterly meeting with the *Vicarius*. After the formal audience there was a somewhat less formal dinner party at Civilis's private residence. It went on well into the night and some very good wine was sampled. Perhaps a little more than was entirely wise. By and by the guests started exchanging amusing little anecdotes, the sort of things which never find their way into written reports. Somebody – I forget who – brought up the subject of the credulity of pagans and their belief in the powers of the stone and metal idols they make to their false gods.

'And so, most unwisely as it turned out, I mentioned that wretched figurine to my fellow guests, and also Peltrasius's belief – evident to me, even if denied by him – that its possession would somehow make him as rich as you seem to have become. The other guests – good Christians all – thought it most amusing, but Civilis himself became somewhat agitated.

'Strangely, it would appear that the *Vir Spectabilis* was aware of the existence of that particular pagan idol, and wanted to know everything I could tell him about its current whereabouts. Why, I do not know, and I thought it imprudent to ask, but he certainly knew something of the myths and superstitions which apparently surround it. And, although he did not actually say so, I formed the impression that he had seen, and perhaps even handled it, at some time in the fairly recent past. Which, I admit, surprised me somewhat.

'Not that all this really matters. What does matter is that he ordered me to spare no effort in finding the idol and delivering it to him in person. I did hope that by the morning, in daylight, when heads were clearer, he would rescind the order, but in fact he was even more insistent that I find the wretched thing – and as you may have heard, Civilis is not a man whose displeasure one would wish to incur. And if I were to incur his displeasure, you would most certainly incur mine. So, Caninus, be so good as to bring it to me without delay.'

'But as I told you, I haven't got it.'

Sabinus exhaled loudly. 'So you said. But be warned, Caninus: should I be forced to suffer the *Vicarius's* anger by failing to deliver that idol, I have it in my power to make life very difficult for you. For one thing, there is the little matter of your supposed Aunt Peregrina's will bequeathing you that fortune in gold coins – oh yes, the late Macrinius Lunaris told me all about that.'

'That will is absolutely genuine, as I'm sure you know. If Lunaris really had thought it was a fake, then he would have attempted to prove it, to make blackmailing me easier.' Sabinus looked as if he were about to demur, but before he could do so, Canio continued, 'But it isn't a fake, so he couldn't prove it.' *And neither can you, you bastard, or you'd have done so by now.*

'And yet, Caninus, you still did his bidding. Why was that?' Without giving Canio a chance to reply (which was fortunate: he might have struggled to produce a plausible answer), Sabinus added, 'In any case, in my position I would have little difficulty in finding the necessary documentary proof that the will is indeed a forgery.'

Like the documentary proof you forged and then "found" to prove that Antoninus was implicated in Valentinus's conspiracy? Canio thought, but was not unwise enough to actually say.

'Also,' Sabinus continued, 'it lies within my power to overrule the *Rationalis's* assessor and determine myself the amount of tax payable by your estate, in coin and grain and fleeces.'

And Canio, like Aurelius Charax before him, enjoyed a mutually beneficial relationship with the local tax assessor, something which he most definitely did not want jeopardised. He gave an ambiguous shrug. 'Very well, since you say the *Vicarius* himself wants it, I shall attempt to find it – wherever it may be.'

'Oh, you must do much more than attempt, Caninus. You must succeed.' There was a long pause, and then Sabinus said slowly, as if weighing every word, 'Are you aware that Civilis has been in post now for some two years?'

'It must be at least that since he was appointed *Vicarius* at the request of our glorious saviour, *Comes* Theodosius.'

'Quite so,' Sabinus said coldly. 'Although what you are probably unaware of is that, with the so-called *Barbarica Conspiratio* long over and the traitor Valentinus's attempted rebellion crushed, Civilis is anxious to return to the milder climes of his native Hispania. He is not a young man, and finds the prospect of spending yet another winter here in Britannia distinctly disagreeable.'

'So?' asked Canio.

'So, the post of *Vicarius* of the diocese of Britannia is likely to become vacant early next year.'

'And you're thinking —?'

'I'm not thinking anything, Caninus. Appointment to the vacant post of *Vicarius* will be made by the emperor, on the recommendation of the Praetorian Prefect of the Gauls.'

'But you consider it possible that if you hand Civilis that figurine of Hecate, which he seems so keen to acquire, he'll put your name at the top of any list of suitable candidates which he might feel inclined to pass to the Prefect?'

Sabinus smiled – a smile which never came close to reaching his eyes. 'You understand the situation perfectly, Caninus. It would be very much to both our advantages for you to provide me with that figurine. After all, it never hurt anyone to have friends in high places, particularly when such friends are in a position to overlook misdemeanours, future as well as past. Don't you agree?'

'Certainly,' said Canio. *And enemies in high places are also to be avoided, if at all possible.*

'Good. Today is the nineteenth day of October, fourteen days before the kalends. So, I will give you until that date – the kalends of November.'

Canio decided to take a chance, reasoning that he had nothing to lose. 'Fourteen days isn't nearly enough; it's bound to take me longer than that, seeing as I've no idea where it is.'

Sabinus stared at him and gave an exaggerated sigh. 'You want longer?' There was a long moment of silence, then, to Canio's surprise, he said, 'Very well: I can be a reasonable man – you may have until the nones. That's another four whole days. But... do not disappoint me, Caninus, because if you do the consequences for us both will be unpleasant – and in your case, very unpleasant.' And before Canio could reply, he continued, 'So farewell, Caninus, until we meet again – on, or preferably well before, the nones of November. Castor will escort you to the gatehouse.'

As he rode the ten miles back to Villa Canini, the great fiery sun sinking slowly in the south-west sky, Canio held a disjointed and one-sided conversation with Antares, in which he voiced his opinion that, among other things, Sabinus's entire female ancestry had been members of the oldest profession.

Antares, a good listener but no conversationalist, did not reply.

CHAPTER FOUR

20th & 21st October

Canio spent the night at Villa Canini. Next day, at first light, carrying bread, a joint of cold mutton and a goatskin full of that rather pleasant South Gaulish wine, he rode the seven miles back north to Leucesca's temple, hoping to speak with Vilbia again.

The place appeared deserted, but reasoning that she could not be far away he settled down to wait in the doorway of her little house, eating, drinking and watching squirrels plundering beechmast in the sunlit treetops, where sprays of yellow and brown leaves showed here and there among the green, silent reminders of summer's unstoppable passing.

It was mid-afternoon when Antares' soft neighing and the restless pricking up of the horse's ears alerted Canio to the sounds of somebody or something coming up through the wood from the lowland plain below. Silently he got to his feet and drew back from the doorway, twice hearing the soft cracking of a rotten twig, the first faint, the second louder. Then silence. Noticing that Antares was looking towards a point a few yards to the left of the house he walked out of the building and peered round the corner.

But it was not Vilbia who stood hesitantly at the edge of the clearing, but a scrawny young boy. Canio guessed his age to be around seven, give or take a year.

32

'Who in the name of sweet Venus are you?' he asked, not bothering to hide his irritation. He glared at the boy, taking in his ragged tunic, bare legs and the filthy rags bound around his feet to serve as shoes.

'My name's Maximus,' said the boy. 'What's yours?'

'Maximus? You look more like a Minimus. What do you want here?'

'I've come to ask the priestess something. What's your name?' the boy asked again.

'That's my business. What priestess?'

'The priestess they say lives here.'

'She's not here, so you've had a wasted journey.'

'Then I'll wait till she comes back,' the boy said defiantly.

'Please yourself,' said Canio, 'but you might have a long wait.' He settled down in the doorway and took a bite out of his joint of mutton. After a while he glanced up, to see the boy staring at the mutton joint as if he had never seen food before. He looked down and carried on eating. Several bites later he looked up again. The boy was still eyeing the mutton joint covetously.

'You hungry?'

'Not particularly,' said the boy.

'So you don't want a bite of this then?'

'Only if you've finished with it,' said the boy with apparent indifference.

Canio hesitated, then tossed the half-eaten joint over to him, then watched as the boy caught it in mid-air and straightaway began tearing into it with his teeth. He looked on in silence as the joint was rapidly reduced to white bone, and the bone sucked for the last traces of meat juice.

When the boy had finished and was licking his fingers, Canio wordlessly passed the three-quarters-empty wineskin (it had been a long day) over to him.

The boy unstoppered it and gulped down several mouthfuls, paused and choked slightly, then gulped down several more.

'Good stuff, eh?' said Canio, holding out his hand for the wineskin's return.

'Better than the snake piss that Vario serves.'

'Who's Vario?'

'Oh, nobody – just a man who sells wine,' the boy replied, turning away and looking towards the temple.

Canio got the impression he regretted mentioning the name. 'Sells it where?'

'Corinium.'

'Corinium? That's a coincidence: I seem to remember that there used to be a man by the name of Vario who kept a ratty little *popina* that sold the foulest wine in Glevum. Must have moved to Corinium. What is it you want to ask the priestess?'

'Where someone's gone... where they are now.'

'What someone?' Canio asked, passing the wineskin back to the boy.

The boy took another drink. 'Do you think the priestess will come today?'

'Maybe. What someone?'

'How much does the priestess charge?'

'To find someone? Maybe five *siliquae*. Have you got that much?'

'Yes.'

'Really?'

'Don't you believe me?' The boy fished down the front of his ragged tunic and from a hidden pocket drew out a twist of cloth, knotted at the top, which he untied to reveal a dozen or so small silver coins.

'How did you come by those?' Canio asked.

'My mother gave me them, before she went away.'

'Is it her you're trying to find?'

The boy hesitated, then nodded.

'How long's she been gone?'

'Sixteen days now,' the boy almost whispered, looking at the ground.

'Didn't she say where she was going?'

'No, not to me or anyone.'

'She just went off on her own and left you?'

'She went with a man, so I was told.'

'Ah, like that was it?' The boy said nothing, so Canio asked, 'What about your father?'

'Haven't got a father.'

'So where have you been staying these past two weeks?'

'At the *popina* where my mother worked... I thought she would be coming back for me.'

'Vario's *popina* in Glevum?'

The boy hesitated again, then mumbled, 'Yes.'

'And she never said when she'd be coming back?'

The boy shook his head, and Canio caught the glint of tears in the boy's eyes. 'She never even said she was going.'

'Which way did they go?'

'I don't know, not for sure. North, perhaps – a week after she'd gone a man drinking in the *popina* told me that the man she went with had said something about Eboracum. But he couldn't remember whether the man said he was going there, or had come from there. I asked him how far Eboracum is, and he said it's two hundred miles away to the north. Is it really that far?'

'Must be all of that – it's certainly a long way from Glevum. What's her name, your mother?'

'Marcia – have you heard of her?'

The name was not uncommon, but it was one which brought back memories of his own childhood. Bad memories. 'Liar – her name's no more Marcia than yours is Maximus.'

'It *is* Marcia, it really is,' the boy protested, again close to tears. 'Have you heard of her?' he asked again.

'No, why should I have?' Canio replied, aware that the words came out harsher than he had intended.

The boy must have picked up the anger in his voice, because

he fell silent and walked across the clearing to sit on the stone threshold of the temple.

Time passed. Over towards the south-west the sun sank below the treetops, and still Vilbia did not come. Reluctantly, Canio decided to wait through the night.

After unsaddling and tethering Antares, he carried saddle and bridle into Vilbia's house, kicked off his boots and prepared to stretch out on her little bed. In the gathering dusk he saw the boy still sitting at the temple threshold.

He looks much as I must have looked at his age, came the thought. 'Hadn't you better be heading for home?' he called over to him, although he was next to certain what the answer would be.

The boy stood and walked over to the house. 'I haven't got a home, not any more.'

'What about that *popina* in Glevum?'

The boy shook his head. 'I can't go back there. Vario only let me stay for as long as he did because he thought my mother might be coming back… some nights she used to go to his room.'

Canio didn't need to ask why.

'Even before she left he used to hit me sometimes, and after she'd gone he'd try to kick me whenever he caught sight of me… Do you think the priestess will come tonight?'

'Her name's Vilbia, and I've no idea whether she'll come or not. But I'm going to wait for her anyway – all night if I have to.'

'What is it you want to ask her?'

Canio scowled. 'Where I can find a lost lamb.'

The boy looked puzzled. 'But there aren't any lambs at this time of year.'

'That's probably why I can't find it,' Canio replied, lying down on Vilbia's bed.

The boy curled up on the bare, stone-flagged floor like a cat. Faintly shamed, Canio tossed him one of the blankets.

From time to time Canio woke, hearing again through the small, shuttered window the sighing of the wind through the treetops and the strange nocturnal woodland noises.

He woke at sunrise, but still Vilbia had not come. Then his stomach decided it was time to return to Villa Canini. The boy wanted to remain at the temple, fearful of missing Vilbia, but Canio's offer of as much food as he could eat proved too tempting to refuse. By the look of him, Canio guessed that he had not eaten a decent meal for several days, maybe longer.

As the boy sat jogging up and down behind him on Antares' back, Canio, voicing a suspicion that had come to him during the night, asked the boy if his mother, Marcia, really had given him those shiny silver *siliquae*? Or had he perhaps found them in a place where they were not actually lost?

'Yes, she gave them to me,' the boy answered promptly.

'Vario must pay good wages for a ratty *popina*.'

This time the boy did not reply immediately, and when he did it was so quietly that Canio barely heard him. 'She was given some of those coins by other men, not Vario.'

'What other men?' Canio asked.

'Other men… you know,' the boy said awkwardly.

Canio knew. He let the subject drop.

When they reached Villa Canini, Canio propelled the boy into Regina's kitchen, the boy gazing warily all around as he went.

'This is – what did you say your name was?'

'Maximus,' replied the boy, sounding surprised that Canio should have forgotten.

'Of course it is. Maximus, this is Regina. She's going to give you all the food you can eat, aren't you, Regina?'

'If you say so, Master,' said the cook, eyeing the boy's unwashed person and filthy tunic with distaste.

'Good, that's settled then. In the meantime, I'm off to see Aniceta – do you know where she is?' Canio asked, picking up a large bunch of plump black grapes and nibbling them off the stalks one by one.

'Not at this moment I don't, Master,' Regina replied. 'But I'm sure she's not far away...' she called out to Canio's retreating back.

Once inside his bedroom, Canio began searching through the great chest where his clothes were stored. From near the bottom he pulled out an old, plain tunic and a pair of *bracae* trousers of his that had seen better days.

From the adjoining chest, which contained the clothes left behind when Trifosa had fled away on that July night, he chose a pair of her everyday shoes, the ones she had worn when out gathering flowers and herbs. Studying them at arm's length, the memories they brought back started him wondering once again where she was now. Or even if she were still alive. Unwelcome thought.

Carrying the clothes and shoes, he found Aniceta in the great aisled barn and steered her back to the kitchen, where, to Regina's amazement, the boy was still eating like a starving wolf.

'This,' he said to Aniceta, 'is Maximus. First, you and Regina are to take him to the bathhouse and wash him. Then, you're to cut down these old clothes to make them fit him as best you can. If the shoes are too big, stuff some clean rags inside them. After I've packed some food and wine, young Minimus, I'm going back to the temple. You, are to stay here – if Vilbia does turn up, then I'll come back and tell you... Agreed?'

The boy, his entire lower face greasy from the mutton joint he was feasting on, hesitated, then nodded assent.

It was well after midday when the boy, now dressed in reasonably respectable (if somewhat baggy – Regina and Aniceta had evidently allowed for growth) tunic and *bracae* trousers, came scurrying down the path from the plateau and halted at the side of the temple. Canio frowned at him, but was not altogether surprised: he had anticipated that the boy would disobey him and come anyway, not trusting him to report Vilbia's return. Secretly, he was not displeased. 'Usually best to trust no one,' he murmured to himself, although to the boy he growled, 'What in Hades' name are you doing here?'

'Same as you, Canio – I've come to see if Vilbia's returned. Has she?' the boy asked, apparently unconcerned by Canio's less than friendly welcome.

Canio reflected that he had probably received much worse greetings. Also, that he now knew his name, so it had been pointless not to have told him earlier. 'No, she's not here. And my name is Claudius Caninus, not Canio.'

'But she will come, won't she?'

'Who knows?' Canio shrugged. He was himself beginning to wonder whether she would.

'Have you ever seen her?'

'Of course I have. Many times.'

'What's she like?'

'Vilbia? Nothing special,' he answered carelessly. 'Two legs, two arms. Only one head though. But she has got a huge black hound that eats ungrateful little shits for supper and spits out the bones to crunch up for breakfast next morning… are the new shoes comfortable?'

'They're a bit big for me,' the boy replied, 'but they're much better than what I had before,' he added hastily.

'Glad to hear it. Don't feel you have to thank me.'

CHAPTER FIVE

21st October

The boy heard her first, perhaps even before Antares, so silently did she arrive. 'Is that the priestess?' he whispered to Canio, pointing to the woman who stood in the middle of the clearing looking curiously at the horse.

Canio, who had been half asleep, sat up and yawned. 'No, that's not Vilbia. I don't know who she is.'

The woman must have heard him, because she turned and frowned. She was, he guessed, in her mid to late thirties with a weather-tanned face framed in a nimbus of abundant reddish-brown hair, beginning to grey.

'So you've come again, have you?' she said. 'I thought you might.'

'What? Who are you?'

'I'm Bodicca. Vilbia asked me to look after the temple while she's away.'

'Where's she gone?'

'Oh, just away... I don't know where.'

'So when will she be back?'

'Next week perhaps, or maybe the week after. She never says: perhaps she never knows herself. I didn't know you had a son, Canio.'

'He's not my son... and how did you know my name?'

'I know lots of things. I've seen you before.'

'Where?'

'Oh, here and there,' the woman replied vaguely.

And then Canio remembered: 'Bodicca – aren't you the woman Saturninus told me about? He said you were a strange woman.'

'He said that, did he? Well, strange or not, he found Caelofernus in the place where I said he would, didn't he?... Well, didn't he?'

'Who told you that – Vilbia?'

'Who else? Are you sure he's not your son? There's a lot of you in his face.'

'His name's Maximus, and I'd never seen him before yesterday. He's come to ask Vilbia to help him find his mother. And to save you asking, his mother's name is Marcia, apparently, and I've never met the lady.'

'So what is it that you want to see Vilbia for, *Domine* Canio?'

Canio looked over to where the boy sat, silent and still, apparently fascinated by this reputedly strange woman. 'Go and untether the horse and take him over to the stream and let him drink,' he called out. 'Well, go on – Antares won't bite you.'

When he judged that the boy was out of earshot, Canio whispered, 'Has Vilbia still got that little *orichalcum* figurine of Hecate?'

Bodicca pulled a mystified face. Theatrically mystified, Canio thought. 'Whatever would Vilbia be doing with a thing like that?'

'Keeping it safe.'

'Ah, that must be why she's never told me about it.'

'Look, I was the one who gave it to her – she must have told you that.'

Bodicca shook her head slowly from side to side. 'No, she's never told me anything about it.'

Realising that he was getting nowhere, Canio tried another approach. 'All I want is to see it for a few moments, so I can remember exactly what it looks like. Somebody – a very important somebody – is demanding that I find him a replica, an exact copy, of the damned thing.'

'But surely you must know what it looks like, if it really was you who gave it to Vilbia?'

'That was over two years ago, and I can't remember every detail,' Canio protested. 'But I do recall Vilbia herself saying that copies of the figurine exist, so she might know where I can find one. And if I do, I've got to be sure it looks just like the one I gave her.'

Bodicca looked up at the almost-cloudless autumn sky. 'A month ago I saw the last swallow leave,' she said wistfully. 'Some say they dive down into the mud of the Great Marshes and spend the winter there, but that's untrue. I happen to know that they fly away to the Isles of the Blessed, which lie far across the western ocean, near the place where the sun sets below the rim of the world.'

'And how do you know that?' Canio asked, stifling his irritation and thinking to humour her.

'Because he told me so.'

'Who did?'

'The last swallow, of course. Every September he comes to me and promises that he will return next spring, and he always does, because that swallow never dies.'

'Pity he's not here now; then I could ask him where to find a copy of that Hecate figurine which you know nothing about.'

Bodicca looked pensive. 'Eutherius might know... have you heard of him, Eutherius?'

'I've heard of him. Apothecary in Corinium.'

'And he might know where Vilbia is too.'

'Yes, I suppose he might.' *But even if he does, he certainly won't tell me*, Canio thought morosely, for reasons he was not prepared to share with Bodicca. It seemed that they would both keep their secrets.

42

By late afternoon he had decided to return to Villa Canini. He asked the boy, Maximus, if he wanted to come back with him.

The boy hesitated and looked at Bodicca, who smiled comfortingly. 'No, I'll stay,' he replied. 'Vilbia might come back before next week, mightn't she?'

'Well, it's possible, I suppose,' Bodicca replied. 'All things are possible: listen...' And she lay down and pressed her ear against a patch of dry earth at the edge of the clearing, a place where the grass grew sparsely in the shade of the great beeches. 'I think I can hear Persephone slowly journeying back to her winter home, deep under the earth. And there she will stay, all through the cold and dark and wet and misery of winter, until she returns in the spring.'

Canio shook his head. 'Mad as a chicken with its tail feathers on fire,' he whispered to the boy. He took the remaining food and a half-empty wineskin (this time not containing his best South Gaulish) from Antares' saddlebag and handed them to the boy. 'When you want more, come to the villa and ask Regina. And if Vilbia does return, come and let me know – but not before telling her that there's something I want to ask her.'

'Won't you be coming back?' the boy asked.

Canio thought he detected a note of anxiety in his voice. 'Yes, I'll be back, but maybe not for a day or two.'

As he rode beneath the archway into the walled courtyard of Villa Canini he saw, over on the far side, two horses with military saddles. One had polished copper *phalerae* medallions adorning the leather strapwork. He recognised that horse.

Dismounting, he handed Antares' reins to Austalis, who had followed him up from the stables at one end of the great aisled barn, then walked across to the villa, where the pair of great entrance doors stood open. He walked up the steps and turned right, into the long corridor.

Meeting him there, Regina whispered, 'There are two soldiers in the *triclinium* waiting for you. What with Felix and Senuacus being out over Guito's Wood way, I couldn't rightly stop them, and I felt I had to give them wine. One of them's—'

'I know,' said Canio, 'I recognised his horse. Don't worry, I'll deal with them.' He shooed her back into the kitchen, then walked on down the corridor, rounded the corner and pushed open the *triclinium* door.

Castor and a soldier that Canio did not recognise were sitting in two of the high-backed wickerwork armchairs. Castor had his booted feet on the polished table; the table on which Canio had laid Antoninus's body and where Trifosa had washed the dried blood from the murdered man's wounds. Castor's helmet, with its blood-red crest stood on the table beside the booted feet.

For a moment Canio felt a near-uncontrollable impulse to snatch the *spatha* from the scabbard at his left hip and take a swipe at Castor's unprotected head. The moment passed: in any case, Castor's head was probably too far away across the broad tabletop.

But perhaps that flash of anger had shown on Canio's face, because Castor, as if realising his vulnerability, swung his feet off the table and levered himself out of the chair.

'Ah, Caninus, I was beginning to think you'd never arrive. Where have you been? – None of your minions knew where you'd gone, or so they claimed.'

'Been? I've been riding untold miles around the countryside trying to find that damned figurine of Hecate, that's where I've been.'

'Now why would you need to do that, seeing as it's been in your possession since the day you retrieved it from wherever it was that Peltrasius so unwisely threw it?'

Canio shook his head in exasperation. 'How many times do I have to tell you? The one and only time I saw it was when it was flying through the air towards a large tangle of bracken and brambles. I've never seen it since.'

Castor sighed. 'You disappoint me, Caninus. I thought you might have invented a more convincing lie by now. Both I and the *Vir Perfectissimus* know you have that figurine – so why not hand it over here and now, and save me the trouble of coming again? Because I will keep coming back until I have it.'

'Well, it's a pleasant ride, if the weather's fine and you have nothing better to do.' And before Castor could reply, Canio reminded him that, 'Sabinus gave me until the nones of November. That's still fifteen days away. With any luck I should have found it by then.' But he couldn't resist adding, 'Probably,' just to annoy Castor.

'Probably? No, Caninus – certainly. On or before the nones, Sabinus will have that figurine, or you will have made an enemy who will make your life intolerable. Do you understand that?'

Canio said nothing, simply fixed Castor with an expressionless stare.

'Do you understand?' Castor repeated.

'Enjoy your ride back to your kennel. If you start now you should be there before your *dominus* starts sounding his horn.' Canio was well aware that it was unwise to provoke Castor, but he enjoyed it, so did it anyway.

'One day, Caninus, you will goad me too far, and then—'

'I'll become so frightened,' Canio interrupted, 'that I'll wet my *bracae* before running away and hiding – and then your master will never get that little figurine that Civilis wants so badly. Then they *will* both be pleased with you, won't they? Goodbye, Castor. Your *dominus* will have it on the nones, or maybe even before. Tell him that.'

'Oh, I will, Caninus. But if the nones come and you do not, I'll come looking for you, and then...' Castor drew his finger across his throat.

'Yes, you're good at that sort of thing – as I'm sure Lunaris could testify, if he wasn't so dead.'

Unabashed, Castor gave him a humourless grin. 'Believe it, Caninus, believe it.'

That night Canio came to a decision, and in the morning he set off to ride the twenty miles south to Corinium.

CHAPTER SIX

22nd October

There were two roads that led to Corinium from the north: the Fosse Way and the Via Alba. Canio chose the latter, the less-travelled, lonelier route. He rode Protus, the horse normally used by Felix. He would have much preferred Antares. Antares had always brought him luck, but Antares' size and red-brown coat were too distinctive. On this particular visit to the city he wished to pass as anonymously as water through a stream.

And so, a mile from the city, he took a long, hooded cloak, a *cucullus*, from a saddlebag and wriggled into it as he rode. Soon after that he left the Via Alba and rode a circuitous route along meandering paths until he came to the Glevum Gate on the north-west side of Corinium, where the Via Erminus entered and became the *Cardo Maximus*, the main street of the city.

His face in shadow under the hood of the *cucullus*, he rode slowly and unchallenged beneath the main archway of the massive stone gate, then continued on past the old, now derelict, semicircular theatre, until he came to *The Rising Sun*, one of the city's *stabula*. There he stabled Protus and ate a meal of what the landlord described as mutton, washed down with a vinegary watered wine.

From *The Rising Sun* he made his way on foot through the side streets, still wearing the *cucullus*, until he came to the small stone house of Eutherius the apothecary.

He tried to unlatch the heavy door of weather-stained oak, but found it unyielding. Tapping produced no result, so he knocked, and finally, impatiently, he hammered – although not before shooting quick glances left and right to check that nobody was in the immediate vicinity.

Moments after the last hammering he heard a bolt being slowly drawn back and the door creaked open by the width of an open hand. Framed in the gap was the old man's creased face.

'What do you want?' Eutherius asked irritably.

'It's me, Canio.'

'I can see that. What do you want?' the old man asked again.

'Let me in and I'll tell you.'

Eutherius appeared to hesitate, but Canio's boot was now in the crack of the door. Also, Canio towered a head or more over him. He sighed and motioned his visitor to come in, then closed and re-bolted the door behind him.

The only light came from a metal brazier pan with fancy openwork sides, set on a tripod base in the centre of the small room. The glowing charcoal cast lurid orange light and black shadows around the remembered walls, with their tiers of shelves crowded with rows of glass bottles and pottery jars.

Eutherius slowly settled himself back into his chair, behind a worktable littered with several mortars and pestles and bunches of aromatic dried herbs. 'So, Canio, what is it that you want from me?' It seemed that the old man had no illusions that this might be a social visit.

'Vilbia hasn't been near her temple for several days now – do you know where she is?'

'Vilbia? No idea whatsoever. I haven't been there since last midwinter... you do remember our meeting there, don't you?' Eutherius asked blandly.

Canio suspected that the old man was being less than candid. 'Yes, of course I remember: you told me then that she was dead.'

'Did I? I don't recall saying that – not exactly. Although to you perhaps she should be dead, given the way you left her to die beside that lake in the Great Marshes.' And before Canio could protest, he added tonelessly, 'The gods gave you a simple choice, Canio: you could have saved either her or all that lovely gold, but not both. And you chose the gold.'

What choice? Canio thought bitterly. *Something malevolent was driving me that day. I know that now – and I'm damned well sure you do too.*

'But she forgave me – didn't she tell you that?' he asked, probing.

Eutherius ignored the question. 'So why do you want to find her so urgently now?'

'That little figurine of Hecate, the one Vilbia always carries with her—'

'The one you gave her, thinking it was worthless?' Eutherius interrupted.

'I was hoping she could tell me where I can find a copy – an identical copy.'

'Why?'

'Because *Praeses* Sabinus is convinced that I still possess the original one, and apparently his master, the *Vicarius*, wants it.'

'And why would Civilis want such a thing?'

'I neither know nor care. All that matters is that he wants it, and Sabinus thinks I have it.'

'*Vicarius* Civilis and *Praeses* Sabinus,' Eutherius mused. 'My, you are moving among the great of the world these days, Canio. But why would they think that you still have it – or indeed ever had it?'

'Because a bastard called Peltrasius, a soldier who was with me when I first saw the infernal thing, told them so.' When the old man did not reply immediately, Canio added, 'Vilbia said that there were fakes made.'

'Did she now – I wonder who could have told her that?'

'Yourself, perhaps?'

'I don't remember doing so.'

'Memory going the same way as the rest of your carcass?' Canio didn't wait for a reply before asking, 'So have you got one of those fakes?'

'No, I certainly have not.'

'Do you know anyone who has?' Canio persisted.

The old man pressed both palms together under his chin, tilting his head slightly upwards, the light from the brazier creating whole new patterns of light and shadows across the ancient landscape of his face. At last he said, 'There is someone who *might* know where a copy of that figurine could be found.'

'Who?' Canio asked.

'His name is Fraomarius, and he lives here in Corinium, in the *Street of the Three Vine Leaves*. Do you know it?'

'Yes, of course I know it. I can't say I've heard of Fraomarius though.'

'No. He's a very' – Eutherius hesitated – 'solitary man. I believe he was once a priest at a little temple dedicated to Mercury and Rosmerta, which was destroyed in the troubled years that followed the crushing of that fool Magnentius's rebellion, when devotion to the old gods rendered a man vulnerable.'

'So how does he earn his living now?'

Eutherius shrugged. 'I couldn't say. Ask him when you see him. You'll find him on the north side of the street, at the last house but one that you come to from here.' And with a sweep of his outstretched arm towards the door, the old man indicated that the unwanted interview was over.

The *Street of the Three Vine Leaves* shared its name with a dingy *popina* located halfway along it. As he hurried past, Canio caught the less than savoury odours of frying fish and stale urine, the latter presumably from the inevitable latrine at the rear of the premises.

50

Fraomarius, when he eventually answered his door, turned out to be an oldish man – mid to late forties, Canio guessed – with lank, greying hair. He wore an ankle-length tunic which might once have been a rich blue, but now had faded unevenly to a patchy blueish-grey.

Still on the threshold, with the hood of his *cucullus* pulled far enough forwards to obscure his face, Canio introduced himself by the name of Geta. He said he had heard that Fraomarius might be able to obtain something that he wanted.

'Heard from who?' Fraomarius asked warily.

'A man in Glevum.'

'What was his name, this man in Glevum?'

'That I don't know. He didn't volunteer it, and I didn't ask. Sometimes it's better that way.'

Fraomarius hesitated, then nodded and ushered Canio into the front room of the little house, where a solitary tallow candle burned smokily in a sconce driven into a mortar joint between the bare stone blocks.

The sometime priest hurriedly pulled a curtain across the doorway leading to another room. From what he briefly glimpsed, Canio was fairly sure that in that back room there was a collection of cult objects which the man had presumably managed to salvage from the destruction of his temple. Objects worshipped, at a price, by men and women who still venerated Mercury and his Celtic consort Rosmerta.

Canio turned and made sure that the door was firmly closed, before saying, 'The man in Glevum said that you might know where I could buy a copy of a certain *orichalcum* figurine of the goddess Hecate, identical to one I once saw years ago.'

'Did he now...? And why would you want such a thing?' Fraomarius was still wary, understandably so, Canio conceded, in this little city which, for several years now, had been the seat of the province's Christian bishop.

'That, my friend, is my business,' he replied, and smiled in an attempt to take the edge off his bluntness.

Fraomarius shrugged, as if to say that it was of no particular interest to him anyway. 'So what exactly did it look like, this figurine?'

'As I remember, it was some five or six inches high, and the Dark Lady held a torch in one hand and a sword in the other, both pointing upwards. And curled around her feet was a hound of some sort.'

'How many heads did the lady have?'

Interesting that you should ask that question, Canio thought. 'Just the one.'

'So she was made a long time ago.'

'The original probably was, but I'm only looking for a copy. Have you ever come across such a thing?'

'Perhaps,' Fraomarius said slowly. 'I seem to recall seeing something of the sort, although that was a good few years back. Tell me, how much would you be prepared to pay for such an object – assuming, of course, that I could find it for you?'

Canio reached under his *cucullus* for his belt pouch, from which he extracted a *solidus*, holding it up between thumb and forefinger so that it gleamed in the hazy candlelight. 'And there will be two more of these little beauties waiting for whoever brings me the Dark Lady, so long as she's exactly as I've described her.'

Fraomarius seemed mesmerised by the little gold coin: Canio guessed that it was a long time since he had seen one. 'Come back tomorrow, no earlier than noon, and it's possible that I'll have what you're looking for – or, at the very least, I'll be able to tell you where you can find it.' He paused, flicked his tongue over his upper lip, and added, 'That being so, could you see your way to giving me a small advance – for the expenses which I'll undoubtedly incur, should I locate it?'

Canio's first instinct was to refuse. His second was that his need to acquire the figurine was too great to risk losing it for the sake of a few coins. He handed the *solidus* to Fraomarius, together with five little silver *siliquae*. 'Until noon tomorrow then.'

He considered adding a warning – that any attempt to cheat him might prove exceedingly painful. As it was, he only bared his teeth and treated Fraomarius to his best wolfish smile, something which he usually found sufficiently intimidating to act as a deterrent.

CHAPTER SEVEN

Canio had already decided that it would be unwise to linger for too long in Corinium. He was uncomfortably aware of the ever-present danger that somebody would recognise him, and the awkward questions that might follow. But the prospect of a twenty-mile ride back to Villa Canini, and then another twenty miles back again next morning was distinctly unappealing.

So, having collected Protus from *The Rising Sun*, he ambled the horse though the city and out onto the Via Erminus via the Calleva Gate. From there he followed the arrow-straight highway across the flat lands until he reached the settlement of Criccus, some seven miles south-east of Corinium, where the Via Erminus crossed the infant Flumen Tamesis.

Arriving well before sunset, he took a room in the little *stabulum* there. After unsaddling Protus and checking the quality of the hay, he ordered a meal and went up to his room to wait until it was ready.

The bed was a pallet stuffed with straw, and the solitary blanket looked and smelt as though it hadn't been washed for years, if ever. He guessed that the rooms were mostly taken by wayfarers coming from Calleva, people who were overtaken by nightfall before they could travel the final miles to Corinium. And by then they were probably too tired to be fussy.

Downstairs in the main room he found a dice game in noisy progress. At first, seeking anonymity, he ate his meal of roast wood pigeon seated at a table in a far corner of the room. But as time passed, and several cups of watered wine disappeared down his throat in an attempt to take away the gamey taste of the pigeon, he began to be drawn into the excitement of the game.

Eventually he sidled over and stood behind the two players, observing each throw of the dice and the whoops and groans they elicited, both from the players themselves and their audience of some dozen shabbily dressed and faintly malodorous men.

After a dozen more throws, one of the players gave a loud sigh of exasperation and tossed the shaker cup back onto the table. 'That's enough for me – I'm nearly a *siliqua* down. Oh Fortuna, my once-beloved goddess, where oh where have you been today? Certainly not with me,' he murmured bitterly, before pushing his way through the crowd and walking out into the gathering dusk.

'So who else wants to try their luck?' asked the other player, whose name, Mettus, Canio had picked up from voices in the crowd. 'Come on, there must be somebody – what about you, stranger?' he asked, pointing to Canio.

And Canio was not unwilling. Seeing that they were playing for coppers, he dug a handful of *nummi* out of a belt pouch and arranged them in a neat pile on the table. 'Same rules – one *nummus* a throw?' he asked.

'Same rules,' the man confirmed. 'Highest score wins each round and Venus scoops the pot. You can throw first.'

Canio examined the three dice critically and rolled each one several times on the table, noting that they showed different numbers every time.

'They're honest dice are those,' remarked Adventus, landlord of the *stabulum*, as he walked past carrying a taper with which he was lighting candles in various parts of the room. 'I won't allow any other sort in my house.'

'Glad to hear it,' Canio grunted, as he dropped the three dice into the shaker cup and gave it a good rattling, before tipping the dice out onto the table. Two 4s and a 5.

His opponent, Mettus, who Canio learned during the course of the game was a carpenter by trade, threw a 1 and two 5s. 'Thirteen beats eleven,' he sighed, as he flicked a copper *nummus* from the pile in front of him to form the first coin in Canio's pot.

On the second round, Canio threw 4, 2 and 1. Mettus threw 6, 2 and 5. Seven to thirteen, so it was Canio's turn to put the first *nummus* into Mettus's pot.

On the third round Canio only managed a 4 and two 1s, while Mettus threw 3, 2 and 6, so Canio pushed another copper from his pile into Mettus's pot.

But he then came back to win the next three rounds, only to see Mettus win the subsequent three.

And so it continued, until after fifty rounds there were some twenty-five *nummi* in Canio's pot and only about twenty in Mettus's (there had been five draws). So Canio and the surrounding crowd, who were keeping a noisy running score, reckoned that Mettus was some five *nummi* down.

At that point they changed around, with Mettus throwing first, and it was on the sixty-ninth round that it happened. Mettus threw a 4 and two 3s, but Canio threw three sixes.

'Venus!' three or four people in the crowd shouted simultaneously, and somebody added that it had been weeks since anyone had thrown one of those.

Canio reached across the table and began raking in the two pots, totalling around sixty *nummi* (there had been another three draws). As he did so he glanced up at Mettus's face. The man appeared stunned, and Canio realised that while thirty-three or so *nummi* were nothing to him, to Mettus they were probably several days' wages. And perhaps the man had a wife and children? Afflicted by an unaccustomed prick of conscience, he was seriously considering giving at least some of the coins back, when a voice from the crowd made itself heard. A voice he had not heard before. A woman's voice.

'Don't hurry away, stranger. It's my turn to play you now.'

Surprised, Canio turned and looked in the direction of the voice, seeing an old woman with a sharp, weather-tanned face, creased like a winter apple and framed in a shock of whitish hair. 'Who are you?'

'My name's Diodora. And yours is…?'

'Geta,' Canio replied smoothly, faintly surprised that nobody had asked him before. 'So how much do you want to lose?'

By way of reply, the old woman held up a handsome silver coin. It was a *miliarense*, a double *siliqua*. 'Twenty-one games, and the first to win eleven is the winner. Talus rules,' she added, 'and Venus takes all.'

'Talus rules?' Canio queried. 'Have you got a set of knucklebones?'

'No, but I've got an extra die.'

'So? I haven't played knucklebones for years, but I remember that tali have only four flat sides, numbered one, three, four and six, as I recall. So how can you play to talus rules using six-sided dice?'

'Easily,' replied Diodora. 'Any die showing a two or a five is thrown again until it shows a talus number. And here's the fourth die,' she said, holding out the bone cube for Canio's inspection. 'Go on, roll it yourself to check that it's not weighted.'

Canio took the die, scrutinised it, then rolled it three times. Every time it came up a different number. He shrugged. 'Talus rules it is then.'

He dropped all four dice into the shaker cup and rolled 3, 4, 3 and 2. He put the last die back into the cup and threw a 1. 'That makes eleven,' he announced to no one in particular.

Diodora took the shaker cup and threw 2, 4, 1 and 5. Replacing the 2 and 5 in the cup, she threw 1 and 3. 'Nine,' she sighed. 'You win, Geta.'

In the second game, Canio eventually threw a 4, two 3s and a 6: total sixteen. Diodora threw two 4s, a 6 and a 5, but throwing the 5 again produced a 6: total twenty.

But Canio won the next four games, nineteen to seventeen, seventeen to twelve, fourteen to thirteen, and sixteen to thirteen, and seemed to be galloping towards the winning total of eleven games.

Then his luck changed for the worse, with Diodora winning the seventh, eighth, ninth and eleventh games, with Canio only managing to claw back the tenth.

So it was that, at the beginning of the twelfth game, Canio was now ahead by only one game: six to five.

After that the game flowed backwards and forwards fairly evenly, but by the beginning of the twentieth round Canio was still ahead by ten games to nine: just one more to win outright.

Canio threw 6, 4 and two 2s. Throwing the 2s again produced a 3 and a 5. He threw the 5 again and it came up 6. So, 6, 4, 3 and 6 – total nineteen.

Diodora threw 3, 4, 1 and a 2. She threw the 2 again and it came up 5. So she rolled it again, and this time it came up 6. So, 6, 4, 3 and 1 – total fourteen.

So Canio thought he had won, by eleven games to nine. He kept a straight face, but was inwardly crowing as he held out his hand for the *miliarense*.

But Diodora smiled conspiratorially and shook her head. 'Oh no, Geta – look again.'

So Canio looked again, but her dice still added up to 14, and he was sure his had totalled 19.

The uncertainty must have shown on his face, because at that point a voice in the crowd, which had steadily increased in size as the game progressed, said in a loud, excited whisper, 'It's a Venus, man – she's thrown a Venus!'

And then at last Canio remembered: under talus rules Venus was not four 6s, but 6, 4, 3 and 1. 'Hades' arse!' he swore under his breath, hesitated, then shrugged and pushed his pot of sixty *nummi* over to Diodora's side of the table.

The old woman smiled again, more broadly now, revealing a distinct lack of front teeth, as she pounced on the coins like a hawk on its prey, her bony fingers hurriedly scooping them from the table and into the capacious leather purse which dangled from her belt.

It was only as he was walking back to his corner table, with the intention of pouring himself another cup of the execrable wine, that something stirred in his memory. In the fifth game – or it might have been the sixth, he wasn't quite sure – he remembered that he too had thrown a fourteen. And the more he thought about it, the more certain he became that the fourteen had been made up of a six, a four, a three, and a one – definitely not two fours and two threes. But neither Diodora nor anyone else in the throng around the table had uttered so much as a single word.

He hesitated, then, having almost made up his mind to challenge them all, slowly turned around, only to see Diodora standing no more than a yard behind him. The lines and creases of her mobile face had arranged themselves into a look which conveyed twinkling amusement. And that look convinced him: he *had* thrown a talus Venus – of course he had!

She came closer, patted him on the hand, and said quietly, 'You may have lost a few *nummi* tonight, but you've gained wisdom, which is infinitely more precious.'

'And what wisdom would that be – never to play dice with cunning old women?'

'That too, of course, although a man of your age should have learnt that lesson long ago. But, young or old, remember this: never be drawn into playing a game if you don't know all the rules.'

Good advice, as far as it went. Its fatal flaw, he reflected later, is that in life you are usually given no choice as to which games you have to play. And nobody knows all the rules.

CHAPTER EIGHT

23rd October

Canio arrived back in Corinium at a little after midday, having whiled away the morning in solitary drinking in the lee of a beech wood some quarter of a mile off the Via Erminus. He had extracted a goatskin of half-decent wine from Adventus (at an exorbitant price) and sat beneath the sighing trees, from which the occasional yellow leaf drifted down, slowly drinking and wondering irritably why life was not turning out to be as happy and carefree as he imagined it would when he first became rich.

He left Protus at *The Rising Sun*, the same *stabulum* near the Glevum Gate that he had used on the previous day. Then, with the hood of his *cucullus* pulled well forward, he made his way back to the *Street of The Three Vine Leaves*.

Fraomarius snatched open the door at Canio's first quiet knock. 'Come in, come in,' he said hurriedly, closing and bolting the door as soon as Canio was over the threshold.

'Have you got it?' Canio asked.

'You mean that copy of a figurine of the goddess Hecate which you asked me to find?'

Strange question. 'Of course that's what I...' But as his eyes began to accustom themselves to the dim light, Canio noticed the sheen of perspiration on Fraomarius's face. Something definitely wasn't right.

Instinct took over. 'No, not Hecate. Why would I, or anyone else, want a figurine of Hecate? A figurine of Rosmerta is what I asked for… Rosmerta. If you haven't been able to find one yet I can come back tomorrow – I've still got a few enquiries to make here in Corinium,' he added casually.

He heard a faint metallic clink from the curtained-off back room. Someone was there, listening. His fingers began groping behind his back for the door bolt.

Too late. His fingers had scarcely found the bolt when the curtain was snatched aside and Julius Castor strode into the room followed by Peltrasius, both soldiers carrying unsheathed *spathae*.

'You disappoint me, Caninus… or should I say, Geta?' Castor shook his head slowly from side to side in mock reproach. 'I really didn't think you would be so stupid as to attempt to cheat Sabinus.'

Canio thought that Castor didn't look disappointed. In fact, the man seemed rather pleased. His brain racing, he decided that indignant bafflement was his best defence. 'What do you mean, "cheat"? I've been searching day and night, trying to find that wretched figurine for him.'

Castor pointed an accusing finger at Fraomarius. 'You asked this man to find you a *copy*, Caninus. A copy – not the original. I call that attempting to cheat, and so, I'm sure, will Sabinus.'

'Of course I said I wanted a copy,' said Canio, injecting what he thought was just the right amount of irritated exasperation into his voice. 'Because I didn't want friend Fraomarius here thinking it was anything valuable. Look, I reasoned that, if you couldn't find it at the place where it was thrown away, then someone else must have found it – agreed? So, if I sought out all the figurines of Hecate in this part of the province – and there can't be many – then among them would probably be the one which our hero managed to lose.' And he shot Peltrasius a contemptuous glance.

Castor chuckled humourlessly and shook his head. 'But this wretch won't be finding anything for you – will you, Fraomarius? Tell him why – well go on man, tell him.'

Fraomarius licked his lips and said, 'I... I lied about the figurine of Hecate: I don't know anyone who has one.'

Canio wasn't sure that he believed him, but realised there was no point in arguing, at least not in Castor's presence. He gave Fraomarius his best intimidatory stare. 'That really was very unwise of you – very unwise indeed. Still, my brave lads, all I can do is keep looking.' With his left hand he reached behind him again and slid back the door bolt.

Castor wagged the forefinger of his free left hand. 'No Caninus, I've got a better idea. You're coming with us, to a place where we can talk more freely.'

'And where would that be?'

'Your old home – the guards' barracks.'

'You'll be among friends there,' Peltrasius added, although he didn't say it as if he really meant it.

With Castor leading and Peltrasius close behind, both still carrying their drawn swords, the three men walked through the puddle-dotted streets of the autumn city.

On the way, Canio briefly considered making a run for it. Then decided against, aware that the *cucullus* would slow him. And besides, he was still confident of his ability to talk his way out. It was only when he realised that they were heading for the back of the barracks, where the guardroom and cells were located, that he began to feel uneasy.

As soon as they reached the place, Castor gave three raps on the massive door, waited a few moments until he heard a voice from within, then, with his mouth almost touching the dark iron grille, hissed, 'Sagittarius.'

Today's password, thought Canio. *Worth remembering.*

Several bolts were drawn back, the door swung open and the soldier on guard duty saluted Castor. Once inside, Castor whispered something to the man, who nodded and scurried out. Castor shut the door himself and bolted it behind him. Canio noticed that the door also had a large iron lock, but there was no key in it, or none that he could see.

'Sit down, Caninus,' Castor ordered, pointing to the bench that ran down one side of the room. 'And then tell us where you've hidden it.' And before Canio could speak, he added, 'We know you went back and found it in the place where Peltrasius threw it those three summers ago, so don't annoy us by continuing to insist that you didn't.'

But Canio still reckoned he was bluffing. 'How many more times must I tell you? – I haven't got it and never had it, which is why I'm trying my best to find it for you. Anyway,' he added, 'what does it matter if the Hecate figurine I find isn't the one which Peltrasius managed to lose? Even if Civilis did once see it, that must have been years ago, so the chance of him spotting the difference is almost non-existent.'

'But that, Caninus, is not a chance which the *Vir Perfectissimus* is prepared to take. He is most definitely not going to risk becoming a victim of Civilis's volcanic temper by being caught attempting to dupe him with a fake. So, the sooner you hand over the genuine figurine, the one which Peltrasius threw away, the sooner you can get back to enjoying the fruits of your illegally acquired riches.'

Canio shook his head in what he thought was well-counterfeited exasperation. 'But I haven't got it, and never had it!'

'Oh, but you have got it, Caninus, you have. I'm certain of it – although it seems that you've forgotten where it is at this precise moment. That, however, is not an insuperable problem – I know just the man who can stimulate your failing memory.' And Castor strode over to the guardroom's one internal door, opened it a few inches and barked, 'Crotilio!'

Moments later the door opened wider and Crotilio waddled in: Canio reckoned he must have been told to expect the summons. He was not a short man, his eyes being about level with Canio's chin, but what made him appear shorter was the extraordinary width across his shoulders, making him appear from some angles almost as broad as he was tall. His bull-head continued without any discernible narrowing down into his neck, which in turn spread like the roots of an oak into a pair of massive shoulders. By way of clothing he wore what appeared to be a blacksmith's leather apron over a standard army-issue uniform.

He seemed pleased to see Canio, although the feeling was not mutual.

'Caninus here – you know Caninus, don't you? – is suffering from a temporary loss of memory. But I'm sure you can cure him of that, can't you?'

'I'm sure I can, sir – we're old friends. Is there anything in particular you wish to know?'

'That, is between me and Caninus. Your job is to bring him to the point where memory comes flowing back like a river in flood. Do you understand?'

'Perfectly, sir. You wish me to start now?' One look at Crotilio's face told Canio that the man was eager to begin.

'Of course,' said Castor, and he swung round and gave the seated Canio a vicious kick in the stomach.

It took several moments before the waves of agony hit him, and in those moments Canio managed to gasp, 'I can't be tortured, you bastard! I'm a *honestior* now, remember – the law doesn't allow it.'

Castor seemed to find that amusing. At any rate, he laughed. 'You, Caninus, are whatever I say you are. And I say that you are a thief and a liar, and here you have no rights at all. In fact, you're not even here.' He turned to Crotilio and pointed at the man's waist. 'Put those on him and drag him into one of the middle cells.'

"Those", Canio saw, were a set of heavy iron manacles hanging from Crotilio's belt. It took only moments for the man to pull the hinge open, encircle both of Canio's wrists, and then snap the twin bracelets shut by pushing the spring-barbed end opposite the hinge into its slot in the lock-box, until the barbs sprang open inside it with a loud click, locking the manacles into one rigid whole.

Crotilio then looped the end of a substantial iron chain around the centre of the manacles, secured it with a heavy-duty plunger padlock pushed through two links, and he and Peltrasius together then used it to drag the struggling Canio into the cell. There, Crotilio threw the free end of the chain over a ceiling beam and then hoisted Canio up until he was standing with his arms above his head, before securing the chain with a large bent nail between the links.

'So, Caninus,' Castor asked, 'are you ready to tell me what I want to know?'

Still in pain from the kick, Canio snarled, 'How in Hades' name can I tell you what I don't know?'

Castor hit him again in the stomach, this time with his clenched fist. 'Memory not returned yet? Ah well... Crotilio, see what you can do to help the poor fellow remember. But be careful not to do any permanent damage – not just yet anyway.'

Canio saw Crotilio's punch coming and tried to twist away, but the man's fist hit him over his left kidney like a kick from an angry mule.

He grunted with pain and tried to kick Crotilio, but the man stepped back surprisingly quickly for a man of his bulk.

'Temper, temper,' Castor jeered. 'Remember we're only trying to cure your failing memory.' He nodded to Crotilio, who punched Canio again, this time in the stomach, then again over his left kidney. 'Hurts, doesn't it?' Castor remarked.

After three more punches in the stomach he asked Canio if there was anything he wanted to tell him.

Struggling to breathe, Canio gasped, 'All right, I'll tell you.'

'Leave us,' Castor said sharply, and Crotilio shrugged and retreated back into the guardroom.

'Well,' Castor asked. 'Where is it?'

'It's hidden.'

'Where?'

'In a place miles from here. In the morning I'll take you there.'

'Why not now?'

'It's deep in a wood… I'd never find it in the dark.'

'What wood?'

'It's called Guito's Wood – a big wood a couple of miles north-east of my villa.'

Castor blew out a long breath of exasperation. 'Very well, Caninus; I can wait until morning.' He called Crotilio, and when the man was back in the cell, said, 'Give him another reminder of what will happen if he tries to deceive me again.'

And Crotilio – public executioner and private torturer – punched him so hard in the stomach that, despite his determination not to, Canio cried out in pain.

'Chain him up for the night to reflect on his sins. No food, no water. And in the morning we'll go to—' Castor broke off abruptly, apparently not wanting to tell Crotilio anything that he was not supposed to know. 'See to it, man,' he concluded, and walked out of the cell, followed by Peltrasius.

Crotilio reached up and pulled out the bent nail securing the chain to the ceiling beam, causing Canio to collapse onto the stone-flagged floor. His arms and wrists numb, he watched through half-closed eyes as Crotilio briskly extracted the plunger padlock at the manacles end. The man then tugged, none too gently, at this now-free end, making a raucous iron-on-iron chatter as the chain rasped over the centre of the manacles, until the chain was in two almost equal lengths. He then threaded one of the free ends through a massive iron ringbolt set in the wall, before completing the loop by means of the plunger padlock threaded though the last links. After jerking the chain several times to make sure it was secure, Crotilio then ambled out of the cell, although not before giving Canio a hard kick to his right thigh and muttering, 'Pleasant dreams.'

Alone in the gathering darkness, Canio saw the cell door close, heard first the massive bolt slam home, and then another door open and close and a key turn in a lock. Then silence. He waited and waited, but still silence: it seemed that there was no one else in the guardroom.

Did Castor want as few people as possible to know that he was in the cell? If so, why involve Crotilio? Presumably because Crotilio was a master of the dark arts of extracting secrets from the recalcitrant. Also, Castor must be reckoning that the fear of what Crotilio would do to him, if given his head, would ensure that he would have no second thoughts about leading them to the Hecate figurine in the morning.

'I'll see you all on the other side of the Styx first!' he muttered savagely. His stomach still felt as though it had been run over by a quarry wagon, but that didn't stop him uttering an animal growl of anger, before hissing, 'Bastards! Bastards! Bastards!! Come the morning, my brave lads, I'm going to lead you on such a merry dance, until we find ourselves deep in a very dark wood, and then...' He gave a wheezing chuckle, picturing in his mind what he would do to Castor once his hands were free and locked around the man's throat, his thumbs crushing the windpipe. It was fantasy, and he knew it, but it helped dull the pain.

CHAPTER NINE

24th October

Alone in the darkness, Canio tried everything he knew to break free. But the rigid manacles made it difficult to grip the chain or its padlock two-handed, and the iron ringbolt was set so securely into the thick stone wall that no amount of tugging could jerk it free. Eventually, exhausted and aching, he fell asleep.

The grey dawn light was seeping through the cell door grille when he woke to the sounds of someone moving out in the guardroom. Moments later the bolt rasped back and Crotilio entered the cell.

Canio decided to feign sleep: perhaps Crotilio would not be staying? That hope was dispelled when the man drew back a heavy-booted foot and kicked him in the ribs.

Canio grunted with pain and curled into a foetal position.

'Get up, Canio. Your friend Castor has instructed me to make sure your memory hasn't deserted you again during the night, and also to give you a little reminder of what will happen if it has.' And Crotilio kicked him again.

With the pain in his ribs spreading and making it painful to breathe, Canio struggled slowly to his knees, then fell backwards as Crotilio yanked the chain viciously to slacken it, before crouching to open the padlock securing it to the wall. The chain rattled shrilly through the ringbolt and Canio felt his wrists lighten as the free ends of the chain dropped away and clattered onto the stone floor before Crotilio could catch them.

The man cursed and stooped to pick them up, but before he could do so, Canio, ignoring the pain, sprang up and smashed the heavy iron manacles, still with the chain looped around them, savagely down on the man's bare head – once, twice, three times, four times, five times – then lost count in what was a cathartic release of anger and fear.

Crotilio staggered, crab-like, crumpled onto all fours, fell forwards, twitched half a dozen times, and finally lay still, face-down on the stone flags. And then, at last, Canio stopped hitting him. Fearful that the commotion might at any moment bring Castor or Peltrasius rushing into the cell, Canio dragged the chain free from the manacles before fumbling the dagger from Crotilio's belt. With his left hand he then began desperately rifling through the man's belt pouch for a key that would unlock the manacles. There were coins and other oddments, but nothing else.

Realising that Crotilio must have dropped the plunger key he had used to unlock the heavy-duty chain padlock, Canio scrabbled around on the floor, found it, and immediately saw that it was too big to fit the manacles' lock.

Then he remembered the large chatelaine ring that he'd seen hanging from Crotilio's belt on the previous evening. In the poor light he heaved on the man's thick leather belt, turned him half over and spotted the ring beneath his belly.

With cramped fingers he tried to unfasten the belt buckle and failed, so he grasped the dagger as best he could with one manacled hand and slashed at the leather until it parted. Pulling the chatelaine ring clear he selected the first plunger key and, contorting his fingers, tried to push it into the hole in the bottom of the manacles' lock-box. It was too large.

He swore, then frantically tried the next key. This one fitted the hole, and with the key resting on the floor slabs he pushed the manacles gently down on it, feeling the resistance as the key compressed the spring barbs of the lock. When it felt as though the key would go in no further he jerked one wrist upwards. To his intense relief the spring barbs popped up out of the hole in the top of the lock-box, the hinged manacles swung open and his wrists were free.

He instinctively began rubbing his sore, aching wrists where the cruel iron bracelets had left deep, purpling weals. Then he stopped and listened intently, but still could hear nothing from the guardroom: if there had been anyone there, then surely the noise of Crotilio crashing to the floor would have brought them running?

Castor had taken Canio's own belt pouch, *spatha* and dagger, so he hurriedly transferred Crotilio's pouch, dagger and sheath to his own belt, then paused as he considered what to do about the man, still sprawled unconscious on the stone flags. His instinct was to kill him: he had never liked the turd, and his body still ached from the punches and kicks.

But what was really driving that instinct was not so much the lust for revenge, but rather the thought of what Crotilio might do to him if he were to be recaptured before he could find a figurine of Hecate which would both fool and placate Sabinus and Civilis.

He placed the point of the dagger against Crotilio's neck, an inch forward of the earlobe and inhaled deeply as his grip tightened on the hilt. *Thrust hard in, slice sideways out* – the way the army had taught him, fifteen years before.

It was neither compassion nor squeamishness that made him first hesitate, then change his mind, but more the realisation that by killing the man he would be adding another, provable, crime to those of which he was already suspected. Which Sabinus might find very useful.

To avoid further temptation he swiftly pushed the dagger back into its sheath, and it was only then that he noticed the dark blood seeping from under Crotilio's prone face. Grasping the man's collar he dragged his head off the flags and saw that his face was a mask of blood, some still dripping from his nose and mouth. He felt for a pulse and found none.

He sat back and gave a grunt which mingled sardonic amusement with fatalism. 'And I thought you must have had a skull an ox would envy,' he murmured. 'But it seems that Atropos had already chosen me to be the one to cut your thread.'

He suddenly became aware that his bladder was at bursting point. Untying the cord of his *bracae* trousers he looked for somewhere to relieve himself. There was a large clayware pot in the corner. He started to piss into it, then noticed that there was blood in his urine, a legacy of those punches to his kidney. 'Bastard!' He contracted the muscles of his lower stomach, walked back to Crotilio's body and let the rest of the urine splash down over the dead man's head, mingling with the blood.

Picking up his *cucullus* from where Castor had thrown it on the previous evening, he cautiously opened the cell door and peered into the guardroom. As he had suspected, there was nobody there. There was no lock on the cell door, only a bolt, which he shot behind him anyway, for no particularly logical reason.

Pulling on the *cucullus*, he tried the outside door and found that it too was unlocked. It seemed that Crotilio had come in that way and had been so confident of the helplessness of his chained prey that he hadn't bothered to re-lock it. He eased the door open and saw that the street outside was shrouded in a thick autumn mist. It seemed that Fortuna was still smiling upon him.

Closing the door behind him (and regretting that he had not thought to search Crotilio's body for the key – the locked door might have slowed discovery of his escape) he began hurrying through the back streets of the city, spectral in the misty half-light, towards *The Rising Sun stabulum* where he had left Protus.

On the way he briefly considered paying a visit to Fraomarius, firstly to find out if he really did know the location of a Hecate figurine, and secondly to discover who had betrayed him. He suspected Eutherius, but wanted confirmation, even if that meant roughing up Fraomarius a little to persuade him to talk. The idea died almost as soon as it was born: time was now too precious.

Reaching *The Rising Sun*, he roused the sleepy landlord, paid him what he owed (with Crotilio's money) and hurriedly saddled Protus.

He was acutely aware that he had to get out of the city, and get out fast: in the streets he was beginning to see Castor's face on every figure that came looming out of the mist. The obvious exit points were the Glevum or Verulamium Gates, but were Castor to learn that he had left through either he would suspect that the fugitive was heading back to Villa Canini – which was indeed Canio's intention.

So he held his nerve and calmly trotted through the streets until he came to the Calleva Gate on the south side of the city. He had told the landlord of *The Rising Sun* that he was due to meet somebody in the forum of Cunetio, some thirty miles away to the south-east, late that very afternoon, an appointment which he was anxious to keep. For good measure, he had also added that this mythical person was in possession of something which he was keen to acquire. It was possible – perhaps more than possible, he hoped – that the story would reach Castor's ears.

As he approached and then passed under the archway of the Calleva Gate he expected at any moment to hear a harsh shout from one or more of the soldiers guarding the gate. But his luck held; the guards seemed only interested in inspecting the contents of a covered cart drawn by a pair of long-horned oxen which had just trundled into the city.

Through the gate and out onto the Via Erminus, he resisted the temptation to urge Protus into a fast trot, even though they were still hidden by the mist. He continued steadily on, past the remaining massive, lichen-blotched tombs and tombstones of the honoured and forgotten dead, until he was at least a mile beyond the city walls.

Only then did he stop and look all around to make sure that no one was watching, before branching off onto a series of rough trackways which led him north until he came to, and crossed over, the Fosse Way. There he turned west and hurried on until he came to the Via Alba, where the mist was condensing and dripping like rain from the wayside trees.

Once on the Via Alba he urged Protus into a fast trot, and by mid-morning had covered the twenty miles north back to Villa Canini.

By the time he reached home the sun, climbing higher in the south-east sky, had long since burnt off the mist. And Castor, he reflected, would long since have found Crotilio's body. Time was definitely not on his side.

He approached his villa cautiously, mindful that it was just possible that Castor and a troop of soldiers, galloping furiously along the Fosse Way, could have reached it before him. But if they had, there was no sign of their horses, and the various people he observed seemed to be going about their normal occupations unconcerned.

So he rode up to the great aisled barn, turned Protus over to Austalis and ordered him to saddle Antares. Then he went to the villa and told Regina to pack food for a long journey – and a goatskin of wine.

Felix caught up with him in the kitchen and tried to ask him questions about estate business, but Canio shooed him away. 'I've got to go away for a little while. You and Senuacus will have to run the estate between you and sort out any problems.'

'Just like we did in Aurelius Charax's day, you mean?'

'Not quite – unlike Charax, I know exactly how much of everything there is in the barns and on the hills – grain, sheep, everything, it's all in here.' And Canio tapped his forehead. 'So if any of it goes missing, I'll know who to come after with a big stick.'

'I understand, Master,' said Felix, contriving to look hurt that his honesty should be doubted.

'Good. So tell Senuacus.'

In his bedroom he hurriedly changed his clothes, strapped on his second-best *spatha* (and cursed Castor for taking his best one), and pouched a quantity of gold *solidi* and silver *siliquae* from the strongroom.

After calling Felix, Senuacus, Regina and Aniceta together, he told them that he was going to Glevum, and then perhaps going on further west from that city, maybe as far as Ariconium – he wasn't sure. In any case, he might be gone for a week, possibly longer.

He had originally planned to tell Felix and the rest to deny that he had returned to the villa at all; in fact, that they hadn't seen him for several days. What changed his mind was the near-certainty that other people had seen him arrive, and if Castor caught Felix and the others in the act of lying to him, then he would have no compunction in using torture to force the truth out of them.

He realised, with a twinge of guilt, that the swine might do that anyway, and there was absolutely nothing he could do to stop him. Ignorance would be their best defence. Or perhaps their only one.

And yet, and yet... Suddenly he realised that there *was* something he could do. Grabbing a small sheet of parchment, a bronze split-nibbed pen and a phial of ink, he shook the phial vigorously, then scribbled a letter addressed to Castor, telling him that if he harmed any of his people, then neither he nor Sabinus – or the *Vicarius* – would ever see the Hecate figurine.

He paused for a moment, then hastily scrawled a postscript to the effect that he, Canio, would personally hack off Castor's head and stick it on top of the tallest pole he could find. He signed the letter *Aulus Claudius Caninus, honestior*, then flapped it dry before rolling it into a tight scroll and pushing and twisting it into the narrow neck of a pottery flagon, until it dropped down into the globular body below.

'If Castor comes looking for me, tell him the truth as to where I've said I'm going, and also give him this. Tell him that there's a letter for him inside, but you have no idea what it says – he will have to break the flagon to get it out.' And he handed the flagon to a mystified Felix before scrambling up onto Antares' back.

To lend credibility to the pretence that he was heading for Glevum, when he rode away from the villa he headed west down the coomb, then up towards the high ground that led to the ancient burial mound of Maglocrouco and the gorse-studded wilderness beyond.

Only after several miles did he turn Antares' head towards the north and head downhill into the valley of the little Flumen Isbournis. He followed that shallow river for a short while, then began the long climb back up to the high plateau of the hills, where he eventually reached the path that led to the temple of Leucesca, the goddess of the spring.

He still thought it possible that Vilbia had returned, despite what Bodicca had said. Or if she hadn't yet come back, then perhaps that strange woman herself could be persuaded to tell him where she was. In his experience, the sight of a gold coin often had a wonderful way of loosening recalcitrant tongues.

CHAPTER TEN

24th & 25th October

He reached the temple in the early afternoon. At first it seemed that the place was deserted, but then the boy who called himself Maximus emerged cautiously from the surrounding wood.

'Has she been here, the priestess?' Canio asked.

'No, never – not in all the time you've been away.'

Canio heard the distress in the boy's voice, but ignored it. 'And the weird woman, Bodicca, is she anywhere around?'

'Not now she isn't. She came this morning and said she'd be back in the evening.'

'Then it seems I'll have to wait... Have you been getting food from my villa?' he asked, as an afterthought.

'I've been back every day. Your Regina said I could have as much as I could carry,' the boy added defensively.

'Could you carry much for seven miles?'

'Bodicca came with me. She waited up on the hill above the villa, then helped me carry it all back.'

Canio noted the "all". 'Has Bodicca said when she thinks Vilbia will return?'

'She still says she doesn't know.'

'Really – now there's a surprise.'

The clearing was already in shadow when Bodicca at last appeared from the edge of the wood, beside the stream.

'Did you go and see Eutherius?' she asked, the moment she spotted Canio.

'Yes, I saw him.'

'And?'

'And nothing. He didn't know where Vilbia is, and didn't know where I could find a copy of that Hecate figurine either.' Which was true, as far as it went: he had decided against complicating matters by mentioning his dealings with Fraomarius or his subsequent encounter with Castor.

From a belt pouch he pulled half a dozen gold *solidi*, minted no more than a year or two before at the Treveri mint, the lettering and images still as sharp and fresh as the moment the hammer fell on the die. He crouched and arranged all six coins in a line on the ground before picking one up, flicking it into the air, catching it and slapping it down on the back of his left hand. 'Call – heads or the two emperors sitting on their thrones?'

Bodicca cocked her head to one side. 'Emperors.'

Canio lifted his right hand. 'Heads,' he declared, without letting Bodicca see whether it was or not, then dropped the coin back into his pouch. Picking up another *solidus*, he spun it into the air. 'Call.'

'Heads,' said Bodicca.

'Emperors,' said Canio, and back went the *solidus* into his pouch unseen. 'Where's Vilbia?'

'I don't know – really I don't.'

'And a copy of that figurine?' Canio flicked the third *solidus* into the air.

'Heads.'

Canio shook his head. 'No, emperors again. No idea at all where I can find a copy?' he asked as he pouched the *solidus*.

Bodicca looked thoughtful. 'There is somebody who *might* know.'

'Who?' He spun the fourth *solidus* and slapped it down on his left wrist.

'Her name's Pacata.'

'And what makes you think she'll know?'

'Oh, she knows lots of things,' Bodicca replied airily.

And all of them probably useless, if she's anything like you, Canio thought. But he asked, 'So where can I find her?'

'She lives six miles or so to the east of here. I can take you there.'

'All right. If we start now we can be there not long after sunset. Call.'

'Emperors.'

'Correct.' And Canio tossed the *solidus* across to her.

'But we can't go now,' she said, looking down admiringly at the shiny little gold coin as it lay in her open palm.

'Why not?' Canio asked, trying not to let his annoyance show.

'We'd never find where she lives in the dark.'

'There'll be plenty of moonlight – the moon's only two or three days past full.'

'There will be precious little moonlight – can't you see all those clouds drifting in from the west?' said Bodicca, looking up and pointing at the sky.

Canio too looked up, and to his irritation saw that she was right. 'So we'll start at first light then – agreed?'

'Agreed,' replied Bodicca, casting another admiring look at the *solidus*. 'I was going to spend the night here anyway.'

Canio did not spend the night at the temple. A paranoid suspicion that someone might have seen him riding this way, despite his precautions, made him lead Antares into the depths of the wood. There he spent an uncomfortable night wrapped in his *cucullus*, not the one he had worn in Corinium but a blue-dyed one brought from Villa Canini. (He never called the place Arcadia now, not since the night that Trifosa had disappeared.)

Leaving Antares in the wood, in the grey half-light of dawn he crept back to the edge of the clearing and waited there until he was certain that no one but Bodicca and the boy were present. Then he went back for Antares.

'Are you ready?' he asked Bodicca.

'I've been ready for quite some time, waiting for you.'

Canio noted the accusation, but let it pass. 'Then lead the way.'

She started on the path that led up to the plateau, the boy, Maximus, walking beside her.

Canio frowned. 'He's not coming with us.'

'Yes he is. I'm sure that Vilbia won't be returning here for days and days – or quite possibly for weeks, even. Besides, north is the way his mother might have gone – and we might even meet Vilbia somewhere on the way.'

Canio knew that they would not meet Vilbia. He was certain now that she was deliberately avoiding him, and he suspected that Bodicca knew why. 'He's not coming,' he repeated. 'He'll slow us down.'

'She won't go if I can't come with her,' Maximus piped up. 'Isn't that so?'

'It is,' Bodicca confirmed.

Under his breath, Canio muttered a curse on them both, but he wanted to be gone, and gone now. 'All right,' he said to the boy, 'I'll let you come – on one condition.'

'What?'

'That you tell me your real name.'

'It's Maximus, like I told you,' said the boy, looking at the ground and shuffling his feet.

'Nobody's called Maximus, except a tribune I once had the misfortune to serve under – and that wasn't his given name.'

'Then why did you call him Maximus?' the boy asked.

'Because he was the biggest fool in the army,' Canio replied briskly. 'And believe me, he had a lot of competition for that title. So tell me, Maximus Junior, just what is your real name?'

The boy continued to stare at the ground, but Bodicca said quickly, 'It's Nectovelius – that's what you told me, didn't you?... Didn't you?' she repeated.

More shuffling of feet, then a muttered, 'Yes.'

'So why...?' Canio began, then changed his mind. Precious time was passing. 'Well Nectovelius, or whatever your real name is, let's get started.'

Up on the undulating plateau the grass blades, where not recently grazed by sheep, were long and lank, dark green and beaded silver with tiny droplets of dew. Not the dew that burns off quickly under the summer sun, but the kind that lingers miserably all day under the late autumn clouds.

Although Canio had feared that Nectovelius would slow them down, in fact the boy easily kept pace with Bodicca as she strode out in front of Antares. To keep the dew from soaking her shoes she insisted on following the narrow sheep paths whenever they led in roughly the right direction, although this inevitably meant that their progress north-eastwards was a meandering one.

They encountered few people, other than the occasional shepherd, who waved and eyed the little party curiously as they passed. In sheltered spots on the edges of the small woods that dotted the plateau, Nectovelius managed to find a few ripe, sweet blackberries, which he plucked from the briars with nimble fingers and devoured immediately, not offering to share them with either Bodicca or Canio.

After about four miles they came to the Via Ricnild, which there ran south-east to north-west from the point where it had branched off the Fosse Way just north of the town of Vadumleucara, some eight or nine miles away to the south. At Canio's insistence they waited, concealed in the lee of a clump of beeches, until there were no travellers within several hundred yards in either direction. Then they quickly crossed over the highway and continued on eastwards.

CHAPTER ELEVEN

25th October

Some two miles east of the Via Ricnild, Bodicca halted and pointed to a wood which lay several hundred yards to the north of the path they had been following.

'Pacata lives in that wood over there. Come with me and I'll show you.'

Dismounting and leading Antares by his reins, Canio followed Bodicca up to the edge of the wood, then deeper and deeper into it, following an overgrown path that meandered between the trees. There was no sign of any dwelling, but after several hundred yards he saw ahead what appeared to be a clearing, but which, as he came closer, he realised was in fact a large abandoned quarry pit.

Roughly circular and some fifty yards across, the quarry's vertical sides were dotted with hart's tongue ferns, their long, strap-like leaves growing out of crevices and fissures in the greying stratified limestone. Peering over the edge, Canio saw that the uneven bottom of the quarry, some forty feet below, was a mass of brambles and small hazel bushes which had germinated in the weathered rock and wind-blown soil. Curiously, the large, serrated-edged leaves of the hazels were still as green and fresh as they must have appeared back in late May.

'Well, here we are,' Bodicca announced. 'Pacata lives down there.'

Canio looked again, but could see no building down on the quarry floor. 'Where?' he asked impatiently.

'Come with me and I'll show you,' Bodicca replied. She walked around the edge until she came to a place where, half hidden by undergrowth, a broad ramp, carved out of the quarry face, led down to the bottom.

Walking behind Bodicca, Canio led an uneasy Antares down the ramp, while Nectovelius trailed behind, gazing all around as he went. As he reached the bottom, Canio noticed a weathered wooden door, set a foot or more back into the rock face and reached by a couple of stone steps. From above, the door would have been almost impossible to spot.

'This is it – this is where Pacata lives,' said Bodicca, pointing to the door with a magician's flourish. 'I'll see if she's at home.' And she rapped on the door, first once, then twice, then three times.

At first nothing happened, and Canio was just about to tell Bodicca to knock again, when the door slowly creaked open a few inches.

'Pacata – it's me, Bodicca. I've brought someone to see you… there might be some money in it for you.'

The door opened wider, and Canio caught a glimpse of an elderly woman with a sharp, leathery face and short, spiky hair, white as snow. 'Who is it that you've brought?' Canio thought her voice sounded as rusty as the door hinges.

'Just two friends,' Bodicca said soothingly.

'What is it they want?'

'Let us in and they can tell you themselves.'

There was a pause, then the door opened fully and Bodicca entered, beckoning Canio and Nectovelius to follow. Canio released Antares' reins and did as bidden.

Inside the cave it was twilight, what little light there was coming from four hitherto unnoticed holes cut through the rock at high level, two on each side of the door. As his eyes adjusted to the gloom, Canio saw that the cave was about ten feet square with a barrel-rounded ceiling. Beyond was an archway leading to another room, where a glow suggested that an unseen lamp or candle was burning there.

'This,' said Bodicca, 'is Canio. He wants to know where he can buy a little figurine of the Dark Goddess.'

'Not just any figurine,' Canio interrupted. 'This one must be a copy of one I once saw. It was about five inches high, made of *orichalcum*, and the lady was holding a raised sword in one hand and a torch in the other. And there was a hound curled at her feet.'

The old woman slowly shook her head, the look on her face conveying mystification. 'I don't think I've ever come across such a thing. Who's he?' she asked, pointing a bony finger at Nectovelius.

'My name's Maximus – did you make this cave yourself?'

Pacata cackled. 'No, of course I didn't, you young fool. It was made hundreds of years before I was even born – and I was born so long ago that even I don't know how old I am. These rooms were hacked out of the living rock by the men who once worked this quarry. This is where they lived.'

'What happened to them?'

Pacata sighed. 'Time happened to them, boy. Time the destroyer blew them away like leaves in the winter wind, and now they're all gone. Long, long gone. Would you like to see the other rooms?'

'How many are there?'

'Three, counting this one. Come, I'll show you.'

'Are you sure you've never seen a figurine like the one I described?' Canio called to her retreating back. There was no reply. 'Do you think she has?' he muttered to Bodicca, shooting her an exasperated glance.

'It's possible. She's probably just being cautious,' Bodicca replied serenely, as she followed Pacata and Nectovelius into the next room.

There, Canio could just make out in the gloom a bed, table and numerous alcoves cut into the limestone walls, most of them crammed with clay bowls, mortaria, flagons and pots of various sizes, all with lids.

By then he had realised that the glow was coming from the third chamber which, when he had squeezed through the narrow archway, turned out to be smaller than the other two. In this chamber a little wood fire burned in a tall recess cut into a side wall. There was no smoke in the room and the small bright tongues of flame rose vertically upwards. This he found puzzling, until he glanced up at the ceiling and saw a wide fissure in the rock. It seemed that any smoke must somehow be finding its way out through cracks in the bedrock to the surface, forty feet above.

'Who's that?' Canio heard Nectovelius ask, and craning around the two women he saw an arched niche cut deeply into the rock of the other side wall. Standing in the niche was a free-standing altar made of the same limestone, on the front of which, carved in deep relief, was the figure of a young man with curly hair, naked to the waist, carrying a cornucopia in one hand and a *patera* sacrifice dish in the other.

Pacata pointed to the letters incised neatly into the stone above the young man's head. 'Look, it says there who he is.'

'I can't read,' the boy admitted. Canio peered, and in the flickering light read the inscription, "*GENIO HUIUS LOCI*".

'He's the Guardian Spirit of this place, boy,' Pacata explained. 'You see, the men who worked this quarry, long, long ago, went in fear that, by taking his stone, they were offending him. And if they were to anger him, there was no telling what he might do. Quarrying work is always dangerous, even without a malevolent god seeking to do quarrymen harm. So, even before they started digging into the earth, they set up this altar and made sacrifices to it – or so I was told. And later, much later, when they had carved out these caves, they set the altar up in here.'

84

'Do you make sacrifices to him?' the boy asked.

'Of course I do,' said Pacata, and Canio thought she sounded shocked that the question should even be asked. 'Even after all these years he might take offence if I didn't. And sometimes, in the middle of the night, I hear little groans and creaks as the rocks above me shift and settle. But I'm not afraid, because I know that the Guardian will keep me safe.'

There was a small table and two decrepit chairs in the outer room, and after Pacata and Bodicca had sat gossiping about local happenings, past and present, and drunk freely from Canio's goatskin of wine while he waited with increasing impatience, he asked the old woman again if she knew where he could obtain a figurine of Hecate like the one he had described.

'Why would you be wanting a thing like that?'

'Bodicca knows.'

'Because a very important person has asked him to find a good copy of the original – although I've never seen that original myself, or even heard of it before,' Bodicca said. A statement which, Canio suspected, was somewhat lacking in candour.

'What person?'

Bodicca looked questioningly at Canio, who said, 'I'm not allowed to say, but if he ever discovered that you knew where a copy was and hadn't told me...' And Canio drew his forefinger across his throat, making a hissing sound as he did so.

'Then it's just as well that I don't know, isn't it?' said Pacata testily. 'Vilbia might know though,' she added, looking at Bodicca.

'She might,' Bodicca agreed, 'but just now she's away on a journey somewhere, so we can't ask her.'

'Well, if you can't find one, then you'll have to get one made,' said Pacata, stating the obvious. 'A good coppersmith is what you need. What's that man's name – Ivo... something, isn't it?'

'Yes, I know the man you mean,' Bodicca replied, nodding enthusiastically. 'Ivomandus I think he's called, or at least that's one of the names he goes by.'

'So where in the name of sweet Venus can I find this Ivomandus?' Canio asked, conscious that time was slipping away and he seemed to be getting nowhere.

Bodicca shook her head slowly from side to side. 'I can't say for sure. I once heard someone say that he has a home in Vertis, but he travels from town to town – anywhere that a coppersmith's skills can earn him a few *siliquae*.'

'If I were you though, I would try Alauna first,' said Pacata sagely. 'Then Salinae, perhaps.'

Canio sighed. 'So what does he look like?'

'Oh I've never seen him, only heard of him, but I believe he's quite old,' Pacata said.

'I think I saw him once – and he's not so old,' Bodicca demurred. 'And I'm fairly sure I'd recognise him if I saw him again,' she added, looking directly at Canio in case he hadn't taken the hint.

'And to get to Alauna you just follow the Via Ricnild north,' said Pacata.

'I know the way,' Canio muttered. He was beginning to realise that having a copy made was probably the only way he could be sure of getting a Hecate figurine by the nones of November. And that would involve tracking down a coppersmith whose present location was unknown and whose very name was not entirely certain. Wonderful.

More to keep Bodicca happy than from any real sense of obligation, Canio gave Pacata a couple of *siliquae* before bidding her farewell, gathering Antares' reins and leading the horse up the ramp and out of the old quarry, Nectovelius and Bodicca following behind.

When they came to the Via Ricnild again, Canio told Nectovelius to go back to the temple of Leucesca, saying it was possible that Vilbia might have returned.

'Do you really think she might have?' the boy asked Bodicca uncertainly.

'Oh, I shouldn't think so,' she replied. 'When she goes off on one of her journeys she usually stays away for weeks and weeks. And we're going north, to Alauna, to find Ivomandus the coppersmith, aren't we, Canio?'

He gave her a hard look.

'And north was the way my mother might have gone,' Nectovelius reminded him, half pleading, half defiant.

Canio looked at them both. Bodicca smiled and Nectovelius stared at him, as if willing him to agree. He was about to insist that the boy returned the way they had come, when it suddenly occurred to him that if Castor had sent out search parties, unlikely though that was this far north, they would be looking for a lone horseman, not a man travelling with a woman and boy.

He shrugged. 'Very well, young Nectovelius, you can come with us.' But then couldn't stop himself from adding, 'For a while, anyway.'

CHAPTER TWELVE

They travelled north along the straight but undulating Via Ricnild, where the potholed surfaces and the undergrowth encroaching from both sides, including ash saplings taller than a man, spoke of years of neglect. After four miles they came to the point where the highway began its zigzag course down the steep descent from the Long Limestone Hills to the lowland plain below.

Shortly before they started on the downwards gradient, they overtook a stationary four-wheeled wagon loaded with small blocks of limestone. One carter stood at the head of the team of longhorned oxen, holding them steady, while the other was busy kicking into position under both rear wheels the iron dragshoes which hung by chains from the wagon bed. Neither man paid any attention to Canio as he passed, which, in the circumstances, he found oddly comforting.

At the top of the incline Canio reined Antares to a halt, and for a few moments sat gazing at the broad panorama of the lowlands spread out before him. Countless small fields, woods and individual trees stretched out to the far horizon, becoming ever bluer and indistinct. Villages and even towns were invisible, although he knew they must be out there somewhere.

And somewhere too in that vast landscape there might also be a man who might be able to make him a copy of the Hecate figurine that would fool both Peltrasius and Civilis. All he had to do was find him. Kneeing Antares' flanks he started the horse ambling down the incline.

High above, in the north-west wind that rushed up and over the scarp slope of the hills, four ravens were croaking as they performed aerial acrobatics; twisting, diving, and then soaring upwards again in the cool autumn air.

Halfway down they met another wagon, this one pulled by a team of eight shorthorned oxen. The leading two pairs, according to Bodicca, who claimed to have been this way before, would have been hired from the *stabulum* at the foot of the hills. A man sat on the back of one of the third pair of oxen, both hands holding a long goad made from a withy pole tipped with an iron spike. With this he was prodding the hindquarters of each of the two lead pairs in turn, which produced the occasional bellow as the poor beasts strained to slowly haul the heavy wagon up the long and wearying climb to the plateau.

The wagon was covered by a barrel-shaped canopy of stitched hides stretched over a wicker framework, which hid most of the interior from view. But as it passed Canio glimpsed, through the open back, piled sacks of what he guessed to be wheat, since he could catch no whiff of the distinctive, slightly oily scent of barley.

Shortly afterwards they met two packmen trudging up the hill at a steady, energy-conserving pace, heading, they said, for Vadumleucara. When he learnt they had come from Alauna, Canio asked if they knew whether a travelling coppersmith called Ivomandus was there.

'I've heard the name Ivomandus,' volunteered one, 'but whether he's at Alauna today I couldn't say.'

'We only stayed there the one night,' the other explained, looking back but not breaking the steady rhythm of his mile-eating tread.

Nearing the foot of the incline, they encountered a youth sprinting up the hill as though, Canio remarked, old Hades himself were chasing him. He rode on, but Bodicca and Nectovelius turned and watched, apparently intrigued, until the youth vanished from sight around one of the zigzag bends.

As Canio rounded the last curve of the descent he saw below him the *stabulum,* a substantial two-storey building, with walls built of the warm, yellowish local limestone and roofed with split limestone slates, which the years had weathered to grey. Behind the *stabulum,* stretching into the middle distance, he noticed a series of small paddocks in which pairs of shorthorned oxen were grazing.

'That will be a good place to spend the night,' Bodicca pointed out. 'We can eat and rest there, and then start for Alauna first thing in the morning.'

Canio had other ideas: he wanted to put as many miles as possible between himself and Castor. 'How far is Alauna from here?'

'Oh, it must be a good fifteen miles: too far to reach before sunset.'

Canio suspected she was exaggerating the distance. He looked up at the sky. The sun was hidden behind whitish-grey clouds, but a faint glow betrayed its position. 'It's not long past noon. We can get there by dark, if we don't spend too much time here.'

'You can't expect the boy to walk another fifteen miles today.'

'He can ride up behind me – would you like that, young Nectovelius?'

'Yes – but I'm not tired,' the boy declared. 'I can walk another fifteen miles to Alauna. Bodicca can ride if she needs to… Do you think my mother might be there, at Alauna?'

'You were told she might have gone north, and Alauna's north of Glevum,' Canio replied obliquely.

'So she might be there?' the boy persisted.

'It's possible – you'll see when we get there tonight, won't you?' Canio turned and grinned at Bodicca, who returned him a stony look of disapproval.

Over the door of the *stabulum* was a newly-painted sign, depicting what Canio at first took to be an odd-looking red apple, until Bodicca pointed out that it was probably supposed to be a pomegranate, that being the name of the establishment.

Standing in the yard outside *The Pomegranate* was a smart barrel-roofed carriage with polished copper animal-head fittings and two jet-black horses harnessed on either side of the shaft. Tethered alongside the carriage was a matched pair of saddle horses, also black. Canio regarded them uneasily: he recognised neither carriage nor horses, but that did not mean that their wealthy owner would not recognise him. He dismounted, tied Antares' reins to a rail and then walked into the *stabulum*.

In the wide dining room a man and a woman sat at the largest of the tables, while two men dressed in identical livery were arguing with the large, tough-looking woman who stood behind the bar counter, so that only her top half was visible.

She was trying to convince them, apparently with only limited success, that coupling oxen to their carriage to pull it up onto the hills was a complicated task, one which only her husband could perform. From what Canio could overhear, it seemed that the husband had been with the wagon which they had passed going up the hill as they came down. She was, however, assuring them that she had sent a man to fetch him back, so he should be arriving shortly. And hearing that, Canio recalled the running youth they had encountered near the foot of the incline.

The seated pair were splendidly dressed, both enveloped in fur-trimmed cloaks made of cloth as white as newly-fallen snow and pinned at the shoulder with great gold crossbow brooches. Evidently a very rich man and his considerably younger wife – or perhaps his daughter?

The wife, or daughter, had a glacial beauty, her dark hair moulded around her head like a helmet and sculpted at the front into a series of waves. Canio wondered how many hours it must have taken her maids to achieve that effect, and how many times she had threatened them with a whipping before the desired appearance had been achieved?

But he should have kept his eyes on her companion, because when he glanced away from the young woman he realised that the man was looking directly at him. He told himself that it was only natural when a stranger walked into a room. And yet… he could not rationalise away the impression that the man's face had worn that faintly puzzled look which comes with tentative recognition.

With deliberate casualness Canio eased the hood of his *cucullus* forwards as far as it would go, before ushering Bodicca and the boy to a table in a shadowed corner of the room. From there he covertly studied the older man, now whispering something inaudible to the young woman. Was he whispering about him? Had he been recognised?

Over the last two years, ever since he had bought Aurelius Charax's villa, he had mixed, willingly or otherwise, in the society of such men and their imperious wives, and there *was* something vaguely familiar about the man. But where and when – or indeed if – he had seen him before, he simply could not recall. Which troubled him more than if he had positively recognised the man: at least then he would have been spared the gnawing uncertainty.

He was still wondering when one of the retainers approached his master and asked if he should go after the missing husband, only to be waved impatiently away.

Fortunately, it was only moments later that the husband himself at last arrived – panting and full of ungraciously received apologies for keeping the great man waiting. The two retainers were then brusquely ordered to accompany the husband outside to assist in the harnessing of a pair of oxen to the carriage.

Taking advantage of the interruption, Canio whispered to Bodicca that she should call him Julius while they were in the presence of strangers, then gave her a *siliqua* and sent her to order food and wine. She gave him a puzzled look, then walked over to the bar, from where she returned shortly afterwards with two flat loaves and a wooden platter on which sat a large blob of soft, smelly cheese.

'There you are, Julius,' she said in a stage whisper.

The proprietress followed with a flagon of wine and three coarse pottery cups. Canio caught the wife/daughter eyeing their meal with chilly distain as it was carried past her table.

Halfway through the meal one of the retainers came back into the dining room and announced that the oxen had been harnessed to the carriage. The man in the white cloak nodded in acknowledgement, and without a word to the proprietress he and his female companion rose and swept out of the *stabulum*.

At the door Canio saw him hesitate and half turn towards the corner where he sat. But a moment later he had turned again and was gone, and an uneasy Canio was left wondering if he really had been recognised.

Either way, he decided that it would be wise not to linger at *The Pomegranate*. He badgered a reluctant Bodicca to finish her bread and cheese quickly, and drank the remaining wine himself to prevent her from lingering over it. And by the way that the boy kept staring northwards, Canio guessed that Nectovelius was even more eager than he was to reach Alauna.

Outside, he saw that the carriage had gone. He relaxed a little, and back on the Via Ricnild let Bodicca and Nectovelius ride Antares, she in the saddle, the boy clinging on behind her, and himself leading the horse by the reins.

CHAPTER THIRTEEN

25th & 26th October

Some two miles north of *The Pomegranate* it began to rain. At first only a misty drizzle, it soon turned into a steady downpour which forced them to seek the shelter of a wood, where the trees came to within twenty yards of the highway.

The trees were mostly oak and still in leaf, so providing reasonable sanctuary, at least for a while. But before long the rain that had fallen on the boughs and leaves above began to plop heavily down onto the travellers below.

Canio was debating with himself whether he would get less wet by staying under the trees or by venturing back out on the highway, when he heard the sound of distant hooves. The sounds rapidly drew nearer, and moments later a troop of half a dozen cavalrymen, all wearing iron nose-guard helmets and long riding cloaks, clattered past.

He only glimpsed the lead rider for a moment, but that was long enough to see that the man's helmet bore a red crest, not that Castor's was unique. He tried to hold the image of the man in his mind, attempting to visualise the face below the helmet, but the harder he tried the quicker the image faded.

Back on the highway he tried again to capture the fleeting image, but it had irretrievably gone, leaving nothing but paranoia.

When they were some four miles south of Alauna they came across a small settlement stretching along the east side of the Via Ricnild. The buildings were all of timber, some of their thatched roofs in good repair, others dilapidated. There was a thin woman sitting beside a stall selling wickerwork baskets, and on the west side of the highway Canio noticed a small cemetery with wooden grave markers, many of them algae-stained and leaning at odd angles among the tall, dead grasses.

Just beyond the northern edge of the village they crossed the Avon, splashing through a broad, gravel-paved ford, where the grey-brown water came up to Antares' hocks. At Bodicca's insistence, Canio first ferried Nectovelius across, sitting behind him on the horse's back, then went back for her. Canio wondered if she really thought that he might be tempted to leave the boy behind, but decided not to ask. Which was probably wise.

It was about a mile south of Alauna that he finally came to a decision. The soldier in the helmet with the red crest *could* have been Castor, in which case he dared not risk going into the town. So he decided to send Bodicca and Nectovelius on ahead, with instructions to return and tell him if the soldiers were still there.

Bodicca gazed doubtfully at the western sky. 'It'll be night by the time we get there,' she said. 'We won't be able to search properly.'

Canio looked towards the west, where the low sun was half-hidden by clouds, and reluctantly conceded that she was right. 'So go into the town, spend the night there and look around at first light. Meet me back here an hour or so after sunrise.'

'I'll need money for a room and supper.'

'And breakfast too,' Nectovelius reminded her, evidently thinking with his stomach.

Canio considered reminding her of the *solidus* with which he had attempted to bribe her back at Vilbia's temple. But then he handed her three *siliquae* anyway, before watching until both she and the boy had walked out of sight.

95

He then turned and rode back to the place where he remembered a broad track branching off the highway. He followed the track where it weaved between trees, and after half a mile came to a farmstead – a house with a thatched roof and wattle and daub walls, and several outbuildings of the same construction.

The farmer was around thirty, the years of toil etched on his face. His haggard-looking wife came out of the house as he approached, a girl-child behind her. The girl was about five years old, with a plain dress of the same undyed wool as her mother's and a rope of black briony berries – red, orange and green – hung around her neck. As he gazed around, Canio noticed two little grave mounds, over one of which the grass had yet to grow.

'*Salve*. Can you find me a bed for the night, and something to eat and drink?' By then all of the food and wine he had carried from Villa Canini had gone, much of it into Bodicca's and Nectovelius's stomachs.

'Alauna's not much more than a mile up the highway, you can—'

But his wife touched the man's arm and said quickly, 'We can, although it will only be in the cow byre – but it's dry, and there's fresh straw on the floor.' She must have seen the less than enthusiastic expression on Canio's face, because she added quickly, 'Our two cows are still in the field, so you'll have the byre to yourself.'

So, for a silver *siliqua*, both Canio and Antares spent the night in the byre, and in the morning he ate a bowl of wheat grains soaked in milk. It was not very tasty, but by then he was too hungry to be fussy.

Before he rode off he threw the little girl another *siliqua*. Hearing a childish shriek he glanced back, only to see the father cuff her again before prising her little fist open and taking the coin. He was halfway back to the highway when the thought came that they had never once asked his name, nor he theirs.

After waiting at the side of the highway for what seemed at least a summer hour, attracting the unwelcome curiosity of other travellers, he at last saw Bodicca and the boy approaching from the north. They seemed to be in no hurry.

'Slept well, did you both?' he asked.

'The bed was nice and warm and I had as much venison stew as I could eat,' Nectovelius crowed, either not recognising or caring about sarcasm when he encountered it.

'And all for a single *siliqua* too,' said Bodicca. She did not offer to return the other two.

'Well, that is good news. What did you find out?'

'Those soldiers we saw yesterday aren't in the town any more. They were there last night, but they'd all gone by this morning.'

'Which way did they go?'

'North, I think. Letocetum way probably.'

'And the soldier in the helmet with the red crest, did you discover his name?'

'I didn't ask: I didn't want to appear too interested in case they came back.'

Canio blew out a long breath of exasperation. 'So what about the coppersmith – Ivomandus, or whatever he's calling himself today?'

'Apparently he had been in Alauna a couple of days ago, but now he's gone.'

'Gone where?'

'Salinae; or at least that's the road they said he took.'

'How far is that from Alauna?'

'About sixteen miles that way,' Nectovelius broke in, pointing towards the west. 'I asked Bodicca because I thought you'd want to know.'

'Right – so if we hurry we can be there by noon.' And Canio urged Antares into a gentle trot that left Bodicca and the boy hurrying to keep up.

Some three hundred yards south of Alauna, the Via Ricnild

crossed a little river which, Bodicca informed Canio, was called the Sagitta, and then continued on, with the town to the right and a large cemetery to the left.

What appeared to be the oldest part of the town, the part nearest the highway, consisted mostly of a disparate jumble of wooden buildings and a sprawling grid-iron of animal pens. Further over to the north-east Canio saw what appeared to be a more affluent area of newish buildings, encircled by a defensive wall. He didn't linger, but rode on until he came to the point where the road branched.

'That's the road to Salinae,' Bodicca announced, pointing westwards.

'Where we should be by noon,' Canio muttered. His wheat grains in milk breakfast had left a sour taste in his mouth, and the South Gaulish wine brought from Villa Canini had run out on the afternoon of the previous day.

About eight or nine miles along the road to Salinae, Canio, who was leading Antares by the reins while Bodicca and Nectovelius rode for a while, became aware of some sort of activity three hundred yards ahead. Several farm carts were standing at the roadside beside a cluster of tile-roofed buildings. As he drew nearer he saw that the carts were loaded with sacks, and several men were moving around them. Nearer still, and he realised that the place must be a collection point for the *annona* grain tax, and said as much to Bodicca and the boy.

As they passed he saw a man dressed in the quasi-military uniform of a minor government official, complete with *cingulum* leather belt, the strap-end of which, studded with tiny medallions, hung down almost to his knees. He appeared to be supervising the pouring of grain from a sack, which had been unloaded moments before from one of the carts by an unhappy-looking farmer, into a polished bronze *modius* measure.

When the *modius* was full, its contents were tipped into

another sack by one of several soldiers, most of whom were simply lounging around. Canio noticed a whole row of full sacks stacked against the side of the large timber building, which he guessed was an imperial *horreum* grain store.

The polished *modius* sparkled in the weak sunshine. Nectovelius peered at it as they passed, his sharp young eyes apparently taking in every detail. 'What are those marks scratched on the side for?' he asked Bodicca.

'They're the *rationales*' – the tax gatherers' – symbols. They show that it holds exactly one *modius* of wheat or barley when filled either right up to the top, or up to a line marked on the inside.'

Canio snorted with amusement, and when he judged they were out of earshot of the official with the *cingulum*, said to Nectovelius, 'But you can bet a *solidus* to a *nummus* that it holds quite a bit more than a *modius*. Most of them do.'

'Why would it do that?' the boy asked.

'You tell him.'

'Because,' sighed Bodicca, 'each one of the local farmers is down in the records of the local *rationalis* to provide so many *modii* of grain every year. And if that bronze tub holds more than a *modius* then the farmer gives more than he actually owes.'

'So the farmers are being cheated... What do the *rationales* do with the extra grain?'

'What would you do with it?' asked Canio.

'Sell it?... And keep the money for myself?'

'You catch on fast,' Canio said approvingly. 'In good harvest years they do just that, but in bad years they use the extra to make up the shortfalls of other farmers. You see, if they don't collect the amount of grain they've been ordered to, then they'll lose their jobs, or worse. Much worse. And it doesn't help that most years the targets go up, with nobody knowing or caring whether the farmers are actually able to grow more. So the farmers hate the *rationales* who cheat them, and the *rationales* hate the farmers who try to evade the *annona*, and they all hate the *Comes Sacrarum Largitionum* in faraway Treveri, who sets the targets in the first place.

'And in the end some farmers give up and run away – they mostly don't own the land anyway – so the *rationales* get nothing and extort the shortfall out of the remaining farmers, who also give up and run away. A stupider system has yet to be devised, but I'm sure somebody somewhere is trying their best to come up with one,' Canio concluded sardonically.

And he reflected on how fortunate he was that the senior *rationalis* of the Corinium district was a reasonable man when it came to assessing, among other things, the annual quantity of fleeces which his estate was liable to supply. Admittedly such reasonableness did not come cheap, but at twelve *solidi* a year he considered it a bargain.

It was a couple of miles further on, Canio riding again, that they met a solitary mounted soldier trotting along the highway, coming from Salinae way. From his uniform, Canio could see that he was no officer, only an *eques*, a ranker cavalryman. But as the *eques* was about to pass he slowed and stared at Canio. It was an automatic reflex that caused Canio to return the man's gaze, and for a few moments their eyes met. And in those moments Canio read first uncertainty, then something that could have been recognition.

But neither man stopped or spoke, and then they had passed, the distance between them increasing with every clop of Antares' hooves. For fifty yards or so Canio held to his resolution not to look back, but then the temptation to do so became too great and he turned in the saddle.

By then the *eques* was nearly a hundred yards distant. Only the back of his helmeted head was visible above his riding cloak, but Canio had the curious impression that, in the moment before he himself had turned, the man had been looking back at him – as if trying to remember who and where.

He rode on, but the more he thought about it, the more certain he became that he had seen the man before, although he couldn't put a name to the face or remember where they had met. Worse, he was left with the gnawing suspicion that the man had recognised him too. And if he had, who would he tell?

He smelt Salinae almost before he saw it. The wind, still coming from the north-west, was blowing low, rolling clouds of mixed woodsmoke and water vapour towards him. It bore a faint resemblance to the salt smell of the wind from the sea – the wind that had sighed around himself and Vilbia as they had walked along the shore beside the Great Marshes, on that summer day that was little more than two years gone, but now seemed a lifetime away.

Closer, and he saw clusters of large wooden sheds, some thatched, others with dull-orange tiled roofs, and beyond them a large area of small rectangular pools which glinted when the cool October sun caught them. And around the pools and the buildings men were working, some pouring buckets of water into the pools, some scooping water from other pools and carrying them towards the areas from where the smoke and vapour were billowing.

A highway ran north to south along the east side of the salt works, and the road from Alauna joined it just south of a sluggish little river.

'That's where they boil off the water from the brine to leave the salt,' Bodicca told Nectovelius, pointing across to the sheds.

'You've been here before then?' Canio asked, thinking she might know where the metalworking area of the town was.

'I've been to lots of places,' she replied. 'And everybody knows that Salinae is where the salt in those rough clay pots they sell in markets like Fonscolnis comes from.'

The driver of a wagon loaded with firewood bound for the salt works directed them to an area of workshops south of the river, where it took Canio only a short time to establish that Ivomandus was no longer in Salinae.

'He was here yesterday, but he left for Vertis this very morning,' Canio was told by a cobbler at work in the entrance to his little shop.

Bodicca then took the opportunity to point out that Nectovelius's pair of Trifosa's old shoes had not stood up well to the rigours of the highway, and badgered Canio into buying the boy an off-the-shelf pair of new boots with proper hobnail-studded soles.

He then made the mistake of enquiring sarcastically if *her* footwear was in good condition, and ended up buying a new pair of stout *calcei* boots for her too.

They ate a meal of what was alleged to be beef stew at a run-down *popina* fronting the highway, where he learnt that the town of Vertis lay only some seven miles to the south.

'So we can be there well before nightfall, if we don't hang around here,' Canio told them both.

'Aren't we going to look for my mother?' Nectovelius pleaded.

'You can stay and look if you want,' said Canio. 'Myself, I need to get to Vertis.'

'If Marcia were your mother you'd stay and search,' Bodicca said reproachfully.

'But she's not,' he replied brusquely, before the accusing thought came, *Although that other Marcia was the nearest thing to a mother I ever knew.* Another thought: 'Did you look for her at Alauna? – You never said.'

'Because you never asked: of course we looked and asked around.'

'All right, then we'll ask around for her here as well – but not for long.'

Bodicca smiled approvingly. 'Which part of the town do you want to search?'

Canio did not reply. He was staring at the terrified face of that other Marcia, the Marcia who stood chained to a stake on a snowy plain outside the grim old walls of a city beside the Rhine. Her eyes were locked on his, even though he was hidden among an immense crowd. Those eyes were pleading with him to do something, anything, to save her, even as the blazing torches were thrust into the piles of tinder-dry brushwood and the flames roared up like ravenous wild beasts. But there was nothing his twelve-year-old self could do. Nothing. And yet, after nearly twenty years, the guilt still lingered, and by now he knew that it would never leave him.

Aware that both Bodicca and the boy were looking questioningly at him, he said abruptly, 'You take this side of the river, I'll take the north side. Meet me back here in time for us to reach Vertis well before sunset.'

So he rode around the salt works and various houses and workshops north of the river, asking everyone he came across if they knew anything of a woman called Marcia who might have come to the town in the last three weeks or so. Nobody had. It occurred to him that perhaps she was now going by another name, which only compounded what he suspected was the hopelessness of their search.

Meeting up with them back south of the river, Bodicca and a downcast Nectovelius reported that they too had found no one who remembered Marcia, or even a woman who resembled Nectovelius's description of her. It seemed that Marcia had never been to Salinae.

Canio was not entirely unsympathetic. 'Well, we tried – and perhaps we'll have better luck in Vertis. Now let's get there before nightfall: I want to sleep in a proper bed tonight.'

CHAPTER FOURTEEN

26ᵗʰ & 27ᵗʰ October

Vertis, as Canio soon discovered, was an unwalled, run-down industrial settlement straggling along the east bank of the great Flumen Sabrina. Sunset was no more than an hour away when he rode into the town, a tired and dejected Nectovelius perched on Antares' back behind him and Bodicca walking alongside the horse.

They passed endless dark mounds of iron slag, abandoned-looking iron smelting furnaces, and a handful of furnaces that were still in use, their smoke and lurid flames staining the evening sky.

Most of the buildings that he could see were made of timber, and displayed much the same mixture of thatched and clay-tiled roofs as those in Salinae. The first *stabulum* he came to stood a little way back from the highway and bore a weathered sign which proclaimed its name to be *The Full Moon*.

At *The Full Moon* he first arranged stabling and feed for Antares, then rooms for himself, Bodicca and Nectovelius. Recalling that Bodicca might once have seen the man, Canio intended to take her with him as he set about trying to find the elusive coppersmith who went by the name of Ivomandus.

Ironically as it turned out, finding the coppersmith proved surprisingly easy and Bodicca's assistance was not required. The landlord of *The Full Moon* not only knew the name, Ivomandus, but said that the man himself was a regular customer of his. He directed Canio to a cluster of workshops-cum-dwellings no more than a hundred yards back along the street where, at the first one he tried, a man meeting the description that the landlord had given answered his rap on the door. It seemed to Canio that Fortuna was beginning to smile upon him again.

The two men stood in the doorway for a few moments appraising each other. What Canio saw was a short, strong-looking man with piercing blue eyes set in a wrinkled face and with enormous hands, so stained and engrained that every line and fissure in the skin was highlighted.

'Ivomandus?'

'Who's asking?'

'I am – my name's Baculo.'

'So?'

'So, I have a small but well-paid job that only a skilled coppersmith can do.'

'And what would that be?'

'Let me in and I'll tell you.'

Ivomandus appeared to consider for a moment, then stood back and ushered Canio into his workshop, a room considerably larger than he had expected from the narrow frontage. In the moments before Ivomandus spoke, Canio gazed about him at the racks of tools hanging from the walls and at the great timber workbench, its surface scarred by myriad tiny nicks and scratches.

'What is it you want done?' the coppersmith asked, adding quickly, 'I don't melt down cut-up silver plate into little ingots, if that's what you're after. I never have done.'

'Nothing like that,' Canio assured him, well aware that, in the aftermath of the *Barbarica Conspiratio* and the anarchy which accompanied and came after it, a considerable amount of looted silverware had found its way into the hands of soldiers roaming the countryside while claiming to be on extended leave.

'I want you to make a replica of a small *orichalcum* figurine of a woman. Can you do that?'

'Perhaps,' Ivomandus said cautiously. 'How big would this figurine be?'

'No more than five or six inches high.'

'You have the original here?'

'No, but I remember what it looks like.'

'Ah, it's a pity you haven't got the original: it would make the job much easier. Can you describe it – or better still draw it?'

Canio hesitated. 'Yes, I can describe it – or have you anything here that I can draw with?'

Ivomandus went across to a shelf and came back with a large pair of hinged wooden tablets and a copper stylus. He opened the tablets in front of Canio to reveal two smooth surfaces of yellowish beeswax. Handing the stylus to Canio he said, 'Sit down at the bench over there and draw it for me as best you can.'

And that is exactly what Canio did, or tried to do, while Ivomandus sat on the other side of the bench fettling a batch of cast copper brooches. In the gathering dusk the light inside the workshop rapidly worsened, but Ivomandus poked a taper into the still-hot charcoal at the base of a small kiln built into a corner wall, and when it ignited used it to light six tallow candles, two set in wall sconces and four in pottery candlesticks sitting on the workbench.

After much use of the spatula end of the stylus to erase what he had previously drawn with the point, Canio at last managed to produce what seemed to him to be a reasonable full-sized likeness of the front and back of the Hecate figurine.

'Can you make that?' he asked, holding up the wax tablets for Ivomandus's inspection.

The coppersmith studied them critically. 'I think so,' he said.

'How long will it take?'

'Well, if I start on the wax model in the morning—' Ivomandus began.

106

'Why not now?' Canio interrupted. 'I'll make it worth your while.'

'How much worth my while?' Ivomandus said warily. 'I've got a commission for twenty brooches and forty belt buckles to complete by the kalends.'

Canio reached under his *cucullus* and from a small pocket in his tunic drew out two gold *solidi*. 'These two now, and two more just like them, when the figurine's finished to my satisfaction.'

'Plus materials.'

'What materials?'

'Wax for the model, fine clay for the mould, copper for the figurine itself—'

'*Orichalcum*,' Canio corrected him. 'It's got to be *orichalcum*.'

'And charcoal for the kiln,' Ivomandus concluded.

Canio exhaled past his front teeth, making a prolonged hiss, then, 'Very well – provided you start now.'

'Agreed,' said Ivomandus. 'Come back in the morning and see how far I've got.'

Canio hesitated, aware of the possibility that both the coppersmith and his two *solidi* might vanish into the night, never to be seen again. But then he reflected that he really had no choice but to trust the man. And besides, the tools in the workshop must have been worth considerably more than a couple of *solidi*.

'Until the morning then. Only... don't disappoint me.' And saying that, he casually lifted the hem of his *cucullus* to rub off a spot of dried mud, "accidentally" letting the coppersmith see the scabbarded *spatha* hanging at his waist.

Back at *The Full Moon*, Canio ushered Bodicca and the boy into a quiet corner and told them both that, as far as anyone here in Vertis was concerned, his name was Baculo. 'Baculo – got it?... Any word of your mother?' he asked Nectovelius.

'Not yet,' the boy said defensively. 'But we're going to search around the town in the morning, aren't we, Bodicca?'

'Indeed we are, my lamb. And don't worry: if she's here, we'll find her.'

Canio said nothing.

The sun had barely risen in the eastern sky before Canio was tapping softly on Ivomandus's door. 'How's it going?' he asked, as the door creaked open revealing that two candles were still burning smokily in the interior of the workshop.

'It's over there on the bench. What do you think of it?' said the coppersmith.

Canio walked over and examined the model. It was moulded in yellowish beeswax, and was remarkably true to the sketches he had made the previous evening. But it was still some way from the figurine he remembered. 'It's good, but not quite right yet. Sit down and I'll tell you what's wrong.'

'I'm tired, man,' Ivomandus objected. 'I've been up all night.'

Canio didn't argue, mindful that you can catch more flies with honey than vinegar. 'It won't take long,' he said soothingly. 'Start with the face – she should be beautiful, but stern. Unsmiling.'

Ivomandus shrugged, picked up a bronze tool, not unlike the stylus Canio had used to draw on the wax tablets, except that the pointed end was shaped like a tiny knife. With a few minute strokes, alternating with smoothing using the spatula end, the face was transformed into the one he thought he remembered from that bitter cold dawn nearly ten months before, when Vilbia had held out the original figurine for his wary inspection.

'That's good, very good,' Canio said encouragingly. 'Now make the hound curled at her feet more fierce-looking – draw the lips back to show more of the teeth.'

Wordlessly, Ivomandus sliced back the lips and then, with remarkable dexterity for a man with hands like shovels, incised a double row of pointed teeth. 'There,' he said, 'is that how it should be?'

Canio studied the adjusted figure. The sword in her right

hand and flaming torch in her left were both as he recollected, their tips level with the lady's eyes. But it was still not quite right. And then it came to him: 'The whip,' he murmured. Then, louder, to Ivomandus, 'Sorry, I forgot: she had a coiled whip hanging from her belt.'

'Which side?'

Canio thought for a moment. It had been on his right when Vilbia had held it out, so… 'Left – on her left side.'

Ivomandus carved a thin sliver of beeswax from the small block at his side, rolled it on the workbench into a tiny rope, coiled it neatly and then transferred it to her hip with the spatula end. 'Is that right?'

Canio surveyed it critically. 'Just work a pommel on the handle and stroke a few fine diagonal lines on the whip, then it'll be just like the original.'

Ivomandus made the required adjustments, then opened both palms, as if to say, *Any more?*

'Perfect: just as I remember it. How long will it take to build up the clay mould around it?'

'It'll take as long as it takes,' Ivomandus replied testily. 'After I've had a few hours' sleep.'

Canio reached under his *cucullus* and drew out another shiny *solidus*. Holding it between thumb and forefinger he tilted it back and forth so that it winked in the candlelight. 'Sleep after you've put the clay on.'

'It's a delicate job,' the coppersmith protested.

'Then do it delicately,' said Canio. 'Have you got the right clay here?'

'Over there,' said Ivomandus, pointing to a small mound covered in damp sacking at the other end of the workbench.

Realising that the coppersmith was not about to move, Canio walked over, pulled off the sacking and twisted off a lump of the smooth white clay, which he placed on the bench in front of Ivomandus.

The coppersmith gave him a sour look, then sighed in resignation, shaved off a sliver of the soft clay and began stroking it gently onto the surface of the beeswax model.

Slowly and infinitely carefully he continued applying the clay, sometimes dampening it until it was almost a paste as he coaxed it around the sword and the torch, the most vulnerable parts of the figurine.

When the entire figurine was covered with a layer of clay about half an inch thick, Ivomandus turned to Canio. 'There, that's the hard part done. Now I'm going to bed... If you're feeling brave, you can put the rest of the clay on yourself – another two inches all round at least. Oh, and don't forget the straws.'

'What straws?'

'The ones you have to poke through the clay to the top of the lady's head and the tops of her sword and torch, so as to form escape channels when the molten metal's poured – otherwise the *orichalcum* might not run all the way through to those furthest points. The straws are over there, next to the clay,' Ivomandus added. And with that he gave a mighty yawn, stretched, levered himself up out of his chair and ambled through the doorway at the back of the workshop. Canio heard him clumping up an unseen flight of wooden stairs, then a short period of scuffling, then silence.

Left alone, Canio decided that he was feeling brave and so started, very cautiously, to build up the clay mould to the thickness suggested by Ivomandus. When at last he had finished, by which time it was late morning, he took three straws and very carefully twisted them down through the soft clay until he felt the faint resistance of the beeswax beneath. Then, realising that the hollow centres of the straws must now be blocked with clay, he eased them out and replaced them with fresh ones.

He was aware that the next stage was to gently dry the clay, until it could be heated to melt out the beeswax without cracking. But how gently? He went to the doorway and called out, 'The mould's finished – how do I dry it?'

No answer came from above. He called again, louder this time, and was about to ascend the stairs and, if necessary, shake Ivomandus awake, when he heard the coppersmith's irritable voice. 'Just leave it where it is: I'll be down shortly.'

So Canio went back and sat at the workbench and waited. And waited. He was just about to shout up the stairs again when he heard them creaking, and moments later Ivomandus appeared in the doorway.

He inspected the mould critically, added a little more clay here and there, then made a tiny hole with an awl and inserted another straw through the clay over where he judged the head of the hound to be, as the beast lay curled at Hecate's feet.

The small clay kiln was reddened and hard as stone from many firings, the charcoal in its base still warm from what Canio assumed was usage at some time during the previous day. Ivomandus held his hand over the thick, flat tiles that covered the top of the kiln, then dabbed his palm on them. 'It'll dry on here, nice and slow.'

'How slow?'

Ivomandus appeared to consider for a moment. 'Come back this evening after I've slept some more: maybe it'll be ready then.'

'Only maybe?' Canio queried.

'You can't hurry these things.'

'Can't you?' Canio replied, patting Ivomandus on the shoulder. 'Not even when you're thinking of those lovely gold *solidi*?'

CHAPTER FIFTEEN

27th & 28th October

Back in *The Full Moon*, Canio found Bodicca and Nectovelius waiting for him, seated in the communal area.

'If Marcia ever did pass through Vertis, it could have been as much as three weeks ago,' Bodicca sighed, when he asked if they had discovered anything about the boy's mother. 'People have told us of several couples who could have been her and the man she went off with, but after three weeks memories fade and they couldn't remember exactly what the woman looked like. And nobody could recall the name Marcia.'

Which did not surprise Canio.

'But we'll go down to the wharves this afternoon and ask around there,' Bodicca added, perhaps not wanting to crush the boy's hopes completely. 'I'm told that ships come up the Sabrina from Glevum carrying charcoal for the iron smelting furnaces, and sometimes they carry passengers too.'

'So I've heard,' said Canio, as he walked over to the bar counter and bought a flagon of what passed for wine in that *stabulum*. Carrying the flagon and a beaker he went upstairs to his room and settled down to wait. And drink.

Sunset was at least an hour away when he decided that he had waited long enough. Down in the communal room, where he found Bodicca and the boy had still not returned from the Sabrina wharves, he handed back the beaker and the now-empty flagon, went to check that Antares had plenty of hay and water, then strolled over to Ivomandus's workshop.

'Is it dry enough for firing yet?' he asked, when he had roused Ivomandus from his bed.

The coppersmith shrugged. 'Probably, but better to wait a while longer to make sure.'

But Canio, remembering the soldier they had passed on the road to Salinae, the soldier he felt increasingly sure had recognised him, replied, 'No, let's not wait.'

'Your choice,' said Ivomandus, and from a roughly-made wooden box he took several handfuls of charcoal and tossed them into the still-warm ashes at the bottom of the kiln. 'Now we'll have to wait for the heat to build up. Come back around sunset.'

So Canio, having sighed his impatience, went back to *The Full Moon* and ordered a meal of roast wood pigeon. While he was there, Bodicca and Nectovelius returned from the Sabrina. He didn't have to ask: the look on Nectovelius's face told him that they had learned nothing of Marcia.

By then the communal room was filling up with people, mostly men and mostly locals, judging by their conversations, although a few were travellers passing through on their way to Glevum in the south or Salinae in the north.

Canio overheard one man asking if there were any ships going downriver to Glevum in the next few days, but someone, evidently a local, said that he knew of none. Also, that the traffic on the river was markedly less than it had been even five years before. This produced a grunt of agreement from another local, and the despondent comment that the iron trade was nowhere near as brisk as it had been when he was a boy.

At sunset, back in the workshop, there was a warm red glow coming from the kiln, into which Ivomandus was feeding more charcoal.

'Ready?' Canio asked.

'As ready as it ever will be.'

'Then start.'

Ivomandus drew aside the two tiles at the top of the kiln and placed a clayware bowl over the gap between them. Then he placed the figurine in the bowl, raised up on a couple of stone cubes like large tesserae.

After a while Canio noticed melted beeswax slowly dripping from the underside of the mould and accumulating in the bowl. 'Waste not, want not,' Ivomandus murmured.

When the wax has ceased to flow, Ivomandus picked up the mould with a pair of tongs and set it on the workbench to cool, before blowing through each straw in turn to ensure that all the wax was gone. Then he placed the mould inside another pottery bowl, took the tiles off the top of the kiln and with the tongs gently lowered the bowl into the glowing heart of the charcoal.

'That's to make sure the heat is the same all the way around the mould, so it doesn't crack,' Ivomandus replied to Canio's unasked question. 'And come the morning it should be baked hard and ready for the metal pour.'

So once more Canio returned to *The Full Moon*, where he spent a restless night waiting for the dawn. The eastern sky was still orange-red when he went back to the workshop, where he found Ivomandus waiting for him, the baked clay mould standing on the workbench. There were holes where the straws had been burned out.

'Is it all right – not cracked or anything?' Canio asked anxiously.

'It's fine,' the coppersmith assured him, before adding, 'as far as I can tell. Are you sure you don't want the figurine cast in bronze? It's cheaper.'

Canio frowned. 'No, it must be *orichalcum* – I told you that.' A sudden suspicion: 'Have you got any here?'

'Some.'

'Enough?'

By way of answer, Ivomandus reached under the workbench and lifted up a bulky leather bag. Opening the drawstring he tipped out a stream of big, heavy coins onto the bench.

Canio picked up a handful and examined them. They had been struck in *orichalcum*, once as bright as gold, but now tarnished in shades ranging from dull yellow through dark brown to black, the emperors' heads and the reverse designs of gods and goddesses and temples mostly worn down to mere shadows by the rough hands of thousands of men and women, now long vanished from the earth.

'There's scarce one of those that's less than two hundred years old,' Ivomandus informed him. '*Sestertii* and *dupondii* – ever heard of them?'

'Vaguely,' Canio replied. 'They stopped making them years and years ago, didn't they – long before I was born?'

'More's the pity,' Ivomandus grunted. 'They knew how to make coins worth having in those days, unlike the miserable little copper runts the mints churn out now.'

A row of clay crucibles was arranged along a shelf on one wall. Ivomandus selected a mid-sized one and clinked a good number of the old coins into it, filling it almost to the brim. Then, gripping it with a long-handled pair of tongs, he carefully stood the crucible upright in the glowing heart of the kiln and arranged more charcoal around it. 'They'll take quite a time to melt,' he observed.

He walked around to the other end of the workbench and dragged from beneath it a stout timber box, some twelve inches square and full of dry sand. Kneeling, the coppersmith scooped a hollow in the sand and placed the clay mould upside down inside it, with tile slips underneath, positioned such that the holes left by the straws had small voids beneath them. Then he packed the sand tightly around the top of the mould before levering himself upright, drawing up a stool and sitting down.

'So how long *will* it take for the old coins to melt?' Canio asked.

Ivomandus shrugged. 'Hard to say. Sometimes ages – depends on the quality of the charcoal.'

And then Canio remembered the pomegranate seeds. He cursed under his breath and said out loud to Ivomandus, 'There's something else, something I forgot. The figurine must make a slight noise when it's shaken – as if something is trapped inside.'

Ivomandus looked at him curiously. 'What sort of something?'

'Something that makes a rattle – a soft rattle.'

'If you put something inside it'll become embedded in the molten metal.'

'Not if you put some bits of grit inside a hollow clay ball. Then pour the metal into the top half, drop in the clay ball, then pour the rest of the metal.'

Ivomandus appeared to consider this for a few moments. Then he said slowly, as if speaking more to himself than Canio, 'Clay would be no use, not unless you waited for it to dry. The molten metal would turn the water in the clay to steam and the whole thing would explode. But what I could do is make a little tube of copper, hammer one end closed, drop in some tiny fragments of hard pottery, then hammer the other end closed as well.'

'Won't the copper melt when you pour the *orichalcum* onto it?'

'Shouldn't do: copper has a higher melting point than *orichalcum*.'

'But I thought *orichalcum* was mostly copper.'

'It is – copper and a little bit of zinc: strange that, isn't it?'

Canio was dubious, but couldn't think of a plausible reason why Ivomandus should lie. 'Well, if you think that will work, then do it.'

So Ivomandus went over to one of his shelves and selected a small sheet of copper, out of which he cut a rectangle with tinsnips. He rolled it into a tiny tube, scarcely more than half the length of a woman's little finger, then neatly hammered one end flat.

'Here, you make the fragments the way you want them,' he said, skidding a piece of broken black pottery and a small hammer across the workbench to Canio. 'Tell me, exactly what is it that I'm making?'

Canio had been waiting for a question like that, and was faintly surprised it hadn't come sooner. 'Just a gift for a friend. He collects such things – I don't know why,' he added casually.

Ivomandus glanced up at him, and in that glance Canio read disbelief. But the coppersmith said nothing and did not raise the subject again.

Ignoring the hammer, with the edge of a blunt knife-like tool he had found lying on the workbench, Canio started chipping off pieces of the hard pottery and splitting them down into ever smaller fragments until he had about ten, each so tiny that they could all have sat on his thumbnail with room to spare.

Carefully picking them up and placing them on the palm of his left hand, Canio took them to Ivomandus, who tipped them into the open end of the little copper tube and hammered it closed.

Canio held the tube close to one ear and shook it, hearing a satisfyingly clear falsetto rattle from inside.

Time passed. Occasionally Ivomandus walked over and inspected the kiln, before shaking his head in response to Canio's unspoken question and returning to his seat.

To break the oppressive silence that had developed, Canio asked, 'You live here in Vertis then?'

'This is the place I call home – insofar as I have a home. I often travel around the country doing jobs in other men's workshops, but I always end up back here.'

'Does your wife look after this place while you're away?' Canio asked, fishing.

'My wife's dead, five years gone. The people from *The Full Moon* keep an eye on the workshop while I'm away.'

'No son to pass your skills on to?'

Ivomandus did not reply immediately, and Canio, suspecting he had touched a nerve, did not repeat the question.

But a little while later the coppersmith said, 'I only had the one son, a big, strong lad... There were other babies, but none lived to see their first birthday. He was taken in one of the army drafts a few months after his mother died. The last time I ever heard from him he was being sent north to one of the forts on The Wall. That was nearly four years ago. And three years ago The Wall was overrun by those Pictish savages. Even the *Dux*, Fullofaudes, was killed or captured – I never heard for sure what became of him. Not that I care. I know my son's dead though: if he wasn't he'd have got word to me by now.' There was another long silence, before he murmured, 'I often wonder if his mates buried him, or whether his gnawed bones are still scattered in some bleak wilderness. I don't suppose I'll ever know.'

Canio said nothing, reasoning that there was nothing meaningful that he could say.

'Were you ever there – on The Wall, I mean, you being a soldier?'

'I'm not a soldier,' Canio demurred.

'But you were once, weren't you, Baculo?' And before Canio could deny it, he added, 'You have the look of a soldier, and that's a soldier's sword you've got hidden under your *cucullus*.'

Canio could have lied, but in the circumstances he didn't feel inclined to do so. 'Yes,' he said, 'I was a soldier once, but I was never anywhere near The Wall. In the so-called *Conspiratio* I was stationed at Corinium to protect the *Praeses'* precious arse.'

Ivomandus nodded slowly but said nothing. Canio wondered if he believed him, or if he was too deep in his own thoughts to care.

More time passed in silence, and then the coppersmith suddenly looked up, sniffed the air, and said, 'They should be melted by now.' He went over to the kiln and peered inside, shielding his eyes from the heat as he moved aside the tile blocking the entrance. 'Yes, they're ready,' he said quietly.

Gripping the top of the crucible with his tongs, Ivomandus rapidly lifted it out of the kiln. Then, in one smooth movement, he poured the molten metal, glowing like the setting sun, into the base of the upturned mould.

Working frantically fast now, he pushed the crucible into the sand beside the mould, gripped the little copper tube with another, smaller, pair of tongs and inserted it vertically into the top of the molten metal, halfway down the body of the figurine. He checked that the tube was still upright, then picked up the crucible again and poured more metal until the mould was filled almost to overflowing.

A flame hovered over the top of the molten metal for several moments, before subsiding and dying. Ivomandus blew out a long breath, before setting the almost empty crucible back into the sand a little way from the mould and slowly wiping his sweating face with a piece of sacking.

Canio waited until the coppersmith was sitting down before asking, 'How long before it's cool enough to break open the mould?'

Ivomandus rubbed the sacking several times over his damp hair before replying, 'Not long. Noon, probably. '

'Right: I'll be back by then,' said Canio. 'Don't start without me.'

CHAPTER SIXTEEN

28th & 29th October

It seemed that even Nectovelius had given up hope of finding his mother in Vertis. He and Bodicca had apparently been wandering around the town again, enquiring in places they had missed the day before. But they were still no nearer to locating the elusive Marcia.

'One of those women we were told about could have been my mother, couldn't she?' the boy asked.

'Well, I can't say for sure that she wasn't,' Bodicca said tactfully. Then, to Canio, she said, 'Did you know that there's an army guard post on the other side of town?'

Canio did know, and had been keeping well clear of it. 'I'm aware of it. Anything else I should know?'

'Yes: earlier this morning we saw half a dozen soldiers come riding in from the Glevum road, didn't we, Nectovelius?'

'We did,' the boy confirmed. 'And they stopped at the guard post and talked to the two soldiers who live there.'

'Then they rode off and took the road to Salinae,' Bodicca added.

'So?' Canio asked.

'So after they'd gone, the two soldiers stationed here started walking around the town, looking as if they were searching for something or somebody. Poked their noses in here too.'

'Did they say who they were looking for?'

'No. They didn't say anything, just looked.'

'They probably do that most days, just to show their faces and prove that they're still awake,' said Canio, as much to himself as Bodicca. 'Nothing to worry about.' But, in truth, Canio was worried: he wanted to be away from this town.

'How's the figurine coming along?' Bodicca asked.

Canio thought it curious that she hadn't asked before. 'The metal was poured into the mould a little while ago. When it's cooled, Ivomandus will break it open, but the gods alone know what the figurine will look like. From what little I know of coppersmithing there's a hundred things that could have gone wrong. Maybe the clay won't have taken all the detail of the wax model, or maybe the molten *orichalcum* hasn't flowed to all parts of the mould. And that's only two of the hundred – I don't even want to think about the rest.'

'And did you remember,' Bodicca asked, 'to put something inside the mould to…?' Her voice trailed away, as if something else had occurred to her.

'To sound like seeds when the figurine's shaken? Yes, I remembered – although whether what we put in will sound like the real thing when the *orichalcum's* cooled I have no idea.'

It was only later, when Canio was back in Ivomandus's workshop, that he realised he had never mentioned the seeds to Bodicca – the pomegranate seeds inside the original figurine, which she said Vilbia had told her nothing about.

Back in the workshop, Ivomandus informed him that the metal had cooled and that the mould could be broken.

'Then go ahead,' said Canio, trying not to let his anxiety show.

Ivomandus nodded, picked the mould out of the sand box, examined it from all sides, set it down on a thick pile of sacking, then took a tiny hammer and began giving it gentle taps all around. Fine cracks appeared in the baked clay, cracks which widened slightly with every tap of the hammer. He then took a small knife, inserted the blade into one of the cracks and cautiously levered it sideways.

A small section of the mould came loose. Ivomandus turned it over and let the piece drop away. 'The first bit is always the worst to shift,' he remarked. 'The rest should be easier.'

He tapped some more, inserted and gently twisted the knife blade again, and slowly, piece by piece, the mould dropped away. When the top of the figurine was exposed there were three ragged rods of *orichalcum* projecting from the top of the head and the tips of the sword and torch, with another sticking out of the body of the hound. 'See those jets,' he said, holding the figurine up for Canio's inspection. 'That's a good sign – it means that the metal flowed all the way through the mould, just as it was supposed to.'

When the last of the fired clay was lying in small lumps on the workbench, Ivomandus cradled the figurine lovingly in his huge hands. But, to Canio's disquiet, it looked raw and crude. In addition to the jets, there were numerous tiny projections and other blemishes on the metal, not the smooth surfaces he had been expecting.

Ivomandus must have read the disappointment on his face. He grinned. 'Don't worry,' he assured him. 'She'll look much better after I've cut off the jets and fettled her. And listen...'

He held the figurine an inch from Canio's right ear and shook it gently, and Canio heard a faint rustle as the pottery fragments moved freely inside their little copper tube.

'That sounds about right. How long will it take to fettle it?' Canio asked, trying to imagine how it would look after the coppersmith had finished, hoping desperately that it would be identical to the picture of the original that he still retained in his mind.

'Probably the rest of the day – as I said, these things can't be hurried, not if you want it done properly.'

And of course, Canio did want it done properly: it had to

be done properly. 'One thing more: after it's fettled, I want it treated so that it looks old. Really old – black with age.' And then a thought came. 'If something was mostly black with age, but with one spot still yellow, then lay out in the open for a year or two, what colour would that spot be now?'

'A something made of *orichalcum*?'

'Yes.'

'Difficult to say. It would depend on how sound the black patina was. If sound, the black areas would probably stay black, but the bare spot might turn any colour – green, brown, black – who knows?'

Canio considered this for a few moments, then said, 'Right, just turn it all black – can you do that?'

'Perhaps – I remember doing something similar years ago. But I'll need the right ingredients.'

'Which are?'

'Oh, mostly things I've got here in the workshop,' Ivomandus replied guardedly. 'And urine.'

'Urine?'

'Piss, piddle – or whatever you care to call it.'

'I call it lots of things – especially when I miss whatever I'm aiming for,' Canio replied.

'Good. Then I'll leave you to collect a pot full. Meet me back here an hour before sunset. I should have the lady properly fettled by then.'

So Canio returned to *The Full Moon*, "borrowed" a fair-sized clay pot, and installed it on the floor of the malodorous latrine in the outhouse at the rear of the premises. He also stationed a reluctant Nectovelius outside the door, telling him to request all who entered to urinate into the pot. After that he retired to the communal room, where he spent the afternoon drinking the establishment's foul watered wine and, in due course, contributing to the contents of the pot.

In conversation with an old man, who introduced himself as a master ironmaker, he was told how, twenty years back, the furnaces of Vertis were producing a wagonload of blooms of raw iron every day. And shiploads of charcoal for the furnaces used to arrive on the Sabrina daily; charcoal brought from the great forests on the western side of that river, way below Glevum. Nowadays, it was one, or at best two, wagonloads of blooms a week. Even the wine in *The Full Moon* was not what it was (although that did not deter him from accepting several beakers of the stuff from Canio).

For old men, Canio reflected, yesterday was always better, because yesterday they were young. But today they are old, and tomorrow they will be dead. He also reflected morosely that, at thirty-one, he was himself no longer a young man. This autumn, more than in any other that had gone before, his eyes seemed to be drawn, unwillingly, towards the things which showed the inevitability of the descent into the cold and dark and desolation of winter.

When he judged that sunset was an hour away, he carried the pot and its fragrant contents back to Ivomandus where, to his relief, he saw that the raw casting had been transformed.

Gone were the jets of waste metal and other imperfections, and all the surfaces were now polished smooth. Even the tiny golden face was as he thought he remembered it, the features sternly beautiful.

'It's perfect,' he murmured.

'So are you still sure you want it blackened?' the coppersmith asked.

It looked so exquisite now, gleaming bright as gold, that Canio was tempted, but... 'Quite sure,' he confirmed, still gazing at that unsmiling face. Now cast in *orichalcum*, it was only to be expected that the figurine should look more like the original than the wax model had done. Or perhaps – unsettling thought – that was only because the copy was now shaping his memory of the original into its own image?

'So what, beside piss, will be in this brew you reckon will turn the surface black?' He had noticed a small clay pot containing what looked like salt on Ivomandus's workbench – a pot which, he was fairly sure, had not been there before.

Ivomandus gave a foxy smile. 'That's one of the secrets of my craft. Come back early tomorrow: the lady should be ready then.'

'Well?' asked Bodicca as they ate in a corner of *The Full Moon*'s communal room. It was (allegedly) chicken stew and, as usual, Nectovelius ate everything placed in front of him, as if it were the last food he would ever be given. Perhaps, Canio wondered, life had taught him that it might be just that.

'Ivomandus says it should be finished by morning.'

'Good. And then?'

'Then we go back south, to Glevum.'

'Not north?' Nectovelius sounded dismayed, or as dismayed as anyone with a mouth full of chicken stew could sound.

'Not north,' Canio confirmed. 'Look, if your mother travelled north from Glevum, then here in Vertis is the most likely place she would have stopped, at least for the night. But in all your searching and asking you haven't come across one single person who's even halfway sure they saw her.'

'I'm not giving up,' the boy said defiantly.

'So where will you look next?' Canio asked distractedly. However hard he tried, he could not stop his imagination from picturing the damage Ivomandus's foul brew might, even then, be doing to the metal of the figurine. 'The road north from here leads back to Salinae, and you've already searched there.'

Nectovelius did not reply, but sat silent, obviously unhappy. And Canio had enough imagination to know what must be going through the boy's mind – that not to take the road back to Salinae and beyond was to accept that he would probably never see his mother again.

'You never know,' he said, trying to sound encouraging. 'Perhaps Marcia's gone back to Glevum herself because now she's realised how much she's missing you.'

And still Nectovelius did not reply.

In the morning, in the spectral grey light just before sunrise, Canio went to Ivomandus's workshop, after an unquiet night spent imagining the worst. The place stank of urine. Canio pointed to the pot and the dark, turbid liquid within. Even as he watched in the candlelight a bubble rose to the surface and burst. 'Is it still in there?'

'It is.'

'When will it be ready?'

'I took it off the top of the kiln a little while ago, so I'd guess it's as ready as it will ever be. Shall I stop the process?'

'Yes – straight away,' said Canio, worried that perhaps it should have been stopped long before.

Ivomandus picked up the pot, opened the outside door and poured the foul-smelling liquid over the uneven cobbles of the street. Back in the workshop he fished out the figurine, swished it around vigorously in another two pots filled with what Canio assumed was plain water, then held out the still-dripping figurine for Canio's inspection.

To Canio's relief the details of face, sword and torch appeared undamaged.

'Satisfactory?' the coppersmith asked.

Canio took the figurine, turning it over and examining it from all sides. He rubbed the smooth black patina, gently at first, then more vigorously: it remained intact. 'It appears to be,' he said cautiously.

'Then perhaps we can conclude our business, if that's all right with you?'

'Two *solidi* paid, two more to come. That was the arrangement, I believe.'

'Plus materials,' Ivomandus reminded him.

'And how much are they worth?'

'Well, there was the beeswax, the fine clay for the mould, the old coins for the *orichalcum* – and they're very hard to come by these days. Then there's the charcoal for the kiln, and the ingredients for the blackening process.'

Canio was about to remind him, sarcastically, that the urine had been free, then thought better of it. 'So how much is all that lot worth?'

Ivomandus blew out his cheeks. 'It's got to be the better part of another *solidus*.'

Canio guessed that a few *siliquae* would have more than covered the cost. He stared at Ivomandus, just to let him know that he wasn't deceived, but then said, 'Very well, three more *solidi* it is – on one condition.'

'Which is?'

'That all this never happened: no figurine, and no Baculo either. Neither it nor I ever existed – agreed?'

'Agreed,' said Ivomandus, apparently surprised that Canio was not going to haggle.

Canio felt in his belt pouch, drew out a soft leather bag, shuffled out three of the lustrous little gold coins and dropped them one by one into the outstretched palm of one of the coppersmith's great grimy hands.

'They look as bright as new-polished *orichalcum*,' Ivomandus remarked.

'Yes, and almost as valuable,' Canio replied.

Ivomandus just grinned.

As he was leaving, the Hecate figurine carefully wrapped in several layers of woollen cloth and hidden in one of the inner pockets of his tunic, Canio considered expressing the hope that Ivomandus's son would, even after all this time, return safe from the North Country. He couldn't do it: both men knew that his son would never return.

CHAPTER SEVENTEEN

29th October

Bodicca met him outside *The Full Moon*. 'Isn't Nectovelius with you?'

Canio frowned. 'No – why should he be?'

'Because he's not with me, that's why.'

'When did you last see him?'

'Just before I went to sleep last night, and that was long before midnight. Do you know what I think he's done? – He's gone back to Salinae.'

'I thought we'd talked the young fool out of that.'

'Well, it seems we didn't. You've got to go after him.'

'He can look after himself. I did, when I wasn't that much older than him.'

'You were about twelve then, weren't you? Not seven.'

'Who told…?' But it could only have been Vilbia who had told this strange woman tales about his childhood in Germania, tales that he had never meant to tell even her. 'It was his choice to go, not mine,' he said coldly. Yet even as he spoke he knew that his annoyance was not so much with Nectovelius, but more with his own wretched conscience. He wanted to be away from Vertis without further delay, but in Nectovelius he recognised too much of his young self to leave the child to his fate, alone and with winter approaching.

In any case, Bodicca was ignoring his apparent disinclination to go back north. 'If you hurry you might catch him before he reaches Salinae.'

'It's only seven miles away, and you reckon he's been gone half the night – so he's probably there by now,' Canio pointed out.

'Then the sooner you get there the better. If he starts out on one of the roads leading north from Salinae you may never find him.'

He knew she was right, that he had to go. But he still could not stop himself from giving her a look intended to say that, if the ground were to open up and swallow her, he would be less than heartbroken.

The eastern sky was still a lurid orange-red when Canio had urged Antares into a smart trot along the highway that led back to Salinae.

He was already more than halfway to that town before he met the first traveller heading south, an ox-drawn wagon loaded with big, roughly-made clay pots full of the salt from Salinae's brine pits.

'Have you seen a small boy – no more than seven or so – heading towards the town?' he asked the driver.

The man shook his head. 'No, I've seen nobody – you're the first person I've met on the road this morning.'

But just as he was entering the town he came across a woman carrying a large basket of flat loaves. She said that she had seen a small boy she didn't recognise, but that was some time ago and she didn't know where he was now.

Encouraged, Canio rode slowly through the streets of the already-bustling town, looking this way and that, catching sight of several young boys, most in ragged tunics, but none of them Nectovelius.

Just beyond the point where the road from Alauna joined it, the north-south highway crossed the remembered sluggish little river by way of a ford. Antares splashed through the muddy waters, and a hundred yards further on came to the spot where the highway forked.

Spotting a man carrying an armful of firewood in the salt works opposite, Canio called out, 'Have you seen a young boy on this road, heading north?'

The man halted briefly. 'I did, yes – but that was a while ago.'

'Which fork did he take?'

The man shook his head. 'That I couldn't say.'

'Where do they lead to?'

'The road due north leads to Viroconium, the other one goes north-east to Letocetum.'

'How far?'

'To Viroconium? A good forty-five miles.'

'And to Letocetum?'

'Thirty – maybe thirty-five.'

So Canio had to guess which fork Nectovelius had taken. For no particularly obvious reason he decided that the boy was most likely to have taken the road to Letocetum. He was about to start along it when he suddenly thought of the coin which always hung from a cord around his neck. It was the big copper coin of the Emperor Julian – the same one that Saturninus had given to Vilbia, and which Vilbia had then given to him for safekeeping, before she dived into that lake on the south side of the Great Marshes to retrieve the looted gold – and the Hecate figurine which he had, moments before, thrown out into the water as the dying Orgillus had begged him to.

He pushed back the hood of his *cucullus* and worked the cord over his head. Untying the knot, he pulled the cord through the hole drilled through the coin above Julian's head.

'Heads for the Letocetum road, bull for Viroconium,' he murmured. He spun the coin high in the air and caught it adroitly on the open palm of his right hand. It showed the great Apis bull standing beneath twin stars. He frowned, then shrugged.

'Viroconium it is then.' He patted Antares and started the horse trotting briskly along the north-leading fork.

He had gone little more than two miles before he spotted a small figure trudging along the road far ahead, clad in the oversized *cucullus* which Bodicca had somehow managed to acquire for him in Alauna. For a moment – and afterwards he swore to himself that it was only a moment – a little voice whispered that he should halt, turn around, and return to Vertis, telling Bodicca that the boy had apparently disappeared into thin air.

Perhaps she wouldn't have believed him, but that in itself would not have greatly worried him. What made him knee Antares into a smart trot was disquiet that the thought should ever have come: he remembered only too well his own harsh and precarious childhood.

When he caught up with Nectovelius he reined in Antares and ambled alongside the boy at his own pace. 'Where are you heading for?'

The boy looked sideways at him, then fixed his eyes back on the road ahead. 'Viroconium. I was told that's where this road leads.'

'It's forty-five miles away. It'll take you two days at least.'

'I'll get there.'

'Do you really think your mother will be there?'

'She might be.'

'And if she isn't?'

Nectovelius hesitated. 'Then I'll keep on walking,' he said doggedly.

'All the way to Eboracum?'

'If I have to.'

'Maybe the man she went off with did come from Eboracum, but that doesn't mean they're going back there. After three weeks she could be anywhere, even back in Glevum. In fact, if she regrets leaving you she could be there at this very moment, sobbing with grief and guilt, desperate to see you again.'

The boy said nothing, just kept on stubbornly walking northwards.

Canio waited, giving the boy time to reflect, then said, 'Do you think you could climb that tree?' He pointed to a huge old ash, the only large tree in sight. It stood about fifty yards from the road, nearly all its leaves fallen and lying in wind-sculpted yellow drifts around it.

'Of course I could,' the boy replied, clearly puzzled by the question.

'Go on then, climb it.'

'Why?'

'There's something up there that you should see.'

'Up there?'

'High up there,' Canio confirmed.

Still looking puzzled, the boy pulled the *cucullus* over his head, handed it to Canio, then scampered over to the tree, jumped up, grasped the lowest branch with both hands, swung one leg over it and pulled himself up, as agile as a squirrel.

Canio tied Antares' reins to the same branch, pulled off his own *cucullus* and followed Nectovelius up the tree. Halfway up, the boy paused. 'How high should I go?'

'As high as you can.'

Nectovelius was about forty feet above the ground when Canio caught up with him. Standing on a branch and steadying himself against the trunk with one curled arm, Canio pointed to the north through the bare branches. 'Can you see your mother?'

Nectovelius stared northwards, seeing only what Canio himself could see – the road ahead dwindling to nothing in the distance, and beyond it tiny trees blurring into an immense sweep of blue-grey haze, which itself merged almost indistinguishably at the far horizon with the blue-grey of the autumn sky.

Canio watched the boy's face as he gazed; watched as hope fought a losing battle with despair. 'You can't see her, can you?' he said quietly. 'Maybe she is out there somewhere, lost in the vastness of the world. More likely she's not there at all.' He let the words sink in, then said, 'If she doesn't want you back, then you'll never find her... Do you think she will want you back?'

'Yes, of course she will... of course she will.' The words were intended to sound confident, but Canio detected uncertainty.

'Then the best chance you'll ever have of seeing her again is in Glevum, if she's gone back there to find you.'

'Do you think she might have?'

'There's only one way to find out, and that's where I'm going.'

'To Glevum?'

'Of course to Glevum.'

'Bodicca will be going too, won't she?'

Canio had anticipated that question. 'Yes, she'll be going – if she's still in Vertis by the time we return. Come on, let's get back there before she decides to leave on her own.' He started climbing down the tree.

For a few moments more Nectovelius continued gazing northwards, then began following Canio down.

Once on the ground, Nectovelius wriggled back into his *cucullus*, before Canio lifted him up onto Antares' back.

But before he could himself remount, Canio became aware of an old woman carrying a large wicker basket standing at the side of the highway, watching him intently.

'You're not from these parts, are you?' she asked in high, cracked voice.

Canio confirmed they were not. 'Why do you ask?'

'Because nobody from around here would dare climb that tree, not since what happened to Firminus.'

'Who's he?'

'He isn't anybody, not any more. But years ago, when I was a girl, he was in charge of getting firewood for the salt works, and that was the last big tree for miles around that hadn't been chopped down. People warned him not to touch it though.'

'Why?'

The old woman shuffled her feet. 'Because they said a god lived in it.'

'What god?'

'One of the old gods. A god as old as time itself – so old that nobody alive knew his name.'

'But Firminus didn't chop it down,' said Canio, stating the obvious.

'No, but he was going to. They say that he started walking towards it, with an axe in his hand, when all of a sudden he stopped and stared at the trunk, like he'd seen something to freeze his blood. Then he just dropped down dead – stone dead. And from that day to this, nobody has dared to snap so much as the tiniest twig off it.'

'Then it's lucky the wind isn't superstitious,' said Canio, pointing to several big twigs, crusted with yellow lichen, scattered among the fallen leaves.

'Oh, you can mock,' said the old woman, 'but there's something strange about this place, always has been. I'd never go near that tree, especially at night, and I don't know anyone else who would either.'

'Did you believe her?' Nectovelius asked anxiously, twisting round and staring at the tree as they jogged back towards Salinae.

'No, of course not,' Canio replied. And then, for devilment, he added, 'Gods don't live in ash trees. Now if it had been an oak, a really big old hollow oak, I might have half-believed her. I once heard someone say that dryads live in their hollow trunks.'

'What are they?'

'Dryads? They're wood nymphs – pretty women who are supposed to live in and around oak trees and watch over and protect them, or so the tale goes. Didn't your m—' He stopped himself just in time.

It was late morning before he and Nectovelius, the latter now half-asleep, arrived back at Vertis. By the time Bodicca had scolded and fussed over the boy, then waited while he wolfed down a bowl of the inevitable chicken stew, it was as near to noon as anyone could tell, the sun being hidden behind featureless grey clouds from horizon to horizon.

CHAPTER EIGHTEEN

'How far is Glevum from here?' Nectovelius asked. They were half a mile south of Vertis, out on the stoned highway, the boy sitting on Antares' back behind Canio, Bodicca striding along beside the horse.

'Twenty-five miles or so,' Canio replied.

'That far? Will we get there before dark?'

'But not as far as Eboracum,' Canio muttered. Then, louder, 'No, of course we won't. We would have done, if you hadn't gone running off back to Salinae. As things stand it'll be dark long before we get there.'

'But we will get there eventually, my lamb, don't you worry,' said Bodicca. She was setting a brisk pace, but the great puddle-filled potholes and muddy stretches made hurrying difficult. So it was that sunset was no more than an hour away when at last they reached the little town of Confluens, where the Flumen Avon from the north-east met and merged with the great Flumen Sabrina flowing southwards.

On the outskirts of the town they crossed the Avon on a large but algae-stained wooden bridge that had seen better days, the sodden planking creaking ominously under Antares' hooves.

Stopping briefly to rest and eat, they found only one small bakehouse in Confluens, from where Canio bought half a dozen small loaves. There was not even a *popina*, so he was forced to drink the foul watered wine he had taken the precaution of carrying from Vertis.

As the slow miles passed he had spent the time planning his next moves. First, he would leave Glevum and stealthily make his way to the place, some five or six miles south of Corinium, where Peltrasius had thrown away the original figurine on that June day in 368. There, after much (witnessed) effort, he would "find" his fake in the middle of one of the large patches of brambles he vaguely remembered. A bramble patch which he would have heroically hacked apart with his *spatha*, acquiring several prominent scratches on his face and hands in the process.

That same day he would present the still slightly muddy figurine to Sabinus, and then explain how he had come by it. He would say, with well-counterfeited indignation, that it was lying, concealed under a few dead leaves, in the very same place where Peltrasius had so carelessly tossed it away. That would make those two dog turds, Peltrasius and Castor, look fools – a little retribution for all the trouble they had caused him.

Every time his imagination pictured Peltrasius squirming beneath Sabinus's contemptuous stare he could not suppress a fierce snort of laughter. Which must have puzzled both Bodicca and Nectovelius, if the latter happened to be still awake, which, beyond Confluens, he rarely was.

On the road between Confluens and Glevum, with Bodicca now riding Antares and Canio leading the horse by its reins, he could not resist occasionally taking the figurine from under his tunic and sneaking a look at it. Which was when the doubts began to surface.

Each time he looked, seen in harsh daylight rather than the softening, sympathetic candlelight of Ivomandus's workshop, he could not shake off the uncomfortable suspicion that, if the original and the fake were placed side by side, then the differences between them would be all too obvious.

Did that really matter? Vilbia would know original from fake: of course she would. But surely Peltrasius – the man who had only held it for a few moments – wouldn't? That left the

Vicarius, Civilis: he was the real unknown factor. But it must be two and a half years at the very least since he had last seen it, so would he remember exactly what it looked like? Canio simply didn't know; couldn't know, and that worried him. And kept worrying him.

They had only rested at Confluens for as long as it took Canio to seek out and buy the bread, but even so it was long after sunset when the outlines of the city walls of Glevum at last came into view, a deeper black against the dark night sky, where the cloud-obscured moon had just entered its last quarter.

Inevitably, when the weary trio reached the North Gate they found it long closed, and no amount of pleading with the solitary guard on the walkway above the gate could persuade him to open it.

'Hades take you!' the guard yelled down at them. 'I'd be flogged if I opened this gate before dawn, for you or anybody else. Try *The Caduceus*, near the docks, if you want a bed for the night.'

It occurred to Canio that the man probably received a commission for every benighted traveller he directed there. Or if he didn't, then he had missed a trick.

So they trudged through the dark streets of the extensive extra-mural settlement that lay between the city walls and the Sabrina docks, until they found *The Caduceus.* The light spilling from the open doorway of the *stabulum* dimly illuminated a badly executed picture of Mercury's serpent-entwined wand painted on the stuccoed wall above the arch.

After seeing Antares settled, Canio paid the proprietor's daughter, an otherwise plain young woman with an enchanting smile who said her name was Postima, for two bedrooms, an evening meal and stabling for the horse.

In the communal dining room they ate a meal of salmon, which might have been delicious if it was freshly caught.

Nectovelius however, who claimed to know about such things, sniffed it and reckoned the fish had expired the best part of a week before.

All three were tired after the journey from Vertis, Canio especially so after the previous fretful night spent worrying while the figurine stewed in its malodorous bath.

Smothering a yawn, he went to his bedroom immediately after the meal, although not before hearing Nectovelius trying, for at least the third time, to persuade Bodicca to let him go to Vario's *popina* to see if his mother had returned. It was, he assured her, near the docks and not so very far away.

And once again he heard Bodicca tell him that it would be wiser to wait for daylight, because the night-time streets held many dangers.

Sleep hopeful, my boy, Canio thought. *Disappointment will wait patiently until tomorrow: it always does.*

He climbed the stairs and groped his way along the corridor, where one small tallow candle burned darkly. Once inside his bedroom he closed and bolted the door before flopping down onto the bed. Tugging off his boots, *cucullus* and sword belt he crawled under the solitary blanket, grimacing at its foetid odour. Despite the smell, he fell asleep almost immediately.

When he woke he was standing in the dimly-lit *triclinium* of Villa Censorini. He felt no surprise to be there, for in dreams nothing that happens seems irrational. Sabinus was there, sitting in front of the remembered dining table of polished fruitwood, in a high-backed wickerwork armchair of throne-like proportions.

Castor was also there, and Peltrasius too, standing behind Sabinus's right and left shoulders respectively. The eyes of all three men were closed, but as Canio walked soundlessly towards them, across the great Bacchic mosaic, Sabinus's eyes flickered open and he held out his left hand, palm uppermost.

Canio took the Hecate figurine from his belt pouch and placed it in Sabinus's open palm. The *Praeses* gazed wonderingly at it, and then his eyes closed again and his fingers curled around the figurine as gently as a lover's holding his beloved's hand.

Time passed, and then Sabinus opened his eyes and handed the figurine to Peltrasius, who, eyes now open, took it and began examining it minutely, slowly turning it over and over in his hands.

Then he looked up and stared questioningly at Canio, before turning to Sabinus and slowly shaking his head. 'No, this is not the figurine I took from the deserter, Orgillus.'

The expression on Sabinus's face changed, like a dark cloud passing across the sun. 'Are you sure – absolutely sure?'

'Yes, *Vir Perfectissimus* – absolutely sure.'

Canio tried to protest that Peltrasius was lying, that the figurine was indeed the one they had taken from Orgillus on that June day in 368. The words formed inside his head, but his tongue was paralysed and he could make no sound. He tried again, was sure he was speaking, but could hear no words coming out of his mouth.

Sabinus was studying him now, with the cold eyes of a dead fish in an expressionless mask of a face. 'So you thought to deceive me, Caninus... you actually thought to deceive me,' he said softly, as if he still could not quite believe that anyone would dare do such a thing.

Not taking his eyes off Canio, he murmured, 'Castor, take this man away and extract from him the whereabouts of the genuine figurine. I don't care how you do it: cut off his toes one by one, then his fingers, then gouge out one of his eyes if you have to – make him scream in agony. But, don't kill him, not yet. Perhaps that can come later, when I am absolutely certain that I have the genuine figurine – the one which Peltrasius possessed so briefly those two years ago.'

Castor and Peltrasius, faces like thunderclouds, both drew their *spathae* and began walking slowly towards Canio. He groped beneath his *cucullus* for his own *spatha*, but it had gone, vanished. He tried to turn and run, but his legs were as stone and he couldn't move.

And then Castor was raising his *spatha*, its blade gleaming in the lamplight, his arm drawing back to jab the cruel point into Canio's right eye. He felt an unstoppable scream of terror rising in his throat.

CHAPTER NINETEEN

29th & 30th October

Waking again, he found himself staring out into the darkness, heart pounding, his face beaded with sweat. Had he screamed? Had anyone heard him? Wild, disjointed fragments of the dream were still replaying in his head when he became aware of the sounds of rapidly approaching footsteps outside in the corridor. He scrabbled wildly for his *spatha*, his fingers finding it just as somebody began hammering at the door.

Fully alert now, he stayed silent, his right hand grasping the hilt of the *spatha* and drawing it smoothly and almost soundlessly out of its scabbard.

'Canio, Canio – it's me, Nectovelius!' The boy sounded desperate.

Still Canio stayed silent.

The pounding on the door continued. 'Canio! Canio!'

Noiseless in his bare feet, he crept across the rough floorboards, eased back the bolt and flung open the door with his free left hand as he stood concealed in the darkness at the right-hand side of the doorway.

Nectovelius shot out of the dim light of the corridor, landing on his hands and knees with a thump. Canio ignored him and stepped quickly out into the corridor, the point of his *spatha* tracking the movement of his eyes as he looked up and down the empty passageway. From behind the door of another room a sleepy, angry voice bellowed something about stopping the infernal noise.

Ignoring the angry voice, Canio turned to Nectovelius. 'What in the name of Hades do you want?' he hissed. 'And where's Bodicca?'

'She's dragging Vario off towards the docks.'

'What?'

'Vario – she's dragging him off towards—'

Canio grabbed the tallow candle from its sconce on the corridor wall, went back into his bedroom, jammed the candle into a pottery candlestick, then shut and bolted the door. 'Sweet Venus, what have you two been up to? Tell me – and make it quick. And make sense.' By the candle's smoky light he noticed for the first time a gash on the boy's forehead. He thought he'd also been crying, but couldn't be sure.

'I went to look for my mother—'

'You were told to wait till morning,' Canio interrupted.

'But she might have been here, in Glevum,' the boy wailed.

'And did you find her?'

Nectovelius shook his head. 'No. I tried to sneak into Vario's *popina*, but as soon as I put my head round the door the pig spotted me. I tried to get away, but he came running after me through the streets, yelling and calling me bad names. I tripped over something in the dark and he caught me and started kicking me. I curled up in a ball like a hedgehog and tried to roll away. When he stopped kicking – only because he was out of breath – I asked him if my mother had come back. But he just laughed, and said she would never be coming back, because she never wanted to see me again. Not ever. He said she'd often told him that I'd been hanging around her neck like a quern stone for years, and the only reason she'd kept me was because she thought my father might come back to her one day.' The boy paused, then said quietly, 'That was all lies, wasn't it…? It was, wasn't it?'

143

Canio said nothing, and the boy started sobbing. Remembering himself a quarter of a century ago in that cold city beside the Rhine, Canio felt a twinge of something close to pity. 'I simply don't know, boy – how could I know?' He waited until the sobs had subsided into snivels, then asked, 'But if you were on the ground and Vario was standing over you, how did you get away?'

'Bodicca came... I didn't see what happened, not properly, it was so dark. I think Bodicca must have hit him with something, because all of a sudden Vario was lying on the ground too, and then Bodicca was pulling me upright and telling me to run back here.'

'So where is she now?'

'I don't know. The last I saw of her she'd reached down and grabbed Vario by the neck of his tunic and was starting to drag him away, like he was only made of straw. I think she was going towards the docks, but I'm not sure because it was so—'

'Dark.' Canio finished the sentence for him. He knew he ought to go and find her, but before he could say as much to the boy he heard more footsteps in the corridor. The footsteps halted outside his door.

'Canio?' It was her voice.

He opened the door and Bodicca walked in, saw Nectovelius still on the floor and crouched down beside him. 'There's nothing to fear now, little man, you're safe here – Vario will never find you.' She looked up at Canio. 'Did he tell you what happened?'

'He told me. What did you do to Vario?'

'Do...? I just held him off long enough for the boy to run away. I don't know where he is now: still searching, I suppose.'

Canio was on the point of repeating what Nectovelius had told him, but then decided against: he had other things on his mind. 'Best take him back to your room.'

So Bodicca shepherded Nectovelius out into the corridor and Canio heard her door open, then close, and then, to his annoyance, heard her returning.

144

'Did he tell you what Vario said about his mother?' she whispered, sitting on the bed beside him.

'That she never wanted to see him again? Yes, he told me.'

'Do you think Vario was telling the truth?'

Canio shrugged. 'She abandoned the boy, didn't she?'

'So you do believe Vario?'

'Does it matter what I believe?' he sighed. 'Perhaps in the morning I should go and find this Vario and kick the truth out of him. Do to him what he did to Nectovelius – see how he likes it.' He noticed how the lazily swaying flame of the candle was casting his and Bodicca's enlarged black shadows onto the wall of the dingy room, magnifying the slightest movements of their heads as they spoke.

Bodicca seemed to hesitate, before saying, 'Yes, perhaps you should... if you can find him.'

'Any reason why I might not?'

'Who knows, with a man like that. He'll probably be drunk by morning, if he isn't already.'

'On river water? It never had that effect on me.'

In the dim light Canio more sensed than saw the enigmatic smile on Bodicca's face, but she stood up and left the room without replying.

With Bodicca gone, he wedged the candle back into its sconce on the corridor wall, then groped his way back to his bed. But sleep would not come: that terrifying dream of Peltrasius and Sabinus rejecting his copy of the Hecate figurine as a fake had been too vivid. He attempted to convince himself that it was meaningless, nothing more that the product of his own doubts and fears. The attempt failed: his rational mind may have told him that the dream had no significance, but his instinct was screaming that he should heed its warning. And life had taught him that, in some situations, instinct was a more trustworthy friend than reason.

So just how close a match was his copy to the original figurine? Back in Vertis he had thought it perfect, but now…

Vilbia would know. With her he could compare the two and know in a moment. But he was now certain that she must somehow have foreseen what was coming, and feared he might attempt to take the genuine figurine from her. The realisation that she still did not trust him was painful, but that must be the reason why she had gone away. And why he would not see her again until this business was over – or perhaps not even then.

Bodicca? Had she seen the original figurine? At their first meeting at Leucesca's temple she had denied all knowledge of it. Now he was certain that she had been lying, but equally certain that, for reasons he could only begin to guess, she would never admit it.

Eutherius? Canio was almost certain that Vilbia had shown the genuine figurine to the old apothecary. But he also suspected that if his copy were a good likeness, then the malicious old bastard would probably say it was not. And if it were not, then he would almost certainly say that it was – he had not forgotten that somebody had informed Castor about his visit to Fraomarius.

And then he remembered something that Peltrasius had said – about the old priest at the temple of Apollo, far away in the Niger Hills. The man whose obsessive need to steal back the genuine figurine had led to the sacking of the temple and the theft of the figurine by Orgillus and his fellow deserters – and to the murders of Apollo's priests who lived there.

Peltrasius had said that the priest was still living in the ruins a year ago. So if he were to show his copy to that priest, and if the man were to believe it to be the genuine figurine, then surely that would prove that the copy was good enough to fool both Peltrasius and the *Vicarius*?

Back in January, Eutherius had told him that the temple was situated in the remote, hilly country that lay some way to the south-west of the Great Marshes.

And Peltrasius had said that it was some miles to the west of Lindinis, in the Niger Hills.

'Somewhere in the Niger Hills,' Canio murmured. He had never been to those hills – was not even quite sure where they were – and it would mean a long journey. But it would be worth it, if the priest thought his copy was the real thing – as he was increasingly confident he would. And yet… *"Men believe what they want to believe,"* as he had heard someone – it might have been Saturninus – once say. He wished he hadn't remembered that.

Soon after daybreak, in a quiet corner of *The Caduceus's* communal eating room, it occurred to Canio to ask Nectovelius why Vario had been so angry with the boy that he had jumped up and chased him through the dark streets the moment he had set eyes on him. He was beginning to suspect that the man's violent reaction must have been due to something more than simple dislike of the boy.

Nectovelius mumbled something to the effect that Vario was always angry, and had beaten him several times for no good reason after his mother had left.

Bodicca nudged him. 'Better tell Canio the other reason as well.'

Nectovelius said nothing, so Bodicca nudged him again. 'Tell him.'

'These *siliquae*… the ones I've got to pay the priestess,' the boy began hesitantly, pointing to the place in the front of his tunic where the twist of cloth containing the coins was hidden, 'not all of them were given to me by my mother.'

Which began to confirm Canio's suspicions. 'You borrowed the rest from Vario?' he asked sardonically.

The boy nodded.

'Without telling him?'

Nectovelius nodded again.

Canio grinned and cuffed the boy lightly around the side of his head. 'Nothing I wouldn't have done myself. Sometimes you have to take what you need from this hard world, because nobody's going to give it to you.'

For a moment Nectovelius grinned back, but then his face turned solemn again and he said, 'I still don't know if my mother came back to Glevum, not for sure.'

'Then I'll go and find out. What's the name of Vario's *popina*? – *The Dirty Dog*, isn't it?'

'*The Brindled Hound*,' Nectovelius corrected him.

'Knew it was something like that,' Canio replied. 'Wait here, both of you. This shouldn't take long.'

Even at that early hour there were several men drinking in *The Brindled Hound*. Canio went up to the bar and ordered a cup of their best wine from the youth standing behind the counter. There appeared to be no tables or chairs, so he retired to a corner and spent a little while leaning against the wall and listening to the conversations of his fellow drinkers.

One of the topics under discussion was Vario. It seemed that he had not been seen since the previous night, when he had apparently caught sight of somebody in the doorway, uttered several profane expletives, then gone running off into the night after that somebody. And that was the last that anybody in the *popina* had seen of him.

The general consensus was that the somebody must have been a woman of his acquaintance, and that he was still with her somewhere. Which prompted several coarse comments, and even coarser speculations as to what he had been doing all night, and perhaps was still doing.

After waiting for the time it took him to swallow the wine (which, he guessed, was locally produced: it was certainly vile enough), Canio sidled back to the counter and said to the youth, 'Last time I was here – back in the summer it was – there was

148

a woman, quite pretty, standing behind the bar where you are now. Metta, or Marcia, I think her name was. Is she still around?'

The youth gave him a sly look, as if to say, *I know what you have in mind*. 'Marcia? She's been gone for the better part of a month now. Ran off with one of her best clients, if you take my meaning.'

'Ah, like that was it? Do you have any idea where she went?'

'None at all. Vario might, but I don't know where he is at the moment.' The youth hesitated, then lowered his voice and added, 'If it's a woman you want, try Julia Brica at *The Yellow Sun*, inside the walls, near the East Gate. Tell her it was me who sent you.'

'Julia Brica,' Canio mused. 'Thanks.' He spread five *nummi* on the counter and left.

Back at *The Caduceus* he gave Nectovelius the bad news. He had expected tears, but none came. It occurred to him that Bodicca might have cautioned the boy against hope. *Always wise advice,* he thought. He was fairly certain now that what Vario said had laid bare a truth so painful that the boy had smothered it and tried to bury it deep in his young soul. But truths like that can never be killed, no matter how deeply they are buried. That was another thing that life had taught Canio.

He briefly considered asking Nectovelius directly if his conjecture was correct. A glance at the boy's face, set rigid with unhappiness, dissuaded him: he would have to wait for the boy to acknowledge it in his own time and in his own way.

Changing the subject, he said casually to Bodicca, 'I'll be going south for a few days. There's someone I have to see.'

She appeared strangely unsurprised. 'Aren't you in a hurry to give that figurine to the very important person you said wants it?'

'I want to make sure it's exactly right before I do. That's why I'm going south.'

'And will this someone you have to see tell you if it's right or not?'

'Perhaps.'

'So who is he – or is it a she?'

Canio couldn't think of a logical reason not to tell her. 'He's a priest – at a temple of Apollo that was raided during the *Conspiratio*.'

'Not the one at Urticager – the one beside the Fosse Way, north of Aquae Sulis?'

'No, this one's much further south, in the remote, hilly country that lies to the south-west of the Great Marshes – or so I was told.'

'Ah, that one in the Niger Hills. That is a long way from here – you've never been there yourself, I take it?'

There was something knowing in the way she asked, something that made him say, 'No – have you?'

'When I was a girl we lived near the shore of the Sabrina Estuary, and my mother took me there once. It's difficult to find.'

'So the temple's near the Sabrina?'

'Oh no, it took us two whole days to walk there. You'd better take us with you, otherwise you might wander around for days without finding it.'

'Us?'

'Well, you can't leave Nectovelius here, not with Vario looking for him.'

'Do you really think he is still looking for the boy?'

'Bound to be.'

Canio looked her in the face, but that face betrayed nothing. *I've a growing suspicion, Bodicca,* he thought, but didn't say, *that Vario's not looking for anyone any more, but before long people are going to start looking for him. In which case, we'd best all be gone from Glevum before they fish him out of the docks, or wherever it was that you left him.*

150

'No, I suppose we can't leave him here. You and the boy wait in your room, but be ready to leave as soon as I get back.'

'Where are you going?'

'To see a man about a horse.'

There was, Canio remembered, a horse and mule dealer called Proxsimus, whose yard and stables stood a little way outside the North Gate. They had passed the place as they arrived in the dark from Vertis.

For three *solidi* he bought a sturdy pony, and for another *solidus* acquired a saddle to put on it. He made sure that the saddle fitted and none of the straps was worn, then led the pony back to *The Caduceus*.

CHAPTER TWENTY

30th October

By the end of the first hour after sunrise, or as near to it as Canio or anyone else could guess, they were already two miles south of Glevum, trotting briskly along the metalled road that led to Aquae Sulis, some forty long miles distant.

Canio was riding Antares; Bodicca and Nectovelius were jogging along on the pony, the boy swathed in his oversized *cucullus*.

For the first seven or so miles they travelled past corn stubble and plough lands, which over the next seven gave way to flat grasslands where sheep and cattle grazed, occasionally in distant sight of the ever-widening estuary of the Flumen Sabrina, way over to the west.

In the third seven miles the road and the estuary gradually eased away from each other, and over to the east it was the scarp edge of the Long Limestone Hills that remained their constant, though ever-changing, companion.

In those twenty or so miles they met no more than a score of other travellers, and only one roadmender. He was a man who could have been of any age between mid-twenties and late thirties. As they approached he was loading limestone rubble from a roadside pile into a large, dilapidated wickerwork basket, using his hands as shovels, prior to tipping it into one of the numerous potholes in that stretch of road. As was the custom, Canio tipped him a few copper *nummi* as they passed.

'May the blessings of your god be with you,' the man called out in a weary monotone to their retreating backs. It was the usual benediction, calculated not to offend, whether the giver was a follower of one of the old religions or the new.

Canio looked back, intending to wave acknowledgement, but the man was already trudging back towards the stone pile to collect another basketful.

When he had travelled this same road, in the days before the *Conspiratio*, he would have met a roadmender every three miles or so. Times were changing, and generally not for the better.

A mile further on they passed an ash tree, the lower branches of which supported a large, luxuriant mass of ivy, much of it caught in a pool of late autumn sunlight. It seemed to fascinate Bodicca, who reined in her pony and peered benevolently at it, as though it were a long-lost friend.

The leaves on the flowering shoots were fresh-new, glossy mid-green and spear-shaped, in striking contrast to the fading, dying vegetation all around. The branched stalks, extending above the leaves, were each topped with a mass of pale green globular flower buds, some of which had opened to reveal a coronet of pale yellow stamens.

And around these flowers the air was filled with a gentle hum produced by the masses of little flies, worker bees, hoverflies and a few wasps, all plundering this, the last nectar they would find before the winter cold killed most of them.

As Canio waited, with growing impatience, a large red and black butterfly fluttered past and settled to join the feast. As bright and fresh as if it had emerged from its chrysalis that very morning (which perhaps it had), its hair-thin black tongue uncurled and began probing the ivy flowers for the life-giving nectar.

Perhaps noticing the look of exasperation on Canio's face, Bodicca explained, 'I always tell myself that autumn's not yet over until the last ivy flowers have gone and the last of those red and black butterflies have disappeared.'

"And I've seen the last bumblebee on wayside flowers of white deadnettles, searching for the last drop of nectar." Isn't that what you once told me, Trifosa?

At around noon they reached the little town of Forum Termini, where there was a substantial stone-built *mansio*. Although supposedly only for the use of travellers on official business, Canio was well aware that most *mansionarii* welcomed any extra trade they could attract. And judging by the scarcity of official-looking travellers they had met so far, he reckoned that they would have no trouble getting a meal there.

And so it proved: the *mansionarius*, a man who wore a tunic and *cingulum* belt that gave him the appearance of a minor government functionary in the imperial civil service (which indeed he officially was), greeted them as though they were members of the emperor's own family.

They ate a meal of hare and beans stew, and Canio drank the first decent wine he had tasted since leaving Villa Canini. Nectovelius, for once, ate little, and Canio guessed that he was still brooding on the previous night's events in Glevum. It seemed to confirm his suspicion that what Vario had said was indeed the bitter truth, and that, deep in some lonely place in his young soul, the boy knew it. *And had always known it? But if so, why...?*

While they were eating, Bodicca herself remarked on how few travellers of any sort they had met on the highway so far.

'That's because, unlike the Fosse Way, this road's not regularly patrolled by the army any more,' Canio told her. 'A lot of people going from Glevum to Aquae Sulis prefer the longer route along the Via Erminus to Corinium, then down the Fosse Way to Sulis.'

Remounting, they trotted through the outskirts of Forum Termini, Nectovelius gazing from side to side at the handsome stone houses that lined both sides of the highway.

Beyond the houses, Bodicca pointed out the dark heaps of iron slag scattered in the fields. 'Look at those – they're just like the ones at Vertis,' she remarked to the boy sitting behind her.

Nectovelius didn't answer, but Canio said, 'There used to be several iron smelting furnaces here. I was once told that they brought the ore and the charcoal from the great forests on the far side of the Sabrina. Not any more though: I don't think a single furnace has been lit since the *Conspiratio*.'

'How far now to Aquae Sulis?' Nectovelius suddenly asked.

'About twenty miles – isn't that right, Canio?' Bodicca replied, adding, 'Didn't you hear me ask the *mansionarius*?'

'That's right, no more than twenty miles,' Canio agreed. 'Or maybe less,' he added reassuringly.

Some dozen miles further south they came to a three-way crossroads, where their road from Glevum in the north merged with another which ran from the port of Abona in the west towards Aquae Sulis in the east. There they halted briefly to rest their mounts. As they moved off again, on the road which led eastwards, Canio casually remarked to Bodicca that he had heard that Hecate was the goddess of crossroads, especially ones where three ways met. 'Is that really so?' he asked.

Bodicca, riding alongside, glanced across at him, but her face gave nothing away. 'So some people say. Did Vilbia tell you that?'

'No, it was another woman, another Marcia... long ago, when I was no older than Nectovelius.'

They splashed through a ford crossing a little south-flowing river, and shortly afterwards the road began to follow the north bank of the much larger Flumen Abona, whose valley led them through the remaining six or so hilly miles up to the West Gate of Aquae Sulis.

By the position of the hazy sun in the south-west sky behind them, Canio reckoned that dusk was less than half an hour away when they rode wearily into the town, past two soldiers standing guard on either side of the gateway in the high stone walls.

Nectovelius, who had seemed half-asleep for the last few miles, suddenly came to life and began looking all around in the fading light, gazing intently at the great houses that lined both sides of the road for the first hundred or so yards inside the gate.

Further into the town, on their left they passed a temple with a triangular pediment supported by tall stone columns, and just beyond it, on rising ground, stood a great semi-circular structure with tier after ascending tier of stone seats, which Bodicca informed Nectovelius was a theatre.

'What's a theatre?' the boy asked.

'It's where people come to see actors perform plays and the like,' she replied.

'They say some actors came to Glevum a year ago, but I never saw them. I heard that the *Decuriones* sent them away.'

'No, the City Fathers – especially the Christian ones – don't like plays, or pretend they don't.'

'Why?'

'Because they tell stories about the old gods, or they're rude – or sometimes both,' Bodicca replied.

It seemed that Nectovelius hadn't noticed it until they were almost past the theatre, half-hidden as it was behind a surrounding wall, but suddenly the boy looked back and shouted, 'Look! Look at that!' and pointed with outstretched arm towards another great temple, this time on their right. 'There's a head on that wall!'

Canio reined Antares to a halt and twisted round in the saddle, seeing the tops of four great Corinthian columns, and above them a triangular pediment. And in the centre of the pediment was the remembered great carved head of a man with moustachioed face and staring eyes. A man whose luxuriant hair and beard combined to make a snaky nimbus radiating out all around his head.

'That, is a gorgon,' Bodicca said. 'A male gorgon, guarding the temple of Sulis Minerva.'

'Sol, the sun god?' Nectovelius asked, apparently mishearing.

'No, the goddess Sulis,' she corrected him. 'Sulis Minerva is the goddess of the hot spring that feeds the baths.'

'What baths?'

'Those over there, of course,' Canio replied impatiently, conscious that the sun was now rapidly sinking below the south-western horizon. 'Do you see those big halls with barrel-shaped roofs, right opposite where we are now? Well, those are the baths, and people come from all over the province and beyond to bathe in the warm water, or ask the goddess of the spring to do things for them.'

'What sort of things?'

'Lots of things – like making them well if they're sick,' said Bodicca. 'Or sometimes to find things they've lost or had stolen.'

Canio glanced covertly towards Nectovelius, wondering if the boy would want to ask Sulis Minerva to find his mother.

But Nectovelius was silent, although the thought must surely have entered his head. And when he did speak it was only to ask if they could see more of the town.

'No – not now we can't,' Canio replied, kneeing Antares into motion again. 'We've got to get to the North Gate before it closes.'

'Can't we stay here in the town for the night? There's so much to see,' the boy pleaded.

'No – the *stabulum* where we're going to spend the night is in the northern suburbs, outside the walls.'

'Perhaps we can see more of the town in the morning, or on our way back,' Bodicca said consolingly, glancing towards Canio, as if to say, *Isn't that so?*

'If we've got time. Have you ever been here before?' he asked Bodicca, wondering, not for the first time, if she really did know the way to that far-off temple of Apollo.

'Of course I have – I've been to lots of places,' she replied. 'Look, that's the *tholos*,'– this to Nectovelius, as she pointed to the right where, inside the low-walled enclosure they were passing, there stood a circular stone structure with a domed roof supported by a ring of columns.

But Nectovelius, the fatigue of the long journey south catching up with him again, appeared to be nodding off, his arms still wrapped around Bodicca's waist.

Shortly after passing the *tholos*, their road in from the West Gate intersected with another major street, which Canio informed the unresponsive Nectovelius was the Fosse Way. Here he turned left, and after a hundred or so yards they came to the North Gate. Moments after they had trotted under its massive stone portal, Canio glanced back to see the guards on either side beginning to drag the iron-studded gates closed.

As Canio remembered from previous visits, the northern suburbs outside the walls of Aquae Sulis were more extensive than the town itself. Once past the palatial houses which lined both sides of the Fosse Way for some two hundred yards beyond the North Gate, the highway swung sharply to the right and soon afterwards crossed over the greeny-grey waters of the Flumen Abona via a handsome stone bridge.

On the far side of the bridge the highway forked. Seeing Nectovelius wake and look about him, startled, as if wondering where they were, Canio nodded towards the fork and said, 'The left hand road's the Fosse Way, leading north to Corinium; the other is the road east to Cunetio, and that's the one we want.'

Drawing ahead of Bodicca's pony, Canio trotted Antares a little way along the Cunetio road, then stopped outside a *stabulum*, over the doorway of which hung a sign depicting a standing woman wearing an ankle-length *stola* and holding a long palm frond in one hand and a cornucopia in the other.

'This is it, *The Hilaritas*. This is where we'll be spending the night.'

'You've stayed here before?' Bodicca asked.

'Once or twice,' Canio replied casually. 'Wait here and I'll see if they have rooms free.' He swung himself out of Antares' saddle and walked into the *stabulum*.

As he entered the large communal room he briefly scanned the various people sitting at the tables, before his eyes settled on the woman standing behind the bar counter. 'Fortunata! It's been a long time… how are you?'

'Canio? Is that really you?' said the woman, peering into the gloom of the doorway. 'I haven't seen you for half a year or more. I thought you must have found somewhere else to stay in Sulis.' She was just as Canio remembered, a slightly plump but distinctly attractive woman in her mid-twenties, with raven-black hair, smiling eyes and full lips.

'What?' said Canio pulling a hurt face as he walked up to the serving area, well lit by the sparkling light of several oil lamps. 'When the best food in Sulis is right here, and…' he glanced round to make sure he was not overheard, 'the warmest beds too.'

Fortunata gave him an arch look, but before she could reply he continued, 'Have you got a couple of rooms for the night?'

'A *couple* of rooms? Who have you brought with you?'

'A woman and a young boy – neither of them related to me in any way, to save you asking.'

'Two rooms it is then. And stabling for how many horses?'

'Two. I'll take them round to the stalls myself.'

'Still got that big red horse?'

'Of course: Antares only gets better with age – just like me. I'll be back as soon as I've seen him bedded down for the night.'

Back outside, he saw that Bodicca and the boy had both dismounted. 'Go in and order whatever you fancy for all three of us. The owner's a widow called Fortunata – she knows me.'

With that he took both sets of reins and led the tired horses into the stable yard, where he waited to see them both unsaddled while he checked the quality of the oats, the hay and the water.

'It's all good stuff,' said the ostler, whose name, Canio vaguely remembered, was Ulpius.

'Good. Then give them as much as they can eat: they've a long way to go tomorrow.' And Canio flicked him silver *siliqua*, which the man caught adroitly.

When Canio walked back into the communal room he saw that Bodicca and Nectovelius had already started eating. He went and sat beside them, and a short time later Fortunata brought him a steaming bowl of lamb stew, flavoured with coriander seeds and *liquamen* fish sauce.

'So you're only staying the one night then – can't you stay longer?' she asked.

Canio shook his head, and when he had swallowed a mouthful of stew said, 'No, we'll be off at dawn. I must be in Lindinis by tomorrow evening.'

'So what's Lindinis got that Sulis hasn't?'

'Nothing: it's just a place on the way to somewhere else.'

'What somewhere else?'

'I'll know when I get there,' Canio replied enigmatically.

Fortunata pouted. 'Better make the most of my hospitality while you're here then,' she murmured as she walked back towards the bar, giving him a sly wink as she went.

By the sidelong glance Bodicca gave him, Canio realised that wink had not gone unnoticed.

Later, when they had finished their meals and she was showing them to their rooms, which were, Canio noticed, some distance apart, Fortunata said, 'If you're leaving at first light, perhaps you'd better settle your account now. I don't like getting up until the sun's shining through my bedroom window – not that there's much sun at this time of year.'

'So what do I owe you?' Canio asked.

'Five *siliquae* should cover it.'

'Everything?'

'Everything,' Fortunata confirmed, and for the briefest of moments half an inch of pink tongue caressed her upper lip.

'Five *siliquae* it is then,' said Canio as he counted out the five little silver coins, then whispered, 'When?'

'As soon as all those who aren't staying the night have gone, and I can lock up – sometime before midnight,' she whispered as she moved away down the corridor towards the stairs.

Canio, observing that Bodicca and Nectovelius were already halfway through the door of their room, objected, 'But that's a long time away.'

'But good things are always worth waiting for, aren't they?' Fortunata murmured. And she blew him a kiss as she disappeared into the gloom.

In the near-darkness of his room, Canio kicked off his boots, took off his *cucullus*, sword belt and tunic, washed his face and hands in the bowl of water provided, stretched out on the bed and promptly fell asleep: it had been a long day.

It was, he reckoned afterwards, well before midnight that he was woken by a light tapping on his door. He waited, silent in the darkness, as the door opened and the silhouette of a woman appeared, a deeper blackness against the single-lamp gloom of the corridor.

The door closed and Canio heard soft footsteps moving towards the bed. The footsteps stopped, and he heard the soft rustle of cloth that ended with a barely audible sigh as Fortunata's *stola* slid down onto the timber floorboards. He stretched out an exploring right hand and his fingertips touched her naked shoulder as she leaned over the bed.

His fingers moved downwards, first lightly stroking her breasts, then gently massaging the soft curve of her stomach with the flat of his hand. His fingers began moving even lower, but as they touched the luxuriant curled hair he felt her fingers interlace with his own, before drawing them up to her lips.

'Where have you been since you were last here, Canio?' she murmured. 'You come to Sulis, you stay for a day or two, and then you disappear again for months on end.'

'Oh, here and there – wherever my business takes me. Does it matter? I'm here now.'

'And tomorrow you'll be gone, and I may never see you again.'

'Nor I you. So all the more reason why we should enjoy each other's company while we can.' And he cupped his left hand behind her head and drew her face down towards his own.

CHAPTER TWENTY-ONE

31st October

When he woke, the grey dawn light was filtering into the room between gaps in the window shutter. Fortunata had disappeared and somebody was rapping at his door.

'Canio – aren't you awake yet? You said you wanted to be off at first light.' It was Bodicca's voice.

He swore almost silently and called out, 'Go downstairs and eat – it's already paid for. I'll join you as soon as I've dressed.'

'We've already eaten, and that ostler, Ulpius, is saddling the horses.'

He heard her footsteps retreating down the corridor, swore again, louder this time, splashed water from the bowl onto his face and dressed hurriedly. Carrying his *cucullus* he trotted downstairs where he found Bodicca and Nectovelius waiting in the communal room.

There was still no sign of Fortunata, and he assumed that she was in her own bedroom, sleeping soundly. Recalling the lady's performance during the hours of darkness he could understand why: Venus herself would have blushed to witness some of the tricks in Fortunata's repertoire.

After a quick visit to the latrine at the back of *The Hilaritas* he joined Bodicca and Nectovelius, pulled himself up into Antares' saddle, and together they rode back along their route of the previous evening, through the North Gate of Aquae Sulis and into the walled town itself. But this time Canio carried straight on, and after riding for some four hundred yards along the wide street they passed through the South Gate and back out onto the Fosse Way.

'How far is Lindinis?' Nectovelius called out to Canio's gently bobbing back.

'About thirty-five miles,' Canio called back.

'And then where do we go?'

'To a temple – a temple of Apollo. Bodicca will guide us there, won't you, Bodicca?'

'I will; never doubt it,' she replied.

'I wouldn't dream of doing so – is there any reason why I should?'

Bodicca did not reply: perhaps she hadn't heard him.

Near the halfway point of their journey down the Fosse Way they came to a crossroads, where their road met another which, as Canio vaguely recalled (although Bodicca insisted on telling him), ran from the mines in the Lead Hills away to the north-west, down to Sorviodunum in the south-east.

The first twenty miles were hilly, the climbs and descents tiring for their mounts. Every few miles they stopped to rest them, but even so it was past noon when they arrived at Ovilmalleus, a small unwalled town at the eastern end of the Lead Hills, some two miles south of the crossroads. Here they found houses and workshops, some stone-built, some of timber construction, lining both sides of the highway for half a mile. There was also a *mansio*, and there they stopped for a meal of mutton stew, this time flavoured with an abundance of mint leaves, probably to disguise the fact that the meat was, Canio guessed, at least a week old.

Feeling inside one of his belt pouches for a *siliqua* to pay for the meals, he realised that the little bag of soft leather containing his cache of gold *solidi* was no longer there. With increasing anxiety he hunted for it through all the pockets of his tunic and *cucullus*, then looked up, just in time to see Bodicca nudge Nectovelius.

The boy grinned, and with the air of a conjuror, dipped his fingers into a pocket of his own tunic and brought out the missing leather bag.

'That wasn't funny, you young rat,' Canio growled, attempting to snatch the bag with one hand and to give Nectovelius a hearty cuff around the ear with the other.

With the alacrity of one well practised in avoiding blows, the boy dropped down below the table, still clutching the bag, and Canio's open palm halted in mid-air, waiting for him to bob up again.

'No!' Bodicca jumped up and leant over Nectovelius, shielding the boy with her body. 'He didn't steal it.'

'Then who did? You?'

'Tell him – well, go on, tell him,' she said to Nectovelius, whose head was slowly appearing above the table top.

'It was that woman you were with last night,' the boy said, warily eyeing Canio's large right hand, which was still poised above his head like a sword of Damocles.

'Fortunata?'

'Who else?' Bodicca said crossly. 'Unless you found another vestal virgin to continue the poetry reading with after she'd gone? Tell him, Nectovelius, tell him what you saw and did.'

'I saw her coming out of your room,' Nectovelius began, slowly retreating until well out of range of Canio's hand. 'She closed the door very quietly, then turned towards the lamp, and I could tell she was trying to see inside something that looked like your money bag – this little *follis*...' And Nectovelius took a cautious pace forwards and held it out to Canio, who promptly snatched it, tipped the contents out into his palm and started counting the coins. There didn't seem to be any missing.

'Go on,' Bodicca prompted.

165

'I crept after her and saw which room she went into, and then I waited. And when I thought she must be asleep—'

'Exhausted, no doubt, by her labours – poetry reading being such a strenuous activity,' Bodicca murmured.

'— I opened the door and saw your *follis* on the table beside her bed—'

'You saw it in the dark?' Canio interrupted.

'After a while my eyes can see as well in the dark as they can in twilight – can't yours?' the boy asked, sounding surprised at Canio's scepticism. 'Anyway, I saw your *follis* and I knew you wouldn't have given it to her.'

'So you stole it back?'

'Yes – and nobody saw or heard me do it,' Nectovelius said proudly.

'So why didn't you tell me before we left Aquae Sulis?'

Nectovelius looked uncertainly at Bodicca.

'Because I told him not to.'

'Why?'

'To see the look on your face when you realised they were gone, those little gold coins which you prize above everything – even above people you imagine you care for.'

So she knows, does she, what happened at that lake? Was it Vilbia or Eutherius who told her? Canio wondered. Struck by a sudden attack of conscience, he tipped a *solidus* out of the *follis* and handed it to Nectovelius. 'The reward for virtue,' he announced.

Nectovelius looked down wonderingly at the little gold coin lying in the palm of his hand. Then he frowned: it seemed that a thought had struck him. 'But if I'd kept that *follis*, and all the gold coins in it, I wouldn't have been virtuous, but I wouldn't have been cold or hungry for a long time either. So gold must be more worth having than virtue, mustn't it?' He looked at Bodicca for confirmation.

Bodicca looked at Canio, her thick eyebrows rising as if to say, *Now there's an interesting question.*

166

And Canio looked at the boy, seeing himself twenty years and more ago. 'You're becoming wiser by the day, young man.'

Four or five miles south of Ovilmalleus the Fosse Way descended a steep slope and the land became flatter. And as they journeyed ever further southwards, Canio caught occasional glimpses, far away to the west, of what he thought was the eastern edge of the Great Marshes. He did not seek confirmation from Bodicca, uneasy as to where such a question might lead, certain as he now was that she knew what had happened there between himself and Vilbia in the high summer of 368.

About a mile from the walled town of Lindinis the clouds at last slid away and the light of the low sun shone almost horizontally, casting the monstrously elongated shadows of trees across a landscape illuminated with eerie clarity.

For several hundred yards outside the town walls the Fosse Way was lined on both sides with stone and timber houses, shops and workshops. As they passed the various premises Canio breathed in the distinctive smells and stenches of butchery and the tanning of leather. Away to the west, through gaps in the buildings, he caught glimpses of a large cemetery with grass-covered mounds, stone tombstones and the occasional circular stone mausoleum, the latter lit transient gold by the last rays of the sun.

Perhaps it was that late sunshine which persuaded the soldiers on the North Gate not to swing the two great iron-studded gates closed until the last blood-red rim of the sun had sunk below the western horizon.

Whatever the reason, they were able to clatter over the stone bridge which spanned the little river flowing immediately outside the walls, pass between the twin semi-circular gate towers and enter the town of Lindinis itself.

A few yards inside the gate the cobbled street branched, the Fosse Way carrying on south-westward and the other branch, which Canio was fairly sure was the road to Durnovaria, heading off towards the south-east.

Looking for somewhere to spend the night, they rode through the wide streets, laid out gridiron pattern. Glancing from side to side at the sumptuous houses which lined both sides, Canio remarked to Bodicca that he would bet a *solidus* to a bent *nummus* that they were the town houses of those rich men whose villas they had seen dotting the flat countryside in the miles approaching the town.

Thinking to spend the night in comfort, and testing her local knowledge, Canio asked Bodicca if she knew where the *mansio* was.

'Don't you know?' she said. And before he could stop her she had reined in and asked an old man hobbling past carrying a bundle of sticks.

Appearing surprised that anyone in that place should not have known where it was, he directed them towards a substantial stone-built house in the next street.

Not being, or even appearing to be, travellers on state business, Canio wondered if they would get beds in what was clearly a considerably more important town than Ovilmalleus. But, as usual, money talked.

This *mansio* turned out to be the most impressive that Canio had ever been in, even more opulent than the two that Corinium boasted. The walls of the large communal room were plastered and adorned with brightly coloured frescoes, depicting what appeared to have once been scenes from mythology, but which, on closer inspection, he realised had been overpainted here and there to give the subjects a distinctly Christian character.

One scene, originally showing what seemed to have been Venus standing naked between two winged cupids, the goddess's hands strategically placed to cover her modesty, had been overpainted to give the goddess a robe and wings, so that to Christians she could appear as an angel. Those not so enamoured of the new religion could presumably imagine her to be Victoria, goddess of victory. Both Christian angel and pagan Victory were, Canio reflected, uncannily similar in appearance.

After they had eaten, and he had seen the horses stabled for the night, Canio got into conversation with the *mansionarius*, a fortyish ex-soldier who introduced himself as Priscinus. The man had a stiff right arm, the result, he claimed, of a spear wound received in a skirmish with Pictish invaders back in 364 (although later that evening another guest whispered to Canio that he had actually received the injury in a knife fight over a woman: what the truth of the matter was, Canio never discovered).

What he did discover, from Priscinus, was the reason for the *mansio's* unusual splendour. Originally, he said, it had been the town house of a rich man who had owned a large villa estate over towards the Polden Hills. This man, Didius Gallus, had backed Magnentius in the latter's rebellion in the early 350s: an unwise decision. When Magnentius was finally defeated in 354, both estate and town house had been confiscated by the state.

Gallus himself was one of several local landowners who had been arrested and dragged away in irons to Londinium on the orders of the imperial notary, Paulus, nicknamed *Catena, The Chain*. Gallus and his immediate family were apparently never heard of again. And to make quite clear what he believed had happened to them, Priscinus drew the index finger of his right hand across his throat as he concluded the tale.

'See that,' said the *mansionarius*, pointing to the image in the central roundel of the mosaic floor of what Canio had by then come to realise must have been the *triclinium* of Gallus's house. 'Who do you think that's supposed to be?'

Canio peered among the tables and chairs that partially hid the figure and saw a seated man with one arm raised, extended fingers spread as if in greeting or blessing. In three concentric rings surrounding the man there prowled various beasts and birds. Canio made out a lion, a leopard and several peacocks.

'Orpheus?' he suggested. As he well knew, the demigod had been a popular subject with those villa owners who patronised the Corinium guild of mosaicists.

Priscinus shook his head. 'Look again.'

So Canio walked over and examined the seated man more closely. The man had once been Orpheus – he was certain of that – but a skilled mosaicist had removed his Phrygian cap, his lyre, and probably the fox that usually sat beside him. Now his head was surrounded by a nimbus of honey-coloured limestone tesserae, and on each side of that nimbus was a pomegranate and a chi-rho monogram. 'Christos?' he asked.

'Correct,' Priscinus replied. 'Christos blessing the beasts of the fields and the birds of the air.'

'I suppose it wouldn't do to have an old pagan like Orpheus sitting in the middle of a place like this, not in these changing times.'

'Indeed it would not,' Priscinus replied. 'Here in Lindinis, Orpheus wouldn't be at all welcome, if you understand my meaning.'

Canio understood, although he was about to point out the irony that, in and around Corinium, the provincial capital, there were a number of rich men who still believed in the old gods and regarded the encroachments of Christianity with something less than enthusiasm.

But, at that moment, the *mansio's* only official guest, an imperial courier carrying despatches from Isca Dumnoniorum to Corinium (as Priscinus later told Canio) came down from his room demanding a jug of the best wine in the house, and the *mansionarius* jumped up and hurried to serve him.

Later, when he, Bodicca and Nectovelius were eating, seated at one of the tables, Canio noticed that one of the men who had come into the *mansio* later that evening kept glancing towards them, a puzzled look on his face. Had the man recognised him?

He was fairly certain that he had never seen him before, but nevertheless the unwanted scrutiny was beginning to make him uneasy.

He stood up and was about to suggest to Bodicca that it was time they went to their rooms, when the man also got up and hurried over to their table.

'Decima?' he asked. 'It is Decima, isn't it?'

It was Bodicca's turn to look mystified, perhaps exaggeratedly so, Canio thought.

'No,' she said. 'My name's Bodicca.'

'Bodicca? How strange... You look just like the Decima I remember – although it must be the better part of twenty years since I saw her.' Turning to Canio, he added, 'I was only a boy then.'

'Did she live here in Lindinis, this Decima?' Canio asked.

'Oh no,' the man replied, now looking curiously at Bodicca again. 'I met the woman I knew as Decima on one of the old paths that wind over the Niger Hills.'

'Twenty years ago I was twenty years younger, and would have looked twenty years younger, wouldn't I?' Bodicca pointed out.

'Yes... yes, of course you would,' the man said. 'But you are so like the woman I remember.'

'But I can't be her, can I?'

'No... of course you can't be.' Realising that he couldn't argue with Bodicca's logic, and perhaps embarrassed, the man muttered, 'I'm sorry to have bothered you and your husband,' turned and walked slowly back to his table. Although just before he reached it he turned again and looked back at Bodicca, as if still not wholly convinced that he had been mistaken.

Canio, recalling their previous conversation, whispered, 'You said it was your mother who once took you to that temple of Apollo – what was her name?'

171

Bodicca smiled at him coolly, a smile which seemed to say, "*Nice try, but the dice all show ones.*" 'Not Decima,' she replied, adding, 'and she looked nothing like me.'

'But you're still sure you can find your way there?'

'Of course: I wouldn't lie to you about such a thing.'

CHAPTER TWENTY-TWO

1st November

The heatless sun was only halfway above the horizon when they rode out through the South-West Gate of Lindinis and back onto the Fosse Way, where they found more suburbs stretching for a quarter of a mile on both sides of the highway. The houses there were mostly built with the same honey-coloured limestone walls and split-stone roof slates that Canio had seen elsewhere in the town, and behind them stood timber barns, cattle sheds and sundry other outbuildings. When the suburbs ended the highway carried on, arrow straight through a flat countryside in which herds of cattle grazed in vast open pastures.

Passing a spinney of hawthorns, the remaining shrivelling leaves a forlorn mixture of yellow and brown, they disturbed a small flock of fieldfares plundering the plump, dark red berries. The birds flew off, chattering crossly, only to circle and return to the berries as soon as the riders had passed.

'"When the winter thrushes arrive, I know that winter itself will not be far behind them" – my mother taught me that,' Bodicca explained to Nectovelius.

'Alternatively, she might have noticed that the weather was turning colder, the nights were becoming longer, and the leaves were falling off the trees,' Canio muttered. Although not quietly enough it seemed, because Bodicca, who at that moment was

173

riding a little way ahead, turned her head and gave him a sharp look.

After some seven miles on the stoned highway, and about a mile after crossing a little river via a broad, stone-paved ford, Bodicca, who had again eased her pony a little way ahead of Antares, raised her right hand as a signal that Canio should halt.

'I think we should take that path.' And she pointed to a track that led westwards across the flat meadowlands.

'How far now?' Canio asked.

She shrugged. 'Twenty miles, perhaps. After ten miles or so we should reach the eastern end of the Niger Hills, but then we'll still have a long way to go before we reach the temple.'

'Will we get there before nightfall?'

'We should do, if the weather holds.'

So they turned onto the track, unstoned and deeply rutted in places by the wheels of heavy carts that had trundled along it in wet weather. Fortunately, the autumn in those parts seemed to have been fairly dry, so the track had not yet been churned to mud, the ruts still almost stone-hard.

They had gone no more than half a mile when Nectovelius pointed to two horsemen cantering towards them from the south. 'Look – over there! They're coming this way.'

'I see them. Keep riding.' Out of the corner of his eye, Canio watched the two horsemen as they rode onto the track about fifty yards ahead of him, their horses snorting through flared nostrils. A large, mean-looking wolfhound loped up and stood beside them, growling low in its throat and looking as if it might launch itself towards Antares at any moment as Canio continued riding steadily towards them.

'Halt!' ordered one of the horsemen, the bigger of the two. Both wore identical blue tunics with rope-pattern decorative bands sewn on at cuffs and hems. 'Do you realise that you are on the estate of Calpurnius Receptus – have you any business here?'

'We're on our way to my wife's brother's farm, about ten miles that way,' replied Canio, pointing vaguely westwards.

'So you're trespassing. Go back to the highway.'

'This is the way we went before. I don't know of any other route – is there one?'

'I neither know nor care: just get off this land.' This from the shorter of the two bailiffs.

Canio eyed them coldly: he had not the slightest intention of turning back. He had already noted that the big man was armed with a boar spear, carried in a leather case strapped to his saddle. Also, that both men had whips attached to their belts. Nevertheless, his instinct was to draw the *spatha* concealed beneath his *cucullus* and inflict a few painful lacerations. They didn't have the look of ex-soldiers, so he reckoned it wouldn't be difficult to give them a lesson in manners that would take several weeks to heal.

His fingers were edging towards the hilt when Bodicca said, 'Surely you've heard of the new law which gives travellers such as ourselves the right to use established tracks, no matter who owns the land?'

'New law – what new law?' said the big bailiff contemptuously.

Worth a try, I suppose, thought Canio. *I can always make a few holes in their hides if it doesn't work.* 'Why, the *Lex Valentinianus*, of course. You must have heard of it, even in these remote parts,' he said, feigning astonishment at their ignorance. 'Our beloved emperor, who, as I'm sure you're aware, is said to have a particular dislike of rich landowners who tyrannise the poor, issued the edict several months ago. That being so, if you don't want to risk bringing Valentinianus's wrath down on your master's head, I suggest you allow us to continue peacefully on our way.'

By the look on his face, Canio could see that the big bailiff was uneasy; worried, even. He glanced uncertainly at his companion.

But the shorter bailiff was sceptical. 'You're lying,' he said flatly. 'If there were such a law Receptus would have heard of it and told us. Now, are you going to turn back, or do we have to give all three of you a thrashing?' And he began untying the whip attached to his belt.

Canio grinned: he was going to enjoy this. Pushing back his *cucullus* he grasped the hilt of his *spatha*. 'I really wouldn't try that, if I were you.'

The shorter bailiff recoiled, tugging the reins and forcing his horse to back, stiff-legged, for a yard or more. It seemed that it had never occurred to either of them that Canio might be armed. They stared at him, and Canio stared back, willing the big man to grab for his spear. At this close range he was confident that he could draw and swing the *spatha* before the spear was more than halfway out of its case.

Suddenly he heard Bodicca say to Nectovelius, 'Go on – play them the way I showed you, back at Vilbia's temple.'

'Like this?' Canio heard the boy ask, himself not taking his eyes off the two bailiffs.

'That's right,' she confirmed.

Canio heard no sound from Nectovelius. He risked a quick look sideways and saw the boy blowing across one end of a small set of wooden pan pipes, his cheeks puffed out.

Antares started prancing nervously, and Canio stroked him between the ears and spoke soothingly to him. Bodicca was crooning into her pony's ear.

But the effect on the bailiffs' hound was dramatic. It jumped up and began barking furiously, snapping at the heels of its masters' horses. They reared and plunged, their riders struggling to bring them under control. And then one bolted, followed moments later by the other, the wolfhound pursuing them, still barking insanely.

Canio stared in astonished amusement at the sight of both horses and men rapidly dwindling northwards across the grasslands, the bailiffs bent low over their horses' necks, legs flailing as they struggled vainly to halt their headlong flight. And then one bailiff fell off: Canio thought it was the smaller of the two. He chuckled as his sharp eyes detected at least one bounce as the man hit the ground.

'Well done,' he said to Nectovelius, reaching across and slapping the boy on the back.

Nectovelius gave a fierce grin of impish delight.

'Where did you get those pipes from?'

'I gave them to him,' said Bodicca.

'Do you think that man hurt himself when he fell off his horse?' Nectovelius asked.

'Yes, with any luck – I certainly hope so anyway,' Canio replied.

'So do I,' said the boy. 'I hate men with whips.'

From the animated way he said it, Canio guessed he had encountered several in his young life.

'Time to go,' said Bodicca, and urged her pony into a smart trot, Nectovelius gripping her around the waist with one arm while still clutching the pan pipes in his free hand.

At a fast trot they rode on across the flat land, taking whatever track or path led them westwards. Some four miles further on they forded a little river flowing northwards towards what, away in the far distance, might have been marshland – Canio could see what he thought were the feathery tops of tall reeds swaying in the wind as the intermittent sunlight caught them.

'Did you recognise that river?' he asked Bodicca.

'I think it was the Insula,' she replied, adding, 'but I could be wrong.'

Right or wrong, Canio thought, it really didn't matter: the name meant nothing to him.

After another two miles or so, in which the once frequently-seen farmsteads with their thatched roofs grew progressively sparser, he saw rising ground both ahead and to the south, wooded and still some three miles distant. 'Are those the Niger Hills?' he asked Bodicca.

'Of course they are.'

'And the temple of Apollo?'

'Ah, that's miles further on. Not easy to find.'

'No, I didn't think it would be.'

They rode on, and as they did so they came across a narrow track which began to lead upwards into a land superficially not unlike Canio's Long Limestone Hills, but wilder and with great expanses of tangled ancient woodland, which they had to detour around as they continued heading westwards.

Along the sides of the track lay drifts of brown and yellow leaves, mostly ash, which scattered and swirled as the fickle wind veered and caught them. Canio noticed, not for the first time, that while most of the ash trees were already completely bare of leaves, a few others, perhaps only yards away from the leafless ones, were still in full green leaf, barely touched by autumn.

Leaves and men, he mused. *Some die sooner, some later, but they all die in the end. Time and winter will kill them all.*

To see their way ahead they tried to keep to the high ground as much as possible, although sometimes the highest points were shrouded in a cold, clammy mist which settled white on their clothes and reduced visibility to only a few yards. So thick it was that they rapidly lost all sense of direction, forcing them to ride down onto lower ground.

Canio had assumed that, once they were in the hills, they would come across someone who could tell them the way to the temple. But they met nobody: the few hovels they chanced upon appeared deserted, and although they occasionally spotted a distant human figure, it had disappeared into the trees or the mist long before they came within hailing distance. It seemed a strange, empty land.

CHAPTER TWENTY-THREE

It was mid-afternoon and the open areas between tracts of woodland were becoming more numerous, when suddenly Bodicca reined her pony to a halt and pointed to a huge, solitary oak at the side of the track. The tree was still in almost-full leaf, although those leaves were a mixture of green, yellow and warm brown. 'If that's the tree I remember, then the temple isn't far away.'

Canio was sceptical. 'We've come across a good few oaks like that today.'

'But not with dead branches quite like those,' she replied. 'Look – they're like antlers.'

So he looked, and saw two bare, twisted branches that stuck up above the top of the canopy for the height of a man, their tips weathered to points. Knowing that such trees could stay seemingly unchanged for decades made him inclined to believe her.

And glancing around, Canio realised that the track they were now following, although now fighting a losing battle with the wilderness encroaching from both sides, appeared, not so very long ago, to have been frequently used. 'So we're nearly there then?'

'Nearly there,' Bodicca confirmed. She urged her pony on a few dozen yards, until the track turned abruptly left into the head of a small, south-facing valley.

After pausing to let their horses drink from the stream which rose from a spring a little way down the valley, they then rode on for some two hundred yards until, rounding a slow curve, Canio saw the roofless shell of a large building.

Pausing Antares, he asked, 'Is that really it – the temple of Apollo?'

Bodicca did not reply immediately. She sat silent, staring at the ruins, her face set and expressionless. He waited, and at last she said quietly, 'Yes, this is the place.'

He urged Antares past her, rode on down and slowly circled the octagonal temple. Most of the stone walls still stood to a height of twelve feet or more, although blackened and reddened in places by the fire that had destroyed the roof.

Still in the saddle, he peered in through what had once been the main entrance doorway. Most of the floors were hidden beneath uneven heaps of smashed clay roof tiles, out of which poked the ends of charred roof timbers. Hosts of opportunist weeds had already begun to flourish on top of the rubble, chief among them patches of ragwort, still with a few tattered little yellow flowers, even so late in the year.

Projecting from seven of the eight sides of the main hall were low-level annex rooms, apparently accessed from the interior of the main hall. On one of these annexes the lean-to roof appeared to have survived the fire. Dismounting and drawing his *spatha*, Canio walked through the wide main entrance, skirted the debris in the main hall, and entered the roofed annex via its arched doorway. As his eyes accustomed themselves to the dim light of the interior it became evident that somebody still lived there.

Against one wall was a bed of sorts, consisting of a pile of brushwood covered with a thick layer of dead bracken and a couple of coarse-weave blankets. There was a small table and one wickerwork chair, the scorch marks on both bearing mute witness to them having been salvaged from the ruins. In one corner were stacked various pottery vessels. A large clayware pot on the table was full of water: Canio dipped a finger into it, licked the finger and reckoned the water was fresh, quite possibly taken from the stream earlier that day. But the old priest, the man he had come so far to find, was nowhere to be seen.

As he came out of the room he heard Bodicca saying, in reply to what must have been Nectovelius's unheard question, 'It's Apollo, of course.'

And looking over to the far side of the main hall he saw the boy balancing agilely on top of the rubble, watching Bodicca as she carefully pulled aside the carbonised ends of roof timbers to expose more of the greater-than-life-size stone statue of a curly-haired young man which stood a few feet in from one of the walls. The fire had scorched red blotches on the once-pale marble, but the bent right arm was still attached, its curved fingers drawing back the invisible string of a bow that the missing left hand must once have held.

Vestiges of frescoes, ravaged by smoke and rain, were still visible on the lower parts of several of the temple's plastered walls. Most of them depicted standing figures, the heads and torsos either completely vanished or mere blurs of smeared colour. But enough remained to make Canio aware that the great hall must once have been a magnificent sight, before Orgillus and his fellow deserters sacked the place on that spring day, now two and a half years past.

'That was Artemis – or Diana, if you prefer the Roman name. She's Apollo's sister.' Bodicca must have been following his gaze.

'And that crowd of women over there?'

'Those? – Those are the Muses, all nine of them, or what's left of them.'

'The Muses?'

'The goddesses of the gentle arts – music, poetry, dancing and the like. They were Apollo's handmaidens... even you must have heard of them, haven't you?'

'Of course I have – in the army we talked of little else... Are you sure it's them? As you say, there's not much left.'

'I told you; my mother brought me here when I was a girl. I remember them when they were as fresh and perfect as the day they were first painted.'

'And you've never been here since?'

Bodicca appeared to hesitate, then replied simply, 'No, not since then.'

Canio wasn't entirely sure he believed her, but realised that there was no point in saying so.

'Have you found the priest?'

'Not yet, but he can't be far away,' Canio replied. 'Someone's been sleeping here, and there's fresh water in a pot on the table.'

'No, he's not far away,' she said quietly, gazing southwards towards the valley.

'So we'll just have to wait.'

'Here, or further up the valley?' she asked.

'Here's as good as anywhere. I'm sure he won't run away if he spots us – apparently he welcomes visitors, always hoping that they'll tell him where he can find the Hecate figurine that was stolen from this place. He even seems to have knocked a small stone out of the wall of his room, so he can spy on anyone coming up or down the valley.'

'No, he won't run away, but it seems that we'll be spending the night in these hills.'

Canio looked towards the south-west, where the low sun was visible as a hazy brightness though the clouds. He shrugged. 'It can't be helped. Not scared of the dark, are you?'

She gave him a strange look. 'It's not I that should be afraid of the dark, Canio. The night was always my friend.'

And if he wondered what she meant by that, some self-protective instinct warned him that it was better not to ask.

Time passed. Canio was eating some of the bread and cheese they had brought from Lindinis when he heard the rapid beating of wings. He looked up, and moments later a small covey of grey partridges came whirring up the valley, caught sight of him and the horses and veered off towards the cover of the trees.

'He's coming,' Bodicca observed.

Canio nodded. 'Him, or someone else.'

'No, it's him,' she murmured. 'I'm sure of it.'

They waited in silence, Nectovelius standing behind them. And then, rounding a curve some way down the valley, an old man appeared. He was walking surprisingly quickly, and when he saw them he even broke into a shambling run. As he came closer Canio guessed his age to be at least fifty, quite possibly more. His hair and beard were long and grey and ragged, his skin brown and creased. But his eyes, when he was near enough for Canio to see them clearly, were as bright and alert as those of a young bird.

He had half-expected the man to be dressed in rags, so was surprised to see that the robe he wore was richly embroidered with what he was vaguely aware were the symbols of Apollo – cithara, plectrum, bow and arrow, sacrificial tripod – and tolerably clean too, except for a dark stain at stomach level.

Then he remembered what Orgillus had said – about him and his fellow deserters slaughtering all of Apollo's priests, after the man who now stood before him had guided them to this place. He told himself that it didn't matter, that only the present and the future mattered – and what use now did those dead priests have for their fine robes?

And then the strangest thing: before he could even say a word, the old priest exclaimed, 'So you've come – the woman, the man and the boy! Last night I dreamed that you were coming, but I thought you would arrive from the south... Have you got it – is it here?' His voice seemed unused to speaking: it put Canio in mind of the creaking of a rusting scale cuirass.

Then he realised that the priest was addressing Bodicca, not himself. He glanced towards her and saw that she was looking intently at the old man. 'Yes, we have it,' she said quietly.

'Where... Where is it? Let me see!'

Wordlessly, Canio took the Hecate figurine from inside his tunic, unwrapped it and held it up for the priest's inspection.

The old man uttered a strange little cry and held out both hands. Canio hesitated, then let him take the figurine and watched as his trembling fingers caressed it from the top of her head to the snarling hound at her feet. 'She told me that she was returning,' he murmured, 'but I was afraid that she was only taunting me again.'

'Do you recognise her?' Canio asked, trying not to sound even slightly anxious.

At first the old priest did not answer, seemingly wholly fixated on the figurine, his eyes studying every minute detail. Then he whispered, 'Of course I recognise her – of course I do.'

He seemed so certain that Canio, on a sudden, reckless, winner-take-all impulse, said, casually, 'I'm not sure it's the original one though: it may only be a copy.'

The old man looked up sharply, then held the figurine close to his right ear and shook it gently. He gave Canio a sly look. 'A copy? Liar! This *is* the original one: I know it is, because I've seen her before... held her before. Those thieving soldiers took her from me, but her image has been locked in here' – he tapped his forehead – 'ever since the first moment I saw her. The soldiers even came back and stole the little casket she'd been hidden inside for all those years, but I'd know her anywhere.'

'So you're certain that this is the original, genuine one – not a copy?' Canio asked, just for the pleasure of hearing the old man confirm it again.

'Yes, yes – it's the original one, the ancient one!' The old man sounded exasperated that Canio should still doubt him.

'Well, that's good to know,' said Canio, holding out his hand for the return of the figurine.

'No! It's mine. The soldiers stole it from me once, but now it's mine again.'

184

'Why – because you stole it from this temple first? Oh yes, I know about that. And I also know that, thanks to you, Apollo's priests were all slaughtered and this temple burnt.'

The priest shook his head, 'No, no, that wasn't my doing,' he muttered. 'It was the soldiers – stupid men hunting for gold.'

'But who led them here? Who encouraged them to rob the place?'

The priest stared at Canio. 'Who told you that?'

'Does it matter?'

'But I need it more than you ever could.'

'For what?' Canio felt a masochistic compulsion to ask the question, even though he was hoping that what Eutherius had told him back in January had been a lie.

The priest hesitated, then said, 'To bring my daughter, Pascentia, back from the Lower World. With that figurine, I can bargain with Hades and—'

'Pascentia? But she isn't dead,' Bodicca interrupted. 'That's what we've come here to tell you. She survived the shipwreck and swam ashore, and now she's living near Burdigala, in the villa her late husband, the wine trader, once owned.'

'Near Burdigala? But that's in Gaul.'

'South-western Gaul.'

For several moments the old priest's face registered open-mouthed astonishment. Then it changed to doubt, hardening into disbelief. 'How can you possibly know that?'

'Because,' explained Bodicca, 'I saw her there not long ago – saw her and spoke to her in a villa surrounded by endless rows of vines. We're in the wine trade too, and that's how I came to meet her. We spent nearly a week at her villa, and one day she told me that her father had been a priest. And it was then that I remembered where I'd heard the name Pascentia before.'

'You had – where?' The old priest was still suspicious, but Canio could tell he was hooked by the tale Bodicca was telling. What he couldn't understand was why she was telling it.

'Be patient and I'll tell you,' Bodicca replied. 'Some months before our journey to Burdigala I met a soldier. Short of money, he begged me to buy that figurine of the goddess Hecate from him. I asked him how he had come by it, and he told me that he'd been given it by another soldier who had stolen it from this temple. According to this other soldier, they were led here by an old priest who claimed he wanted the figurine to bargain with Hades to bring his daughter, Pascentia, back from the Lower World. Apparently the priest believed that she'd drowned in a shipwreck several years before.'

The old man shook his head in apparent confusion. 'I don't remember telling them that.'

'But you must have done, or how else could I have known about it?' Bodicca replied. 'Anyway, when Pascentia told me that her father had been a priest – or so her mother had confessed to her, just before she sold her to the wine trader, the man who was to become her husband – I realised that I'd stumbled on the two halves of the same story.'

The old man said nothing, but stared over their heads towards the great fiery sun setting in the south-west. Finally he murmured, 'I could have saved her from being sold, if only... And all this time I thought she was dead... all those miserable, lonely, guilt-ridden years.'

'And she had thought you must be dead too. With the grape harvest approaching she couldn't leave Burdigala, but knowing that I was returning to Britannia she begged me to find you and let you know that she was still alive. It seems that Pascentia's mother had never told her your name, but we reasoned that if you recognised the figurine then you must be the man we were seeking. Oh, and she also asked me to give you this.' Bodicca reached under her *cucullus* to her belt pouch and extracted a gold *solidus*, which she held out to the old man. 'It was only meant to be a keepsake,' she explained. 'She couldn't have known that you'd become so poor.'

186

The old man's left hand shook slightly as he took the coin. 'But who are you – what are your names?'

'My name is Aelia,' Bodicca replied, not hesitating for even a moment.

'And mine's Geta. Can I have her back now?' Canio said, pointing to the figurine that the old man still clutched in his right hand.

The old priest looked down at the figurine and said in a voice so soft that Canio barely heard him, 'So she's alive. Pascentia is alive... All through these six long years while I thought her dead, she has been alive and well... and happy.' He smiled, then handed the Hecate figurine back to Canio.

'Burdigala is so far away – much too far for me to travel. And anyway, it doesn't matter now; not now that I know. And I understand the meaning of the other part of the dream too, the part that promised—' He closed his eyes and smiled again, looking blissfully happy. Then he turned and walked into the ruins of the temple.

Canio waited, wondering what the other part of the dream might have promised. He was still wondering when the old man emerged, said nothing, and began walking away up the valley. But after a dozen yards he stopped, hesitated, then turned and said to Bodicca, 'Swear again, swear on her, on Hecate, that Pascentia survived the shipwreck, and is alive and well and happy. Swear it's true... swear it, I beg you.'

Canio looked at Bodicca, who shrugged almost imperceptibly. She took the Hecate figurine from Canio and held it up so that it caught the light of the setting sun. 'As this is the true image of the Dark Lady, so I swear that everything I have told you is likewise true.'

The old man closed his eyes again and gave a great sigh, like a traveller who, after a long journey, has at last shrugged off the heavy pack that had burdened him all day. His eyes opened and he looked all about him, at Bodicca, at Canio, at Nectovelius,

187

and finally back at the ruined temple. 'If you wish,' he said, 'you can sleep in my room in the temple tonight. I won't be needing it.' And with that he turned again and walked off up the valley, not once looking back.

They watched until the curve of the valley had hidden him, and then Nectovelius asked, 'Where's he going?'

Bodicca did not reply, so Canio said, 'No idea. Perhaps he has to be somewhere else tonight. Anyway, let's make ourselves comfortable. It's going to be a long, dark, cold night.'

They let the horses drink again from the little stream that bubbled down the valley, and then, in the dying light, unsaddled and tethered them so that they could crop the lank grass.

After eating more of the bread and cheese, Bodicca produced six apples from a saddlebag and they ate some in the darkness, the old priest apparently not possessing either lamp or candle, or none that they could find.

The old man's apparently unshakable conviction that his figurine was indeed the original one had put Canio in a generous mood, and he let Bodicca and Nectovelius share the bed. Wrapping himself in his *cucullus*, he spent the night sleeping on the mosaic floor of red, cream and grey-blue tesserae. It had once been beautiful, that floor, with a large stylised flower set in the centre of two interlaced squares of guilloche rope, all now partly obscured by the furniture and the dried mud that had been trodden onto it over the past two years.

CHAPTER TWENTY-FOUR

2nd November

The old priest had still not returned when the morning sun at last struggled above the south-eastern horizon. They washed their hands and faces in the chill, clear waters of the stream (Nectovelius with some reluctance), saddled the horses and set off to return to Lindinis.

At the head of the valley they turned east, and had gone no more than a hundred yards before they found him, as Canio came to realise he had intended that they should. He lay on his back, furred with dew, and with what, in other circumstances, might have been taken for a faint smile on his face. Scattered around his body were the chewed remains of the bright red berries that he must have spat out before swallowing the seeds.

Canio glanced at Bodicca, trying and failing to read from her impassive face what was going through her mind as she looked down at the dead man. Neither spoke, and it was Nectovelius who at last asked, uncertainly, 'Is he asleep?'

'He's dead.' By then Canio had dismounted and laid the flat of his hand on the old priest's ice-cold face.

'How?'

'Yew seeds, child,' Bodicca replied calmly as she too dismounted. 'They're deadly poisonous – you eat them and they stop your heart from beating.'

'But why would he have done that?' the boy asked, the distress evident in his voice. 'He was happy, wasn't he, when you told him his daughter was alive and well... he did believe you, didn't he?'

'Oh yes, I'm sure he did. Quite sure,' Bodicca said softly.

'And perhaps he wanted to believe it, which always helps,' Canio added, still looking at the dead man. 'Another miserable winter of endless darkness and wet and cold in this place couldn't have been anything to look forward to. And at this time of year next summer seems as distant as the moon. Besides, it's best to die while you're happy, because happiness never lasts – something will always come along to destroy it. He'd lived long enough to know that.'

He walked back to Antares and grasped one of the saddle horns, but before mounting he turned to Bodicca, out of earshot of Nectovelius, and whispered, 'Why?'

'Why what?' she replied, as if she did not understand the question.

'Why did you...? Eutherius told me that old man was so crazy that he actually believed he could bribe Hades with the figurine – the real one – to allow his daughter to return from the land of the dead. If you hadn't convinced him that Pascentia was still alive, do you think he would have tried again?'

'We'll never know, will we? Not now.' Bodicca was herself now looking down at the dead man, and before Canio could reply, she asked 'Aren't you going to bury him?'

'With what? I haven't got a spade hidden under my *cucullus* – have you?'

'I remember seeing a mattock in the corner of his room.'

Canio considered asking her if she thought the man had buried those priests of Apollo that Orgillus and his friends had slaughtered? Then he became aware that Nectovelius, now dismounted and standing beside Bodicca, was looking anxiously at him. 'Wait here,' he sighed. 'I'll go back for it.'

The mattock was a poor tool, the iron head small and rusty, the wooden shaft split along the grain. 'I won't be able to dig much of a grave with this thing,' he pointed out, showing it to Bodicca.

'There was a hollow back there, not far from the stag-headed oak. Perhaps you could deepen that?' she suggested.

The hollow was roughly circular, about eight feet across, the bottom already covered with windblown ash leaves, brown and yellow. Canio took off his *cucullus*, scraped the leaves aside and began hacking through the turf and into the mottled, silty earth below. The soil was wet and full of roots, making digging difficult. After little more than a foot he hit the flinty clay subsoil.

'That's it,' he growled. 'I can't dig any deeper with this useless tool.'

'Then let me try,' said Bodicca. 'Perhaps I can.'

His manly pride irritated, Canio declined her offer, and after much further hacking, scraping and cursing the unyielding ground, the hole was almost four feet deep.

Between them they carried the body back to the hollow and laid the old priest in the grave. Searching through the meagre contents of the old priest's belt pouch, Bodicca retrieved the *solidus* she had given him. Easing down his stiffening lower jaw, she placed the coin on his tongue, then tried to push his mouth closed. It would not shut completely, leaving his yellow, uneven teeth showing in a sardonic grin.

Canio looked down at the old man's withered body and remembered what Eutherius had told him, when they had met at Vilbia's temple on that bitterly cold night back in January. About how, some thirty years before, when he was a young man, the priest had had a passionate affair with the young, pretty woman who, nine months later would become Pascentia's mother. How they had made love on a summer's day in a hay meadow full of flowers, the sun hot on their naked bodies. He must have been handsome then, and full of life and energy. Only thirty years ago, and now... *vita brevis*.

He found himself hesitating to throw the wet earth directly onto the old man's face, and wondered if he should turn the body over before backfilling the grave? Or perhaps, back in his room in the sacked temple, there was another robe or something, anything, that could be used as a shroud.

But before he could say as much, Nectovelius had jumped into the hollow with an armful of fallen ash leaves and began heaping them over the dead man's head. So he stood aside and let the boy and Bodicca together gather more leaves from under nearby trees and scatter them until the entire body was covered several inches deep.

Using the mattock, Canio then carefully pulled the dug earth over the leaves, then hacked topsoil from the edge of the grave downwards, then more soil from the surrounding area, until at last the sometime hollow had been transformed into a low mound. He stood looking sombrely at the trodden raw earth, wondering if the body was now buried deeply enough to deter wolves and foxes, and concluding that it was. Probably.

'What was his name?' Nectovelius asked. 'You never said, either of you.'

'His name?' Oddly, until that moment, the question had never occurred to Canio. He had always been *"the old priest"* or *"the mad priest"* or *"Pascentia's father"*. 'I don't know: I never heard anyone say,' he admitted. He looked to Bodicca, but she shook her head, and he was past wondering whether that was the truth or not. 'Does it matter?' he asked Nectovelius.

'But after we've gone, without a name to mark his grave, nobody will remember him. It will be like he never lived.' The thought seemed to trouble the boy.

'With or without a name, we'll remember him,' said Bodicca.

'Whether we want to or not,' Canio muttered. 'And anyway, time is always passing, always destroying, and we'll all be forgotten one day.' In his mind's eye he kept picturing the old priest's last, lonely moments of life.

Squatting down, he tried to clean his hands on a tussock of grass, weighed down and silvery with beads of cold dew. He noticed how the earth-stained water highlighted the numberless tiny fissures in the skin of his palms and fingers: not a young man's hands any more. 'Come on,' he said, louder, 'let's try to get back to Lindinis before nightfall. I want to sleep in a decent bed tonight.'

But Nectovelius seemed reluctant to leave and stood looking at the grave, still troubled. He took out the pan pipes that Bodicca had given him and began playing a slow, simple series of notes. It could hardly have been called a tune, but those single notes, lingering in that forlorn place, possessed a haunting, melancholy quality that seemed oddly fitting in a way that a more polished and complex melody could never have been.

As if the thought had just occurred to him, the boy suddenly stopped playing and said, 'If we hadn't come here and told him those things, he'd still be alive, wouldn't he?'

Neither Canio nor Bodicca answered him, and the boy did not repeat the question. Perhaps he thought that their silence was answer enough.

They retraced the route they had taken on the previous day, back the twenty or so miles to the Fosse Way, at first meeting few people other than cattle minders on the flat grasslands east of the Niger Hills. Glancing back towards the hills, Canio saw wreaths of thin grey clouds, smoke-like as they drifted rapidly across the upper slopes, driven by the brisk south-west wind.

Before he had lived with Trifosa, Canio had scarcely noticed flowers. She had tried to teach him the names of those which they came across when they had walked together in the hills near his villa, and some of those names had stuck in his memory. Now, on that second day of November, in the dying of the year, when there were few flowers to be seen, he found his eyes straying towards those that they happened to pass.

White deadnettle, white yarrow, white hogweed – the flowers of winter – the monopoly of white only occasionally broken by a late-surviving yellow ragwort or the tiny pink flowers of a plant with red and green feathery leaves that nestled in hedgerows and at the edges of woods and whose name was lost in his memory.

Ever since leaving the place where they had buried the old priest, whose name he would never now know, Nectovelius had been uncharacteristically quiet. Thinking to cheer him up, Canio said, 'Now that we're in November the beezlebums will soon be flying.'

The boy did not respond immediately, but after some fifty yards curiosity apparently got the better of him and he asked, 'What are beezlebums?'

'You've never heard of beezlebums?' said Canio, affecting surprise. 'They're bumblebees that fly backwards, of course.'

'I've never seen them,' the boy said doubtfully.

'Well, you wouldn't: they only fly on winter nights.'

'But why backwards?'

'To keep the cold night air out of their faces.'

There was a long silence, broken only by the clopping of the horses' hooves, before the boy asked, 'But how can they see where they're going?'

'They can't – that's why they keep crashing into things. In my soldiering days, when we had to march at night, I'd wear my helmet back to front, so that if one flew into me arse-first I wouldn't get stung in the face.'

'So how could you see where you were going?' Nectovelius persisted.

'Smell,' said Canio. 'After weeks without a chance to wash even our feet we all smelt so bad, in our own peculiar ways, that all I had to do was sniff the air to recognise the man in front of me.'

Bodicca, who it seemed had been listening with growing exasperation, twisted around as best she could in her saddle and said in a loud whisper to Nectovelius, 'Don't take any notice of him – he's the biggest liar in all Britannia Prima.'

'But still not as big a one as you, I suspect,' Canio murmured softly, too softly for her to hear.

CHAPTER TWENTY-FIVE

2nd & 3rd November

At first the weak sun crawled across the southern sky. Then, at around noon, dark clouds began drifting across from the west under a strengthening, chilly wind.

At Bodicca's suggestion, after fording the Insula, they diverted north-eastwards so as to join the Fosse Way well beyond the point where they had encountered Calpurnius Receptus's bailiffs.

In other circumstances Canio would not have minded meeting those two again, and having some more amusement at their expense. But he was conscious that in three days' time (he was keeping a careful reckoning of their passing) it would be the nones, the day he and Sabinus had an appointment which he was determined to keep. Also, there was something else that he was planning to do in Aquae Sulis.

Despite the time spent burying the old priest, they managed to reach Lindinis before sunset and trotted under the South-West Gateway in the dying light.

Once again they stayed the night in Priscinus's *mansio*, their host regaling Canio with more well-polished tales of his soldiering days, and early next morning, under a leaden sky, they set off to ride the thirty-five miles back to Aquae Sulis.

They broke their journey atthe *mansio* at Ovilmalleus, grimacing at the same mutton stew, the rank flavour again disguised with plentiful mint leaves.

A mile or so from Aquae Sulis, Bodicca asked Canio where he intended to spend the coming night.

'At Fortunata's *stabulum*, of course.'

'*The Hilaritas* – after she robbed you?... Are you going to tell her you know what she did?'

'Certainly not.' Canio waited until they had ridden another hundred yards along the metalled highway, weaving between the potholes, then said, 'She once told me that she believes the goddess Minerva is her protector. Even has a little shrine in her bedroom – I saw it once.'

'So?'

'So, I'll let Minerva punish her.'

'How?'

'You'll see. And Nectovelius...'

'Yes?'

'You're not to tell anyone that you filched my money back from her. Nobody at all – understood?'

'But she must know that somebody did,' the boy protested.

'Somebody or something did. But not you or me or Bodicca. I'm going to tell her that I think the money disappeared at Lindinis, and look distinctly unhappy about it.'

'Why tell her that?' Bodicca asked.

Canio looked at her and smiled. 'So she'll never even begin to suspect that we know it was her who stole it.'

They reached Aquae Sulis in the dusk of that louring day. Seeing that the gates were about to close they didn't try to enter the town, but trotted around the outside on a well-worn track between the high stone walls and the Flumen Abona, and kept on until they reached the northern suburbs and Fortunata's *stabulum*.

The lady herself was standing behind the bar counter and, to Canio's eyes, seemed distinctly startled at the sight of him walking through the doorway.

But he greeted her warmly, remarking that it was good to see a familiar face again, before arranging stabling, rooms for the night and a meal for himself and his two companions.

Several times as they sat eating the fish (said to be trout, but the number of bones suggested pike) cooked in its own juices with coriander seeds and sour wine vinegar, he caught Fortunata glancing uncertainly towards him.

After the meal, when Bodicca had ushered a reluctant Nectovelius upstairs to their room, Canio sat alone with a fresh jug of wine. As the contents of the jug slowly disappeared down his throat, he contrived to make the expression on his face that of a man weighed down by his sorrows. To further enhance this air of melancholy he gave the occasional deep sigh.

As he had hoped it would, after a while Fortunata's curiosity, or guilty conscience, or perhaps both, got the better of her and she sidled over and sat beside him, the small pottery oil lamp on the tabletop, casting a warm yellow light and dark shadows over the contours of her face as they talked.

'You don't seem your usual cheerful self tonight, Canio… The fish wasn't off, was it? The man I bought it from swore it had been caught this morning.'

'The fish was fine.'

'But something's troubling you – what is it?'

'When I was last here,' Canio slowly began, 'I was on my way to Dunum… have you heard of Dunum?'

'Yes, I've heard of it – a big old hill fort near Durnovaria.'

'That's the place. Well, I was on my way there when it vanished.'

'What did?'

'The money – a *follis* full of gold *solidi* I was taking to Dunum, to the new temple being built there on the high ground inside the hill fort.'

'You were carrying money intended for that temple?' Canio, listening for it, detected the growing note of apprehension in her voice.

'I was indeed.' He sighed again. 'Several months ago, when I was in the *laconicum* of the baths, here at Aquae Sulis, I had a vision. A sort of waking dream it was, and in it I thought I saw the goddess Minerva telling me to give fifteen *solidi* for the making of a statue of herself, to stand in the temple that's just been built on the hilltop at Dunum. The vision passed so quickly that, like a fool, I told myself that it was nothing but the product of my imagination. Some sort of brain fever, brought on by the heat and steam of the *laconicum* – and perhaps, if I'm honest, by the amount of wine I'd drunk the previous night.'

'But now... you don't think it was?' she asked hesitantly.

'No. A few days ago, when I was staying in Corinium, I had another dream, the like of which I hope never to have again. The goddess herself appeared for a second time, demanding to know why I hadn't done as she had ordered. She was terrifying, Fortunata, terrifying – her face twisted with an anger I had never seen on the face of any mortal man or woman. If I close my eyes I can still see that face...' And he gave what was intended to be a horrified shudder.

'And now you've lost it – the gold?'

'I didn't lose it: it was stolen.'

'Stolen? Are you sure?'

Canio nodded.

There was a slight pause, as if, he thought, Fortunata was willing herself to ask the question. 'Where?'

'I don't know. It might have been at Ovilmalleus, or more likely at Lindinis – that's where I first missed it, and then spent two whole days searching for it.'

'So you still had it when you left here?' The relief in her voice was almost comical.

Canio nodded. 'Yes – I'm almost certain the *follis* was inside my purse when I left.'

'So what will you do now? Return home for more gold?'

And give you a second bite at the cherry? What a wag you are. 'I suppose I'll have to,' he sighed. 'But first I want revenge on the thieving bastard who stole those fifteen *solidi*.'

'But you don't know who took them… do you?'

Nervous again? 'I don't, but the goddess surely does. And in the morning I'll go to her temple here in Sulis and seek her help.' He hesitated, then asked, 'Would you come with me – I've never been inside that temple or met any of Minerva's priests.'

Fortunata did not reply immediately, and Canio thought she was about to refuse. But then she said, 'Yes, of course I'll come,' and gave him her brightest smile.

It seemed that, although she might speculate nervously all night (or so he hoped) as to exactly what his intentions were, at least come the morning she would find out.

'You will? I'd be most grateful… if you're sure you can spare the time?' He didn't give her time to reconsider, but gave an enormous yawn and said, 'And now I really must get to my bed: it's been a long and anxious four days.'

For as long as he thought she might be watching, he feigned an air of dejected weariness as he climbed the stairs. But after going into his bedroom and bolting the door behind him, sitting alone in the darkness he rubbed his palms together and permitted himself a fierce grin. The grin faded as conscience-prompted doubts surfaced. He smothered both conscience and doubts, kicked off his boots and wriggled under the blankets.

CHAPTER TWENTY-SIX

4th November

Well before the end of the first hour, Canio, Bodicca and Nectovelius, with Fortunata leading, entered Aquae Sulis via the North Gate and began walking down one of the main streets of the town, the continuation of the Fosse Way.

After about a hundred yards on this street, Fortunata turned right onto the wide street leading to the West Gate, through which they had entered the town five days earlier. Passing the *tholos* on their left, they came to the high wall which surrounded the temple precinct. Turning left beside this wall, which there was fronted by a colonnaded portico roofed with lichen-blotched red tiles, they came to an arched opening through which, at Fortunata's prompting, Canio walked and found himself standing in the temple courtyard.

Paved with slabs of blue-grey stone, badly worn in places, the courtyard had another colonnaded portico running around all its sides, except in those places where the paving butted up against the walls of adjoining buildings. The courtyard was, by Canio's rough reckoning, some thirty double paces wide by half as much again deep.

In that early morning the place was almost deserted, except for two men and a solitary woman, who were deep in animated conversation and seemed oblivious to the four newcomers. Unusually, there were no beggars soliciting alms.

Twenty double paces in front of Canio, standing on a podium as high as a tall man and built of huge blocks of dressed stone, stood the great temple of Sulis Minerva. It towered upwards, its great triangular pediment resting on top of four massive fluted stone columns, each more than four times as high as that same tall man.

He watched in amusement as Nectovelius stared up wonderingly, and a little uneasily, at the great moustachioed head of the male gorgon carved in the centre of the pediment, his snaky hair and beard radiating outwards and completely encircling his face like the sun's rays, while his piercing eyes glared down at everyone standing before him in the courtyard.

'Come on,' he said to the boy, 'I've got business inside the temple. You can look around here later.' And with the two women beside him, Canio began walking towards the podium steps, only to be checked by the boy's voice from somewhere behind them asking, 'Who are they?'

Turning, he saw that Nectovelius was pointing to the large stone altar, almost two double paces square and a hand's span taller than the boy himself, which stood in the courtyard midway between the entrance and the temple. "They" were the two standing figures, some three feet high, carved on each of the four corners of the altar, one naked, the other clothed, all different.

'I don't know,' Canio said impatiently.

'They're gods and goddesses,' said Bodicca, ignoring Canio. 'The ones I can see from here are Jupiter, Hercules, Apollo playing his lyre, and what looks like a river goddess pouring water from a big jar.'

'And her?' asked Nectovelius, indicating the life-sized statue of a woman wearing a strange sort of military helmet set high on her head. She stood on a plinth in front of the altar, holding a spear upright in her right hand, with her left hand resting on a shield grounded on the top of the plinth.

'That's the goddess Minerva, of course – don't you know anything, child?' Fortunata scolded.

By then Canio was at the foot of the wide flight of stone steps, worn concave in places by the passage of innumerable feet over the centuries, by which visitors climbed up to the temple podium. At the top he waited for the two women and the boy to reach the steps, then walked alone across the flat top of the podium, passed between the central pair of towering columns and through the high double doors of the temple, which then stood wide open.

The interior of the temple was dimly lit by the light which filtered through the rows of small windows set high in the side walls. As his eyes accustomed themselves to the gloom, Canio became aware of the gilded bronze cult statue of Sulis Minerva herself.

She stood on a high plinth at the back of the great hall, and in the semi-darkness appeared to be of greater than human-size. Clad in a long robe, she carried a spear in her left hand, and in the other something which he was too far away to properly make out.

As he walked slowly towards the statue he had the curious illusion that Minerva was becoming larger: actually larger, not merely seeming that way because the distance between them was decreasing. When he was only a few paces away a previously unnoticed brazier below her plinth flared into life, perhaps stirred by a draught from the doorway, the flames casting flickering orange light and dark shadows over the statue.

Now he could see clearly Minerva's great Corinthian helmet, with its blank eye holes, set high on her head above a ring of abundant hair. And standing on the extended palm of her right hand was what Canio now realised was a bird, its heart-shaped face clearly recognisable as that of an owl.

As he stared up at the golden face and the eyes that seemed to stare out into infinity, Fortunata's voice, coming from close behind, startled him.

'Did you know that she is the goddess of wisdom and healing, as well as battles? And poetry and weaving and all manner of other arts and skills?'

'Of course,' Canio replied, which was not strictly true. Knowledge of the various attributes of the deities in the classical Roman pantheon was not something he had burdened his memory with, mainly because he had never really believed that any of them actually existed.

Except for Hecate: belief in the existence of that dark goddess had been breathed into his soul by another Marcia, the nearest thing to a mother that he had ever known, when he was no older than Nectovelius. And ever afterwards he had been unable to rid himself entirely of that superstitious belief, no matter how hard he had tried.

He became aware that Bodicca was now standing beside him. 'And Sulis, the goddess of the sacred spring, and Minerva, the goddess of wisdom, act as one to avenge crimes committed by mortals – isn't that so, Fortunata?' she asked brightly.

Fortunata hesitated, but before she could reply a widening column of light appeared in the gloom behind the statue as a door opened and a long shadow emerged. Canio heard slow footsteps, and into the light of the brazier came a man. He was middle-aged, tall and gaunt, and wore the ankle-length decorated robe and conical headgear of a priest.

'*Salve*, Fortunata. What brings you here today?'

'Business for you, Calpurnius. Canio, this is Calpurnius Antigonus, priest of Sulis Minerva. Calpurnius, may I introduce you to Can... to Claudius Caninus and his companion, Bodicca.'

'And how may I be of service?' the priest asked Canio.

'Somebody – I don't know who – has stolen a considerable sum of money from me.'

'And you want it back, of course.'

'I most certainly do, every last *solidus*. But, if that's not possible, then at the very least I want the person, or persons, who stole them punished. Can you arrange that?'

'Certainly. Or rather, the goddess can, through a humble intermediary such as myself.'

'Can it be done now?'

'It can, if you wish. Be so good as to follow me.' And the priest led them back into the room he had emerged from.

It proved to be surprisingly large, this room, with several chairs, a rack of scrolls covering one whole wall, and a solid-looking table with elaborately carved legs. A large pottery oil lamp burned on the table, and there were several other lamps, all unlit, sitting on stone brackets protruding from the walls.

'I assume you wish me to make a *defixio* – a curse tablet, as the vulgar call them?'

'If that's the way these things are done,' said Canio, feigning ignorance.

Calpurnius Antigonus settled himself into the chair next to the table and picked up one of several large wax tablets and a bronze stylus. 'Right, let us begin then. Have you decided on the wording you require?'

Canio sat down in one of the other chairs and began, slowly and thoughtfully, giving the impression that he was weighing every word.

'To the great goddess Sulis Minerva: I beg you, Goddess, to inflict upon the person who stole the fifteen *solidi* from me the most cruel and hideous torments, whether that person be man or woman...' Canio paused, as if unsure of the formula of words to be used.

'Slave or free?' the priest suggested.

'Slave or free, pagan or Christian. May they never again find rest, neither by day nor night, until they either return the fifteen *solidi* to me, or confess their crime, naked, before your altar at Dunum, and perform whatever penance your priests there may demand.'

And before Calpurnius could ask, Canio explained, 'The goddess came to me in a vision, in the baths here at Aquae Sulis, commanding me to pay for a statue to herself in the new temple on the hilltop at Dunum.'

'You actually saw Minerva?'

'I did, standing as close to me as I am to you now, or so it seemed.'

'Remarkable!' The priest seemed impressed, as Canio intended him and Fortunata – especially Fortunata – to be. 'I have heard of such things, of course, but only once before have I met a man to whom the goddess actually appeared.'

And I'll wager he was lying too, thought Canio. 'Which makes it all the more shameful that the money – her money – was stolen,' he sighed. 'How soon can the *defixio* be made?'

'It should not take long, if I begin immediately. I have an engraving tool and several sheets of pewter here.' The priest hesitated, as if considering how to frame the request, then murmured, 'Of course, such things cost money... did the thief take everything you had?'

'Only the *follis* containing the *solidi*,' Canio reassured him. 'What's your standard fee?'

'For the pewter sheet – it's superior to lead – and my expertise and blessing of the *defixio*, my fee is normally ten *siliquae*.'

Canio was not convinced that it really was that much. However, time was passing, so... He fished under his *cucullus* into a pocket of his tunic, pulled out a small gold coin and held it up for Calpurnius's inspection.

The priest looked at it curiously, in uncertain recognition.

'It's a *semissis* – a half-*solidus*,' Canio explained.

'A half-*solidus*? So it's worth—'

'All of twelve silver *siliquae*,' Canio assured him. 'And it will be yours, *if* the *defixio* is ready by the time I return – which will be in no more than the length of a winter hour.'

'It will be ready by then, never fear,' said Calpurnius, his eyes still on the little gold coin.

CHAPTER TWENTY-SEVEN

Back out in the temple courtyard, Canio and the others sat down to wait on one of the stone benches inside the colonnaded portico, which gave some shelter from the chilly north-east breeze and the spits of rain mixed in with it.

After a while Nectovelius grew restless and began asking Fortunata questions about the novel things he was seeing all around him. But the lady seemed distracted, answering only in monosyllables, or sometimes not at all.

So it was left to Bodicca to explain to the boy what the large building abutting the south side of the courtyard was, the one with the barrel-roof which he had gazed at from the top of the temple steps.

'That covers the pool in which the sacred spring rises. When the priest has finished making it, Canio will throw the *defixio* into the pool so that the goddess can read it... That is right, isn't it, Fortunata?'

Fortunata nodded.

'So who are they?' Nectovelius asked, pointing to the figures carved on the tympanum of the stone porch sheltering a small door in the wall of the building which covered the spring.

'Those are two water nymphs, and that head above them is Sol, the sun god. You've heard of Sol, haven't you?'

'Yes, of course I have,' the boy replied. He stood up and walked over to the centre of the courtyard, near the altar. 'And those women over there – who are they?'

'Where?'

'On that wall,' said the boy, pointing to the stone building on the north side of the courtyard, opposite the building which housed the sacred spring.

Having nothing better to do while he waited, Canio got up and followed the two women who were already standing beside Nectovelius.

The wall had three fluted pilasters on either side of a central door, and in each of the four spaces between them was carved a life-sized relief of a woman seated in a niche under a shell canopy, with a cupid flying overhead. The figures seemed to have once been painted in bright colours, now badly faded.

To Canio, the whole courtyard gave the appearance of having seen better days. Although perhaps, he reflected, it was only the pervasive melancholy he always felt in the dying of the year that made it seem worse than it really was. In the warmth and brightness of high summer he would probably have scarcely noticed its imperfections.

'I think they represent the four seasons,' Bodicca was saying. 'You would know, wouldn't you, Fortunata?'

'What?' It seemed that Fortunata's thoughts had been elsewhere.

'Are those the four seasons?' Bodicca repeated.

'Yes... yes, of course they are. You can tell by the cupids – there's Spring bringing the flowers, Summer with an ear of wheat, Autumn a bunch of grapes, and Winter... Winter carrying a bill-hook for cutting firewood.'

'So who's the fierce-looking lady in the circle up there, with her hair twisted and piled high on top of her head, the way my mother sometimes did?' Nectovelius asked, pointing to the bust of a woman carved on the tympanum above the door.

'Ah, she must be the goddess Luna – can you see that crescent moon behind her head?' Bodicca replied. 'And see how Sol and

Luna face each other across the big altar: sun and moon, day and night.'

Nectovelius looked as if he were about to ask something else, but before he could do so Canio said irritably, 'Sweet Venus, will you stop asking silly questions. Come on – let's see if that priest has finished my *defixio* yet.'

But Nectovelius was now studying the stone base on which the statue of Minerva stood in front of the altar. On it were carved, in four short lines, the words:

"*DEAE SULI / L. MARCIVS MEMOR / HARVSP / D.D.*"

which the boy began to trace with one finger.

Bodicca, ignoring Canio, crouched down beside the boy and slowly expanded each word as Nectovelius ran his finger across it.

'"*To the goddess Sulis*," she read, '*Lucius Marcius Memor, haruspex, gave this gift*".'

'I thought the lady was Minerva?' Nectovelius objected.

'Here in Aquae Sulis,' Bodicca explained, 'Sulis and Minerva are one and the same. That's right, isn't it?'

Fortunata nodded.

'So what's a *haruspex*?'

'A jackass, that's what a *haruspex* is – a man who pretends he can foretell the future by sticking his fool nose into the liver and guts of a dead sheep!' an exasperated Canio shouted from the bottom of the temple steps.

An elderly couple, who had just emerged from one of the two roofed shrines which flanked the temple, looked at each other in apparent disbelief that anyone should say such a thing, there in the temple precinct of all places.

But Canio, ignoring the disapproving looks, carried on up the steps. When he looked back he saw that the two women and the boy were still talking in the courtyard.

The fuel in the brazier which stood in front of the great gilded bronze Minerva was burning brightly now. Canio wondered if the priest, in anticipation of his return, had stirred the fire. And looking more closely, he realised that the fuel was not the usual charcoal, but rather small pieces of the strange, burnable stone occasionally used in those parts. A kind of stone that he had heard of, but never noticed before.

Looking up, he noticed that the flames were illuminating not only the stern, all-seeing face of Minerva herself, but also the grey smoke which was drifting up to and around the timbers of the high roof, and then slowly curling down again in thin, pungent tendrils.

The door of Calpurnius's room was ajar, so Canio pushed it fully open and found the priest still hunched over the pewter sheet, graver in hand. 'Only two more words to go,' he murmured, without looking up.

Canio grunted acknowledgement and went back into the hall, noticing for the first time the rows of unlit oil lamps set in niches down both long walls, and how Minerva seemed almost to come alive in the dancing light of the brazier. There was still no sign of the others, a situation which suited his purpose.

He was still gazing up at the goddess when he heard Calpurnius announce that he had finished. Back inside the priest's room the man indicated, with a magician's sweep of his hand, the *defixio* lying on the table bathed in the yellow light of the oil lamp.

Canio leaned over and read without difficulty the rudimentary straight and curved symbols of the cursive script, the letters ploughed silvery through the dull bluish-grey surface of the pewter. He noted with satisfaction that the wording was exactly as he had dictated to the priest.

'You did not actually say,' Calpurnius began, a tinge of anxiety in his voice, 'but I assumed that you did not want the message to the goddess to be written backwards in mirror writing. If you had,' he added quickly, 'it would of course have taken me much longer.'

'No, normal writing is exactly what I wanted,' Canio assured him. He fished under his *cucullus* and handed over the promised gold *semissis*. 'One thing more: will you sell me one of those blank sheets of pewter?'

'Certainly,' said the priest. He did not ask what it was for, and Canio had no intention of telling him.

'Two *siliquae*?' Canio enquired.

'They cost me that,' Calpurnius replied, an expression of pained regret on his face.

Again, Canio was not sure that he believed him, but gave him three of the little silver coins anyway.

'Do you wish me to show you the way to the sacred spring?' the priest enquired.

Perhaps, Canio wondered, he wanted to charge him a fee for that too? He smiled. 'Thank you, but I know the way – as I said, I've been in the baths before. *Vale,* my friend.'

He walked halfway down the hall before turning to check that Calpurnius had not emerged from his room. Then, taking out one of the pewter sheets, he checked that it was the correct one, before going down on one knee and, with some difficulty, rolling it into a cylinder.

Outside on the podium he met Bodicca and Nectovelius. Fortunata was still standing in the courtyard below. He waved the rolled-up pewter sheet in her direction, then trotted down the steps.

At the bottom he turned right, walked past the western end of the great barrel-roofed building which covered the sacred spring and into the colonnaded portico, where an arched doorway in the back wall gave access to an anteroom of the baths complex.

Just beyond the archway his path was blocked by a large, tough-looking man, nearer forty than thirty Canio guessed, wearing a quasi-military uniform and almost certainly an ex-soldier. Before the man could speak, Canio held out a *siliqua*. The man grinned, took the coin and stepped aside. From previous visits he remembered meeting such doorkeepers at all the entrances to the baths.

He paused briefly, while memory flowed back, then turned left into a gloomy corridor. This corridor first narrowed as the blank end wall of a room projected into it, then widened again and led to a short flight of steps, from the top of which, to his left, he could see the remembered three large openings in the spring pool's wall.

Canio had looked into the pool once before, although then it had only been out of idle curiosity. The outer two openings were some six feet square with horizontal heads, but the central one was considerably larger, ten feet wide at least, with an arched head. The sill level of all three openings was the same, a little below his shoulder height.

Standing beside the big central opening he peered into the cavernous interior of the building which housed the spring pool. By the dim light that filtered down from the large semicircular openings high up in both end walls he could make out the dark green surface of the water, partly obscured though it was by the vapour which swirled above it as the hot waters of the sacred spring, bubbling up from the depths, met the chilly air.

He waited until Fortunata, Bodicca and the boy had caught up, then took out the rolled-up pewter sheet. Holding it out to them all he asked, 'So, who wants to be the one who throws the *defixio* into the sacred spring?... Come on, who wants to have the honour of asking the goddess to inflict upon the person who stole those fifteen *solidi* the most cruel and hideous torments?'

Fortunata, looking pale and tense, said nothing. Bodicca slowly shook her head and gave Canio a questioning look – a look which he interpreted as saying that she thought this game had gone far enough.

'Can I do it?' piped up Nectovelius.

Canio eyed him doubtfully, not least because the top of the boy's head was at least a foot below the sills of the openings.

Evidently anticipating the problem, Nectovelius said, 'I can do it if you lift me up.'

Canio shrugged and handed the rolled-up pewter to the boy. Then he stooped, grabbed him around the waist, lifted him high up over his head and onto his shoulders, before carrying him over to the large central opening.

They both stared into the misty dimness for a few moments, before Nectovelius squawked, 'There are women in there – weird women standing on the water! Five of them on the far side, and two more this side.' Wriggling like an eel, he tried to break free from Canio's grip and scramble off his shoulders.

'They're not women, you damned fool! They're just statues – stone statues of water nymphs and the like.'

'But they're standing on the water,' the frightened boy persisted.

'Of course they're not standing on the water – they're set on stone pillars that stop just below the surface.'

'I'm sure I saw one of them move,' Nectovelius whimpered, still wriggling.

'You couldn't have: statues can't move. It was only the vapour drifting around them – and your fool imagination – that made them seem so.'

'I *did* see one move, I'm sure I did – let me down!'

'Not until you've thrown the *defixio* into the middle of the pool,' Canio snarled.

Then, as if he had just realised the full implications of what he was about to do, Nectovelius wailed, 'Will the person who took your money really be hurt? I don't want—'

'Of course they'll be hurt, and hurt badly,' Canio interrupted. 'That's the whole point of asking the goddess to punish them. Sweet Venus, will you get on with it!'

'No – I don't want to do it! I don't want to hurt—'

Thinking the boy was about to say Fortunata's name, Canio gave a growl of exasperation, hoisted Nectovelius up from his

213

shoulders and set him down, still shaking, onto the stone-flagged floor.

Snatching the rolled-up *defixio* from the boy's trembling hand, he unceremoniously lobbed it out into the centre of the sacred spring's pool, where it made a slight plop and a few tiny ripples in the bubbling green water. And then it was gone, as if it never had been.

Bodicca gave Canio a reproachful look, before kneeling beside the boy and stroking his head. 'Canio's right, they are only stone statues. Nothing to fear.' She did not mention the boy's other concern.

'But one of them did move, I know it did... And will the goddess really do cruel things to the person who stole Canio's money?'

Bodicca looked questioningly at Canio, who shrugged his insouciance at the boy's distress and asked, 'Where's Fortunata?'

'Gone: she said she had things to do back at *The Hilaritas*.'

'Perhaps she's gone to search for those missing *solidi*?'

'That's not funny, Canio. She really believes Sulis Minerva will do something terrible to her now.'

'And you – what do you believe?'

'I believe many things,' she replied. 'Things I doubt you would want to believe.'

'Even that the *Genii Cucullati* exist? A few days before he disappeared, Saturninus told me that you claimed to have seen all three of them together once.'

'And so I did, many years ago. Floating through the air they were, one behind the other, floating like thistledown on the late summer breeze.'

Before Canio could reply that what she had seen probably *were* clouds of thistledown, Nectovelius, the trauma of the "moving statue" seemingly banished by the restless curiosity of youth, piped up, 'Can I see the baths before we go?'

'No, we haven't time.'

214

'Oh, let him look: it won't take long – and he may never get another chance to see them.'

'Do you want to see them too?'

Bodicca hesitated, then said, 'No, I'll stay here. Perhaps Fortunata will return and confess what she did.'

Canio couldn't decide whether she was being serious or ironic. 'Come on then, young Nectovelius; let's go and see the baths.' His change of mind was something less than altruistic: he had realised that it would suit his purpose to delay his return to *The Hilaritas* for a little while.

CHAPTER TWENTY-EIGHT

At the far end of the gloomy corridor that ran beside the sacred spring's pool was a door. Canio pulled it open and light flooded in from the hall of the Great Bath beyond. On the other side of the door a short flight of stone steps led down to the arcaded ambulatory aisles, which ran along both sides of the Great Bath. He started down the steps, beckoning Nectovelius to follow.

At the bottom he turned and watched in amusement as Nectovelius stood staring all about him in wonder – as well he might, for the hall was a vast cavern. Its walls soared up to a roof curved like the inside of an enormous barrel, supported by a row of deep pilasters which ran down both long sides of the hall, the arched heads between them framing the ambulatory arcades.

The Great Bath itself was rectangular, at least twice as long as it was wide, and around all four sides a line of lead-covered steps ran down into the bath, where the same green-tinged water they had seen in the sacred spring lapped faintly against them. Emerging in the corner, close to the spot where Canio stood, the water gushed into the bath from a stone cornucopia held by an exquisitely carved little water nymph reclining on a stone slab set just above the water level. He knelt and stretched out a hand, letting the hot water splash over his fingers.

'It's so…' Nectovelius whispered in awe.

'Enormous?' Canio suggested. 'There's certainly nothing else like it in all Britannia.' He followed the boy's gaze up to the vast unglazed lunettes in the end walls, and the row of smaller ones at high level down both long sides of the hall. Shafts of late autumn sunlight were filtering in through the lunettes on the east and south sides, playing on the lazy curls of vapour rising from the water below.

There were about thirty people in the hall, all men of various ages, either in the water or lounging in the large, shell-like alcoves set into the ambulatory walls on both long sides. The men in the warm waters of the bath were naked; those in the alcoves were mostly wrapped in towels against the November chill. A few were fully clothed. In one alcove Canio spotted a man being pummelled by a masseur.

Canio was about to point out to Nectovelius that it was not only the steps, but also the entire floor of the Great Bath, huge though it was, that was lined with sheets of lead. But before he could do so, a youngish man in a smart white tunic popped his head out of one of the alcoves and came hurrying towards them.

'*Salve*, Master. My name is Lycomedes – may I be of some assistance? A swim perhaps... or a massage... or both?'

'No time, unfortunately – I'm just showing the boy around the place,' sighed Canio, although Lycomedes' offer of a massage had made him remember, wistfully, that when he had visited in the summer of the previous year he had engaged the services of two female masseuses – ladies who, doubtless due to the heat, had discarded their *stolas,* together with most other items of clothing. Admittedly that had not been in the Great Bath hall itself, but in a small, secluded *caldarium* at the western ends of the baths complex.

'You know the baths well?'

'Not that well,' said Canio, instinctively wary of anyone with a Greek name and an accent that suggested that he had never been further south than Durnovaria.

'Then allow me to guide you,' said Lycomedes, and without waiting for a reply began walking rapidly down the north side ambulatory, weaving between the bathers standing or lying on the limestone floor slabs. Nectovelius immediately began following the man. Canio hesitated, sighed an expletive, then did likewise.

When they were halfway down the length of the bath he noticed a small fragment of pink plaster fall from the high barrel vault ceiling and drop into the water, although any splash it made was drowned by the hubbub of voices. But Nectovelius must have noticed it too, because he turned and looked questioningly at Canio.

'Does that happen often?' Canio asked their guide.

'What's that?' said Lycomedes, although Canio was fairly sure that the man must have seen it himself.

'Plaster dropping off the ceiling.' Scanning upwards, Canio saw several other areas where plaster had previously become detached.

'Oh, once in a while – it's nothing to worry about,' their guide said airily. 'But isn't that roof a thing of wonder? People from all over the empire come to stare at it. And I'm told it was built two hundred years or more ago, after they found that the old timber roof was beginning to rot in the wet air rising from the bath.'

In the wall at the end of the north ambulatory was a closed door. 'Where does that lead to?' Nectovelius asked.

'The immersion bath,' replied Lycomedes, pushing the door open. And peering over the boy's head into the dimness, Canio saw a flight of steps leading down to a semicircular bath set into the side wall.

'People sometimes sit in there for hours, up to their necks in the warm, healing water from the sacred spring... though at the moment it's not in use,' Lycomedes added. He did not explain why.

Turning right, they walked beside the far end of the Great Bath until they came to the south-east corner, where an arched doorway led into what appeared to be a smaller version of the Great Bath itself, though orientated north to south. Small it may have been in comparison with the Great Bath, but it was still enormous by the standards of other baths Canio had seen, even in the most opulent of villas.

There was nobody in this smaller bath, and Nectovelius ran over and swished his hands though the pale green water. 'It's almost as warm as the other one,' he announced, sounding surprised.

'Of course,' said Lycomedes. 'The water from the Great Bath flows through a pipe under the floor and into this bath.'

'And from here a drain carries it all the way down to the Flumen Abona,' said Canio, pointing eastwards. He had learnt that on a previous visit.

In the wall on the far side of this smaller bath was a large door. Nectovelius pushed against it, ever eager to see what further wonders lay beyond, but it appeared to be locked. He turned to Lycomedes, who spread his hands apologetically. 'That leads to a truly magnificent suite of rooms – a *tepidarium*, a *caldarium*, an *apodyterium* and several other rooms, all of them heated from below by hypocausts. Sadly, however, they too are unavailable at the moment. '

Nectovelius turned to Canio. 'What's a *tepidarium*, a *cal—*'

'A cool room, a hot room and an undressing room,' Canio interrupted. 'Why are they unavailable?' This to Lycomedes.

'Alas, when the Abona burst its banks after the heavy rain some weeks ago, the water came up as far as this eastern end of the baths and poured through the stoke holes into the hypocausts below those rooms. And although some of that water has now drained away now, the stoke holes are still half under water so no fires can be lit. Also, the water has left deposits of river mud everywhere which... how can I put it?'

'Stinks?' Canio suggested. He had been speculating about the cause of the faint odour his nose detected near the door.

Lycomedes nodded. 'So the *Decuriones* have decided to do nothing until all the water has drained away.'

'The Town Fathers are good at doing nothing,' Canio observed, although he didn't expect Lycomedes to reply, and was unsurprised when he didn't. 'The Abona flooded last winter too, didn't it?'

'Nowadays it seems to flood at least once a year,' Lycomedes admitted, 'although this latest flood was the worst that anyone can remember. At the other end of the baths though, the west end, there's an even bigger and better suite of rooms, and they were untouched by the floods. Would you like to see those?'

'Can we?' asked Nectovelius, looking up at Canio.

Canio exhaled noisily. 'All right, if you're quick.'

Lycomedes led the way, trotting up the ambulatory on the south side of the Great Bath until they came to another arched doorway at the end, beyond which was a wide corridor.

The light in the corridor was poor, Lycomedes reluctantly admitting that the sum of money allotted by the *Decuriones* for oil was such that the lamps could only be lit when the suite was in full use.

However, even the dim light was sufficient to allow them to see the great circular plunge pool, fully nine or ten giant strides in diameter, which occupied the centre of a large room that opened off the right-hand side of the corridor. The pool was empty, exhaling a chill odour of decay: Lycomedes said that it was only filled in the warm months.

On the other side of the corridor was a room which, Lycomedes informed them, was another *apodyterium*, and a little way past that, past an external door, was a circular chamber which their guide proudly announced was a *laconicum*.

'That's a room of dry heat, which makes you sweat and itch worse than a hundred bed bugs,' Canio told Nectovelius, to save him asking.

At the end of the corridor Lycomedes pointed out a suite of rooms with mosaic floors, one of which Canio recognised, even in the poor light, as the *caldarium* of happy memory. Their hollow ring beneath his boots confirmed that the floors had hypocausts below.

Then on past an oblong room containing yet another cold plunge bath, and suddenly they found themselves back at the entrance from the temple courtyard, having made, as Lycomedes proudly announced, a complete circuit of the entire baths complex.

Canio thanked the man and tipped him a *siliqua*, assured him that they had already seen the temple area, then waited until he had scuttled off back into the shadows from which they had just emerged.

The ex-army gatekeeper seemed to have disappeared, but they found Bodicca still in the corridor beside the sacred spring, standing on a small footstool that Canio had not noticed before. She was staring through the central opening into the bubbling, misty water, and as Canio approached he could have sworn he heard voices, women's voices, although Bodicca was the only person there.

Before he could decide whether to mention those voices, Bodicca turned to Nectovelius and asked, 'So, what did you think of the Great Bath?'

Nectovelius appeared to struggle to find the right words to express his wonder at the things he had just seen. 'How could men ever make such a vast building?' he said at last. 'The roof seemed to go up almost to the sky, with little clouds up there. And the water's so warm! They said it's warm all the time, day and night, summer and winter just the same. I never knew there were such places in the world. I hate being made to wash in icy cold water,' he added feelingly.

Bodicca smiled at the boy. 'The world is full of wonders, but you have to seek them out: they don't come looking for you. Back to Fortunata's *stabulum* now?' she asked Canio.

'Yes, back to *The Hilaritas*. And then we take the road to Corinium.'

They walked back through the streets of Aquae Sulis, out through the North Gate, through the northern suburbs and across the bridge over the Abona, Nectovelius lingering behind as he gazed this way and that, and back towards the baths and Sulis Minerva's temple.

Making sure that the boy was out of earshot, Bodicca said, 'You don't really believe that Sulis Minerva will punish Fortunata, do you?' It sounded more statement than question.

'Of course I don't, but she does, and that's what matters.'

'Don't you believe that any of the old gods or goddesses exist?'

He hesitated, then said, 'No, not the old ones, or the new one either.'

'Not even Hecate?'

How much has Vilbia told you? thought Canio, but before he could think of a suitable reply, Bodicca continued, 'Fortunata now thinks that she will, and I quote, *"Never again find rest, neither by day nor night"* – those were your words on the *defixio*, were they not? Believing as she does, she must be terrified.'

'That was the idea.'

'So you've had your revenge, now why not have another *defixio* made – one that cancels out the first? Then show it to Fortunata and let her see you throw it into the spring… it's been done before.'

Canio briefly considered this suggestion, then shook his head. 'No time – I've got to get back to Corinium.'

At *The Hilaritas*, Fortunata was not in her usual spot behind the bar. When Canio enquired, he was told that she was in her room upstairs, packing for a journey.

'Is she now? Do you know where she's going?' he asked casually.

'Durnovaria way, apparently. She didn't say exactly where, or why she's going,' replied the cook-cum-barman.

'No, I don't suppose she did,' Canio murmured.

He paid what was owing, before going around to the stables and checking that Antares and Bodicca's pony were both being saddled correctly. Then, while Bodicca and Nectovelius waited outside, he went back into *The Hilaritas,* took out a pewter sheet and handed it to the cook-cum-barman. 'Sometime, could you give this to Fortunata. Tell her… tell her that it was so dark inside the temple that, by mistake, I rolled up a blank sheet of pewter which I'd bought for another purpose, then threw the blank one into the sacred spring. This one – the one with the writing on – is the one I meant to throw in… By the way, can you read?'

The man shook his head: he was holding the *defixio* upside down.

'No matter. I have to leave for Corinium now – I've got an appointment there that I have to keep. But, when she gets back from her journey down south, tell Fortunata that I'd be most grateful if she would roll up this sheet and throw it into the sacred spring for me. There's no hurry though – it can wait until she returns from Durnovaria.'

Afterwards, Canio reckoned that Fortunata must have recognised his voice and been listening on the landing, coming downstairs the moment he had left the *stabulum.* They had ridden no more than fifty yards back along the Cunetio road, heading for its junction with the Fosse Way, when he heard a voice, her voice, wailing, 'Canio… Canio! You lousy, lousy, lousy baaastard!'

Looking back, he saw that she was furiously waving the *defixio* in one outstretched hand. Raising an arm in acknowledgement, he urged Antares into a smart trot for several hundred yards, until he was clear of the suburbs and the angry voice of the proprietress of *The Hilaritas.*

When Bodicca caught up she gave him a curious look, but said nothing. Had she guessed? He waited for her to ask, but the question never came. A little later though, he heard her in whispered conversation with an evidently puzzled Nectovelius.

CHAPTER TWENTY-NINE

It was already past noon when, some ten miles north of Aquae Sulis, they reached the settlement of Urticager, little more than a straggle of buildings beside the Fosse Way, mostly on the western side of that highway.

The day was now louring and overcast, with the threat of rain, and the stalls selling amulets and charms appeared to have few customers.

'That? – That's another temple of Apollo,' Canio heard Bodicca say to Nectovelius. He turned to see them both looking towards a large, multisided building set on a knoll of rising ground, a little way back from the highway, its tiers of tiled roofs rising to a central eight-sided dome.

'Like the one where the old priest…?' the boy started to ask, then stopped. *Bad memories*, thought Canio.

'Yes, like the one back in the Niger Hills,' Bodicca said quietly. 'Although this one is dedicated to Apollo Cunomaglos.'

'Cuno… what?' the boy queried.

'Cunomaglos, the hound prince – the healer god,' Bodicca explained.

'Which is why the woman on the stall back there was trying to sell me one of her little copper dogs,' said Canio.

'In the temple,' Bodicca continued, twisting in the saddle so that she could see Nectovelius's face, 'the priests keep a hound, and sick people believe that if it licks whatever part of their body is afflicted they will get well again.'

'But the poor bastards rarely do,' muttered Canio. 'I need a drink.'

By then they were outside a shabby-looking *taberna*, which stood only a few yards from the small stone bridge carrying the highway over a shallow brook. Canio dismounted, went inside and emerged shortly afterwards sipping from a clayware beaker of barley beer.

'Don't we get any?' Bodicca enquired pointedly.

By way of an answer, Canio, still sipping, gestured behind him, and moments later a thin girl of about fifteen appeared carrying a beaker in each hand. These she handed to Bodicca and Nectovelius, after they had dismounted.

When they had finished drinking, and leaving Canio to mind the horses, the pair started walking towards the temple, Bodicca saying that she wanted to see if the place was still as she remembered it.

'Don't be long,' Canio called after them. 'We've still a way to go.'

But he was on his third beaker of beer before they returned.

'Well, what did you think of it?' he asked Nectovelius.

'It's got eight sides, I counted them – and Bodicca says it's falling down,' the boy replied.

'Falling down – really?' Canio was sceptical.

'I think it will, before long,' Bodicca confirmed. 'There are great cracks in the walls, some wide enough to put your hand in. And the roofs leak: there were puddles on the floors.' Canio thought she sounded genuinely saddened by what she had seen.

'And the dog died last month, so the priest said,' the boy added.

'What dog?'

'The dog that licked the sick people. And that place over there,' Nectovelius said, pointing to the long, open-fronted building facing the brook, 'is where the sick people slept, waiting for Apollo to send them dreams and make them well again. But there's nobody in there now though.'

'The dog probably licked them and caught something nasty. That's what killed it.'

'Don't you believe that the gods sometimes send us dreams, Canio? Or do you think it's always just our hopes and fears and consciences that weave them?'

'You tell me, wise woman – if you can.'

'I'll tell you what Vilbia told me: that Saturninus dreamed of a tall stone with the name Caelofernus carved on it. A stone which turned into a man, who then killed him. And then, only a few days later, Saturninus disappeared near an old cemetery where there was a tombstone, raised years and years before, over the ashes of a man whose name was Caelofernus. If that dream wasn't sent by a god – or goddess – then where did it come from?'

Canio couldn't answer that one. And didn't want to. He climbed back up into Antares' saddle and said, 'Come on, let's try to get to Alba Muri before the rain comes.'

As they rode across the bridge over the brook, Canio noticed a great crack in the stone parapet, with a little hart's tongue fern growing out of it. He reflected that, only ten years before, it would have been repaired long before that fern had had a chance to grow.

They rode on, past faded straw-coloured tall grasses and miniature forests of the brittle, bleached, broken and desiccated stems of the cow parsley that had made the roadsides a sea of swaying white as the warm May breezes sighed through them.

Ten more miles of riding northwards on the Fosse Way brought them to the town of Alba Muri, which sprawled for the better part of a mile along both sides of the road. The sun, glimpsed through occasional gaps in the low grey clouds, was still some way above the horizon in the south-west sky as they rode along the main street towards the stone bridge that carried the highway over the little river, a tributary of the Flumen Abona, which bisected the town.

Alba Muri lay only fifteen miles south of Corinium, and Canio had passed through it quite a few times in his army days.

When he was still some distance from the bridge he heard loud, angry voices coming from that direction. As he came closer the source became apparent: two large ox-drawn wagons had met in the centre of the bridge, and neither driver would give way to the other.

From the personal nature of the abuse, Canio guessed that the drivers were old acquaintances, although not the best of friends. Each carried a long ox goad, a flexible willow pole tipped with an iron spike, which they were jabbing threateningly at each other, although of course neither goad was anywhere near long enough to reach the other man as he sat on his bench seat.

Canio was tired and the hold-up irritated him. He was still wondering whether to wait for the argument to subside or to try squeezing past, when the man on the far wagon dropped his goad and grabbed a wicked-looking cudgel. Springing down from the seat he started running towards the other driver, shouting that he was going to settle with the bastard once and for all.

Not intimidated in the slightest, the other driver leapt down from his own wagon grasping a club the size of a small tree trunk in both hands and waited for the other to come to him.

By then a noisy crowd of onlookers had formed. Casually scanning across the faces of the onlookers, men and women and children too, Canio saw apprehension on a few, but on the majority only excitement; the eager anticipation of seeing a violent confrontation where blood was going to be shed. Such fights, as he knew only too well, were looked on as the successors to the gladiatorial combats which once, well before his time, had been staged in the amphitheatre at Corinium. And these amateur affairs had the advantage of having no admission charge.

He watched as, grunting and cursing, the two wagoners savagely attacked each other, alternately swinging their cudgels or attempting to block the other's blows. Soon the curses were punctuated with agonised gasps and yelps of pain, as one combatant or the other received a glancing blow from the iron-hard wood.

But by then Bodicca had evidently seen enough. Edging her pony past Antares, she trotted past on the far side of the wagons, easing between the wheels and the stone parapet of the bridge. Canio shrugged and followed.

The *mansio* in Alba Muri was run by a man called Sigilius, a sometime drinking companion of Canio's and a veteran of eighteen years' service with various units on the northern frontier under the *Dux Britanniarum*. Fortunately, for him, his service had ended some four years before the *Barbarica Conspiratio* of 367. If it had not, as he never tired of telling anyone who would listen, he would be as dead as many of his former comrades now were.

Sigilius made them all welcome, coming to sit at their table as they were eating and telling Canio the latest gossip from the surrounding district.

'Any news from the wider world – has anything interesting been happening in the capital of our beloved province?' Canio enquired casually, nodding towards the north, after hinting, but not actually saying, that he had been away for some time. What he really wanted to know was, *Has anyone been looking for me?*

'Nothing important's happened, not that I'm aware of. They say a calf with two heads was born a week ago, not two miles from here, though I never saw it myself. And someone told me that in Corinium an old man called Fraomarius had been found with his throat cut. Thieves, I suppose – although from what I heard he had nothing worth stealing.'

But it seems that Castor killed him anyway. Nothing about Crotilio though, Canio thought, relieved but also puzzled. *Surely he's dead, isn't he? I certainly hit the man hard enough. But if he really was dead, why hadn't word leaked out? There must be*

228

plenty of people who'd be happy to spread the good news if they thought that evil swine had been ferried across the Styx.

The oil lamps and candles had been lit for some time when a man came into the *mansio* and announced excitedly that the fight between the two wagoners had been the best he'd seen in months. And that one of them – a man whose name Canio heard, or misheard, as Donatus – had had an arm broken below the elbow where his opponent's cudgel had caught it.

'Blood all over them both: heads, faces, hands – everywhere,' the man concluded, apparently well satisfied with the evening's entertainment.

CHAPTER THIRTY

5th November

It was the morning of the fifth day of November, the nones, the day of the deadline imposed by Sabinus. But Canio was in no great hurry to leave Alba Muri – something which Bodicca evidently found curious, although she could not have known the significance of the date (and he had no intention of satisfying her curiosity). He continued eating a leisurely breakfast with Sigilius, before paying what was owed and going out to the stables to saddle Antares.

Confident now that he possessed a replica of the original Hecate figurine good enough to deceive both Peltrasius and Civilis, he was determined to make *Praeses* Sabinus wait until almost the last moment of this last day before handing it over to him.

He was well aware that it was a feeble act of defiance, and poor revenge for the metaphorical ox goads that Sabinus and Castor had jabbed into his hide, but it was better than nothing. Or so he told himself.

Despite the slow start, by noon they were within six miles of Corinium, at a place where the Fosse Way passed close to a tract of open woodland.

There Canio halted and looked around. When he was as certain as he could be that this was indeed the place he remembered, he rode alongside Bodicca and said, 'I want you and Nectovelius to go ahead of me into the city. And when you're there, ask around after me – tell people that you'd arranged to meet me in Aquae Sulis a week or so back, but that I'd never turned up. Be discreet though: only ask in one or two *tabernae,* and then sit back and listen for anything that might be of interest to me. I'll wait here until mid-afternoon or so, then I'll follow you to the city.'

As he should have anticipated, Bodicca was mistrustful. 'So, you want me to see what reaction the mention of your name brings? Any particular reason?'

'Well, since you ask, last month I was involved in a slight disagreement with a few people in Corinium, and it's just possible that some of the ill-feeling may still be lingering.'

'What people?' When he didn't reply immediately she added, 'Canio, I'm not going anywhere unless you tell me.'

'Nobody you'd know.'

'Who?' she demanded.

Canio hesitated, then realised that knowing the truth was likely to ensure a certain amount of discretion on her part. 'Does the name Julius Castor mean anything to you?'

'You had a slight disagreement with that evil man? You surprise me, Canio – I thought you would have picked your enemies with more care.'

Canio waited for her to ask if this disagreement was in any way connected with the Hecate figurine, but when she didn't, he said simply, 'I usually do, but the dice don't always fall the way you want them to. Oh, and I may have killed a man called Crotilio,' he added casually. 'Have you heard of him?'

'Crotilio! That must have been quite some disagreement.' She frowned, then asked, 'But why didn't that *mansionarius,* Sigilius, mention it back in Alba Muri? Surely he would have heard if Crotilio had been sent across the dark river.'

Same thought, same river. 'Interesting question that,' Canio replied. 'I don't know, I really don't. Perhaps I didn't kill the evil bastard after all, just gave him a headache that old Silenus would have had to get drunk for a month to achieve.'

'Not dead? That is a pity.' She was silent for several moments, then said, 'Very well, I'll go to Corinium. Ride up to the Aquae Sulis Gate an hour before sunset. If we're there, Nectovelius and myself, standing like mourners among the graves in one of the cemeteries that lie between the amphitheatre and the gate, then you'll know it's not safe for you to enter the city.'

'And if you're not there?'

'It may mean that I have heard nothing, so perhaps it's safe. Or it may mean that the mere mention of your name has caused me to be arrested. You'll have to decide for yourself, won't you? Farewell, Canio... until we meet again.'

And with that Bodicca flicked the reins and started her pony trotting northwards. She did not once look back, but Nectovelius did, turning frequently to watch him, even waving several times, until they had dwindled to insect-size in the distance. He resisted for a while, then waved back.

In reality, he knew that he would be riding into Corinium that evening, whether Bodicca and the boy were waiting in the cemetery or not. He had sent them away because their presence would be a constant reminder that his copy of the Hecate figurine, perfect though he believed it to be, was just that – a copy, not the genuine article.

And instinctively he knew that, from the moment he was to "find" it, the copy must become the original. Not just in the eyes of everyone he met, but in his own as well. He must behave as though he believed the lie absolutely: the lie must become the truth.

Two and a half summers had passed since that fateful meeting with the deserter Orgillus, and woodland that seems scarcely to change from month to month can appear markedly different after the passing of three growing seasons.

If the hacked and slashed and trampled brambles and nettles had not betrayed the place where Castor and Peltrasius must have hunted unsuccessfully for the figurine a few weeks before, Canio realised that he himself would have had difficulty in pinpointing the exact spot.

But such uncertainty was to his advantage, for surely Peltrasius too would have had trouble in identifying the place where he had so contemptuously thrown the original figurine away? (Although Canio was doubtful whether he would have admitted any such uncertainty to Castor or Sabinus.)

Waiting until no other travellers were in sight, he tied Antares' reins to a tree branch some distance from the highway, then walked over to an area where great thickets of brambles and bracken grew, some little distance away from the area that Castor had searched.

Pulling the hood of his *cucullus* over his head for protection and drawing his dagger, he then crawled on his hands and knees, slowly, painfully and with muttered curses, between the vicious thorn-fanged briars, until he was some six feet into the largest bramble thicket.

There, the knees of his *bracae* trousers already stained and soaking, he used the dagger to make a small scrape in the accumulated years of sodden leaf litter. In the scrape, about an inch below the surface, he placed the Hecate figurine, then covered it up, making sure that the newest leaf litter was on top, to match the surrounding debris of the summer just gone.

He then inched his way back out of the thicket, cursing again every time one of the stiff, arching stems snagged his *cucullus* or scratched him, particularly on his exposed face or hands. Once out, he stood and ran a hand across his cheeks, seeing the thin streaks of blood from where the briars had caught him. He grunted with something close to amusement at the thought that those scratches would lend a certain authenticity to the epic tale he would tell Sabinus.

Needing witnesses to the heroic labours which would result in his discovery of the figurine, he walked back to the highway and waited. And waited.

At last, after a dozen or more unsuitable travellers had passed, he spotted three men approaching on foot from the south. And as they came nearer he recognised one of them, a mosaicist who went by the name of Glaucus. He thought he recognised the other two as well, although he couldn't recall their names.

Concealed as he was against the background of trees and bushes, he was fairly confident that they had not yet noticed him. So, drawing his *spatha*, he moved back amongst the undergrowth and began energetically slashing at a clump of brown and withering bracken, stopping every few moments to peer down at the ground he had uncovered, to give the impression that he was frantically searching for something.

When, out of the corner of his eye, he saw that the three men on the highway were almost level with himself he turned and waved. 'Hey, Glaucus – want to earn a *siliqua* or two?'

Glaucus, a small wiry man in his mid-twenties, stopped, glanced at his companions, then called back, 'It's Canio, isn't it? Or should I call you Claudius Caninus now, Master?'

'You can call me whatever you like, if you help me search.'

'Search for what?'

'For a small *orichalcum* figurine – two years ago somebody threw it into the undergrowth somewhere around here, and now I want to find it.'

'Why?'

'Never mind why – are you interested in earning a *siliqua* each, or are you rich enough already?'

One of the other men, younger than Glaucus, in his late teens probably, gave a bitter laugh. 'Oh yes, we're rich all right. Five whole days we've been working for Egnatius Ligur at his villa back there,' he said, gesturing over towards the south-west, 'and in the end all we got were four *siliquae* between the three of us.'

'So come and help me, and maybe you'll earn that much in an afternoon.'

Glaucus looked to his two companions. 'We'll do it,' said one. 'Where do you want us to look?'

'In this area around here,' said Canio, throwing his arms wide and pointing with his *spatha* as he turned though a semicircle. 'Concentrate on the patches of bracken and brambles, places where the figurine wouldn't be easy to see.'

'You're sure it's here though?' Glaucus asked, eyeing the great clumps of brambles unenthusiastically.

'I'm sure of nothing,' Canio said disingenuously, 'but you'll get paid whether you find it or not. Although,' he added quickly, 'I'll give two *siliquae* to the man who does find it.'

With his *spatha* he hacked three stout poles from a small spinney of ash saplings on the other side of the highway, trimmed off the tops and gave one to each of the three men.

In the process he learnt the names of the other two: the youth was called Olondus, and the third, a tallish, stooped, older man, was Cintusmus. *Glaucus, Olondus and Cintusmus.* He committed those names to memory for possible future use: they would add extra credibility to the tale he would tell Sabinus.

Then he set all three to work, moving eastwards away from the highway, in a line about a hundred yards from the bramble patch where the figurine was hidden. Time was passing, but he let it pass, conscious that, in retrospect, it would appear suspicious if the figurine were to be found too quickly.

He himself formed the northern end of the line, setting the pace as he used his *spatha* to energetically push aside the bracken, nettles and brambles and prod the lank grass and leaf litter exposed.

When they had reached a point some hundred and fifty yards east of the Fosse Way, Canio called a halt, saying he was sure that the figurine could not be this far from the highway. He directed the three mosaic workers to move south, and when the line was re-formed they began moving back westwards towards the highway.

As they steadily worked their way backwards and forwards, all the while getting closer to the place where the figurine lay, the featureless grey-white clouds of the morning slid away from the face of the sun. In the near-windless air it became almost as bright and warm as mid-summer. Was it, thought Canio, an auspicious sign? In a superstitious age, even he could not stop himself from noticing things which could be interpreted as omens, good or bad. He even dared to hope that the Dark Lady herself was smiling upon him.

West, then east, then west again they worked, until at last they came to the great bramble patch. There Glaucus and the other two halted, realising that their ash poles, which could push aside bracken and nettles and small patches of brambles with relative ease, would be of little use against the head-high, unyielding tangle of briars.

Canio had anticipated this. Swinging his *spatha* two-handed like a scythe, he began chopping through the bases of the tough, woody stems, before urging the other three to lift the cut briars aside with their poles and begin probing the exposed leaf litter beneath.

Before long they were almost at the place where the figurine was buried, but letting nothing show on his face, Canio kept slashing at the spiteful, arching stems.

And then Cintusmus was searching the actual spot. Canio continued hacking through the brambles, risking the occasional sideways glance and readying himself to express excitement and delight.

But nothing happened. Cintusmus moved on, past what Canio was almost certain was the spot where the figurine was hidden. Of course, the place looked different with the brambles cleared and the leaf litter rooted over, but even so…

Wondering what in sweet Venus's name to do next, he continued slashing away at the brambles, aware that the tough canes were beginning to blunt the cutting edges of the *spatha*, sometimes forcing him to take more than one stroke to sever each cane.

Surely Cintusmus could not have missed the figurine – it was, after all, only an inch below the surface. And suddenly there came a twinge of superstitious unease: perhaps, to punish his impiety, Hecate had spirited it away... but that was ridiculous, wasn't it?

To suggest to Cintusmus that he search the area again would create suspicion, in even the most gullible of minds, that he had always known that the figurine was there. So more time passed, and still he hacked away at the bramble stems and the mosaic workers flicked the cut stems further away from the bramble patch as they waited for him to finish.

It was that hold-up which proved to be his saviour. For want of anything better to do when they had moved all the cut stems clear of the area, the three men again began prodding the ends of their poles into the thick leaf litter that had accumulated over the seasons, flicking lumps of the black soggy mass of compacted leaves into the air.

'What's that?' Canio heard Olondus mutter, and turned to see the man crouching down and picking something out of the wad of black, compressed leaves which he had just stirred through. It was the Hecate figurine: blackened *orichalcum* against black leaves, it had been easy to miss.

Canio hurriedly sheathed his *spatha* and snatched the figurine from a startled Olondus. 'That's it – that's it!' he cried, as he carefully wiped off the wet fragments of decayed leaves. 'I knew it had to be here – I knew it! Whatever that fool Peltrasius said.' And he stood cradling the figurine in both hands and gazing lovingly at it.

He was conscious that he was probably overdoing the rapture, but it was necessary to give a performance which Glaucus and his companions would not forget, and could describe if ever they were asked. Which they might well be.

'So that's what you were looking for, was it?' Glaucus asked, somewhat unnecessarily.

'It most certainly was,' Canio confirmed. 'Well done, all of you, well done! And here are a few tokens of my appreciation.' He dug into his purse and counted out seven *siliquae*: two each for Glaucus and Cintusmus, and three for Olondus who had found the figurine.

He carefully finished cleaning the figurine before stowing it back inside a pocket of his tunic. Then he untethered Antares, mounted, and rode back to the highway.

Before he started the horse trotting north towards Corinium he gave a cheery wave to the three mosaic workers. He was well aware that they must think him brain-sick, paying good silver for a small piece of old *orichalcum*, but it didn't matter. What did matter was that they would remember this day for months to come.

The sun was still shining when he noticed two large peacock butterflies basking on the sun-warmed stones of the highway, their rufous open wings displaying four multicoloured eye-spots. They flew up as Antares approached, but, glancing back, Canio saw them settle again to soak up those last dregs of summer's warmth, before the coming of the long sleep of hibernation or the endless sleep of death.

CHAPTER THIRTY-ONE

That sun, which earlier had been so unseasonably warm, was sinking in the clear south-west sky and steadily cooling on his back as he travelled the remaining miles to Corinium. He rode at a leisurely pace, rehearsing the story that he was going to tell Sabinus.

Approaching the city he rode slowly past the dwarfing green bulk of the amphitheatre, seeing the lank grasses on the upper slopes quivering in the chill evening breeze as he scanned cautiously from side to side.

Just beyond the amphitheatre he reined Antares to a halt and gazed across the cemeteries that lay on both sides of the Fosse Way. In the fading light he saw a woman standing among the mounds, her back turned away from him. Tense, he waited until she turned around. It was not Bodicca.

He should have been relieved by her absence, but instead felt only a nagging uncertainty. Perhaps somebody who knew his recent history really had overheard Bodicca enquiring after him, and that had led to her arrest? If so, her non-appearance did not mean that it was safe for him to enter the city: quite the opposite.

And he was conscious of something else – something which added to the disquiet he already felt. He was fairly certain that beneath one of the anonymous, still-raw mounds lay the body of Eutyches, sometime bailiff of the Villa Censorini estate – the man who had betrayed Antoninus to *Praeses* Sabinus. He wondered too if Macrinius Lunaris, the *agens in rebus* whose obsession with destroying Antoninus had, with a grim irony, led to his own destruction, was also out there somewhere?

Uneasily he remembered that endless July day when, in Tullus the undertaker's workshop, he had angrily tipped the *agens'* stiffening corpse out of its stone coffin, before appropriating that same coffin to give Antoninus a half-decent funeral on the slopes of Coel's Hill. In the weeks that followed he had deliberately never enquired as to how or where Lunaris himself had eventually been buried.

Canio did not believe – or, in truth, did not want to believe – in any form of life after death, fearing that eternal existence as a helpless, disembodied spirit would be far more terrible than merciful oblivion. But in the gathering dusk of that November afternoon he could not stop himself from wondering whether the malevolent shades of those two men were somewhere near, their dead eyes watching him, wishing him ill.

The massive wooden gates of the Aquae Sulis Gateway still stood wide open. Briefly he speculated that it might be wiser to leave Antares and try to sneak into the city on foot. But the only way in was through one or other of the city gates, and if he were to be challenged then his chances of escape would be better on horseback.

Wrapping the *cucullus* around him and pulling the hood as far over his head as it would go, he nudged Antares into motion and began riding unhurriedly towards the gate. There were two soldiers guarding it, one on each side, both with spears. Canio did not recognise either of them, but that did not mean that they would not recognise him.

Suddenly he became aware of the drumming of hooves and the rattle of iron-bound wheels behind him. The saddle creaked as he twisted around to see a carriage drawn by two horses approaching fast, liveried outriders in front and behind. He recognised that carriage: it belonged to Cicereius Felix, a man who owned both a villa estate some miles away to the north and a sumptuous town house here in Corinium.

Realising that Felix would take a dim view of being held up at the gate by guards questioning a traveller in front, particularly if he were trying to get to the Verulamium Gate on the other side of the city before it closed, Canio kicked his heels into Antares' flanks and began riding at a smart trot just in front of the leading outrider. Had he been alone then perhaps the guards would have stopped and questioned him. As it was, he passed unhindered between the high stone watchtowers of the gateway, and so entered the city.

He continued trotting briskly in front of the carriage as it rattled up the *Decumanus Maximus*, as the Fosse Way was designated as it passed through Corinium. At the junction with the *Cardo Maximus*, the other main street of the city – the one which ran past the forum and the *praetorium*, *Praeses* Sabinus's official residence – he turned right. The carriage and its outriders carried straight on, confirming his suspicion that Cicereius Felix was indeed heading for the Verulamium Gate.

Even with night approaching there were still plenty of people about in the streets. He ambled Antares through the crowds, glancing repeatedly from side to side, but failing to spot either Bodicca or Nectovelius, although he was aware that they could have been there somewhere, hidden among the crowds.

At the entrance to the forum he dismounted and led Antares under the archway and into the great paved forum piazza. The shops in the colonnaded porticos on the east and west sides were beginning to put up their shutters, the stalls in the centre were being dismantled and packed into the waiting carts, the crowds starting to drift away.

In the centre of the piazza, great bronze Jupiter stood on top of his soaring limestone column, scarcely changed after more than two centuries, grim and dark against the darkening sky. He found himself wondering how long it would be before Sabinus ordered the statue to be torn down? There were rumours that the newly-appointed bishop was already making outraged noises that such a pagan monument should still be standing in the heart of a provincial capital of an empire that by then had been nominally Christian for over fifty years.

Still leading Antares, he walked towards the northern end of the forum, where a pair of double gates set in a stone ornamental screen wall separated the raised outer court of the *praetorium* from the forum piazza. Outside the gates, at the top of a low flight of steps, two guards stood, spear butts grounded, their wicked steel tips pointing skywards.

He recognised one of the guards, a soldier called Tetrecus, and realised that the man would certainly recognise him too. He hesitated for a moment, but there was no going back now. Pushing back the hood of his *cucullus*, he said in his best parade-ground-impatient voice, 'Tetrecus? That is you, isn't it? Run and tell the *Vir Perfectissimus* that I have an important message for him.'

Tetrecus peered down at him. 'Canio?'

And Canio realised that, after half a month without a trim, his beard was considerably longer and more unkempt than the little-more-than-stubble-length he preferred. 'Of course it's me. Go and tell Caristanius Sabinus that I'm here. And hurry – it really is urgent.'

'I can't – the *Vir Perfectissimus* isn't here.'

'What! So where in the name of sweet Venus is he?'

'At his villa, I suppose. Left in the middle of the afternoon – I saw his carriage go.'

'He's at Villa Censorini?'

'That was the way he was heading.'

'When will he be back?'

'Who knows? I certainly don't – for some strange reason he never tells me these things.'

'No, I don't suppose he does.'

'If it's really important then you'd better go to Villa Censorini yourself, although I wouldn't fancy riding ten miles on a dark November night.'

But Canio, his brain racing, scarcely heard him. He had no wish to be in Corinium now. Apart from the risk of running into Castor, admittedly unlikely since the dog had probably gone to Villa Censorini with his master, he was now as tense as a scorpio ballista's bowstring in anticipation of his appointment with Sabinus. And when, as he had promised himself, he stood watching the sun rise in tomorrow's dawn, he was absolutely determined that this whole damned business would be finished and done with.

Grabbing one of the saddle horns he sprang up onto Antares' back, wheeled around and rode out of the forum, making the remaining stallholders and bystanders scatter and curse.

Back on the *Decumanus Maximus* he headed at a fast trot through the darkening streets towards the Verulamium Gate on the north-east side of the city. As he passed he noticed oil lamps being lit behind the glazed windows of the rich, and stray gleams of feeble candlelight filtering out from between chinks in the shutters of shops and less affluent dwellings.

Despite it being dusk, to his relief he saw that the gates were still open, which would at least save him an argument with the guards. He trotted Antares briskly under one of the two large central archways of the four-arched gateway flanked by its twin towers, waved his thanks to the guards, clattered over the stone bridge which spanned the Churn brook and then, back on the Fosse Way, started northwards into the gathering night.

CHAPTER THIRTY-TWO

For the first quarter mile he rode past the remaining grim old funerary monuments and massive, weathered tombstones that stood, sentinel like, on both sides of the highway.

In that quarter mile he met only a solitary horseman and two pedestrians, a man and a woman travelling together and muffled against the evening chill, all hurrying to reach the city before the Verulamium Gate closed.

Then nobody. The darkening road was deserted as he travelled ever deeper into the land of night, feeling it closing in around him, the only indication of human life the occasional glow-worm of light from a farmstead or shepherd's bothy far away.

As he jogged along in the estranging darkness he felt the nervous tension which had buoyed him up in Corinium slowly seeping away, to be replaced by a vague, gnawing unease. *Why hadn't Tetrecus so much as mentioned the killing of Crotilio?*

It must surely mean that Castor – and Sabinus too – had suppressed the news. But why?

Because, he told himself, Sabinus needed the figurine to ingratiate himself with the *Vicarius*. And Sabinus obviously believed that he, Canio, was the only person who could get it for him. But if Sabinus had alerted every soldier under his command to search for him – giving the killing of Crotilio as the official reason – then there was a very real danger that such a manhunt might result in his death, with the secret of the figurine's whereabouts dying with him.

So, no Canio, no figurine for Sabinus to present to Civilis, and no chance of Civilis recommending Sabinus for the post of *vicarius* when it became vacant. Also, Civilis was reputed to be a zealous Christian, and as such was indeed someone who might well feel compelled to acquire and destroy the Hecate figurine, with its unsettling pagan background.

So Sabinus's stated reason for wanting the figurine, and also for his not unleashing a manhunt to find him, both made perfect sense. And yet, and yet...

In the darkness the slow miles passed.

The night was chill, and becoming steadily colder under a near-cloudless sky. Perhaps, he wondered, there would be a frost before dawn? He glanced upwards. There was as yet no moon, but the great dome of black sky glittered with innumerable stars.

Looking ahead he saw the slight puffs of vapour from Antares' nostrils condensing in the night air. And for at least the fifth time since he had branched off the Fosse Way, some seven miles north of Corinium, the fingers of his right hand strayed under his *cucullus*, feeling the little *orichalcum* figurine now hidden in one of his belt pouches, reassuring himself that it was still there.

The strangely alien shapes of trees and bushes that loomed out of the night were unsettling, but the low murmurs of the Coln, the little river which lisped and swirled unseen in the darkness as it there ran parallel to the trackway, were a comfortingly constant presence.

When, away to his left, he recognised through the gloom the outline of the old temple, dedicated long ago to the hunter goddess Diana and to Silvanus, god of woods and fields, he knew that he could be no more than half a mile from his destination. Unused since Censorinus died, the massive structure of weathered limestone sat brooding on a terrace cut into the hillside above the Coln, dark against the black woods behind it.

245

As he passed by he had instinctively glanced towards it, barely able to make out the row of great cylindrical columns supporting the roof over the portico entrance. In that first glance he thought he had seen something that could have been a human figure, standing beside one of the columns. He had begun to look away before the image fully registered on his consciousness, and when he looked again the figure was gone, leaving him uncertain as to whether it had really been there at all.

Another quarter mile passed and then, through the semi-leafless branches of a wayside tree, he saw flashing pinpricks of light. A hundred yards further and the whole of Villa Censorini came into view, standing in the starlight on the rising ground above the Coln.

He reined Antares to a halt and sat gazing at the great villa, fatalistically aware that, whatever uneasiness he was increasingly feeling, the dice had already been cast out into the darkness, and Hecate alone knew what numbers they showed.

Yet as he reached under his *cucullus* and stroked the head of the *orichalcum* figurine and touched the tips of the tiny sword and torch she held, he felt confidence returning. He told himself that she was perfect, exactly as Peltrasius would remember her. His face relaxed into something approaching a smile, picturing the look on Sabinus's face as he handed him the figurine and told the tale of his heroic quest – a quest which had ended in her discovery in the very place where that fool Peltrasius had thrown her away.

Of necessity the tale would be something less than the whole truth. But, he told himself, Sabinus would believe it anyway, simply because he would want to believe it, because he wanted the figurine. And *"men believe what they want to believe"* – he was now almost certain that it was Saturninus who had said it. Nudging Antares into motion, he began trotting the last few hundred yards up to the villa.

There was still no moon visible. And then it came to him, something which he should have realised long before: that this was the night of the new moon. Hecate's moon. Sometime after dawn tomorrow it would rise, unseen, in the south-eastern sky. And in the evening, not long after sunset, a knife-edge-thin crescent would be briefly visible in the south-west. Whatever happened, he was determined to see that crescent moon slip below the horizon.

The watchtower-flanked gateway into the villa's lower courtyard was ablaze with light from two great torches flaring in sconces projecting from the watchtower walls. As he approached, Canio caught the choking smell of the combustible mixture of sulphur and lime with which the tightly-wrapped rags had been saturated. Antares must have detected it even before he did, whinnying restlessly.

As he came looming out of the darkness, one of the two soldiers guarding the gate shouted, 'Halt! Identify yourself!' and took several cautious paces forward, spear grasped with both hands

'Claudius Caninus,' Canio shouted back. He was fairly sure he recognised the soldier from his last visit, a little over two weeks before.

'And your business here?'

'The *Praeses* wishes to see me – I have a message concerning something which he ordered me to find.'

'What something?'

'Something which he ordered me to find,' Canio repeated. 'Kindly tell him that I'm here.'

'The *Vir Perfectissimus* is not to be disturbed.'

'Then tell Julius Castor.'

'I can't disturb him either.'

Canio felt a near-overwhelming urge to punch the obstructive man's stupid face. 'Go tell Castor I'm here, Hades take you!' he snarled. 'Or I'll see you tied to a tree and flogged – and it will be

Castor who'll be doing the flogging… Unless Sabinus wants to do it himself, which he very well might.'

The soldier hesitated, disconcerted by Canio's anger. He retreated and held a whispered conversation with his colleague, then called to another soldier who had emerged from the lower courtyard. There was another murmured exchange, followed by the sound of running feet which faded into the night.

'I've sent to tell Castor,' the first soldier announced. 'And may the gods help you if you're lying, because nobody else will,' he muttered.

Canio bared his teeth and gave him a contemptuous leer.

They waited, the flickering light of the torches playing on the bodies of men and horse. He heard footsteps rapidly approaching, and suddenly a young officer strode out of the gateway and stood staring at Canio. He carried the knob-topped vine stick of a centurion in one of the old legions, and wore a heavy cloak pinned at the shoulder by an elaborate crossbow brooch of polished silver which sparkled in the torchlight.

'So, you are Claudius Caninus, are you? I'm told you have a message for the *Vir Perfectissimus* – is that true?' By his accent, Canio guessed that the young man was the son of a wealthy family, probably given a position on Sabinus's staff in return for a donation from his father. Gold coins or handsome silver tableware, perhaps? – he certainly had not come up through the ranks.

'Of course it's true.' Canio tapped the side of his *cucullus* below which the Hecate figurine lay hidden in his belt pouch.

'And exactly what is this message?'

Canio shook his head. 'I'm not at liberty to tell you – it's for Sabinus's ears only: go back and check with him if you don't believe me.'

For several moments the young centurion looked as if he might insist, but the night air was chilly and Canio suspected that the man would be nervous about delaying what might be an important official message for Sabinus. If he did think that, then so much the better. The man hesitated for a few moments longer, then said abruptly, 'Very well. Dismount and follow me.'

So Canio climbed out of the saddle and led Antares through the gateway and into the wide lower courtyard, the place where, four short months before, he had brought Antoninus's body back from Corinium. He noticed how utterly different it now seemed, from the warmth of a bright July day to the cold darkness of a November night.

He took off his *cucullus* and draped it over Antares' saddle. At the sight of the scabbarded *spatha* hanging at his hip the centurion stopped abruptly.

'By what authority are you carrying a sword?'

'As a *honestior* I have every right to do so,' Canio replied irritably. For a moment he thought the centurion was going to challenge him to prove he really was a *honestior*. But, standing half a head taller than him, Canio gave the man an impatient glare which was effective in dissuading him.

'Nevertheless, I must insist that you hand it over before I escort you to the *Vir Perfectissimus*.'

Canio complied: he had expected as much.

'Are you carrying any other weapons?'

Canio exhaled audibly. 'No… and take care of that *spatha* – I killed a dozen Alamanni with it at the battle of Argentoratum.' Which he thought might impress the young centurion, or at the very least convince him that he was not a man to be obstructed without risking unpleasant consequences.

But he had no intention of handing over the wicked little sheathed dagger, tucked into the waistband of his *bracae* trousers and hidden by his knee-length tunic.

The young centurion shouted, 'Groom!' and moments later a man materialised out of the darkness from the direction of the lower south wing and led Antares away.

'Give him a good feed of oats,' Canio called after him, although he hoped he would not be staying long.

With the young centurion leading the way and two soldiers following behind, Canio was escorted across the rising ground of the lower courtyard, up the steps, straight through the gatehouse of the cross-gallery, and out into the ornamental gardens of the upper courtyard.

Their feet crunched on the wide gravel paths as they weaved between the geometrically-shaped herb beds which, on that last day of May, the day of Antoninus's homecoming party, had been fragrant with the scents of mint and rosemary.

There had been peacocks then, strutting fan-tailed among the guests. But now, on this November night, there were no scents and no peacocks, although he noticed that the light escaping from lamps burning in the corridor of the west range gleamed dully on one of the remembered bronze fauns in the centre of a bed, its head thrown back in ecstatic mid-dance.

Arriving at the west range's entrance portico, with its flanking stone columns and triangular pediment above, the young centurion strode in through one leaf of the double doors. Turning left, he led the way down the wide, lamp-lit corridor, its floor paved with a mosaic of intersecting red and blue circles, until they came to the opening on the right-hand side which Canio recognised as the anteroom to the main *triclinium*.

'Wait here,' the man ordered abruptly, and disappeared into the gloom of the anteroom.

Canio heard him knock on the *triclinium* door. There was a pause, a muffled voice, then the door opened and light flooded out. There were more voices, louder this time, and Canio heard the young centurion say, 'Yes, sir… Immediately, sir,' before the man hastily returned.

'The *Vir Perfectissimus* will grant you an audience,' he announced, in a tone that implied that it was he who had persuaded a reluctant Sabinus to grant it.

Canio gave the man a humourless grin, then followed him up the short, three-sided flight of stone steps from the corridor into the anteroom where, on his left, the door to the *triclinium* stood wide open.

'Claudius Caninus, sir.'

And in that moment Canio experienced the same dry-mouthed mixture of eager anticipation and stark fear which he had felt before the battle of Argentoratum.

"*Life a battle, an endless exile in a hostile land,*" as he had once heard someone say, probably misquoting somebody else.

CHAPTER THIRTY-THREE

'Thank you, Vibius Natalis. Now leave us, but don't go far – wait in the anteroom.' The speaker was Caristanius Sabinus himself. He sat at the great table of polished fruitwood that Canio remembered from the summer, when the late Antoninus had been his and Trifosa's host in this same room. Opposite Sabinus sat Julius Castor, and behind Castor stood Peltrasius.

The *triclinium* was warm and there was a lingering aroma of food in the air, although only two wine cups and a flagon, all in embossed silver, now stood on the table. As the eyes of all three men fixed upon him, Canio heard the heavy door thud closed behind him, an ominous sound, putting him uneasily in mind of Crotilio's cell.

Sabinus was magnificently dressed in a long robe of white wool decorated with several red vertical *clavi* strips and at least four large *orbiculi* roundels, the latter beautifully embroidered with bunches of grapes and vine leaves. He eyed Canio with a somewhat less than kindly expression. 'Well, well, well – so it really is you, Caninus. I had a suspicion that you might wait until the last possible moment to turn up, just to irritate me. Have you brought it?'

'Yes, it's here,' said Canio, patting his belt pouch. He was both puzzled and relieved that nobody had mentioned Crotilio – not so far, anyway.

Sabinus opened his arms as if welcoming an old friend. 'Then let me see it – let us all see it.'

So Canio walked towards him across the great Bacchus mosaic, the god standing in the central octagon, from which eight pairs of what he had assumed to be satyrs and maenads radiated outwards. Perhaps it was the tension of the moment, but he had never before fully appreciated what strange, sinister figures those satyr-figures were, made more so by the slowly wavering light of a dozen oil lamps hanging from stands down both sides of the room and the darkness of the encircling night outside, visible through the small, high windows.

When he was within a couple of yards of the table, Castor said sharply, 'That's far enough. Raise your arms.'

Canio slowly did as ordered, and Castor roughly unbuckled his belt pouch and pulled out the Hecate figurine.

'Be careful – don't drop it! Give it to me – quickly, quickly!' Canio noticed how the tone of Sabinus's voice had suddenly changed from sarcastic to excited.

Wordlessly, Castor handed the figurine to Sabinus, who cradled it in both hands and stared down at it, seeming to take in every detail, from Hecate's unsmiling face to the raised torch and sword, from the folds of the drapery of her *stola* to the snarling hound curled at her feet.

He held it close to one ear and gently shook it, no doubt hearing the faint rattle made by the pottery fragments inside the copper tube which Ivomandus had inserted into the mould. Canio saw a faint smile of satisfaction appear on the *Praeses'* face. It seemed that Sabinus recalled what Peltrasius had told him about that rattle.

'Is she exactly as you remember her?' Sabinus asked Peltrasius, who was leaning across the table and moving his head from side to side, the better to see it. 'Well, come round here man, and look properly,' he muttered impatiently.

Canio was conscious of his heart beginning to thump uncomfortably in his chest as Peltrasius turned the figurine over in his hands and examined it closely. Logic told him that, since the man had seen it for only a few moments over two years ago, he must simply be putting on a show for Sabinus. Even so, if he were to reject it out of sheer malice…

'The one I saw had a bright spot on it, where the black had been rubbed away to show the yellow *orichalcum* underneath,' Peltrasius said accusingly. 'That's why I thought it might be gold.'

Both Sabinus and Castor looked inquiringly at Canio.

But Canio had anticipated the question. He sighed. 'Of course the bright spot's gone – what would you expect after two years and more on and under the wet earth?' he asked, with what he considered to be just the right degree of sarcasm.

Sabinus clicked his fingers and held out a hand, into which Peltrasius hurriedly returned the figurine. 'But that missing bright spot apart, is it, or is it not, the figurine which you threw away two years ago?' he asked.

Peltrasius hesitated, then said, 'Yes, sir – I'm almost certain it is.'

'Not a copy then?'

Canio realised that Sabinus wanted to be convinced: he could hear it in his voice. This was good. Very good.

'No, sir.'

'So why didn't you bring it to me sooner?' Sabinus asked Canio. 'Instead of waiting until now?'

'Because it's taken me all this time to find it – and I almost never did.'

'Really? So where was it?' Castor demanded.

'Where Peltrasius threw it, of course. I've been hunting all over the province for that wretched thing for the last two weeks and getting nowhere. And then, this very afternoon, on my way back from Aquae Sulis, I passed the spot near the Fosse Way where we met the deserter, Orgillus, those two years back. By then I was desperate, so I started searching the area. And as I hunted around I realised that the place where you'd been looking wasn't the one where Peltrasius threw it away.'

'How did you know where we'd been looking?' Peltrasius interrupted.

'By the mess you'd made, of course. It still looked as if an *ala* of cavalry had charged through the place. Any more silly questions?'

Peltrasius gave him a dirty look, but said nothing, so Canio continued his story.

'Three men – mosaic workers I think they were – happened to come walking past on their way back to Corinium, so I paid them to help me search. And in the middle of a great bramble patch, hidden by two years' accumulation of dead leaves, one of them found it – where it had been all the time. Yes, you heard correctly – it had been there all this time! I've been running myself ragged trying to find it, and it was just lying there covered by a handful of dead leaves!' He realised that he was piling on the indignation, but was now increasingly confident that he could get away with it.

Sabinus's eyebrows rose, and he stared at Peltrasius. 'I thought you said you were certain that you had searched the place where you threw it away?'

Peltrasius evidently saw trouble looming. 'That's nonsense – he had it all the time!'

'If that were so, then why didn't I bring it to you straight away, instead of putting myself through all this misery?'

Peltrasius had no immediate answer to that question, but while he was trying to think of one, Sabinus asked, 'These three mosaic workers you allege helped you search – I suppose you didn't think to ask their names?'

Canio slowly shook his head as if trying to recall. 'I'm sure one of them said his name was Glaucus, and I think he called another Olondus. But if I ever heard the name of the third I've forgotten it.'

'I see. Well, I'm sure Julius Castor can check out those men in due course. They shouldn't be too hard to find.' Even as he spoke, Sabinus's eyes never left the figurine, which he kept stroking gently with his fingertips.

Then he looked up and frowned slightly, as if something had just occurred to him. 'One thing more, Peltrasius: I seem to recall you saying that, when you met that allegedly mad priest, you stole from him the casket that this lady was once hidden in. That is correct, isn't it?'

'I… wouldn't say I stole it, sir, because I don't believe it ever properly belonged to the man.'

'Don't contradict me. If I say you stole it, you stole it. The question I was about to ask is, where is it now?'

'It's in my possession, sir.' It was Castor who spoke.

'Here, or in Corinium?'

'Here, sir: I thought it would be safer.'

'Then be so good as to go and fetch it.'

'Very good, sir.' And Castor swept out of the *triclinium*.

What followed was a strange interlude, with all three men waiting in complete silence: Sabinus still studying the figurine, Peltrasius shooting sour looks at Canio, who himself was wondering uneasily what, if any, relevance this casket could have.

For him, the time passed agonisingly slowly. At last he heard the door open, and turned to see Castor holding a small rectangular wooden box, dark with age. He set it down on the table in front of Sabinus, and Canio saw that it was devoid of any markings or decoration.

Sabinus lifted the hinged lid to reveal that the solid wood of the interior had been hollowed out into the shape of the Hecate figurine. By the intricate way in which the polished wood had been carved, Canio suspected that it must have followed the shape of its original contents very closely: raised arms, sword, torch, hound – everything. He felt a growing sense of disquiet.

Holding the figurine by the waist, Sabinus laid it very gently onto the casket. Apart from anything else, it was about the length of a grain of wheat too long. He tried it several ways, but it rapidly became apparent to all four men that the casket and the figurine were strangers to one another.

Time passed, and still Sabinus sat staring down at the figurine balanced awkwardly on top of the open casket, as if he did not want to believe what his eyes were telling him. Then he looked up at Canio, his face reddening, his voice rising. 'You swine, Caninus,' he said slowly. 'You foul, mendacious swine! You actually tried to deceive me – me, of all people!' He gazed at Canio, as if scarcely able to believe that anybody would dare do such a thing. 'So where did you get this worthless lump of *orichalcum* from? Well, tell me, damn you!'

Canio rapidly decided that the best defence was to attack. 'As I told you – from the place where this jackass threw it!' he snarled, indicating Peltrasius with a contemptuous sweep of his arm. 'It's obvious what must have happened. The Hecate which that deserter, Orgillus, was carrying wasn't the one which some soldiers – not Orgillus, it seems – stole from that temple in the Niger Hills during the *Conspiratio*. And why should it have been? Orgillus was coming down from Glevum, not up from the South Country – isn't that so, Peltrasius?… Well, isn't it?'

Peltrasius reluctantly agreed, but then added, unhelpfully, that the man might have been in the South Country earlier in that year.

Evidently struggling to keep his temper, Sabinus asked, 'So what am I to tell the *Vicarius*?'

'Tell him the truth – the plain, simple truth. That this is the Hecate figurine that Orgillus had in his possession when he was caught, but, unfortunately, it would appear that it isn't the one that was stolen from that looted temple. I dare say that dozens of copies have been made over the years – even the one from the temple may have been only a copy of some long-lost original.'

It was a perfectly logical explanation, and Canio was rather proud of it – thought up as it was at such short notice – so he could see no logical reason why Sabinus should not accept it.

But Sabinus did not accept it. 'You're still lying, Caninus. You were caught trying to obtain a copy from that man, Fraomarius, in Corinium—'

So you know about Fraomarius, Canio thought. *Did you order him killed, or did faithful dog Castor do it on his own initiative?*

'—but it would appear that you nevertheless went on to truffle out another source of fakes, which is where this one doubtless came from. But I'm certain – absolutely certain – that somewhere, hidden away in your villa or elsewhere, you still have the original figurine. And this time I'm going to get it from you, whatever it takes. Seize him!'

Canio's first instinct was to make a run for it, before he remembered that young fool of a centurion and the other soldiers waiting outside the *triclinium* door. And by the time he had decided to continue trying to talk his way out, Castor and Peltrasius had grabbed him, one arm each.

Sabinus picked up the fake figurine, and appeared to contemplate it for several moments. Then he rose slowly from his high-backed wickerwork armchair, walked up to Canio holding the figurine by the base as though it were a knife, and jabbed it into his face, just below his right eye. Canio tried to twist his head away, but Sabinus's second blow still caught him on the cheek. He felt warm blood trickling from the lacerations the figurine had made. He licked his lips, the slightly salt taste on his tongue.

Through the pain he felt a surge of savage anger rising within him. He hadn't wanted any of this, damn them! But now he wanted – needed – to hurt Sabinus, and hurt him badly. With Castor and Peltrasius gripping them with both hands he could not move his arms, but his feet were another matter.

Sabinus was closing in for another jab. 'Where is it – where? No more time, Caninus, no more lies! You're a dead man, Caninus – did you know that? I can, quite legally, have you executed here and now for the murder of Crotilio, that most excellent servant of the empire... Oh, did you really imagine that I'd forgotten that particular crime? No, Caninus, your only hope of avoiding that richly-deserved fate is to tell me now, this instant, where the real figurine is.'

But Canio was scarcely listening. Anger had overcome discretion and he lashed out with his right foot. The two soldiers tried to snatch him backwards, so the toe of his riding boot missed its target of Sabinus's crotch. But it still caught him on the thigh, producing a yelp of agony.

Sabinus staggered back and collapsed into his chair, his face contorted with rage and pain, the fake figurine clattering onto the mosaic floor. 'Take him outside!' he screamed. 'Bind him so he can't escape, then go and wake... what's that bastard's name – the estate blacksmith?'

'Atepaccius, sir,' said Castor, twisting Canio's right arm painfully behind his back, while Peltrasius punched him in the ribs and called him a dog turd.

'Wake Atepaccius and order him to prepare his forge. And when the charcoal is glowing red hot, come and tell me. And then, Caninus, you will tell us where that figurine – the real, original figurine – actually is.'

'How many times must I tell you? I have no idea where—' Canio gasped, before Peltrasius punched him in the ribs again.

'Oh, have you not? Well, it's of no matter: I can assure you that when the smoking iron is applied to various parts of your body, you will experience a divine revelation. A god will whisper into your ear, telling you exactly where the original figurine is to be found – I've seen such things happen, several times.' Sabinus smiled, as if finding the recollection amusing. 'Take him outside and tell me when Atepaccius is ready.'

Castor and Peltrasius together started dragging Canio backwards towards the *triclinium* door. Looking up, with eyes watering and slightly unfocussed from the blows, Canio saw the blurred image of Bacchus in the fresco on the far wall – the god standing in his chariot drawn by two snarling leopards, the satyrs and maenads of his *thiasos* whirling and dancing towards him – images of the happy, carefree life he had once dreamed would be his.

CHAPTER THIRTY-FOUR

He heard the door behind him open and felt a draught of cold air on his neck. There was a babble of voices and then a woman wearing a *cucullus* over a long *stola* swept past him, the young centurion, Vibius Natalis, scrambling after her.

'My apologies, sir,' he explained, flustered, 'but this woman claims she has something which you are most anxious to acquire.'

Squinting, Canio could just make out that the woman was offering something to Sabinus, something which she held in her left hand.

And before Sabinus could speak, she said, 'I believe that this is the object which you have been seeking.'

Canio was almost certain he recognised that voice. *Bodicca?...* He tried to stare directly at her, but the *cucullus* hood was pulled well forwards, hiding her face in shadow.

Apparently fearing that Sabinus was in danger, Castor released his hold on Canio and strode towards the woman. But Sabinus, staring at whatever it was that she was holding, barked, 'No!' and raised an open palm to bring him to a halt.

Using his now-free hand to rub his watering eyes, Canio saw that what she was holding out in front of her was another figurine, one so similar to his fake that it had to be another Hecate.

'This is what you desire, isn't it?' she asked Sabinus.

Hearing her voice again, Canio was now certain that it was Bodicca.

'Give it to me – let me see it!'

Wordlessly she passed the figurine to Sabinus, who took it in both hands and examined it minutely. Even from where he was standing, Canio glimpsed the spot on the drapery of the *stola* where the black patina had been rubbed away, the exposed *orichalcum* dull yellow.

Sabinus held the figurine an inch from one ear and shook it gently. Evidently what he heard pleased him, because a thin smile appeared on his lips. The smile faded, and he said crisply, 'Castor, bring me that damned casket again – quickly, man, quickly!'

Castor hurried to obey, and Sabinus, holding the figurine horizontally in his cupped hands, laid it gently down on top of the casket's carved-out recess.

His view blocked by Castor's body, Canio could not see the result, but he did hear Peltrasius's low murmur of astonishment.

'A perfect fit, I think you will agree,' Sabinus said quietly. Then, looking up at Bodicca, he asked, 'So where did you get it – from where Caninus had hidden it, I suppose?'

'Caninus? Who's Caninus?'

'That man over there, of course,' said Sabinus, pointing to Canio.

Bodicca turned. 'Him? I've never seen him before.'

'Then how did it come to be in your possession?'

'A woman gave it to me, on behalf of a man she once met on the steps of that old temple back there – the one between the woods and the Coln.'

'What woman?'

'You don't know her, and her name would signify nothing to you.'

'And the man – did I know him?'

'No, you never knew him – or not in any meaningful sense of the word.'

'So what was his name?'

'Lucius – his name was Lucius, I believe.'

'Lucius?' Sabinus frowned, his eyes still on the Hecate figurine. 'No, I can't offhand recall anyone with that *praenomen*. What was his full name – surely I deserve to know that?'

'That is the least of what you deserve, *Vir Perfectissimus*. And later this night, when you have witnessed the power of that figurine to give you what you most desire in all the world, then I will tell you his name.'

There was silence for the length of several heartbeats, and then Sabinus said briskly, 'Very well. Leave us, Natalis – and take Caninus with you: I haven't finished with him yet. And do not, under any circumstances, come back in until I summon you – do you understand?'

'Very good, sir,' replied the young centurion, and he and the two soldiers with him dragged Canio out into the anteroom and closed the *triclinium* door behind them.

In the anteroom Canio wiped the streaks of blood from his face with the back of his hand and wondered what in the name of sweet Venus was going on. If, as he now suspected, that really was the original, ancient Hecate figurine that Bodicca had just handed to Sabinus, then she could only have acquired it from Vilbia. Which surely proved that she knew all the time that Vilbia was its keeper, despite her denials when they first met. *But why would Vilbia—?*

And then it came to him – something that he should have realised in the *triclinium*, if his brain hadn't been so addled by the roughing-up he had received. That name, Lucius – Lucius Flavius Antoninus – Trifosa's half-brother, perhaps sometime lover, and almost certainly the only man she had ever really loved: the man that Sabinus and Castor had murdered to gain possession of this Villa Censorini. So was Bodicca playing Nemesis, and if so, why? As far as he was aware she had never known Antoninus.

Did she have a dagger concealed under her *cucullus* – a dagger which she intended to plunge into Sabinus's or Castor's heart when they were distracted by the figurine? But if she did, then surely she could never hope to kill all three men in the *triclinium* before one of them killed her.

If killing Sabinus really was her intention, then the only way to save her life would be for him to rush back into the *triclinium* and stop her before she could draw the dagger. But he was acutely aware that, were he to attempt to do so, the three soldiers detaining him might well kill him, thinking that he himself was trying to attack Sabinus. And if he tried to voice his suspicions to the soldiers, they would either disbelieve him or, worse, believe him and kill Bodicca before she could strike.

So he hesitated. Did nothing. Said nothing. He told himself that he would wait until… until what? In any case, what did he owe Bodicca that he should risk his life to save her?

Coward! hissed a little voice inside his head. He tried to ignore the voice, telling himself that waiting was the only rational thing to do, and that he had not survived for thirty-one years in a harsh world by acting irrationally in dangerous situations. He recalled that most of the reputed heroes he had known were also fools, and frequently soon-to-be dead fools at that.

With the three soldiers and himself standing in it, the anteroom, little wider than the corridor beyond, was crowded. There was a faint smell of stale sweat, much of it his own, and the hint of a curious sort of perfume coming from Natalis. No one spoke.

Coming from behind the heavy door of the *triclinium* he could hear the murmur of voices, rising and falling, but could not distinguish so much as a single word.

From time to time he thought he could hear a woman's voice, which must have been Bodicca's, although, muffled by the door, it sounded subtly different from the voice he remembered.

More time passed. Natalis's two soldiers began shuffling their feet, and Canio realised that the air in the anteroom had become quite chill. It seemed that the *triclinium* hypocaust did not extend under the anteroom.

And then, in the men's voices from behind the door, the words still unintelligible, he heard first a rising excitement, then gasps and cries of… what? Astonishment perhaps, or wonder, or even alarm? Perhaps all three, perhaps none of these – he simply couldn't tell.

He glanced at Natalis, and by the puzzled look on the man's face realised that he too had been trying and failing to make out what was being said behind the closed door.

The voices were growing louder, and now began to sound angry and arguing. Canio edged as near to the door as he could, but still could not make out any words. He saw Natalis glance uncertainly at the two soldiers, who shrugged their indifference.

Then somebody – he was fairly sure it was Sabinus – shouted, 'No, they're mine, don't touch them, any of them – they're all mine!' It was the first time that Canio had been able to make out distinct words.

More raised voices, at least two, perhaps more, but none of them recognisable as Bodicca's.

'I will not be cheated – not by anyone, not even you!' This time the voice was definitely Castor's.

The men in the *triclinium* were all shouting now, a cacophony of raised voices growing louder and more furious by the moment.

And then came a high-pitched scream. And then another. Even the two soldiers looked startled. Natalis's hand wavered towards the door latch, then hesitated, as if, even now, he could not bring himself to disobey Sabinus's order.

Everything before had been conjecture, an excuse for inaction, but not even Canio could ignore the reality of those screams. Thinking that they must have come from Bodicca, he shoved Natalis out of the way, knocked up the heavy latch with one hand and shouldered the door open.

Inside, he found the *triclinium* in twilight, the oil lamps hanging from their stands along both long sides of the room still burning, but all the flames low and wan. And the air was cold, even colder than in the anteroom.

Sabinus was slumped back in his wicker armchair, motionless, a great red stain spreading over the front of his beautiful white robe, his eyes open, staring wide but sightless in the agony of death. His left hand hung down the side of his chair, still clutching the Hecate figurine, the dull yellow spot on her *stola* just visible between his dead fingers.

From somewhere behind him Canio heard a voice, almost certainly Natalis's, whisper, 'Dear Christos!'

Castor stood a few feet away from Sabinus, a *spatha* gripped in his right hand, blood on its blade, splashes of blood on his face and uniform. He was as still as a marble statue, his face expressionless, his eyes blank hollows of darkness.

Then Canio noticed Peltrasius sprawled on the floor, his head and slashed throat lying beside one of the half-naked maenads of the Bacchus mosaic, over which a pool of dark blood was slowly spreading. The maenad's arms were half-raised, as if in horror at what she had just witnessed, weirdly as though this moment had been foreseen at the time of her creation, decades before.

Bodicca was standing several yards back from the table, near the centre of the mosaic, the spot where Bacchus himself stood, his *cantharus* wine cup raised as if he was about to drink to the health of long-gone revellers sitting around the table, mockingly incongruous now. Bodicca, though, stood impassively surveying the scene of butchery, like some immortal goddess out of mythology, a chooser of the slain.

And surely she had seen it too – she must have done. Natalis's horrified eyes had probably been fixed on Sabinus and Castor, but Canio had seen it – at least, he thought he had. Admittedly it had only been for the briefest of moments, because the vision – hallucination? – of that vast pile of *solidi* was already fading fast as he burst into the *triclinium*. It had seemed to cover the entire width of the table, a heap at least three feet high, the thousands upon thousands of little gold coins shimmering in the subdued light of the lamps. And then, in the blinking of an eye, they were all gone, as if they had never been there at all.

Suddenly, like a man startled awake, Castor turned his head to see Natalis and the two soldiers advancing cautiously towards him with drawn swords. He gave a strange, animal-like howl and rushed towards them. Canio saw sparks fly as Castor's and Natalis's *spathae* clashed, and the latter's went spinning from his hand. It clattered across the mosaic floor, where it came to rest over the figure of Spring, a cherub naked but for a sash about its waist.

The two soldiers began desperately fighting Castor, slowly driving him back. Natalis was doubled over, nursing what was probably a broken wrist and yelling for more soldiers.

Canio dodged away from them and turned to Bodicca. 'Are you hurt?' he asked. But she ignored him and darted forward to prise the Hecate figurine from Sabinus's dead hand, then turned and began walking calmly back towards the door. As she neared it, three more soldiers burst into the *triclinium*.

'Castor's gone mad,' Natalis shouted, clearly in pain. 'He's insane – he's murdered the *Praeses* and Peltrasius – seize the man, seize him!'

At that moment one of the original two soldiers failed to fully parry a slashing blow from Castor's *spatha*, and screamed as the cruel steel bit into his upper arm, the bright blood spraying into the air.

'I… will… have… them. I… will… have… them,' Castor kept grunting as he thrust and parried.

The three new soldiers hesitated, seemingly confused, Castor being their commanding officer. But a combination of Natalis's squawked appeals and the sight of the man, face contorted with fury, mouthing apparent nonsense and trying to kill their comrades decided them.

It was now four against one, and not even a man as strong as Castor could survive for long against such odds. Canio watched with grim fascination as first he received a glancing blow to his forehead which made him stagger backwards. He tried to claw the blood from his eyes, but before he could do so the four soldiers had surrounded him like wolves, stabbing and hacking. As he started to turn back towards Bodicca, Canio had a fleeting vision of Castor crumpled to his knees, his face a mask of blood, the soldiers still slashing and thrusting.

Taking advantage of the chaos, Canio stooped and picked up his own fake figurine, quickly hiding it beneath his tunic. The action was more automatic than reasoned, the instinct of a guilty man to conceal the evidence of his guilt. He glanced around: nobody appeared to have noticed.

Bodicca herself was at the doorway, watching. But even as Canio started towards her she slipped through it and disappeared into the anteroom. And before he could follow her, Natalis, grasping his injured right wrist with his left hand, had stepped across and blocked his path.

'In the name of Christos,' the man screamed, 'will you tell me what's—'

Canio bundled him aside and dashed out into the anteroom, only to find it empty and Bodicca gone. He leapt down the steps into the corridor, just in time to catch a glimpse of a figure in a *cucullus* going out through the doorway at the far end.

He hurried after her, but when he was only halfway down the corridor a squad of five soldiers, apparently alerted by the commotion coming from the *triclinium*, came tumbling out of the bath suite at the end of the west range, a couple of them still buckling their sword belts.

Canio halted and flattened himself against the wall to let them pass, but they too stopped.

'What's happening?' one demanded. 'What's all the noise about?'

'Castor's gone mad in the *triclinium*. He's killed Sabinus and Peltrasius, and now he's trying to kill Natalis too.'

'Castor?' repeated one soldier in disbelief. 'Killed the *Vir Perfectissimus*?'

'Yes! Castor killed him, slaughtered him like a damned sheep – I saw it with my own two eyes. He's like a rabid dog – and he's going to kill Natalis too if you don't stop him.'

That did it. All five started running up the corridor, and Canio watched them for a moment before they disappeared into the *triclinium* anteroom. Then he dashed to the end of the corridor, slipped through the doorway and out into the darkness of the upper courtyard.

CHAPTER THIRTY-FIVE

Bodicca had vanished. He was about to call her name, but some protective instinct took over and stopped him just in time. Whether that was to protect her or himself was a question never asked: in such matters he tended to avoid introspection.

On the far side of the courtyard, in the poor light, he could see the dark shapes of people emerging from the cross-gallery, silhouettes against the lit doorway.

To his left he saw a flickering orange glow and heard the crackle of burning wood, both coming from what he realised must be the stoke hole of the west range's baths suite. He walked towards it, halting in the gap between the west range and the north wing.

Some thirty single paces away, motionless in the starlight, he could just make out the figures of two women, both wearing *cuculli*. They were standing in front of the *nymphaeum*, the shrine to a water goddess built over the octagonal stone pool into which the water from her hillside spring trickled.

As he started towards them there was a sudden movement to his right. Instinctively his head turned towards it, and for a moment paralysing fear rushed through his veins as he saw the black shape of what appeared to be a monstrous beast crouching against the wall of the north wing.

The shadow moved again, and he swung round to see a great black hound – Vilbia's hound? – rising up in the arched doorway of the west range bathhouse's roofed stokehole, a nimbus of orange firelight streaming out around it. The hound growled, as if in warning, then settled back onto its haunches.

Casting several uneasy glances back towards the hound, Canio continued walking slowly towards the two women. As he came closer he realised that they were Bodicca and Vilbia, the younger woman holding what could only be the Hecate figurine.

Neither woman spoke, and he stood staring at them both. 'Well – isn't one of you going to tell me what happened back there in the *triclinium* when I was on the other side of the door? And why are you here at all – tonight of all nights?' Even as he spoke he began to suspect that the question was redundant, but he had to ask.

Vilbia did not reply, but looked to Bodicca, who said, mockingly, 'Where else would we be, Canio, tonight of all nights? And aren't you going to thank me for saving your life?'

'Oh, I will – if that's really what you did,' he replied, not bothering to hide his growing feeling of antipathy towards her. His face still hurt from Sabinus's stabs with the fake figurine, and he had a rapidly hardening suspicion that Bodicca must have known about that casket. Known too that it had been most unlikely that his copy of the figurine would have fitted perfectly into it. In which case, she had deliberately let him walk into a trap. And another thing – how had she known that Sabinus was the "very important somebody" who wanted the figurine? He was certain that he had never told her.

'You don't sound very grateful,' Bodicca remarked archly.

'I'd be more grateful if you'd warned me about that infernal casket.'

'Now how could I possibly have known that Sabinus had it?' That same mocking tone.

'But you did know, didn't you? Just as you knew that I'd be coming here tonight.' When she didn't answer, he asked, 'Where's Nectovelius?'

'Safe,' she replied.

'Not here?'

'Not here,' Bodicca confirmed.

'Then where?'

'Where I'm going now. Farewell, Canio... until we meet again.' She started walking up the slope towards the woods that formed a backdrop to the villa.

Canio's mind was racing; questions and suspicions restlessly forming and metamorphosing and re-forming. He considered going after Bodicca, but, before he could decide, the moonless night had swallowed her.

But Vilbia remained, the great black hound now crouched at her side. He wondered if she would confirm what he now suspected.

'Why?' he asked her. 'Why have you done this, you and Bodicca between you?'

'Can't you even guess?'

He hesitated, then said, 'Guessing isn't knowing. I want to hear it from you.'

'Are you sure – quite sure? You may not like what you hear.'

'No, I probably won't – but tell me anyway.'

'Very well,' she said quietly. 'And in any case, it's perhaps only right that you should know... A few short days ago there were eight people alive in this world who knew of the existence of this figurine. Just eight.'

'You, Bodicca, Eutherius—' he began.

'And those three men, Sabinus and Castor and Peltrasius, and that old priest who some thought was mad. And yourself, of course.'

'Nobody else?'

'Nobody else,' Vilbia confirmed, 'that knew either of its existence, or its significance, or both.'

'Which is?'

'Which is... what Eutherius unwisely told you back in January.'

'And which I still don't believe.' *Or want to believe,* he did not add.

'That's good, Canio. Keep disbelieving. But never tell anyone what you don't believe.'

'But what about the *Vicarius,* Civilis?' he asked, testing.

'Civilis? No – did you ever really believe that?'

'Why shouldn't I have believed it? It seemed completely believable at the time.' *And how did you know about Civilis?* he wondered.

'When you were first told, perhaps. But later, possibly much later, you did begin to suspect what Sabinus's real reason for wanting this figurine was, didn't you?' She was looking directly into his eyes then, as if even in the starlight she could see right into his soul.

'Perhaps...' He turned his head away. 'So just eight?'

'Just eight. And now four of those people are dead... Knowledge can be a very dangerous thing, Canio.'

And then he understood. Understood only too well, and the implications were chilling. 'I would never have tried to take that from you,' he said, pointing to the Hecate figurine she held. 'Or tell anyone that you possessed it – not ever!'

'Wouldn't you?' she asked, and Canio heard the note of sadness in her voice. 'Not even Bodicca?'

'But she already knew,' he protested.

'But you didn't know that, not for sure, not when you asked her if I'd still got it, did you?'

'No, but—'

'Would you never tell, not even to keep your villa and all the land that came with it? And the warm baths, the fine clothes, the vineyard, the easy life? How old are you now, Canio – thirty-one? Some men of thirty-one are already well on their way to a miserable old age. Could you go back to soldiering?'

For long moments he was silent, wanting so much to protest that he would never try to take it from her. Not by force – no, he was certain of that. But by cunning? He knew himself too well to be absolutely sure. And he would not lie, not to her. 'I don't know,' he said at last. 'If you had been around I might have asked to borrow it for a little while – but only to have an exact copy made, not to give it to Sabinus.'

'Oh Canio, please, please, for your own sake – as far as this little scrap of *orichalcum* is concerned drink deeply from the waters of Lethe, as I pray Sabinus and the others on their dark journeys have already done. Drink deeply, and so forget everything that you ever knew about it – even its very existence... Do you understand what I'm saying – really understand?'

She was almost pleading, and he suddenly wondered what advice concerning himself Bodicca had given her. He decided not to ask, suspecting, but not wanting to know, what that advice might have been.

Instead, he thought of enquiring if she had a supply of that Underworld river's water to hand, since he would rather not go down to collect it in person. Perhaps, he hoped, the weak joke would make her smile – at that moment he would have given anything to see her smile.

But before he could speak he heard voices coming from the gap between the two bath suites. Somebody called his name, and he turned to see Vibius Natalis walking into the lurid glow thrown out by the west range's stoke hole.

'Who's there? Is that you, Caninus?'

'Damn the man!' Canio muttered savagely. 'Don't let him catch sight of—' then realised that Vilbia had gone, disappeared into the night as silent as a ghost, her great black hound with her. He stood irresolute, instinctively wanting to run after her, but realising that he had already learnt more than he would have wished. Far more.

He turned to face Natalis and called out irritably, 'Yes, it's me.'

'Who were you talking to? Was it that woman – who is she?'

274

Under his breath Canio cursed obscenely, but replied, 'I wasn't talking to anyone – there's nobody here but myself.'

'I could have sworn I heard voices.'

'It was just the wind in the trees. Is Castor dead?'

'Dead? Yes, he's dead – of course he's dead! They're all dead, all three of them! What in dear Lord Christos's name am I to do? This has got to be reported to Corinium as quickly as possible... I'd go myself, but I can't ride with this wrist. The *Praeses* murdered! The *Praeses,* of all people! There'll be an enquiry, one which the *Vicarius* himself will almost certainly head. Dear Christos, do you realise that, with Castor dead, I'm the most senior officer in the *Vir Perfectissimus's* bodyguard present here tonight...? A report... I'll have to write a report... dictate a report. You must come with me and explain exactly why you came here tonight, and what went on when you were alone with the *Praeses* and Castor. And who that strange woman was... and where in the name of the Evil One is she now? I must find her, I must! She's the only one who—'

The man was as agitated as a virgin in a brothel, but Canio was no longer listening. Survival instinct had kicked in and he was already beginning to fabricate a distorted version of the truth. One which would paint himself (and perhaps Sabinus too?) as the innocent and bewildered victim, or victims, of what he had, too late, come to realise was Castor's and Peltrasius's insane belief that the possession of the idol of a pagan goddess would somehow make them rich.

Yes, Sabinus as victim would probably be much more acceptable to the *Vicarius* and others who would be interrogating him. Certainly more so than painting the good Christian *Praeses* as the avaricious and credulous believer in the powers of an idol of an Underworld goddess.

So just why did Sabinus order him to find the Hecate figurine? Because, it seems, he had learnt of its existence – and rumours of its supposed magical powers – from Peltrasius, via

Castor. And, dutiful Christian that he was, he was anxious to destroy this object about which rumours of sorcery were said to swirl; sorcery being something which Emperor Valentinianus himself was known to view with particular horror.

That being so (and despite regarding claims of that pagan idol's so-called magic powers as being laughably ridiculous), he, Canio, had, when commanded to do so by the *Praeses*, felt that he had no choice other than to assist the man in that laudable aim.

Anyway, that was the reason Sabinus had given him, and Civilis would be unlikely to want to believe otherwise. And as for it being the *Vicarius* himself who had ordered Sabinus to find the figurine – it seems that had, quite literally, never happened, so he would never mention it.

The figurine he eventually found – in the bramble patch where Peltrasius had thrown it – had never before been in his possession (he must stress that). And the reason why Peltrasius had thought that he, Canio, had the wretched thing was that the fool had failed to find it when he subsequently went searching for it.

And, irony of ironies, that figurine – the one taken from Orgillus – was apparently a fake anyway, because it would not fit inside the little casket that Peltrasius had produced from some unknown source on that fateful night.

Unlike the figurine which that strange woman in a *cucullus* (whom he had never seen before in his life, as Natalis will testify – he had at least that to thank Bodicca for) had handed to Sabinus after bursting into the *triclinium*.

Yes, not bad for a first attempt – and he would polish and expand it here and there before it went into that idiot Natalis's report, stressing his belief that Castor and Peltrasius were the instigators of the tragedy. And also stressing that the only reason for his involvement was that he had had the misfortune to be present when, on that June day in 368, Peltrasius had stolen the figurine from a deserter called Orgillus, before throwing it away when he realised it was not made of gold.

Or alternatively – and potentially even better – he could omit all reference to the fake figurine, so absolving himself of any charge of feeding Castor's delusion. After all, he was certain that Natalis had never seen him with it. In this version he would have come to Villa Censorini tonight simply to confess his failure to find it.

Ah, but those three mosaic workers knew of the figurine – the fake figurine – and had also witnessed his part in its "discovery". And as soon as news of the circumstances of Sabinus's death – his tragic murder at the hands of Castor – spread, they would be telling the tale of its finding all over Corinium, if they hadn't already begun to do so.

So, best to stick to the (almost) truth. A pity, that.

And anyway, *"Quid est veritas?"* as he had once heard Trifosa ask, quoting from somewhere.

"Whatever you need it to be – so long as no one can prove otherwise," he had replied. He had been jesting then, but there was little to jest about now.

He looked up at the moonless, cloudless sky. The myriad glittering stars were still there. Over to the east he saw the bluish-white cluster of the Pleiades – the Seven Sisters – moving slowly on their endless journey across the heavens, utterly remote from and indifferent to what was happening in the world of men far below. They appeared at around this time every year, unchanged and unchanging, and not even Emperor Valentinianus himself had the power to prevent their coming or hasten their departure.

And in a world where he was uncomfortably aware of sometimes being as powerless to control events as a yellow leaf being swept along by the current of a swollen winter stream on its one-way journey to the great sea of oblivion, he found that strangely comforting.

GAZETTEER AND GLOSSARY

Gazetteer

*Names marked * are my fictional names for real places, the
Roman names of which are now lost.*

Abona: Sea Mills, a suburb of Bristol.

(Flumen) Abona: The Bristol Avon, flowing through Aquae
Sulis.

Alauna: Alcester, Warwickshire. A town on the Via Ricnild.

Alba Muri*: White Walls. A small town on the Fosse Way,
midway between Aquae Sulis and Corinium.

Aquae Sulis: Bath, Somerset.

Argentoratum: Strasbourg. Site of a crushing victory over the
Alemanni tribe in 357 by an outnumbered Roman army led
by the Caesar Julian.

Ariconium: An industrial settlement near Weston-under-
Penyard, Herefordshire. Some 15 (Roman) miles north-west
of Glevum.

(Flumen) Avon: The Warwickshire Avon, flowing through
Vertis (Worcester) and joining the Sabrina (Severn) at
Confluens (Tewkesbury).

Britannia Prima: One of the five (?) provinces into which the
diocese of Britannia had been divided by AD370. Its capital
was Corinium Dobunnorum (Cirencester).

Burdigala: Bordeaux

Calleva Atrebatum: Silchester, Hampshire.

Coel's Hill*: Cole's Hill, which separates the narrow coomb containing Spoonley Wood villa from the main valley running first south-east, then south, from Winchcombe up into the Hills.

Confluens*: Tewkesbury, Gloucestershire. A small town on the road south from Vertis to Glevum, where the Warwickshire Avon joins the Flumen Sabrina.

Corinium (Dobunnorum): Cirencester, Gloucestershire. Capital of the fourth century Roman province of Britannia Prima.

Criccus*: Cricklade, North Wiltshire, seven miles south-east of Corinium on the Via Erminus.

Cunetio: Mildenhall, Wiltshire.

Dunum (or *Dunium*): Maiden Castle, an Iron Age hillfort near Durnovaria. A Romano-Celtic temple was built on the flat top of the hillfort at some time shortly after 367. A fragment of a near life-size bronze statue and a feather-shaped bronze plaque with a repoussé figure of Minerva were found there.

Durnovaria: Dorchester, Dorset.

Durobrivae: Water Newton, Cambridgeshire.

Fonscolnis*: Wycombe, near Andoversford, Gloucestershire. The large number of small denomination coins found scattered over the area suggest it was a thriving market settlement in the later third and fourth century, although its origins go back into Neolithic times.

Forum Termini*: Hall End, South Gloucestershire. A small town on the road south from Glevum to Aquae Sulis.

Fosse Way: Roman road running from Exeter to Lincoln. It passed through Corinium from the Aquae Sulis Gate to the Verulamium Gate as the *Decumanus Maximus* of that city.

Glevum: Gloucester.

(The) Great Marshes*: A large area of what is now Somerset south of the Mendip Hills.

Lead Hills*: The Mendip Hills, North Somerset.

Lethe River: One of the rivers of the Underworld. The shades of the dead were required to drink from it to forget their earthly lives.

Letocetum: Roman settlement at Wall, Staffordshire.

Long Limestone Hills*: The Cotswold Hills.

Lindinis: Ilchester, Somerset. A town on the Fosse Way, some 35 (Roman) miles south of Aquae Sulis.

Londinium: London. The title Augusta *may* have been bestowed on it by Emperor Valentinianus in 368, following the crushing of the *Barbarica Conspiratio.*

Maglocrouco*: Belas Knap Neolithic long barrow in the high Cotswolds, about 1.5 miles west of Villa Canini as the crow flies.

Niger Hills*: the Blackdown Hills, stretching from West Somerset to East Devon.

Ovilmalleus*: Shepton Mallet, Somerset. A small town on Fosse Way, mid-way between Aquae Sulis and Lindinis.

(Flumen) Sabrina: River Severn.

(Flumen) Sagitta*: River Arrow, which crosses the Via Ricnild just south of Alauna.

Salinae: Droitwich, Worcestershire. A town some 7 miles northeast of Vertis. Famous for salt production from its brine springs.

(The) Salt Way: An ancient trackway running from Salinae south-eastwards over the Cotswolds.

Sorviodunum: Old Sarum, near Salisbury, Wiltshire.

(Flumen) Tamesis: River Thames.

Treveri: Trier, Germany, on River Moselle. In the 4th century was one of the largest cities of the empire, a residence of the western emperors, and a mint city.

Urticager*: Nettleton, Wiltshire. A settlement on Fosse Way, some 10 (Roman) miles north of Aquae Sulis. Site of an octagonal temple dedicated to Apollo Cunomaglus (a Celtic epithet meaning Hound Lord), indicating that here Apollo was seen as a god of hunting, as well as his more usual function as a healing god.

Vadumleucara*: Bourton-on-the-Water, Gloucestershire. A small town on the Fosse Way, just south of the point where the Via Ricnild branches off it.

Venta Belgarum: Winchester.

Vertis: Worcester. Town located near a ford crossing the Flumen Sabrina. Its main industry was the smelting of iron ore brought up the Sabrina from the Forest of Dean.

Via Alba*: The White Way: a branch of the Salt Way running north from Corinium. Runs to the west of the Fosse Way and initially roughly parallel to it.

Via Erminus: Ermin Street. Roman road running from Calleva (Silchester) to Glevum (Gloucester). Passed through Corinium from the Calleva Gate to the Glevum Gate as the *Cardo Maximus* of that city.

Via Ricnild: Ryknild Street. Roman road branching off the Fosse Way at Vadumleucara and running north-west to Rotherham.

Villa Canini / Arcadia*: Spoonley Wood Roman villa, two miles south-east of Winchcombe, Gloucestershire. Some ten Roman miles by road north of Villa Censorini and twenty miles north of Corinium.

Villa Censorini*: Chedworth Roman villa, Gloucestershire.

Glossary

Agens in rebus (pl. agentes in rebus): 'Those who are active in matters' – a suitably vague and sinister term for a corps of men with multiple functions, including intelligence-gathering and acting as a sort of secret police.

Alemanni (also Alamanni and Alamani): A confederation of Suebian Germanic tribes living in the area of the Upper

Rhine. In the fourth century they frequently raided into Roman Eastern Gaul.

Ambulatory: The outer area of a Romano-Celtic temple.

Barbarica Conspiratio: (the *Conspiratio*): Circa AD 367/68. The invasion of Britain by seemingly co-ordinated waves of barbarian tribes, principally Picts and Attacotti from north of Hadrian's Wall and Scotti from Ireland.

Bracae (or *braccae*): Woollen trousers, closed at the waist by a drawstring. Originally worn by the Gallic tribes of Northern Europe and later adopted by the Romans.

Bucellarius (pl. bucellarii): Literally 'biscuit eaters'. The private bodyguards of wealthy civilians.

Caldarium: The hot room of a Roman bath suite.

Cardo Maximus: The main north-south (roughly) oriented street of a Roman city. The forum was usually located at the intersection of the *Cardo* and the *Decumanus Maximus*.

Cella: The inner heart of a Romano-Celtic temple.

Clavi: Decorative woven or embroidered strips added to the bottom edges of cloaks and tunics (see also *Orbiculi*).

Conspiratio: See *Barbarica Conspiratio*.

Cucullus: Hooded cape or cloak. The shortest were waist-length, the longest were ankle-length.

Cursus publicus: The state-run service by which officials and documents were transported across the empire. The use of this service was supposed to be restricted to persons who possessed the appropriate *diploma*.

Decumanus Maximus: The main east-west (roughly) oriented street of a Roman city.

Diocese (pl. dioceses): By the early fourth century the large provinces of the early empire had been subdivided, in order to avoid concentrating too much power in the hands of any one provincial governor. These small provinces were aggregated into *dioceses*, each under the control of a *vicarius*. By 370 the *diocese* of Britannia was divided into five (?) provinces.

Its *vicarius* was stationed in Londinium and reported to the Praetorian Prefect of Gaul, who in turn reported directly to the emperor.

Frigidarium: The cold room of a Roman bath suite.

Genius Cucullatus (pl. Genii Cucullati): Rustic deities, depicted wearing hooded capes or cloaks (*cuculli*). Carved representations, often crudely executed, have been found across the Romano-Celtic regions, especially in the Cotswolds, Hadrian's Wall and the Rhine-Moselle regions. In Britain the *genii* often appear as a triad, sometimes in association with one or more of the *Deae Matres* (Mother Goddesses). They were thought to have power over healing, prosperity, fertility, death and rebirth.

Hilaritas: Allegorical personification of Mirth and Rejoicing. On coins she is depicted carrying a long palm branch and a cornucopia, sceptre or patera.

Honestiores and Humiliores: In law, the inhabitants of the later Roman Empire (free, not slave) were divided into either high caste *honestiores* or low caste *humiliores*. *Humiliores*, the bulk of the civilian population, could be tortured as witnesses, flogged and executed by the cruellest means. For the same crimes, *honestiores* could usually escape with banishment. In time, *humiliores* working for the great landowning magnates, either directly or as tenant farmers, came to be legally bound to the land, much like medieval serfs.

Kalends: The first day of all Roman months. Between the Kalends of one month and the Ides of the previous month the days were counted backwards, including the Kalends as the first day. Thus, for example, the 18th of October was the fifteenth day before the Kalends of November.

Laconicum: Baths resembling a modern sauna. Chedworth villa had two bath suites: a laconicum in the western end of the north wing, and the more usual Turkish-type baths in the northern end of the west wing.

Liquamen: A sauce made of fermented fish, much used in Roman cuisine. Also known as *garum*.

Maenads: Ecstatic, immortal female followers of Bacchus / Dionysus, forming part of the god's retinue (*thiasos*). In late Roman art they are often portrayed dancing and playing musical instruments

Mansio (pl. mansiones): Local government maintained hotels for the use of persons travelling on state business on the *cursus publicus*. Usually sited some fifteen to eighteen miles apart along the major roads.

Miliarense (pl. miliarensia): A silver coin. After AD 356 it was tariffed as a double siliqua (approx. 4.5 grams) and struck at 72 to the (Roman) pound of pure silver. Tariffed at twelve to the solidus.

Nemesis: Goddess of retributive justice.

Nones: The seventh day of the months of March, May, July and October, but the fifth day of all other months, including November.

Nummus (pl. nummi): In the novel the term denotes the small copper coins current in the 360s and later decades. Their relationship to the gold and silver coins of the period is not now known.

Orbiculi: Decorative woven or embroidered roundels bearing geometrical patterns, stylised plants, animals, etc, attached to cloaks and tunics. Military men sometimes incorporated the insignia of their units in their orbiculi.

Ordo: A city council, made up of *decuriones* (councillors).

Orichalcum: The Roman name for a type of brass, a yellow alloy of copper and zinc. Yellow brass melts at 930 degrees centigrade, pure copper at 1084 degrees.

Parcae: The Roman name for the three Fates. Clotho, who spun the tread of a man's life; Lachesis, who determined its length; and Atropos, who cut the thread, so ending that life.

Popina (pl. popinae): Low-class drinking establishments, sometimes also serving simple meals.

Praeses (pl. praesides): By the fourth century this term had come to mean a specific class of provincial governor, ranking below *consulares* and *correctores*. (A more generic title for governor was *rector*). In the late fourth/early fifth century document known as the *Notitia Dignitatum*, the governor of Britannia Prima is listed as a *praeses*.

Praetorium: By the fourth century this term had come to mean the residence of a provincial governor.

Satyrs: Immortal male companions of Bacchus. In late Roman art they are usually depicted as wholly humanoid in appearance, except that sometimes they have goat-like ears. With their female companions, the maenads, they form Bacchus's *thiasos*. Sometimes depicted as carefree youths, as on the Mildenhall treasure; sometimes as more mysterious, sinister creatures, as on the mosaic in the west wing triclinium at Chedworth villa.

Semissis: A gold half-solidus. Worth twelve siliquae.

Siliqua (pl. siliquae): The standard small silver coin of the late Roman Empire, tariffed at twenty-four to the solidus. After AD 356 it was struck at 144 to the (Roman) pound of pure silver and weighed approx. 2.25 grams.

Solidus (pl. solidi): The standard gold coin of the late Roman Empire. Struck at seventy-two to the (Roman) pound of pure gold, it was introduced by Constantine the Great in 312 and replaced the aureus of the earlier empire, which was struck at sixty to the pound.

Spatha: The long sword used by Roman cavalry.

Stabulum: An inn for the use of the general public, providing stabling for horses (cf. *mansio*).

Stola: A long, pleated dress, the traditional garment worn by Roman women. Originally sleeveless, but sometimes with short or long sleeves.

Talus (pl. tali): Knucklebones. The pastern bones of sheep, goats or calves. Each talus had only four non-rounded sides, numbered 1, 3, 4, and 6. The game was played with four tali, which were thrown and the numbers counted. The winning throw was Venus (6, 4, 3, 1). The worst throw was Canis (dog, four 1s).

Tepidarium: The gently-heated room of a Roman bath suite.

Thiasos: The procession of revelling satyrs and maenads, headed by Bacchus / Dionysus in a chariot drawn by leopards or panthers.

Thyrsus: The wand carried by Bacchus / Dionysus, consisting of a rod of giant fennel topped with a pine cone and wound with ivy or vine leaves. It was a symbol of prosperity, fertility and hedonism.

Triclinium: The dining room of a Roman villa, so called because the couches or chairs were arranged around three sides of the central table.

Vicarius: A high-ranking civilian official of the later Roman Empire, in charge of a *diocese* (group of provinces). Ammianus Marcellinus records that in c. 368, at the request of *Comes* Theodosius (the man who had suppressed the invasions of 367-8 – the *Barbarica Conspiratio*) a man called Civilis was appointed *vicarius* of Britannia.

Vilicus: Bailiff / overseer of a villa estate.

Vir Perfectissimus: The lowest ranking of a series of honorific titles bestowed on the holders of high office. The *praeses* of Britannia Prima was a *vir perfectissimus*. The *vicarius* of the whole diocese of Britannia was given the superior title of *vir spectabilis*.

The DECEIVERS

Roman Britain
Late Autmn AD 370

Bill
Page